C000304142

# A Suggestion of Scandal

*To Bronagh*

# A
# Suggestion of
# Scandal

*with very best wishes*

## CATHERINE
## KULLMANN

*Catherine*

Willow
Books

First published in 2018 by
Willow Books,
Dublin, Ireland.

All rights © 2018 Catherine Kullmann

| Paperback | ISBN: 978 1 78846 055 2 |
| eBook – mobi format | ISBN: 978 1 78846 056 9 |
| eBook – ePub format | ISBN: 978 1 78846 057 6 |
| CreateSpace paperback | ISBN: 978 1 78846 058 3 |

*All rights reserved. No part of this book may be reproduced or utilised in any form or by any means electronic or mechanical, including photocopying, filming, recording, video recording, photography, or by any information storage and retrieval system, nor shall by way of trade or otherwise be lent, resold or otherwise circulated in any form of binding or cover other than that in which it is published without prior permission in writing from the publisher.*

*The right of the author of her work has been asserted by her in accordance with the Copyright, Designs and Patents Act 1988.*

*This historical novel is a work of fiction. Names, characters, places and incidents are the product of the author's imagination or are used fictitiously. Except where actual historical events, locales, businesses and characters are described for the storyline of this novel, all situations in this publication are fictitious and any resemblance to actual persons living or dead, businesses, events or locales is purely coincidental.*

*Produced by Kazoo Independent Publishing Services, 222 Beech Park, Lucan, Co. Dublin*
*www.kazoopublishing.com*

Kazoo Independent Publishing Services is not the publisher of this work.
All rights and responsibilities pertaining to this work remain with Willow Books.

Cover design by Andrew Brown
Printed in the EU

*For my sons John Carl, Michael and Christopher, with love and thanks for their support and advice.*

# Chapter One

*May 1814*

Sir Julian Loring flicked the thong of his whip encouragingly over the shoulders of his matched greys. It was a clear run from here to Loring Place. With five curricles in play, the fourteen mile drive from Newmarket had inevitably turned into an impromptu race. In deference to his home advantage, he had been handicapped by being the last to leave, with the other four whips drawing lots to determine their order of departure, but local knowledge had stood to him and by Risby he had successfully given all his rivals the go-by. Now he just had to maintain his lead.

He checked his pair slightly at the sight of a laden cart lumbering ahead. Behind him, Josiah sounded the yard of tin. The driver of the cart glanced back and ponderously moved to one side. That should do it! As Julian flew past, he raised his whip in acknowledgement, nodding down to the carter who touched his hat in return.

"Keep them moving, sir," his groom called. "Mr Haldon is catching up on us."

Julian grunted a reply. Once they left the turnpike, there would be no room for another to pass.

He was still in the lead when he slowed his pair for the turn towards the Place. In recent years he had spent increasingly less time at his family home and hadn't been here since he had come for a week's shooting in December. His father neither sought nor welcomed any interest on his heir's part in the administration of his estate and seemed as pleased to see his son go as he was to see him come. Despite this, Julian had obeyed the summons to a house party to celebrate his sire's sixtieth birthday and complied with his stepmother's instructions to bring some bachelors to dance with his half-sister Chloe and the other young ladies.

Through his dead mother he was also heir to the ancient Barony of Swanmere and, on reaching the age of eighty, Lord Swanmere had handed over responsibility for the estates to his grandson with whom he enjoyed an amicable relationship. If it were not for his grandmother and Chloe, combined with an innate stubbornness that refused to be driven away from half his birthright, Julian would have long since stopped coming to Loring Place, instead dividing his time between Swanmere Castle in Huntingdonshire and Swanmere House in London.

This visit would be an improvement on the previous ones, he reflected as he drew up in front of the house. Instead of dull days and tedious evenings of stilted conversation over whist played for chicken stakes, there would be congenial company and plenty to do. For a start, he must put together a cricket team and see that they got some practice in before Thursday.

"And it's Loring before Haldon before Glazebrook

before Whittaker before Raven," Josiah intoned as he scrambled down and ran to the horses' heads. "That's a coach wheel apiece the other tigers owe me."

Julian took off his hat and thrust his hand through his hair before stepping down from the curricle. He stretched lazily to relieve the tightness in his arms and shoulders caused by holding a mettlesome team to a spanking trot and arched his spine, enjoying the sensation of loosening muscles and joints.

"There you are, Julian."

He turned at the sound of his stepmother's voice. Sir Edward's 'pretty little partridge' had grown plumper with the years and frequently looked discontented with her lot. "Were you not expecting me, ma'am?"

"Yes, yes of course. Now, who has come with you?"

"Glazebrook and Spilsbury with their sons, and Michael Raven as agreed. Major Frederick Raven was with his brother. He came home with despatches and has a couple of weeks' furlough. As all his family are here, I told him he should come too."

"Wonderful! Only yesterday, Lady Ransford said that she cannot wait to see him after all these years in the Peninsula. She will be ecstatic."

Julian nodded. "Then there are my friends Jack Whittaker and Ambrose Haldon, and my father convinced his old crony, Sir Jethro Boyce, to accompany him."

She frowned. "Where am I to put a man of his age? The first floor is full, the second floor is all married couples and girls, and he can hardly go in the bachelors' wing with the younger men."

"He might be flattered," Julian said, grinning. "He was widowed last year, I understand. Give him my room, ma'am. I'll go and keep order among the bachelors."

"If you're sure you don't mind, Julian, I should be most grateful. I'll just give the necessary orders and then you may present your friends to me."

"You should have been disqualified for having an unfair advantage," Jack Whittaker, who had taken the fourth place in the race, called as he descended from his curricle.

"It's too late to think of that now," Julian retorted. "Admit that I had not only the best horses but also the superior skill."

"Whittaker was too busy flirting with every female we passed," Ambrose Haldon explained, turning to take a tankard from the tray offered by a manservant. "That's what I call a proper welcome—get the dust out of a man's throat. And here's another," he added as a trio of young ladies came around the corner of the house in a flutter of white muslin and blue ribbons and sashes. They walked linked arm in arm, escorted by a young gentleman, and stopped at the sight of the assembled whips.

"Shepherdesses with attendant lapdog," Jack murmured.

"Say rather lambs," Ambrose remarked as two of the girls came forward smiling, while the third dropped back to walk with the lady who followed some paces behind. "But there is an attendant nymph, a dryad perhaps, judging by her tall willowy figure and gown of greyish green. Who is she, Loring?"

"Miss Fancourt, my sister's governess," Julian replied curtly. "And here is my sister," he added as Chloe, having greeted her father and curtseyed to his friend, came into her brother's arms, her cheek tilted for his kiss.

"Welcome home, Julian. Isn't this exciting? What a good idea of Papa's!"

He hugged her gently. "You're looking blooming, my pet. Who are your friends?"

"That is our cousin Cynthia Glazebrook there at the steps," she glanced over to where an excited group had gathered around the Raven brothers. "I'll make you known to her in a moment and—" she tugged him towards the young lady standing with Miss Fancourt, "these are my cousins Hannah Eubank, and her brother James."

Julian exchanged greetings with the Eubanks before smiling at Chloe's governess. "I hope I see you well, Miss Fancourt."

"You do indeed, Sir Julian."

Jack and Ambrose were at his elbow. "Aren't you going to present us?"

It felt subtly wrong to name his sister and her cousins before their older chaperon who had again retreated into the background. Ambrose's interest had been piqued, he could see, and when the group turned to go into the house, his friend had already engaged the governess in conversation. He must keep an eye on that situation, Julian resolved. She had been little more than a schoolgirl herself when she came to his father's house and over the years she had become— not a friend of course, but he could not look upon her as a servant. More some sort of undefined family member, certainly someone for whom he felt responsibility. When he thought about it, her life had been as sheltered as Chloe's. He wouldn't like to see her head turned by Haldon's attentions.

He looked back over his shoulder. "When do we dine, Miss Fancourt? Have we time for a game of billiards beforehand?"

Jack Whittaker groaned. "Can you never be still,

Loring? I, for one, intend to remove my boots and wash away the dust before I even contemplate doing anything else."

The house has come alive, Rosa Fancourt thought. As long as she had lived here, the second floor bedrooms had been shrouded in dust covers and the ballroom used only for Chloe's dancing lessons. Sir Edward was not given to large entertainments—he preferred to invite a few neighbours to sit down to a neat dinner or the local gentlemen to a shooting party or a hunt supper held in what was known as the hunt room, between the gun room and the billiard room on the ground floor of the bachelors' wing. Sir Edward's mother had been instrumental in the building of that wing, saying that if her husband wished to carouse, he should do so away from her and her children and she was not having his drunken guests sleep off their potations in her good bedrooms.

"Miss Fancourt, will you come and play for me?" Chloe requested as soon as the gentlemen had gone to seek out their rooms. "The other girls have brought their music and we thought we might ensure that we don't all sing the same song or play the same sonata. And would you mind also playing for them? They haven't asked, but Hannah said I was so fortunate to have you to accompany me when I sing."

"If they would like me to and it is a piece I can learn quickly, certainly," Rosa said. It was a sensible notion of Chloe's and should help avoid any unpleasant rivalry between the young ladies.

"Thank you, Miss Fancourt. If you take Hannah and Cynthia to the music room, I'll find Celia and Sophia.

I thought I'd sing *My Mother Bids Me Bind My Hair* tonight," Chloe added over her shoulder as she flitted away.

The girls had all been well taught, Rosa discovered, and if their catalogues of songs were very similar, there was enough variety that they could present a diverse selection each evening.

"Why don't we take it in turns to play a sonata?" Cynthia suggested. "Whoever plays doesn't have to sing that evening."

"We might sing something together as well," Celia said. "When is the best time to practise?"

"Probably before breakfast so it doesn't interfere with whatever plans Mamma may make," Chloe answered. "Shall we meet here at nine o'clock each morning?"

Rosa remained in the music room to practise songs for Celia and Hannah and then hurried to change into her new dinner gown. Not that anyone would notice her dark blue crepe among the girls' pale muslins and the bright silks of the matrons. She was pleased with its trimming of silver ribbon and her new cap was more decorative than her everyday ones, but it could not be denied that she was a drab sparrow among these swans.

No head turned when she entered the drawing-room. Lord Swanmere sat alone on a sofa and she went to speak to him. He and the dowager Lady Loring were on very good terms, but tonight she was surrounded by her family, including her widowed daughter, Eloisa Lady Undrell, whom she had not seen for some years. Earlier, two new great-grandchildren had been presented to her. To know not only your children's children but the third generation of your descendants was a rare privilege, Rosa thought, and how wonderful for a child to know itself part of such a family.

Seeing her approach, Lord Swanmere began to struggle to his feet.

"Pray don't get up, my lord."

"Then you must sit beside me, Miss Fancourt. Explain to me who all these young ladies are. They were introduced but in such a babble that I could hardly understand their names and, to be frank, they all look the same in their white muslins."

"You can tell them apart by the colour of their sashes," she pointed out with a smile.

He laughed. "You won't catch me out that easily, ma'am. Tomorrow they will all have changed colours and I shall be in trouble for addressing Miss Celia as Miss Cynthia. Even their names are alike," he grumbled.

"Pay attention when they sing," Rosa suggested. "They all have lovely voices, but each is quite distinctive."

"An excellent idea. I shall make a point of sitting near the pianoforte," he declared, then smiled up at his grandson who had just joined them. "Well, my boy? How was Newmarket?"

"Quite rewarding," Sir Julian said with a sudden grin. "They have added a new race for fillies—the Thousand Guineas. It was run on Thursday on the Ditch Mile."

"Who won?" enquired Lord Ransford, standing nearby.

"Mr Wilson's *Charlotte* before the Duke of Grafton's *Vestal*. There were only five runners in the end, although I believe there were initially ten entrants."

Attracted by the talk of racing, others drifted up to join the conversation and before long Rosa found herself surrounded by a phalanx of gentlemen enthusiastically discussing the exploits of the past week. They crowded around the sofa so that it was impossible to escape, so close that when she looked straight ahead her gaze met an array of masculine thighs clad in clinging inexpressibles that unashamedly delineated the male anatomy. Feeling her cheeks grow warm, she resolutely raised her eyes to above waist-level, distracting herself by looking for the subtle differences that distinguished one gentleman's dress from that of his neighbour—the half inch of waistcoat displayed below the coat, the style of his watch fob or the intricacies of his neckcloth. The men were all freshly shaven and their hair was dressed as carefully as that of any lady. Even Sir Julian, whose attire usually suggested a faint impatience with the whole business of dress, was immaculately turned out, his light brown curls tamed and brushed forward to fringe his forehead. Broad shouldered and deep-chested, he was by far the tallest of the group. Rosa had always thought him most truly the gentleman and seeing him now among a convocation of Corinthians, as young Mr Eubank had irreverently described them earlier, she saw no reason to change her opinion.

Now they had moved on to the prospects for the second Spring Meeting. She looked down and smoothed her skirt over her knee. Two new pairs of evening gloves for this week—white soiled so easily—together with the makings of two new gowns and the ribbons to refurbish her old ones. A costly indulgence, especially as she was to leave at the next quarter-day, but she had had no choice. Lady Loring would expect her governess to be adequately attired but it would not occur to her to wonder how she might meet such expense. Rosa had risen early each morning over the past weeks to take advantage of the daylight hours, sewing at her window until it was time to join Chloe for breakfast. She must still finish the ball-gown. If she got up at six, she would have three hours before she went to the music room. That should do it.

"A penny for your thoughts, Miss Fancourt."

Startled, she looked up at Mr Haldon who drew up a chair and placed it at right angles to the sofa. "May I?"

She gestured invitingly and he sat down, stretching out his legs so that the other gentlemen had to move back a little.

"I hope we have not bored you with all this talk of horses," he said. "Do you ride?"

"Yes. Sir Edward was kind enough to teach me at the same time as he taught Miss Loring. We ride or walk almost every day."

"Perhaps you will permit me to join you one day."

"My sister and Miss Fancourt are capital horsewomen," Sir Julian put in.

"I have no doubt of it if they were instructed by Sir Edward," Mr Haldon said. "I imagine he was a stern taskmaster. But what else do young ladies do with themselves, apart from going to parties, that is? I have often wondered how they occupy their time."

"Have you no sisters, sir?" Rosa enquired.

"Not one," he sighed. "I have been sadly deprived."

"Or are rather to be envied," Mr Whittaker retorted. "I have three and all they seem to do is chatter."

Rosa raised an eyebrow. "In contrast to gentlemen, you mean?" In her admittedly limited experience, gentlemen tended to take over any conversation.

"A direct hit, Whittaker, considering we have been

deafening the lady for the past ten minutes," Mr Haldon said dryly.

"Gentlemen don't chatter, gentlemen converse."

Mr Whittaker's lofty response was belied by a twinkle in his eye that encouraged Rosa to counter, "One could as easily say they prate or even jibber-jabber. *A rose by any other name*, sir!"

"I am sure young ladies' conversation is much sweeter," Mr Haldon said as their listeners chuckled.

Dinner was announced and the little group broke up, the gentlemen seeking out the ladies they were to take in. As the most insignificant ladies present, Rosa and Lady Undrell's governess, Miss Smith, went last, Rosa with Mr Martin Glazebrook and Miss Smith on the arm of Mr James Eubank.

In all her years at Loring Place, she had never seen the dining-room displayed to such advantage. The table, extended to its full length to accommodate thirty diners, was draped in crisp, white napery and set with gleaming plate, glass and porcelain. An elaborate epergne with five cut glass dishes throned in the centre, filled with marchpane delicacies and the choicest fruits the succession houses could provide, and crowned with a green-plumed pineapple. Rosa wondered whether any guest would dare disturb the intricate arrangements. The tulips in the vases of spring flowers she had arranged so carefully that morning had not drooped, she noted with relief, and the little irises were opening nicely.

Meadows looked tense as he supervised the troop of footmen, several of whom had been hired for the week. All were wearing new livery. Had Sir Edward had any idea of what his celebrations would cost him, she wondered idly as Mr Glazebrook held her chair for her to take her place. Opposite her, a few couples down, Chloe quietly removed her elbow-length gloves. She did not appear to be overwhelmed by the occasion, Rosa saw, as she tucked her own folded gloves together with her reticule under the napkin on her lap.

She glanced at young Mr Glazebrook. "Have you been following the progress of the army in France, sir?"

He had, and immediately launched into a discussion of the siege of Bayonne. "Paris has fallen and Bonaparte has abdicated," he said indignantly. "What is the point of continuing fighting? The governor should own they are defeated."

Julian looked down the long table. His stepmother and her household appeared to be coping admirably despite not being accustomed to entertaining such a large number of guests. He still couldn't fathom why his father had decided to host such a party, and at short notice. Including a cricket match. And of course he was expected to lead the home side to victory. Tomorrow was Sunday, so they could not practise, but he could at least select his team. Jack Whittaker had agreed to captain the visitors but Julian might have to arrange for their numbers to be augmented by some neighbours.

Amelia Glazebrook's voice returned him to the present. "Do you plan to go to town after Newmarket, Julian?"

"Probably. And you?"

"Not this year. We shall have enough of it next year, of course, when Cynthia comes out. This is an excellent idea of Lady Loring's. It allows the girls to try their wings in unexceptional company. I must see about doing something before the hunting starts and all the men disappear to Melton Mowbray."

Across the table he saw Miss Fancourt smile and bow as she raised her glass to her neighbour. "Will you take wine with me, Amelia?" he asked his cousin abruptly and beckoned the footman.

# Chapter Two

BEFORE ROSA COULD SLIP UPSTAIRS to her own room to remove her bonnet and pelisse on her return from church, she was summoned to Lady Loring's bedchamber.

Her ladyship drummed her fingers on her dressing-table while her maid set her hair to rights. "There you are, Miss Fancourt. That will do, Hughes. Just give me the cherry-blossom shawl before you go. Now, Miss Fancourt, what entertainment are we to offer the guests tonight? Sir Edward refuses to permit cards or dancing on a Sunday. He is positively antediluvian, as I have told him. It is well known they play cards at Court on Sundays, but he will not be budged."

"Did he say anything else, Lady Loring; give some indication of what would be appropriate?"

"*'They should be content with quiet conversation'*," her ladyship quoted, rolling her eyes in a way that would have elicited a reproof for her daughter.

"I presume we may have some music as usual."

"Yes, but not too worldly—I must tell Chloe. But that is not enough. We must have something else that will involve the whole company, but nothing boisterous like forfeits."

"We could play conundrums or dumb crambo or—what about acted charades?"

"Acted charades?"

"We used play them at school. Instead of posing a riddle, the actors dress up and mime the scenes without speaking and the others have to guess what it is."

"I don't know whether Sir Edward would permit it," Lady Loring said doubtfully.

"Supposing we said they were to take themes from the Bible?"

"An excellent notion. He can hardly object to that. We are to spend the day quietly, he says. A cold collation will be served at half-past one and afterwards those who wish may go for a walk. I must remain here with the older ladies, so you will accompany the younger ones."

"Yes, Lady Loring," Rosa said, resigned to the fact that there would be no rest for her today, and very likely none for the remainder of the week.

A shawl draped veil-like over her head and shoulders, Chloe sat on a cushion and plied a large needle with exaggerated gestures.

"The lilies of the field," Mr Undrell said.

"They toil not," Mrs Glazebrook objected, "and it is spin, not sew."

"The parable of the sower," Major Raven offered.

"That is sowing seed, not sewing a seam," Mr Eubank corrected him.

After a few moments Chloe folded her work and laid it aside while the onlookers resettled themselves in anticipation of the next scene.

Biblical dumb charades had proved immensely successful although Rosa did not know what Sir Edward had thought of the younger Lady Undrell's appearance as a lissom Salomé sinuously dancing before King Herod. Some onlookers had been misled by the choice of Handel's music for the arrival of the Queen of Sheba but the dramatic appearance of Jack Whittaker's head gorily daubed with vermilion and stuck through a cloth spanned between two tables had settled the debate.

Hannah Eubank had been so resolute a Jael that her Sisera had been heard to mutter, "not so hard, Sis," while Cynthia, Mrs Eubank and Lord Ransford had movingly portrayed the judgement of Solomon with the assistance of one of Chloe's dolls.

Now Mr Haldon, resplendent in a plum coloured banyan and turban, took his place on the carpet beside Chloe and began to peruse a stack of banknotes, bills and vowels before turning to count his coins. He took a sheet of paper, wrote in large figures '100,000' and, beaming with satisfaction, displayed it to the onlookers.

"The unjust steward," someone called.

"No. Then he would have to cross out the hundred and write down fifty," Lady Ransford corrected him. "It must be Dives clothed in purple and fine linen."

"Miss Loring hardly represents Lazarus," her daughter-in-law protested.

Mr Haldon stacked his papers and folded his hands. From behind the screen that served as makeshift wings, a columnar figure dressed all in white emerged. It was heavily veiled and wore on its head a diadem of silver wire with an open oval construction rising from the centre.

"An angel!"

"No; Lot's wife—the pillar of salt," Sir Edward's mother declared.

The white figure moved into the centre of the carpet

and knelt upright. An even stranger creature clad in a peculiar costume of mustard-coloured cloth shambled in on all fours. Two cushions covered in the same fabric were fixed to its back and another cushion cover had been cunningly draped so as to conceal the face and neck of the wearer.

"It's no wonder they took so long to prepare," someone muttered.

The creature gingerly pawed at the opening of the silver oval and shook its head violently then looked up at the ceiling, lifting its front paws either in prayer or despair.

"A lion?" someone asked doubtfully.

"*'Be sober, be vigilant; because your adversary the devil, as a roaring lion, walketh about, seeking whom he may devour'*," Sir Edward declaimed sonorously.

"It's the oddest lion I have ever seen," Sir Jethro remarked.

"Something from the Book of Revelation," Lady Ransford suggested.

The beast was now butting its head gently against the column while behind it, Chloe had resumed her sewing and Mr Haldon his counting.

"Oh!" Rosa began to laugh, then felt herself flush as all heads swivelled, looking back to where she sat with Miss Smith. She put her hand to her mouth.

"Come, Miss Fancourt, you must share your supposition with us," Lord Swanmere said encouragingly.

"I think it must be the rich man, the camel and the eye of the needle."

"By Jove, yes!" Sir Jethro slapped his thigh. "Very clever, what?"

The beast nodded vigorously and lifted off its head-covering to reveal a broadly grinning Sir Julian who scrubbed his hand through his tousled hair, shaking his head as he did so.

"Well, this has been most diverting," Lady Loring announced. "Miss Fancourt, pray ring for the supper-tray. I am sure we can all do with some refreshment."

"That was well-spotted, Miss Fancourt," Julian said when he returned to the drawing-room, having divested himself of the camel's garb and made some attempt at tidying his hair. "We were sure we would have you all baffled."

"It was quite ingenious," she admitted, "but I am not sure whether it was entirely fair as the scene itself does not actually occur in Scripture. It is a brief parable."

He laughed. "I am glad you kept your reservations to yourself and did not appeal to have us disqualified after all our efforts."

"How did you contrive something so elaborate in so short a time?"

"Chloe remembered the old bed-curtains and my valet cut and pinned them on to me. And deuced uncomfortable they were, not to mention dusty. I had to remember to move very carefully and do my utmost not to sneeze." He rubbed his nose reflectively. "I need some fortification after that. May I fetch you a glass of Madeira?"

She seemed surprised by the question, but accepted with a small smile.

She looks tired, he thought as he went to the supper-tray. When he had come on to play his part, he had noticed her sitting quietly at the back of the room, her hands folded in her lap. It was unusual to see her idle, not attentive or watchful as she usually was. For a moment her eyes closed, then she snapped them open and sat a little straighter. He had begun to clown, partly to amuse her, and had been rewarded by a delightful chuckle although she had seemed embarrassed when everyone turned to look at her.

He raised his glass. "To your good health, Miss Fancourt."

"Thank you, sir."

"How do you find having the house so full?"

"It is strange, but I like it. It may seem fanciful, but I think the house likes it too. It's very good for Chloe. She grows up a little more each day, I think. It is charming to see her take the lead with the other young ladies and see to their comfort. I hope that she will stay friends with them, especially with Miss Glazebrook and Miss Undrell who are also to make their come-out next year."

"Also?" he repeated sharply. "You don't mean that Chloe is to come out next year? She is just sixteen."

"I understand that is what Lady Loring plans, Sir Julian. Miss Glazebrook is seventeen and Miss Undrell eighteen—she would have come out this year if the family had not been in mourning for her grandfather."

"And you think it would be good for Chloe to have some friends who are a little older?"

She nodded. "You cannot deny that she has led a very secluded life until now."

"As have you, Miss Fancourt. Shall you go to London with Chloe?"

"No," she replied quietly. "I leave at Midsummer when a finishing governess comes to prepare Chloe for her Season."

He stared at her. Somehow, he could not imagine the

Place without her. "What shall you do then?"

"I have not quite made up my mind." Her gaze slipped past him. "Pray excuse me, sir."

Julian watched her go to his grandmother who sat dozing on a sofa. The governess perched beside her, they exchanged a few words and after a couple of minutes the two ladies left the room, the dowager leaning on Miss Fancourt's arm.

Julian bowed politely when he came into the hall from the bachelors' wing the following day. "Good morning, Lady Loring."

As usual, his stepmother appeared irritated by this correct salutation. Fifteen when his father remarried, Julian had refused to accept a woman just ten years older as a 'new mother' and had resisted any efforts on her part to develop a more cordial relationship between them, resolutely addressing her as 'Lady Loring' or 'ma'am'. On his eighteenth birthday she had suggested he call her Delia, but he had 'begged to decline the honour'. Although she had never raised the subject again, she continued to use his unadorned Christian name, even after he had been knighted.

Now she only said, "Pray come into the book-room for a moment."

He raised his eyebrows but obeyed. "What may I do for you?"

"You may ensure that the younger men do not disappear as they did yesterday afternoon," she said bluntly. "Only James Eubank was available to accompany the girls on their walk. It was mortifying, not only for me but for him as well. If you were all going to decamp somewhere, why was he left out?"

Julian frowned. "I spent the afternoon recruiting players for Thursday's cricket match. I don't know what the others did, but if it was as you describe, I agree it was not well done."

"Meadows said they visited the stables and the kennels after church and then repaired to the billiard room where they requested ale and sandwiches. He thought it best to acquiesce. I would have asked you to intervene, but Meadows didn't know where you were and I did not want to bring your father into it."

"That was wise." His father would either have coldly reproved the 'Sabbath-breakers' or flown into a rage at their temerity. "The biblical charades yesterday evening were inspired."

His stepmother tossed her head, apparently flustered by his rare compliment. "Thank you, Julian." She looked pleadingly at him. "I thought today we might ride or drive to Bury to see the remains of the Abbey. May I rely on you to ensure that the men come too? Chloe may not have another such opportunity to become accustomed to masculine company before we take her to town next year. I want her to make the best of her Season and not be so inexperienced that she is frightened if an eligible gentleman displays an interest in her."

"Surely you will not seek to marry her off so soon," he protested.

"I want her to have a congenial husband. Ideally, she should have two or three Seasons to find one, but your father will only agree to one. Hiring a town house, especially one with a ballroom, is too expensive, he says."

"Why not wait until she is a year older?"

She sighed. "I must take what I am offered, Julian. Who

knows what might happen in a year? He promised me he would take me to town the year after we were wed but then your grandfather died and by the time we had put off our blacks—well, suffice it to say that I have not yet been to London. Lady Ransford has kindly agreed to present Chloe and me to her Majesty next year. I am determined that my daughter will have the opportunities and choices that I did not have," she finished fiercely.

Julian felt ashamed that he knew so little about her. Sir Edward had met her in Harrogate, he recalled, where she had lived with her mother. Twenty years ago, it had never occurred to him to enquire what his father had been doing there of all places and there was little point in asking now.

"Well?" she said impatiently.

"You may count on me, ma'am," he replied briskly. He would have to fit in some practice with the bat, but he would work something out.

"Do you not join us, Miss Fancourt?"

"Not today, Mr Haldon."

"That is a pity. I should be happy to take you up in my curricle if you do not care to ride." Mr Haldon spoke quietly, his words just reaching Rosa's ears amid the hubbub as arrangements for the outing to Bury were proposed, discussed, revised, decided and overthrown.

Rosa glanced nervously at her employer. Heir to a considerable estate and blessed with dark good looks, an elegance of manner and an amiable disposition, Mr Haldon must be considered the most eligible of the bachelor guests and she did not think Lady Loring would appreciate her daughter's governess being squired by him. Fortunately that lady did not seem to have heard his suggestion.

"It is very kind of you, sir, but I have some tasks to complete this morning."

His eyes narrowed. "I understand. Perhaps another time."

He has no sisters, Rosa remembered—evidently he is not used to mixing with attendants such as governesses or companions and assumed I was as free as any other lady. Or, what is more likely, he is bored and seeks to amuse himself without risking being trapped into matrimony.

By the time orders were sent to the stables and the ladies had changed into their habits and carriage gowns it was almost one o'clock. Rosa stood under the portico at the front door and watched the cavalcade wind its way down the drive. She exchanged a conspiratorial smile of relief with Meadows when she returned to the hall, then made her way to the morning room where she found the dowager Ladies Loring and Undrell seated amicably at whist with Lords Swanmere and Ransford, while Lady Ransford had abandoned her game of solitaire for the latest newssheets.

"We are perfectly comfortable, Miss Fancourt," Lady Loring said when Rosa looked in. "I suggest you take the opportunity to rest a little."

"Thank you, ma'am." Rosa was fond of the old lady whose trenchant remarks concealed a warm heart and did not misconstrue this instruction as a hint that she was intruding. She knew it was made out of genuine concern.

She left them to their cards and went to renew the flower arrangements for the drawing-room and dining-room. Then she must practise the accompaniment to the song by Mr Linley that Miss Spilsbury wished to sing that evening and after that, if she were lucky, she could finish trimming her new ball-gown. No; first the flowers and then the gown, she thought. It would be acceptable to be found in the music room when the excursion party returned, but it would never do for her to be shut away in her own room. She would not join the others for a nuncheon but ask Mrs Walton for a small tray in the schoolroom. She did not want much; a cup of tea and some bread and butter, perhaps a slice of ham.

# Chapter Three

Loring Place stank of roasting beef. For over twenty-four hours a team of men had turned the huge carcase on the massive spit before a glowing fire, letting the ox revolve slowly as it spat and sizzled, basting it regularly with the drippings so that the skin gradually blackened but did not burn. By Thursday morning the aroma had gone from appetising to nauseating, or so Rosa felt. Although the fire pit had been dug well away from the house, the thick, greasy smell seeped through shut doors and windows, oozing through chinks and gaps so that there was no escape from the all-pervasive reek. But perhaps only the inhabitants of the Place found it so unpleasant. Certainly the tenants, villagers and neighbours who had arrived all morning smiled and licked eager lips in anticipation of the feast to come.

Sir Edward's birthday had dawned sunny but with a chill east wind that set bunting and banners fluttering bravely and sent the ladies back to their rooms to exchange their spencers for warmer shawls and pelisses. Soon over a hundred people mingled on the lawns in front of the house. A marquee had been set up to provide shelter for the nobility and gentry while rough benches and tables waited for the tenants and villagers.

Chloe's eyes sparkled as the fifes and drums of the Bury Yeomanry marched in to the strains of *The British Grenadiers.* "There is something so exhilarating about military music. And here come the players. I hope Julian's side wins. Papa will be so cast down if they are defeated."

She dimpled at Major Raven who brought his hand to his shako with a flourish as he passed, and watched fascinated as the gentlemen, having arrived at the benches set out for the players, proceeded to remove their coats.

"Oh, look; Mr Haldon needs his valet to help him," she giggled.

"What a fribble," her grandmother snapped.

Chloe's eyes rounded when no less a person than her aunt, the dowager Lady Undrell, replied, "You have to admit, Mamma, that he strips better than one would have expected." She nodded towards a sleek, black-haired man of about forty who must have made some quip that had the others laughing. "Who is that beside him?"

"Mr Purdue, the new owner of Old Hall," Rosa said. She had earlier been introduced to this gentleman who had recently inherited the neighbouring property from his uncle. This was his first appearance in local society. Having watched him favour the younger Ladies Loring and Undrell, Mrs Spilsbury and Mrs Glazebrook with the same speaking glance from his dark brown eyes, she had not been flattered when he turned it on her. His eyebrows had twitched together at her cool response but he had bowed as civilly as she and moved on.

"Honestly, Miss Fancourt, is there anything more tedious than a cricket match?" Chloe groaned several hours later. "Only Papa would choose to celebrate his birthday by having wickets pitched on his lawn. It took them forever to begin—all that measuring and fussing about popping and bowling creases—as if it mattered!—and now it seems as if it will never end."

"Sir Edward was a great player in his day," Rosa remarked.

Chloe rolled her eyes. "I know—he has re-lived every single match since he decided to give this party. I vow I'll scream if I have to endure another dinner listening to his tales of notches and catches and bowling-outs!" She looked disconsolately around the marquee where the ladies whiled away the time over glasses of negus to combat the chill and cards and gossip to alleviate their boredom. "I'm tired of sitting. Let us take a turn about the lawn."

A shout went up, accompanied by a groan as Mr Haldon leapt and snatched the ball from the air while Sir Julian and his partner ran towards each other's wickets. The striker left the field and was replaced by a young under-gardener who took up his position opposite Sir Julian.

"That's their last man," Sir Gerard Undrell said. "It cannot be long now."

Rosa's eyes strayed to where a shirt-sleeved Sir Julian now faced the bowler. With a powerful stroke, he propelled the ball over the heads of the onlookers who scrambled out of the way as the fieldsmen ran in pursuit while the two strikers raced to and fro between their wickets.

"Lost ball!"

At the shout, Sir Julian grinned amicably at the under-gardener who stood opposite him and returned to his post.

"Foolish to let it go on so long that we could run another eight notches," Sir Edward said. "We need just six more to carry the day."

"I don't know," Sir Jethro Boyce remarked. "The young lad will soon have to face the bowling. Once he's out, 'twill be all up with you."

"Nonsense. Jem is handy enough with the bat," Sir Edward countered.

"A pony you don't do it!"

"Done!"

Chloe tugged on Rosa's sleeve. "What was that about?" she whispered as her father and his friend moved away.

"Let us stroll over to Mrs Wycliffe and her daughters," Rosa suggested.

"Very well, but what was that about a pony?"

"Sir Jethro was wagering with your father that his team would not win."

"Wagering! I wouldn't have thought it of Papa! And to stake a pony! How could he! My old Firefly is the only pony in the stables. He shan't give her away, and I'll tell him so." Chloe looked as if she were about to whirl around and confront her father instanter.

Trying not to laugh, Rosa put a calming hand on her pupil's arm. "A pony is a vulgar term for a certain amount of money—twenty-five pounds, I think."

Chloe was horrified. "But that is an enormous sum."

A year's salary for me, Rosa thought wryly, but aloud said only, "In terms of gentlemen's bets, it would not be unusual, I believe." She hesitated and then added, "It is better you understand the ways of the world a little, but such language is not ladylike and it would be both foolish and most improper for you to let yourself be tempted into any form of gambling."

"Miss Fancourt! As if I would!" Chloe said indignantly, then smiled at the Wycliffes. "Isn't this exciting? We just need six more notches to win."

The firm thwack of bat against ball drew Rosa's attention back to the lawn where Sir Julian was running again with great loping strides. He touched down his bat and raced back to his own wicket.

"Two more notches," a tenant farmer exclaimed with great satisfaction.

Sir Julian swiped his shirtsleeve across his brow and thrust his hand through his light brown hair. He shook his head vigorously, replaced his tall hat and again faced the bowler. The next ball curved slowly towards him and he stepped forward to send it soaring over the ha-ha. He didn't wait for it to drop on the far side but immediately raced towards the opposite wicket, losing his hat so that his curls bobbed as he ran. He must usually use pomade or macassar oil to control them, Rosa thought, but his hair never looks greasy.

The visiting fieldsmen peered into the depths of the ha-ha. "Lost ball," Major Raven called resignedly, conceding four notches and the match.

The victorious batsman swiped up his hat and flourished it in acknowledgement of the cheers of the home supporters while his team-mates crowded around him, clapping him on the shoulder. Someone handed him a tankard of ale and he drank deeply before passing it to the under-gardener.

Sir Edward pushed his way through the congratulatory throng. "Fifty-one notches! Well played, sir! And well played to all of you! Now you're ready for a bit of dinner, I daresay. They tell me I may carve the first slice of the ox in fifteen minutes. A fine, fat one it is, thirty hours on the spit and done to a turn."

"Well done, Julian!" Chloe exclaimed as her brother passed her. "You won Papa's wager for him."

He smiled down at her. "And what do you know about wagering, Miss?"

She reddened and glanced sidelong at Rosa but stood her ground, retorting, "Is it my fault if he makes bets while I am near?"

"To be fair, it was Sir Jethro who proposed the wager," Rosa pointed out.

"And that's another thing! He is supposed to be Papa's friend. It is most unfriendly of him to bet against us."

"Perhaps, but I believe gentlemen see these things differently, my dear," Rosa informed her.

"Especially wagers," Sir Julian agreed, a wicked glint in his eye. "A little friendly rivalry adds spice to season the victory." He started to walk towards the house. "I must change my clothes."

He sauntered beside his sister, his bat resting on his shoulder. His white stockings were muddy and streaked with grass, as were the knees of his breeches; his neckcloth was loosened and his shirt clung to him beneath his waistcoat. He smelled pleasantly of fresh perspiration, grass and whatever unguents and lotions he used as part of his *toilette*.

Not that he was a dandy, of course—he was too large and too—too male for that. A Viking or an Anglo-Saxon, perhaps, Rosa reflected, admiring the loose-limbed figure moving effortlessly ahead of her. He certainly had no need to pad his calves or shoulders. Who would have thought that a gentleman's rear aspect could be so—arresting? Of course, their posteriors were usually hidden by the tails of their coats. His were firm and neat, tightening and relaxing beneath his pale inexpressibles as he walked. My goodness! What was she doing staring at him like that? She frowned, firmed her lips and resolutely averted her gaze.

"Miss Fancourt?"

He had looked back to address her. Praying he hadn't caught her ogling his backside, she summoned all her composure to reply pleasantly, "Yes, Sir Julian?"

"May I ask you to keep an eye on Lord Swanmere this evening? His deafness means that he easily becomes— removed from the company. He will be with my grandmother at dinner but later, at the ball—"

Rosa nodded understandingly. "Between the music and the general hubbub it will be even more difficult for him to hear."

"That's it."

"I'll look after him, Sir Julian."

"Thank you, Miss Fancourt. I knew I might rely on you."

"I can sit with him," Chloe offered generously.

"But you will wish to dance," he pointed out. "It is your first ball, after all."

It was Rosa's first ball too, but nobody would think of that, or believe it either. Miss Smith, the Undrells' governess, had told Rosa she had frequently attended assemblies at home and Lady Undrell very kindly included her in the Twelfth Night ball she gave every year. But Rosa had gone directly from Mrs Ellicott's Academy for Young Ladies in Bath to Loring Place.

Poor Mamma had remarried so quickly after Papa was killed at Copenhagen. 'I am tired of being alone' was all she had said when she told Rosa she had agreed to wed Mr Kennard and that her daughter would not come with her to his home but would board at Mrs Ellicott's. And then, little more than a year later, she had died in childbed and Rosa was truly orphaned. Her stepfather hadn't even come himself to break the news but had written to a Mr Chidlow who had travelled across England so that he could personally explain the change in her circumstances.

"I could do no less for Captain Fancourt's daughter," he had told her when she expressed her surprise at his presence. "He came to Maidstone especially to tell my dear wife and me of the final hours of our son who served as midshipman under him. Since then I have acted as his man of business and am now your trustee."

"My trustee?"

"In respect of the one thousand pounds he left directly to you, Miss Rosa. Unfortunately your mother's property became this Kennard's outright on their marriage—if she had consulted me, I should have advised a settlement that would have made appropriate provision for you on her death, but regrettably she did not—and he refuses to deprive his infant son of any of what he describes as his rightful inheritance."

"An infant son? The baby lived? I have a brother!" Rosa had jumped up in excitement. "When can I see him? Do you know what he is called, sir?"

"I do not," Mr Chidlow replied shortly. He looked appealingly at Mrs Ellicott who took Rosa's hand.

"Sadly, my dear Rosa, Mr Kennard writes that he does not accept any responsibility for you. He is not your father, he says; you have never lived in his household and he does not wish to receive you into it."

"But where am I to go? I must have a home."

"You must consider this your home for the moment, my dear. Your tuition is paid until the end of this term and after that I shall be pleased to retain you as a pupil-teacher. You will have no fees to pay and will receive an annual allowance of twelve guineas in addition to your bed and board. When you have completed your education and acquired some experience in the class-room, you will be excellently qualified to seek a position as governess in a good family. I am frequently applied to by the best families, you must know, and I am sure I shall have no hesitation in recommending you."

"Might I not look after my brother? I would be no trouble to Mr Kennard, I assure you."

Mr Chidlow shook his head. "I ventured to suggest that you might help care for the child, but he refuses to consider it."

She looked from one to the other. Her surviving parent was dead, she had a new brother whom she would never know and the man who had professed to love her mother denied her daughter the shelter of his home. Tears slipped silently down her cheeks. It had proved impossible to still them and, in the end, Mrs Ellicott had to summon the physician to administer a soporific draught.

"We shall leave your funds untouched, Miss Rosa, until we see what direction your life takes," Mr Chidlow had declared before taking his leave the next day. "In not so many years you may be a happy wife and mother but, should that not come to pass, you will eventually accumulate enough that you can set up your own little establishment. You are far too young to consider that at present."

After a year as a pupil teacher, she had come to the Lorings. And now she was to leave them. It would break her heart to part from Chloe but, no matter how fond she became of her charges, a governess had no claim to them and she must relinquish them smilingly when the time came.

# Chapter Four

THERE WOULD BE NO DANCING for Rosa tonight. She might know all the steps, for she had practised them diligently with Chloe as well as playing the pianoforte when the dancing-master called, but her place was in the background, alert to the beck and call of her employers; a lady, but not an equal.

She tied the draw-string at the top of her chemise and picked up her new, short stays. Behind her, spread out on her bed, was the gown she had made for the evening from an Egyptian brown sarsnet the dowager Lady Loring had given her. The fabric seemed dull, but sometimes it shimmered faintly, especially when it caught the meagre light of her two candles. Rosa had trimmed the high waist and cuffs with cream satin ribbon and cut out brown and cream leaves and stitched them to provide a scalloped finish to the neckline.

At the knock, she quickly wrapped a large shawl around her shoulders and peered around the door before stepping back to admit Dover, the dowager's maid.

"Her ladyship sent me to help you dress, miss. I see I came at just the right time."

She held up the stays for Rosa to slip her arms into the sleeveless garment, then came around to stand in front of her. "Bend forward a little, miss.

Puzzled, Rosa complied.

The maid slipped the long lace into the bottom holes to join the front halves. As she laced them together, she deftly positioned Rosa's breasts so that they were lifted and supported by the intricate seams and gussets. Rosa straightened instinctively as she worked. Finally Dover tied the lace in a firm, flat bow and tucked the ends behind the uppermost lacing.

"It'll do. Back-lacing is better of course, but you have a pretty bosom. Is this your dress?"

She lifted it from the bed, dropped it over Rosa's head and pulled down the rustling skirts while Rosa fastened the matching silk thread buttons over which she had laboured for several hours.

Dover stepped back to assess the effect. "It suits you. Have you any beads or such?"

Rosa produced her mother's modest necklace of seed pearls, a souvenir of some far eastern port. She had Mr Chidlow to thank for these, too—he had persuaded Mr Kennard to deliver up her mother's mementoes of her first marriage. The maid fastened them and took the chair from the little table and set it in front of the chest of drawers that served as Rosa's dressing-table.

"Sit here, miss."

She draped a towel around Rosa's shoulders and unpinned her hair, then brushed it until it shone. "As straight as a poker," she muttered to herself. "There's no time to heat the tongs. Have you any of that cream ribbon left?"

She gathered the long, glossy hair in one hand and pulled it so tight that Rosa's eyes watered, then embarked on a complicated process of parting, twisting and plaiting, working so fast that Rosa could hardly follow what she was doing. Pins and combs were placed and removed until suddenly a braid crossed the top of her head from ear to ear. Then her back hair was pinned up in a stylish knot which the braid crowned, tiara-like.

Rosa gasped. "It's most elegant. Thank you, Dover."

The maid permitted herself a half-smile as she skilfully fixed two narrow bandeaux of cream satin over the smooth hair in front of the braid. "It'll do. If I had had more time, I could have cut a fringe and curled it."

"I prefer this," Rosa answered honestly. "I don't want to have to deal with curl papers every night."

"Most of 'em wear false fronts, if it comes to that," Dover said practically.

Rosa drew on her new evening gloves. A brief pause to check that her reticule contained such essentials as a paper of pins, smelling salts and an extra handkerchief and she was ready. This was the climax of the week's festivities. Tomorrow would be quiet after today's excitement and on Saturday most of the house-party would depart. How long would it take for the Place to return to normal?

Julian smiled at his sister and tucked her hand into his arm. Chloe had called *The Rose* as the first dance. Eight couples had in turn joined hands, revolved, chasséed and progressed through the set until she and her brother had successfully arrived back at the top.

"Well done, imp! So you are out, now."

"Here at any rate, and Papa has agreed I may have a Season next year."

This was said so unenthusiastically that he asked, "Do you not wish for one?"

She sighed. "I just wish Miss Fancourt did not have to leave us—I could face anything with her by my side. But Mamma says I am to have a finishing governess who will 'polish' me. As if I were a piece of tarnished silver!"

"I'm sure she didn't mean it so. And it will help you if you know a little more about the ways of the world. Are you to go to the assemblies in Bury during Fair Week?"

Chloe looked almost frightened by this question. "I don't know. Mamma hasn't said. If I must, promise me you will come too, Julian. I would feel much more comfortable if you were there."

"Of course I'll come," he reassured her. While it might be better for her to find her feet a little in society before she went to London, he felt uneasy at the thought of his little sister exposed to the caprices of a public assembly, no matter how select the promoters claimed their subscribers to be.

A neighbour's son, not much more than twenty, came up to make his bow and Julian relinquished Chloe to him. He had promised his stepmother that he would do his duty in the ballroom but there would be no surprises here tonight unless some neighbouring matron had brought her guests and her ladyship had not mentioned anyone seeking permission to do so. His father would most likely spend most of his time in the card room.

He smiled inwardly at the image of Sir Edward braving the *ton* ballrooms next year and resolved to be on hand to support him and Chloe. Now that he thought about it, his sister's come-out would provide him with the perfect opportunity to survey the latest crop of eligible females without it appearing that he was hanging out for a bride although, at thirty-five, it was high time he fronted the altar. If only he could find a lady who was tall enough to meet his eyes, intelligent enough not to bore him and had that certain something that meant he could imagine spending the rest of his life with her. He shook his head. Where had that flight of fancy sprung from?

Miss Fancourt stopped as she crossed the room. "Lord Swanmere is playing whist, Sir Julian."

"Then he is probably settled for the next couple of hours."

"I think so. I'll look in again just before supper. He may prefer to have something brought to him in the card room. If not, I'll ask Meadows to arrange a quiet table in the supper room."

"Thank you, Miss Fancourt. You think of everything."

She smiled and made a demurring gesture. He watched her as she moved away. During the past week he had become more aware of her, perhaps spurred by Haldon's evident interest. She was in particularly good looks tonight, her graceful figure wrapped in rich, chocolate-coloured silk that gleamed and shimmered in the candle-light. The overlapping brown and white edging of her bodice invited the onlooker to trace its contours with one finger, perhaps allow it to slip onto the sweet curves beneath; to caress the creamy skin that drew the gaze to her beautifully shaped neck and shoulders and hinted temptingly at rounded breasts. She had left off her usual plain cap to reveal raven-black hair dressed in a simple style that emphasised her regal posture and left her forehead bare, drawing attention to fine blue-grey eyes set beneath beautifully arched brows. Unlike the other ladies who were constantly in motion, fluttering their fans, swaying their skirts or tossing their curls, she sought neither admiration nor attention as she proceeded through the throng in a quiet yet business-like fashion.

As he watched, Haldon came up to her. From his bow and inviting arm, he must be asking her to stand up with him. Julian could only see the back of her head, artfully crowned with her own hair, but from the slight shake of her head and Haldon's rueful smile, he knew she had refused him even before she continued on her way. Why the devil shouldn't she dance?

He sighed inwardly and went to solicit the hand of Lady Undrell for the next set. He should lead out Mrs Raven after that, he supposed. As they waited for the musicians to strike up, he saw Miss Fancourt pause to speak to his grandmother who sat in a corner with other older ladies. She left the room, returning a few minutes later with a warmer shawl which she carefully laid around the dowager's shoulders. She was followed by a footman bearing a tray of negus. What a gaggle of grandams, Julian thought, but he was touched by Miss Fancourt's thoughtfulness.

For the rest of the evening he amused himself by tracking her progress through the ballroom. While his stepmother, robed in a dashing ensemble of Pomona silk and blonde lace, chatted and flirted with her guests, Miss Fancourt unobtrusively dealt with the little misfortunes that attended any ball, whether it was a torn flounce, a spilt glass of lemonade or an encroaching ensign who did not seem willing to relinquish Chloe after their dance. Julian had been about to intervene when Miss Fancourt drifted up to the couple and, without undue fuss, detached Chloe from her admirer.

Shortly after midnight he saw her cross the hall from the card-room on Lord Swanmere's arm. He had his own suspicions as to who was supporting whom and not long afterwards she stopped to inform him that his grandfather had retired but was in good spirits and had enjoyed the evening.

"He did not go so far as to boast," she said, a little smile lurking in her eyes, "but he appeared more than satisfied with his winnings."

The musicians played the opening strains of Sir Roger de Coverley and then paused to allow the guests to make up sets for the finishing dance. Rosa smiled to see Chloe on the arm of a youthful officer of the Suffolk Yeomanry. Her pupil had acquitted herself well today. Sir Edward, who had returned to the ball-room for the last dance, approached Lady Ransford while his wife stood up with Mr Purdue. There could be no doubt that the festivities had been a resounding success. Lord Swanmere had already retired, as had the dowager, and Rosa could sit quietly for the final thirty minutes of the ball. It had been a long day with a succession of little tasks and errands to be completed as well as keeping an eye on her charges.

She sighed when Sir Julian walked purposefully towards her. What might he want now? She didn't rise but looked up questioningly.

He smiled and bowed slightly. "May I have the pleasure of dancing this last with you, Miss Fancourt?"

Had she misheard? No, he stood before her, his hand

outstretched. Earlier, she had rejected Mr Haldon's kind offer, saying she would not dance that evening, but she could hardly spurn the son of the house. She rose and placed her hand on his, letting him lead her to the bottom of the nearest set.

They were just in time. The lively, jigging melody began again, she curtsied to her partner and he advanced towards the top lady in the middle of the set and retreated. Now she must advance towards the top gentleman. Rosa skipped and stepped as merrily as the rest, looking forward to the moment in each sequence where she joined hands with her partner to promenade, cast off and re-unite before passing beneath the raised hands of the leading couple. She and Sir Julian were both taller than the average and his broad shoulders made it necessary for them to stoop and press close together if they were to fit beneath some of these human arches. It became a private challenge not to falter but they were almost undone when they came to the second last couple who were as short as Rosa and her partner were long.

"It's fortunate I'm not wearing feathers," she muttered as they waited their turn.

"We'd be completely dished up," he agreed. "I hate the things—they make me sneeze."

Eyes brimming in shared amusement, they ducked their heads and shoulders as they advanced. It was only by tightly clasping their hands and pressing their forearms together that they could maintain their balance while stooping and sidling through. They emerged triumphantly to a ripple of laughter among their fellow-dancers that changed to applause when they rose to their full heights without having missed a step.

"Bravo!" he murmured as they continued to the top of the set.

The figure started again. Rosa found it hard not to giggle when she saw how frequently Sir Julian jerked his head to avoid being tickled by the tall plumes gracing the silk turban of the bottom lady but had to laugh when he returned to her discreetly pinching his nose as if to stop a sneeze. He grinned at her and offered his hand in the grand manner to lead her forward before they cast off. At the bottom of the set they came together again and clasped hands to form the final arch above the heads of their fellow dancers. He stood smiling at her as they passed beneath.

"Thank you, Miss Fancourt," he said as he straightened from his final bow. "I cannot tell you how enjoyable it was to look into the face of the lady with whom I was dancing and not be restricted to a view of the top of her head and a set of bouncing curls."

"Thank you, Sir Julian," she replied but before she could say any more, Chloe swooped down on them. "Isn't it a pity it's over? I vow I could dance 'til morning."

Then there was a sudden bustle as ladies looked for shawls and reticules and Rosa went to assist in speeding the parting guests.

The next morning, Miss Fancourt had returned to her usual subfusc self, appearing at breakfast in a high-necked grey gown that drained the colour from her skin and dimmed the blue in her eyes. Her beautiful hair was again covered by a simple muslin cap trimmed with a narrow band of lace. She had a trick of fading into the background, Julian thought, beguiled by the contrast between this still figure and the spirited woman whose sparkling eyes had met his as they danced. He began to observe her more closely.

She did not put herself forward, he realised as the day went on, but was always on hand if something was required of her. She was never off-duty, not even today when others tended to indolence after yesterday's exertions. Idly he began to count all the tasks he had seen her carry out during the past week. Chaperoning Chloe and the other girls, of course, and accompanying them each evening on the pianoforte. Fetching and carrying endlessly. Early one morning he had passed the flower-room and looked in to see her arranging blooms in a plethora of vases. She assisted Lady Loring at the evening tea-board and officiated at breakfast, a meal which the older ladies preferred to take in their bedrooms. Once she had passed him in the gig, seated primly beside the young groom who was driving.

"Some errands in Bury for the mistress," the head groom had replied to his casual query.

She made up a four at whist if required. On his previous visits she had left the drawing-room with his grandmother after tea had been taken but this week she did not retire until his stepmother did. Despite this, she rose early. As he crossed to the stables one morning, he had glanced up and seen her sitting at an open window, sewing. He had impulsively removed his hat and bowed to her and she had lifted a graceful hand in return.

The day before the ball, she had recruited five gentlemen to dance with the five girls in the music room and played for over an hour while they ran through various country dances and cotillions, suggesting that each girl take turns in calling the dance so as to be prepared if required to do so.

Her embroidery was exquisite, he noticed, picking

up the frame she had laid aside to fetch something for his stepmother. But, even as he admired the delicacy of the white flowers finely stitched onto white linen, he wondered what it must be like to live a monochromatic life in a brightly coloured world.

She returned to the drawing-room and handed Lady Loring a reticule and was immediately despatched on another errand. Beside him, his grandmother frowned. "Miss Fancourt will be pleased when the week is over," she murmured to him. "She rarely sits for longer than ten minutes. I'll miss her when she leaves," she added with a sigh. "She keeps me company in the evenings, you know, reading aloud or playing for me."

"You might offer her a position as your companion," he suggested lightly. Somehow he would like to know Miss Fancourt remained at Loring Place.

"I did consider it, but I am past my four-score years and only Heaven knows how long I shall be spared. Also it would not be fair either to Chloe or this Miss Dismore if the previous incumbent were still here when she arrived. I have written to all the ladies of my acquaintance enquiring if there might be a suitable position in one of their families and you may be sure I shall make Miss Fancourt a handsome present when she leaves."

As if she were a maid or a housekeeper, Julian thought disgustedly. Miss Fancourt is a lady, the daughter of a naval officer who gave his life for his country. Her mother had died just two years later, Chloe had informed him. He had not previously thought to enquire about her governess's antecedents, but it had taken only the mildest of prompts for his sister to relate the brief story.

"Both of her parents were orphans too, so she has no

remaining family," Chloe had added. "It is so sad, Julian. Only think, she was younger than I am now when she was cast upon the world."

Chloe had paused after uttering this dramatic statement and said more quietly, "It is most exciting to read of such things, but quite different when one is confronted with the reality."

Most of the guests left early on Saturday morning, with only the Eubanks, Jack Whittaker, Ambrose Haldon and Sir Jethro remaining. They would depart on Monday when the Eubanks would start their journey home and the gentlemen return to Newmarket in the company of Sir Edward and Sir Julian for the second spring meeting.

Chloe sighed as the last carriage rolled away. "What shall we do now?"

"We could drive somewhere or—do you ride, Miss Eubank?" Julian asked.

The girl's face lit up. "I do indeed, Sir Julian."

"A ride would be just the thing," Chloe agreed. "Where might we go, Julian?"

"I thought over to Lavenham."

"Oh, famous! It the quaintest little town you can imagine," she said to Hannah Eubank. "The streets are crammed with old houses, squeezed higgledy-piggledy together so that you think if one collapses, all must. My nurse was used to say that the crooked man lived there."

"What crooked man?"

"It is just a silly rhyme she knew.

"*There was a crooked man, and he walked a crooked mile.*

*He found a crooked sixpence upon a crooked stile.*

*He bought a crooked cat, which caught a crooked mouse,*

*And they all lived together in a little crooked house.'*

"She always finished by saying 'and that's in Lavenham'. Mamma and I drove over there one day but that is more than ten years ago."

Julian turned to Miss Fancourt. "I hope you will join us, ma'am."

She looked surprised but replied composedly, "Thank you, I should be happy to if Lady Loring does not need me."

"Splendid. Shall we reconvene in half an hour? Can you ladies be ready by then?"

"Of course," Chloe said, "provided you see to our mounts."

Jack and Ambrose readily agreed to join the party. "Although we shall be one lady short," Jack complained. "Haldon, are you sure you would not prefer to remain here and rest?"

Heads together and overlong skirts safely caught up, Chloe and Hannah tripped down the stairs. In their modishly ruffled and frilled riding habits and stylish hats, they suggested nothing more than children dressed up in their mothers' clothes. Behind them, Miss Fancourt descended more sedately, skilfully controlling the rounded train of her dark blue habit with a subtle lift and turn of her left hand. Julian doubted that she realised how the resulting draped folds drew attention to her neat waist and rounded rump.

He noticed an appreciative gleam in Haldon's eye and moved smoothly to escort Miss Fancourt to her horse where he bent and cupped his hands. She glanced swiftly to where Jack Whittaker was assisting Chloe and without further ado put her hand on his shoulder and her foot in his hands. He boosted her slightly and she rose into the saddle where she neatly slipped her right leg around the pommel. He allowed himself the indulgence of setting her narrow foot in the stirrup before releasing her.

She smiled down at him. "Thank you, Sir Julian."

He took his own reins and swung into the saddle. "Lead on, Chloe," he called. "We'll bring up the rear."

"This was an excellent notion, sir," Miss Fancourt said as they clattered out of the yard.

He smiled lazily at her. "I thought you had earned at least a half-holiday, Miss Fancourt. You have been extremely busy this past week, have you not?"

She shrugged. "Otherwise busy perhaps, but overall no more than usual, sir. I enjoyed the change. Also, it was most rewarding to watch your sister take her first steps into society."

He looked ahead to where Chloe chatted happily to Mr Whittaker. "It's strange to think that she has left the schoolroom—it seems no time at all since she was in leading-strings. She did very well, especially for such a young girl. She is still a little shy, perhaps, but that is natural and it was charming to see her grow in confidence over the week."

She smiled. "It was, wasn't it?"

"I am sorry to hear you are to leave her."

She inclined her head. "Thank you, Sir Julian, but my task here is done. As you said yourself, your sister has left the schoolroom."

"She does you proud," he said abruptly. "She has a

certain something, an ease and grace of manner that can never be taught but only acquired by that sort of imitation that is most flattering to its model."

She flushed at his compliment. "You are too kind, Sir Julian."

He shook his head. "On the contrary, I simply give credit where credit is due."

"Then I thank you, sir. I hope Sir Edward was pleased with his celebrations."

"Extremely so. He talks of holding such a party regularly between the spring meetings."

"Good heavens! But without an annual ox roast, I trust. I think I shall never forget the smell! It still lingers, I fancy. The ashes are still warm, I am told, and I don't know how long it will take to restore that patch of lawn."

He grinned. "I have been favoured with Haylett's opinion on the subject. He considers the grounds to be principally his; my father only enjoys them at his pleasure."

She chuckled at this. He glanced sideways, about to make another quip, and swallowed. How had he never before noticed how a mounted lady's skirts clung to her legs and hinted at the secret valley between them? And yet Miss Fancourt sat the side saddle in exactly the same way as any other female. Perhaps it was because she was too tall for a lady's mount and her bay gelding put her almost on a level with him.

"Julian!" Chloe's voice jerked him back to himself. "You must change places with Mr Whittaker. Neither he nor I are sure where we are going."

He touched his hat in a brief salute. "Duty calls. Until later, Miss Fancourt."

As Sir Julian moved forward, Ambrose Haldon wheeled his mount to come up beside Rosa.

"A splendid morning, Miss Fancourt!"

"It is indeed, Mr Haldon."

She chatted politely as they continued along the bridle path. Soon they turned into a wider lane and Sir Julian and Chloe broke into a canter that prevented further conversation. Now she could consider Sir Julian's words in peace. *I thought you had earned at least a half-holiday, Miss Fancourt. You have been extremely busy this past week, have you not?* Surely he had not meant he had arranged the outing for her pleasure? And then had come his praise of Chloe that, in a way, was praise of Rosa herself. This indirect accolade was worth more than any formal compliment.

She gave herself up to the moment. For these few hours she had no duties and no responsibilities. Her horse moved fluidly beneath her. They were old companions. Sir Edward had permitted her to name him and she had called him Captain in memory of her father. She would miss him when she left but even if Sir Edward were willing to sell at a price she could pay, it would be impossible to keep him. Nobody would employ a governess who arrived in tandem with a horse and, even if she set up her own establishment, Captain would be an unaffordable luxury.

So many partings, she thought, and then scolded herself. Don't let the thought of tomorrow spoil today. They rode more slowly now but no one broke the silence. She loved the woods in spring. The world seemed fresh and new; the trees were not yet in full leaf, admitting the sun to gild the fresh green. Birds flitted busily from branch to branch, pausing now and then to flute a warning of trespassers. Two blue butterflies soared together in spiralling flight—courtship, perhaps. Or were they like Chloe and Miss Eubank, just emerged from the chrysalis and still unsure of the world around them? And what was she? A dull moth, perhaps.

All too soon, they left the woods behind them. The riders ahead slowed and Sir Julian raised a hand, signalling a halt.

"We must cross the turnpike here."

A smart coach and four, escorted by outriders and followed by two smaller carriages, passed at a brisk trot. Two farm carts lumbered past on the opposite side and then Sir Julian led the way across. Soon they turned off again into a lane that again went cross-country.

Sir Julian dropped back, leaving Mr Whittaker to ride beside Chloe.

"They can't go astray now," he remarked to Mr Haldon and Rosa. "I hope you are not too tired, Miss Fancourt."

"Not at all," she replied.

"I sent the carriage ahead. A nuncheon in a private parlour at *The Swan* awaits us and if you prefer, you may drive home."

"That is most thoughtful, Sir Julian."

He looked a little sheepish. "It was only when I went to the stables that I realised that you ladies might not be used to spending four hours in the saddle, which is what it will take to ride there and back."

"It is a little more than we are accustomed to," she acknowledged. She would see how the girls fared when it was time to return. Miss Eubank had not ridden her mare before. If she preferred to take the carriage, she could not be left to travel alone.

Mr Haldon rode forward to join the Eubanks and Sir Julian drew nearer to Rosa.

"Your father was a naval officer, Chloe tells me."

"Yes. He was killed at Copenhagen."

"And your mother died not long afterwards."

"Yes," she said again, wondering where this was leading to.

"Forgive me, I do not mean to pry, but it occurred to me that the Place has been your home for ten years and that you have no other."

"No." She blinked and looked away. She was all too aware of her circumstances. Why did he have to spoil her pleasure in the outing by reminding her of them?

He came even closer and put his hand on her reins to halt her. "I have upset you, Miss Fancourt. I am sorry. What I am trying to say is that I hope the connection between you and my grandmother and Chloe will not be lost."

Time stopped. Rosa sat motionless, her eyes fixed on the large hand that gripped the reins above hers. Her utilitarian cotton glove seemed very shabby beside his beautifully stitched doeskin one. His hand lifted and gripped hers.

She looked up into concerned brown eyes flecked with amber. Why had she never noticed the specks of amber before?

"That is not my decision, Sir Julian. I have told Chloe I shall always be glad to hear from her and will of course reply to her letters."

"Excellent." His clasp tightened. "I hope you will not think me impertinent when I say that if in future there is any way I can assist you, I beg that you will call on me. A letter directed to Swanmere Castle or Swanmere House in London will always reach me."

There was a lump in Rosa's throat the size of an egg and a prickle at the back of her eyes. She swallowed hard. "Sir Julian, I cannot tell you what your words mean to me." She would never avail herself of his offer, but that was another matter.

"There is no need, as long as you believe they are sincerely meant."

At her nod, he squeezed her hand comfortingly and released it. "Shall we ride on?"

# Chapter Five

New King Street, Bath

May 1814

My dear Rosa,

I must apologise for the delay in replying to yours of 15th ult. but I wished to be sure that I advised you correctly. I have considered the matter carefully and also taken the liberty of consulting Mr Chidlow who, as you know, always has your best interests at heart. Much as I would welcome your return to Bath, I fear that it remains sadly expensive and your income is not yet sufficient for you to establish yourself here in a genteel fashion. Would you consider removing to Maidstone? Mr Chidlow assures me that you would be able to hire respectable rooms at a reasonable rent and would have no difficulty in securing as many day pupils as you wished. He says that his wife would be delighted to welcome you to their home when you leave Suffolk and suggests you stay with them until you have found suitable accommodation, adding that of course he and Mrs Chidlow will be very happy to introduce you to their friends.

A wave of relief engulfed Rosa. She was not alone. She had somewhere to go and people who cared about her. It would be much easier to find day-pupils if she had the recommendation of a respected local solicitor and his wife, and she would be able to meet new acquaintances on an equal footing without pretence or misunderstandings. When she and Chloe returned from their walk, she would write to the Chidlows accepting their kind offer. Lighter of heart than she had been since Lady Loring had given her notice, she put on her old straw bonnet and picked up her gloves.

"Papa and Julian return today," Chloe remarked as she and Rosa strolled in the dappled shade of Sir Edward's woods. "It's such a pity that Julian and Lord Swanmere must leave on Monday. It will be the real end of our party."

And Rosa would never see Sir Julian Loring again. It was little more than a month to Midsummer and it was most unlikely he would return to the Place before she left. They had always been on good terms but since the ball and the outing to Lavenham there was a new ease between them. She would never forget his kindness or his offer of support. And he had danced with her at her first ball.

"Miss Fancourt? Miss Fancourt?"

She blinked and looked at her pupil. "Oh, I'm sorry, I was wool-gathering. What did you say?"

"That it will be very dull when they are gone. What shall we do all day? Mamma will hardly expect me to return to the schoolroom."

"Probably not, although you will want to continue practising your music, drawing and French. Presumably you will accompany your mother on her calls and visits.

And Miss Dismore will have her own suggestions, I expect."

"I suppose so," Chloe said despondently but then brightened. "I remember now. We turn right here, down this path towards the old gamekeeper's cottage. Lily of the valley is my favourite flower; I noticed the leaves when I came here with Papa last month and resolved to return when it was blossoming. There!" She pointed triumphantly to a carpet of broad green leaves speckled with white flowers that covered the woodland floor.

"How beautiful," Rosa exclaimed, only to wrinkle her nose at the pungent aroma wafted towards them by a sudden gust of wind.

"Ugh! That can't be lily of the valley." Chloe's pretty face was a picture of disgust.

"No, it is *allium ursinum*, literally bear's garlic. Although the leaves are like those of lily of the valley, the flowers—and the scent—are quite different. It's also called ramsons or wild garlic."

Another, stronger gust of wind sent dust and dead leaves scurrying. A chill darkness fell as the sun was blotted out by roiling black clouds. High above, lightning flashed, casting an eerie light over the trees. It was followed by a clap of thunder that had Chloe clutch Rosa's hand. Then the heavens opened.

"How far is it to the cottage?" Rosa asked urgently.

Chloe had to shout to be heard over the pounding rain. "It's in a clearing about two hundred yards further on but no one lives there at present."

"Even if the door is locked, we could shelter in a stable or woodshed. Are you sure you know the way?"

"Yes. These woods belong to Papa and Mr Purdue.

Papa has the part to the left of this path and Mr Purdue to the right."

They ran as best they could, hampered by sodden skirts that wound around their legs, clinging uncomfortably, and dripping bonnets tugged by a driving wind that also dashed rain into their faces. Thunder cracked overhead and they flinched, dazzled by the simultaneous blaze of lightning.

"It's just around that bend," Chloe shouted.

"Thank God," Rosa panted when the little building came into sight.

"I'll try the latch before we go around the back." The door swung open at Chloe's touch. "Come, it's open!" She darted in, tearing off her bonnet as she went.

Rosa was hard on her heels. The cottage was surprisingly well furnished for a vacant gamekeeper's dwelling. A richly coloured turkey carpet covered the stone floor and on the left she could see a glass-fronted cabinet containing expensive-looking china and glass-ware.

Ahead of her, Chloe gasped and stopped short. She looked around wildly, her hand to her mouth and her eyes wide with shock.

Rosa staggered to a halt and stared equally horror-struck at the woman on her knees before Mr Purdue. He sat, head thrown back, his eyes closed and his features taut, in the centre of a chaise longue, his hands fisted in his companion's dishevelled hair. It was not just any woman, Rosa realised, doubly appalled. It was Lady Loring who knelt between his spread legs, her head bent and her hands busy within the open fall of his breeches. Sickened by such a depraved scene, Rosa reached forward to seize Chloe and whisk her away. Anywhere, even the woods in a thunderstorm, were better than this. But she was not quick enough.

"Mam-ma," Chloe stuttered and took another step into the room. Deathly pale, she looked from the man to the woman, as if trying to make sense of what she saw.

Purdue's eyes snapped open. "What the devil!" He pushed his mistress away and jumped up, fumbling at the fastenings of his breeches.

"Come away, Chloe," Rosa said desperately. "This is no place for you."

Lady Loring's face was a mask of rage. Eyes glittering, she scrambled to her feet. "What are you doing here? How dare you sneak and spy on me!"

Chloe defiantly stood her ground. "We weren't sneaking or spying. We merely sought shelter from the storm. But you, Mamma? I need not ask what brought you here. How could you betray Papa so?"

"I'll have no insolence from you, miss!" Her ladyship's hand flashed out to deliver a sharp slap.

"Mamma!" Her hand to her cheek, Chloe staggered back, catching her foot in the loop of a discarded hunting-crop. Arms flailing, she teetered frantically but the crop rolled under her feet and she toppled before Rosa could catch her.

Biting back her panic at the horrific, dull thwack of her pupil's head against the floor, Rosa dropped to her knees beside the motionless girl.

"Chloe."

There was no response. She gently tapped the girl's pale cheek. "Chloe!"

Terrified, Rosa groped for her vinaigrette. As she bent down to hold it under Chloe's nose, the pungent fumes made her own eyes water but Chloe did not respond. Not even an eyelid fluttered. What was that? A scarlet trickle seeped from beneath the girl's fair hair and ran down her neck.

"Get up, Chloe," her ladyship said sharply behind Rosa. "You need not play your tricks with me."

"She is injured, ma'am." Rosa displayed her red-stained handkerchief. "The wound must be on the scalp, hidden by her hair."

"Nonsense! Let me see."

Lady Loring pushed Rosa aside and knelt beside her daughter. By now the collar of Chloe's primrose spencer had turned crimson. She frantically gripped the girl's wrist then turned a ghastly face to her lover. "Simon! I cannot feel her pulse. She's so cold."

Mr Purdue squatted beside her. "Of course she's cold, after such a drenching," he said soothingly. "Let me. There—slow, but steady enough." The long fingers moved to the girl's head. "There doesn't seem to be a fracture," he murmured almost to himself and rose with Chloe in his arms.

"Come and steady her," he ordered Lady Loring once he had laid Chloe on the chaise longue. He carefully turned her head to expose the side upon which she had fallen and gently lifted her hair. "There's quite a gash here. She must have cracked her head against the hearthstone. See how sharp the raised edge is." He folded his own handkerchief and pressed the pad against the wound. "Hold this firmly in place."

When Lady Loring obeyed, he unwound his cravat, then folded the long strip of linen and tied it around Chloe's head.

Lady Loring looked down at the hands stained with her daughter's blood and shuddered. "We must get her home. We'll need a carriage. Miss Fancourt must go for one."

"Miss Fancourt?" Mr Purdue looked over to where Rosa still knelt by the hearth. "Don't be ridiculous, Delia! We can't have her telling her tale to her world."

Rosa shivered under his calculating gaze but squared her shoulders. "Chloe must be our only concern. I will do whatever is necessary to help her. You may be assured of my discretion."

His eyes narrowed. "I have no fear of your babbling, Miss Fancourt. Make yourself useful and bathe her forehead—there is water over there." He jerked his head towards a neat washstand equipped with pretty bedroom china. "I'll fetch a carriage. I'll be fifteen minutes, Delia," he said to her ladyship, "twenty at most."

Lady Loring snatched the damp towel from Rosa's hand. "Set the basin on the floor. I'll tend to her. If you know what is good for you, you will stay out of my way and hold your tongue."

Rosa sat at the small table and rested her head in her hands. What was she to do? She had no wish to act the informer but to say nothing would be to condone Lady Loring's shameless behaviour. But whom should she tell? She could not imagine addressing Sir Edward or even Sir Julian on such a subject. She could speak to the dowager, perhaps. Would she be believed? If not, she would immediately be turned off without a character.

She had already assured the illicit lovers of her discretion. It was probably best to say nothing. It would not be a lie if she just refrained from volunteering information. She glanced over at the chaise longue. Chloe still had not stirred. Pray God she had taken no lasting hurt. What would she remember of all this? Would she say something to her father or grandmother? Rosa could not deny the truth if asked. Perhaps she should simply request to be released early from her employment—there were only a few weeks left. But she couldn't go until she knew how Chloe went on.

Lady Loring rapidly put herself to rights, coiling her hair with quick, jerky movements and jabbing hairpins into it apparently at random, before straightening the bodice of her gown and donning bonnet and spencer. Now she held her daughter's hand. She bit her lip and stared fixedly into the distance, avoiding Rosa's gaze.

Rosa jumped at the sound of a carriage rattling to a halt outside. Through the small cottage window, she saw Mr Purdue alight, looking very grim.

"Any change?" he asked harshly as he came in.

Lady Loring shook her head.

"We'll take her home," he said. "But first—" he came over to Rosa. "I am sorry, but you are deuced inconvenient, Miss Fancourt."

She felt a quick blow on her neck just below her ear and darkness fell.

Rosa swallowed convulsively, unable to lift her head or even turn it to one side. She felt as if it had been split in two and the slightest movement provoked an immediate urge to vomit. Breathe slowly, she told herself. She must have drifted away again and when she next woke, the nausea had receded slightly. She lifted heavy eyelids. Where was she? It was hard to focus at first but then she recognised her location. She was in the gamekeeper's cottage.

Chloe! She painfully turned her head. She was alone. They must have taken Chloe home. But why had she been left behind? The effort to sit up made her dizzy and increased the pain. She didn't think she could manage to stand, at least not yet, and lay down again, her eyes closing despite herself.

The click of the latch roused her. She turned her head and struggled up onto one elbow. Mr Purdue had come in. He was carrying a scarlet cloak of the type country-women wore.

"Time to be on your way, Miss Fancourt," he announced, shaking out the cloak. "Come, put this on."

"What, where?"

"Put it on, Miss Fancourt," he repeated briskly. "In an elopement, time is of the essence."

"What elopement?"

"Yours," he said impatiently. "Surprised with your lover, you have fled the county." He tugged her into a sitting position.

It was as if a knife had been jabbed into her skull. The contents of her stomach rose insistently to her throat. "The basin," she managed to gasp.

Cursing, he picked it up from the floor and handed it to her just in time. She closed her eyes against the sight of the blood-stained water and stopped resisting the implacable need to retch. The effort involved made her head throb and when she was finished, she held out the basin blindly. It was removed from her grasp and she heard the door open. It closed again after a moment.

A glass was put into her hand. "Sip it slowly."

'It' was a weak mixture of brandy and water. She took a few sips to rinse out her mouth and handed the glass back.

He swung her legs over the side of the chaise longue so that she sat and picked up a length of rope. Where had that come from? Before she could say anything he had knelt and hobbled her.

"How dare you!"

He laughed harshly. "You will find that I dare a lot, Miss Fancourt. We can do this the easy way or the hard way. It is your choice."

She made a fist of her right hand and dealt him a blow on the ear. Her hand stung but he simply shook his head and laughed.

"The hard way it is then," he said and tied her wrists as well before drawing her to her feet. He wrapped the cloak around her, drawing the hood over her head and down onto her forehead. When he lifted her, the room spun and she had to shut her eyes against the brilliance of the sun when they emerged from the cottage. The storm was over. The next thing she knew she had been deposited on the seat of a carriage. He climbed in after her and rapped on the roof.

With wrists and ankles bound, it was hard to brace herself against the jolting as they made their way along the woodland lane. Rosa managed to wiggle and wriggle along the seat until she could angle herself into the corner so that her shoulders were supported on two sides. She rested her aching head against the squabs. Where were they going? What route would he take? Would she have the chance to call for help?

Almost as if he had read her mind, he leaned over and drew down the leather blinds, first on her side and then on his.

"What news of Chloe?" she asked weakly.

"None, or nothing good. She is in her bed and the doctor has been sent for, but he will be able to do very little. What a cursed mischance!"

Rosa said no more but closed her eyes and prayed fervently for the girl she loved as a daughter. Soon the jolting of the carriage eased. They must be on the toll road. After some time, she stirred herself to ask, "Where are you taking me, sir?"

"I haven't made up my mind, Miss Fancourt. Somewhere you can do no harm, at any rate!"

"Any harm that comes to you or your paramour you have brought upon yourselves."

He shrugged. "Then it is incumbent on us to minimise it. With you out of the way, who is to know the truth of what happened? Even if Miss Loring comes to her senses, by then it will all be set in stone and there will be no altering it."

❧

# Chapter Six

"A very pleasant few days, my boy, and profitable ones," Sir Edward chuckled as they neared Loring Place. "I haven't lost my eye for a horse."

"Indeed you haven't," Julian replied. "You always were a knowing one. Next year when you are in town, you must come to Tattersall's with me."

His father's smile grew even broader. "I should be delighted to. Do you still spar at Gentleman Jackson's? We could look in there as well. We may have to dance attendance on the ladies in the evenings, but the days will be ours! My lady has the right of it—it is high time we spent a Season in town."

"I doubt that is quite what she meant," Julian answered dryly. "By the way, sir, if you permit, I would like to give a ball for Chloe at Swanmere House. There is a fine ballroom there that remains unused."

"Why, that's uncommonly generous of you, Julian. It will make the whole thing much less costly if we can take a house without a ballroom and it would be a shabby sort of come-out without a ball." Sir Edward smiled reminiscently. "I well remember the ballroom at Swanmere House. It was there that I first met your mother. But I had better not mention that to Lady Loring if she is to consent to your proposal!"

Julian grinned. "I said you were a knowing one."

"Oh, she will be more than happy to agree. She was hoping you would take an interest in your sister but this is more than she ever expected. Ah! Here we are, back at home. I am looking forward to my dinner, I confess."

Julian's valet hurried into the bedroom. "I apologise for the delay in bringing your hot water, sir, but the household is at sixes and sevens due to Miss Chloe's mishap."

"Mishap! What mishap?"

"I'm afraid I don't know, sir. Apparently she has injured her head and Dr Hastings was sent for—he may still be in the house."

Julian washed quickly and pulled on fresh clothes. Determined to learn more, he went first to his father's apartments where Sir Edward sat in a chair in his dressing-room, the doctor holding his wrist.

"The devil with my pulse," he snapped as Julian arrived. "What has happened to my daughter? Julian! Thank God you are come. For God's sake go and find out what has happened." He stopped, clutching his chest.

"Sir Edward, please!"

Julian squatted by his father's side. "If you will only try and be calm, sir, I promise you I'll go immediately in search of information."

Sir Edward put a shaking hand on Julian's shoulder. "Do that, my boy. Talk to Hastings here and Meadows too." He took a long, quavering breath and was silent.

"Try and rest, sir. I'll return to you as quickly as I can. What can you tell me, Dr Hastings?"

"As to Miss Loring's condition, sir, she sustained a blow to her head that caused considerable bleeding as well as a loss of consciousness from which she has now recovered. She is suffering from pain, nausea and a certain confusion of the brain. I have dressed the wound and made up a mild sedative draught and am hopeful we will soon see an improvement. As to the cause of the injury, its appearance and location suggest that it results from a fall rather than a blow."

"How long ago was this?"

"I received an urgent message about half past three o'clock."

It was now after five. "May I see her?"

"There can be no objection, I suppose, as long as you do not disturb her. Rest is the best medicine in such cases, Sir Julian."

Julian hadn't known that Chloe had moved down from the schoolroom floor to a bedchamber more suitable to a young lady, where she seemed lost in the shadows of the big, curtained bed. A young maid who had been sitting beside her rose immediately and he took her chair, troubled by the sight of his sister's still figure. Chloe's head was turned away from him, presumably to prevent pressure on the wound. Her face was as white as the bandages that swathed her head, her stark appearance relieved only by a few wisps of golden hair that trailed across her forehead.

"Pull back the curtains; those at the window as well," Dr Hastings instructed softly and then came to stand on the opposite side of the bed. "It caught her at the right of the crown, sir, above her ear, as if she fell on her side onto something that caused a gash about an inch and a half wide. It is hard to see the extent of the bruising without removing too much of her hair."

"Did you cut some?"

"Only what was necessary." The doctor smiled faintly. "I have two daughters and know how they would scold me if I scalped them!"

The maid opened the curtains at the window. Although Chloe's eyes were shut, the brighter light caused a little pucker to appear on her forehead and she squeezed her eyes more tightly closed. She stirred restlessly and her fingers plucked at the bandages.

Julian took her hand gently. "Don't. Oh, my poor pet, you have been in the wars, haven't you?"

"Julian?" It was the merest whisper and he bent closer to hear her.

"Yes, love."

"My head aches."

"I know," he said sympathetically. "Like Jack, you fell down and broke your crown but here is Dr Hastings with the vinegar and brown paper."

A tiny smile twitched the corners of her lips.

"Can you open your eyes for a moment, Miss Loring?"

Her eyelids quivered and rose over blue eyes dulled with pain.

"How many fingers am I holding up?" the doctor asked.

"Two."

"And now?"

"One."

"Very good!"

Her eyelids fluttered down then up again. "Where is— my mother?"

Julian looked questioningly at the maid.

"Her ladyship went to bathe and change her dress, Miss."

"And—Miss—Fancourt?"

"I'm sure I don't know, Miss."

"Don't talk any more, pet," Julian urged. "Try and sleep." He bent and kissed her cheek.

She turned again onto her left side and winced. "Hurts."

"You'll feel much better in the morning, I promise you. I've taken many a blow to the head, so I know what I'm talking about."

"Not fisticuffs." Her faint smile dimmed. "Mamma."

"I'm sure she will come to you as soon as she is able."

"We'll draw the curtains so you can rest until then, Miss Loring," Dr Hastings interrupted firmly, nodding to the maid.


"Is there someone other than that girl to sit with her?" the doctor demanded once they were outside the room. "A woman of sense who may be relied upon to notice a change?"

"A change?" Julian repeated, alarmed.

"If fever sets in or her wits start wandering. One never knows with head injuries. It's better to be safe than sorry."

"There's her governess, Miss Fancourt."

Dr Hastings nodded approvingly. "An excellent woman; I should have thought of her at once. Together we have seen Miss Chloe through I don't know how many illnesses."

"I'll see to it." Julian immediately felt happier. They

could depend upon Miss Fancourt. "In the meantime, pray be good enough to look in upon my father again. Tell him my sister has spoken to me and is resting comfortably. I shall be with him in ten minutes or so."

Leaving the doctor to find his own way, he ran down the stairs to the library. Meadows would know where Miss Fancourt was and could also provide some insight into what had happened that afternoon.

"Miss Fancourt? Nobody seems to know, sir. She is not in the house. I was under the impression she had left with Miss Loring but it was her ladyship who brought her home in Mr Purdue's carriage."

"Purdue? What the devil had he got to do with it? When was this? Describe exactly what happened."

"It was not long after three o'clock, sir. James reported that a carriage had drawn up and I went to receive the caller. First Mr Purdue alighted and then he took Miss Chloe from the carriage. Her ladyship got down and we could see the blood and when he turned, we saw that Miss Chloe's garments were blood-stained too. Her head was bandaged and her eyes closed." He swallowed visibly. "It was terrible, sir, how she lay lifeless in his arms. For a moment, we feared the worst. Then her ladyship said he should take Miss Chloe upstairs and instructed me to send for the doctor. James ran at once to the stables."

"And Mr Purdue?"

"He came hurrying down almost immediately, sir, and drove away."

Julian frowned. Most likely Chloe had simply stumbled and fallen, hitting her head on a stone. But where had Purdue come into it? And how odd that Miss Fancourt should be out today of all days. He shrugged. These questions could wait. She would return later but until then he must find someone else to care for Chloe. Of course! Mrs Crewe! He hastily scribbled a few lines to Chloe's former nurse who had married a tenant farmer. She could be relied upon to fly to her nursling's side.

"May I enquire about dinner, sir?" Meadows asked as he took the note. "Her ladyship ordered it for six o'clock."

It was now half-past five. "Leave it at that unless she says otherwise," Julian decided. His father should eat and there were his grandparents to consider as well.

Sir Edward frowned as he listened to Julian's report. "Wait here," he ordered and crossed his bedchamber to the door of his wife's room.

"Sound asleep," he said disgustedly a few minutes later. "Apparently she suffered a fit of the vapours and that fool of a woman of hers dosed her with laudanum."

"If you'll excuse me from dining with you, sir, I'll ride over to Purdue and see what he has to say."

"A good idea, but first come with me to see my girl."

When nobody appeared at the sound of hooves, Julian rode around to Purdue's dilapidated stable yard where a young groom emerged to take his horse.

"Is your master at home?"

"I think so, sir. The horses are here at any rate."

"Hmph!"

Julian stalked back to the front door and knocked sharply. After a few minutes he rapped even more loudly. Just as he was about to hammer on the door with his fist, it was opened by a down-at-heel manservant.

"Yes?"

Julian brushed past him. "Sir Julian Loring to see Mr Purdue."

"He's in the library, sir." The man scurried ahead to a room at the back of the house.

"I said I was not to be disturbed," a light male voice complained when he opened the door.

"Yes, sir, I'm sorry, sir. It is Sir Julian Loring, sir."

"Well, show him in," the voice said impatiently, "and fetch up another bottle of port."

Purdue came forward, his hand outstretched. Julian, who knew him as a gamester of dubious reputation who hovered on the fringes of the *ton,* had been surprised to see him at his father's birthday celebrations, but he supposed Sir Edward could hardly exclude his new neighbour. Whatever about his misdemeanours in town, here he had not yet blotted his copybook and must be treated civilly.

"Come in, Sir Julian. Forgive me for being so curmudgeonly; I'm trying to make sense of these papers—but you won't want to know that. More importantly, how does Miss Loring?"

"She is resting quietly, sir. I must thank you for coming to her assistance."

Purdue waved this away. "It was nothing. I am only glad I happened to be passing by when Lady Loring ran onto the lane. But where are my manners? Will you not be seated?" He gestured to a chair beside the smouldering fire and took the one opposite.

Julian waited patiently while glasses were filled and they tasted a rather ordinary port. "To be frank, Mr Purdue, I have come to you for information. My sister is still very weak and Lady Loring has succumbed to the vapours." The two men shared a masculine grin at this remark. "As a result, we have no idea what happened today. What can you tell me?"

Purdue stared into his glass. "There's no gamekeeper here at the moment and I have got into the habit of keeping an eye on things myself. I had just turned into the lane that marks the border between our lands when another rider came pelting towards me. He was wearing some sort of uniform—militia, perhaps, and had a woman up before him. I couldn't make out their faces; his shako was pulled low on his forehead and her head was turned to his chest. She had damn fine legs, though," he added with a reminiscent smile. "I had to jump out of his way and I suppose I stood for a few minutes cursing him before I continued on."

He swallowed and held the decanter up invitingly before refilling his own glass.

"Just as I arrived at old Lambert's cottage, Lady Loring ran out. Her hands and gown were covered in gore. *'Thank God it is you, Mr Purdue,'* she cried. *'You must help me.'*

"*'Of course, ma'am,'* I said and went in with her to find your sister lying on the floor." He shuddered. "I never want to see such a sight again. You know how head wounds bleed, Loring. Her ladyship had tried to staunch the flow. I lifted your sister to a settle and bound the wound with my handkerchief and cravat. She had cut her head on the edge of the hearthstone, I think. She couldn't be left there, of course. I rode back quickly for my carriage and we brought her to the Place."

"Did Lady Loring offer any explanation for what had happened?"

Purdue looked solemn. "She did. I am reluctant to repeat it, for a lady's reputation must be paramount, must it not, and I took Miss Fancourt to be a lady."

"If you mean my sister's governess, there can be no doubt of it," Julian said icily, "and I warn you against suggesting anything to the contrary."

The other man shrugged. "Be that as it may, her ladyship said she and Miss Loring had been walking in the woods when they were surprised by a thunderstorm. They thought to seek shelter at the cottage—there is a little lean-to at the back that would have been better than nothing. But Miss Loring tried the latch first and found the door unlocked. She stumbled in ahead of her ladyship and apparently found her governess in a very compromising position with an officer. I suppose they had not heard anyone approach because of the storm." He held up his hands. "Who knows? Miss Fancourt became irate and accused Miss Loring of spying on her. Miss Loring replied hotly; there was an altercation and your sister fell, hitting her head. Her mother went to her side and the other two fled. I suppose it was they who passed me. She'll have left the county by now, I imagine." He shook his head. "A sorry story and one I had not expected of her."

"Nor I," Julian replied mechanically. He couldn't believe it. But it could not be denied that Miss Fancourt was not at the Place and nobody seemed to know where she was. He rose slowly. "Thank you, Purdue, also for your earlier assistance. I hate to think what might have happened if you had not come along."

"It was only thanks to that storm that I was there at all; I had delayed setting out because of it. Did you ride here? I'll walk around to the stables with you—it is the least I can do after such a surly welcome."

Chatting amiably, he strolled with his guest to the

stables and waited until Julian had mounted and trotted
out of the yard, oblivious to the shadowy figure that beat
desperately against the panes of a small window high
above him.

# Chapter Seven

ROSA HAD NEVER FELT SO abandoned as when she watched Sir Julian ride out of Mr Purdue's stable yard. When she had first caught sight of him, she had been filled with a desperate elation. He had come in search of her. She was sure of it. For what seemed like hours she had strained her ears for the sound of his voice or step outside her prison. Although already hoarse, she had shouted again, but to no avail. Now all was lost. Even if Lady Loring had not already spread her poisonous lies, Purdue would not have hesitated to blacken her character as he had threatened. There could be no hope now of rescue by the Lorings. If anything they would pursue her, seeking retribution for the alleged assault on Chloe.

Her captor had bundled her up a narrow back stairs and thrust her into this small attic room before locking the door from the outside. It must have been a maid's bedroom, she thought, and recently occupied, for there was no accumulation of dust, let alone slut's wool, and Mr Purdue's housekeeper was generally spoken of as a slatternly creature although a good cook. She was not the sort who would think to ensure an empty chamber was swept and dusted.

The room was simply furnished; there was a narrow bedstead with a thin horsehair mattress covered in drugget, a rickety chair and a small deal table on which stood an empty, chipped jug and basin. Two wooden pegs were fixed to the wall behind the door and, to Rosa's relief, she found a chamber pot under the bed. She had not yet brought herself to use it but knew she would have to if she were held here for long.

She had removed her damp spencer and spread it out to dry and, reluctant to take off her clammy gown, wrapped herself in the red cloak and lain down on the scratchy mattress. Just for ten minutes, she had told herself, until your head clears, but in fact she had slept although she did not know for how long, and woken shivering.

She had banged on the door and called until her voice gave out and had then peered down from the window, rapping on the pane when she saw a groom cross the yard. He had not looked up, nor had Sir Julian later even though she had hammered the jug against the thick glass.

She pulled the cloak around her. Without it, she would have felt even more chilled. Judging by the fading light, it must be eight o'clock. Was Purdue going to leave her here all night? She was thirsty—apart from the few sips of watered brandy she had taken nothing since nuncheon. Sighing, she sank down onto the bed again only to spring up when she heard firm footsteps outside her door. It opened just wide enough for a hand to place a tin plate of thick sandwiches on the floor.

"Take it in and I'll give you some wine and water," Mr Purdue said.

She tried to tug the door wider open but he resisted. "Remember, Miss Fancourt, it is your choice. Is it to be the hard way or the easy way? I shall not make you drink if you prefer not to."

Be sensible, Rosa, she told herself fiercely and picked up the plate. It was immediately replaced by two tin mugs.

"You have thirty seconds to remove them," the hateful voice said.

Suddenly, she craved liquid. After a first, hasty sip, she was able to snap, "How dare you hold me prisoner!"

"Now, now, my pet! You will find I dare a lot." He laughed softly, pulling the door shut. Just before it closed, he said, "I almost forgot," and tossed a soft bundle into the room. She snatched it up—it was her reticule and gloves.

The door slammed. She heard the key turn followed by the rattle as it was removed, then his footsteps retreated. She was alone again.

She moved the little table as near the window as she could and placed his offerings on it before taking a couple of slow sips of water, letting the cool liquid rinse and moisten her parched mouth before it trickled down her throat. Then she checked the contents of the reticule. A small comb, her vinaigrette—a bubble of hysteria rose to her throat when she saw that—a coin purse containing a few pence, three shillings, half-a-crown and a guinea, a paper of pins with a threaded needle, a small notebook and pencil and a spare handkerchief. Rosa fell upon this last. She moistened it carefully and wiped her face and neck before scrubbing her hands to remove the traces of Chloe's blood.

She ate as much as she could of the sandwiches but drank the wine sparingly, diluting it with water as she went. Somewhat revived, she unpinned her hair and combed and plaited it for the night. She could do no more. Night was falling. Her spencer was dry and she folded it to form a pillow before lying down again. In the morning she would inspect her prison inch by inch. There must be some way to escape.

Mr Purdue apparently slept late; the sun was high in the sky before he brought more sandwiches and a mug of hot, sweet coffee as well as more water. This time he came into the room but stood with his back against the door, barring her way.

"Chocolate would be more appropriate for a lady, I suppose. I apologise for the deficiencies of my household; we are understaffed at present."

Rosa ignored this sally. "How long do you propose to keep me here?"

"That depends. You cannot return to the Lorings, you know. If you behave yourself, I shall spirit you away in a few days. If not, you may stay here and rot!"

"You blackguard! And I suppose you call yourself a gentleman," she said bitterly.

He shrugged. "Needs must when the devil drives, my dear." He sniffed the air loudly. "However, I do not wish to inconvenience you too unduly. May I offer you a bucket into which you can empty a certain bedroom utensil?"

"You may," she muttered, her cheeks suddenly burning. She had put off using the chamber pot as long as she could, but necessity had finally compelled her.

He raised an eyebrow. "See how gentlemanly I can be, Miss Fancourt? Now stand over there while I leave the room."

Rosa complied with this direction and, more gratefully, with his instructions to 'do the job and be quick about it,' when he placed the bucket on the floor inside the door. The door closed behind him once the unpleasant task was accomplished and silence fell again.

Indeed, the house was unnaturally quiet. Apart from the groom, she had seen only one other servant; a man who drove away in a gig about noon. He was followed an hour later by Purdue on horseback. The household was understaffed, he had said. Had the other servants been dismissed or sent away?

The interior wall beside the bed was a flimsy construction. Now less fearful of discovery, she dragged the bed away and inspected the corner where this partition met the outside wall of stone. The scant layer of plaster was flaking. She worked at it, loosening it, and soon could see thin wooden laths nailed to a corner post. There appeared to be no plaster on the other side. Could she pry the laths loose enough to squeeze through into the next room which might not be locked?

It was worth trying. I've nothing else to do, she thought wryly. But what if he comes before I can escape? She looked around again. The other end, behind the door! He would only notice something if he came fully into the room. Even then, if I spread out the cloak on the two pegs, it will conceal my handiwork. His footsteps are so loud in the silent house that I always know when he's coming. And if he comes as late this evening as he did yesterday, that corner will be quite dark.

Three hours later, she stood back, gasping. She had managed to crack and loosen the plaster by banging it

with the heavy pottery jug and had then used the edge
of the tin plate to pull it away from the wall. The plate
had also served as a lever to prise the nails loose from the
post. Now she must just break the laths free. But first she
must make everything shipshape in case Purdue returned
sooner than expected.

She piled the plaster under the bed, wincing as she
stooped. Her gloves were ruined, her hands scratched
and blistered and her back ached but she would not
give in. Everything must appear unchanged when he
came. When all was tidy again, she carefully hung up the
cloak, spreading it as wide as she could before turning
her attention to her own appearance. She loosened her
hair and bent forward, shaking her head vigorously, then
tossed her hair back and combed and knotted it again.
With her hands, she brushed and beat at her bodice and
skirts to free them as best she could from the flecks and
spots of plaster that speckled them. Finally, she wiped her
face and neck with the moistened handkerchief.

She allowed herself the last of last night's wine and
chewed resolutely on a stale crust. Apart from the groom
who appeared to idle away the afternoon, there was no
sign of life in the yard. She went back to work. The laths
were half rotten, she discovered, and in another hour she
had created a gap large enough to climb through but still
small enough to be hidden by the cloak. She hitched her
skirts to knee level and clumsily made her way into the
next room.

She found herself in a loft from which a small space had
obviously been separated to create the maid's room. There
were no windows but enough daylight filtered through
chinks in the roof that she could look about her. She

went silently to the door and cautiously lifted the latch. It opened! She peered out warily. To her right was the door of her prison and at the end of the passage another door which must lead to the back stairs. She tiptoed towards it. It too was unlocked.

It's too risky to go now, she thought. The groom is below. And where could I go today? Better to wait until early morning, as soon as it is light. *The Fly* leaves from *The Angel* for London at six o'clock. If I take an outside seat, I should have enough money to get to Maidstone.

She looked down at the soiled, wrinkled gown she had worn for almost thirty-six hours and would sleep in for a second night. How could she travel like this? A woman travelling alone in the public coach might be subjected to all sorts of offensive behaviour and in her bedraggled state she would be taken for a drab or worse. Well, it couldn't be helped, she supposed, and Purdue's cloak would cover some of the worst deficiencies. Or—would there be anything in the loft she could use? His uncle had been a childless widower whose wife had died some five years previously. Perhaps some of her garments remained.

She wearily returned to the loft and looked around more carefully. Two trunks were pushed up against the far wall. Heart thumping, she tried the lid of one and suppressed a cry of relief when it opened. It was hard to make out the contents in the dim light, but a faint scent of lavender gave her hope. She reached in and picked up the topmost item. It was a black bonnet with a veil attached to the brim. Heartened, she delved deeper. A black gown, pelisse, gloves, stockings, even a petticoat with a black flounce at the hem. At the very bottom she found black laced boots and a reticule which contained a wedding ring and a coin purse with ten guineas. Some woman's mourning clothes and nest egg. These can't have belonged to Mrs Purdue, she thought fleetingly. But it didn't matter whose they had been. They were a godsend to Rosa and she had no qualms about appropriating them. She would return them if ever the opportunity presented itself but now she silently thanked a benevolent Providence.

Nothing could be more perfect for her purpose. No-one would think it strange if mourning clothes were out-moded or even a little ill-fitting and they would help excuse her exhaustion and distraction. She shook out the garments and refolded them carefully before returning them to the trunk. Tomorrow Mrs Brown would journey to her widowed brother-in-law in Hampshire. With two lively little boys and their new-born sister left motherless, he had appealed to her, his wife's only sister, to come and support him in his bereavement.

Rosa huddled miserably under the red cloak. She dozed fitfully, constantly jerking awake, afraid she had slept too late to set out on the three-mile walk to Bury. When the fluting call of the blackbird announced the first fading of night, she stiffly levered herself up from the bed and rinsed her mouth before washing her face with the remaining water, then ducked through into the loft.

She dressed quickly, pulling on two pairs of stockings so that the borrowed boots fit better. The gown was a little loose on her. It came just to her ankles but would do. She pulled a spencer over it before donning the pelisse and bonnet, grateful for the latter's concealing veil. Then she removed the wedding ring from the beaded black reticule and slipped it onto the fourth finger of her left hand.

She eased the black gloves onto her sore, torn hands and picked up the bandbox into which she had packed her few belongings and a warm shawl. When she stepped into the passage she paused for a moment, listening intently. All was quiet and she silently made her way to the door to the back staircase. She opened it cautiously and felt her way down its murky depths, terrified of falling.

The stairs gave on to a narrow passage that led to an outer door. In a chamber off it, someone snored loudly in a rhythmic rise and fall that ended abruptly with a little snort. Rosa froze. After a deep intake of breath followed by a tremolo snuffle, the sleeper relapsed into a rough, rasping rhythm. Holding her breath, she crept past. She had to put down the bandbox and use both hands to draw the bolt of the back door, but managed without disturbing the slumberer. She closed the door as quietly as she could and quickly made her way around the house and down the drive. The sky was brightening rapidly and she must be out of sight of the house before the sun came up.

She trudged along, impervious to her surroundings unless they impinged upon her comfort, noticing the rising sun only when she had to tug down the brim of her bonnet so that it did not blind her and the change from the woodland lane to a firmer road through the increased discomfort of her borrowed boots. The thin handle of the bandbox cut into her blistered palm and she changed it constantly from hand to hand but walked doggedly on.

Bury St Edmunds was in sight before she met another person. He passed her with a civil, 'Good day, ma'am'. Then she had reached *The Angel* and paid her twenty-one shillings for an inside seat before hiding in a corner of the tap room. At last it was five minutes to six.

"Passengers for the *Bury Fly* to the *Bull Inn* at Bishopsgate!"

There was a brief scramble as people boarded the coach, but there was only one other inside passenger, a morose young gentleman who was not inclined to conversation beyond a grunted, 'Good morning, 'mm'. Despite his sullenness, he correctly took the backwards-facing seat opposite her. The yard of tin blared and the coach rolled on its way. She had done it!

When they stopped to change horses at the end of the second stage, she risked folding back her veil to gulp a scalding cup of tea. The fresh white roll was a welcome change to Purdue's stale bread. Two stages later she managed a dash to the privy and from then sat quietly in her corner until they reached London, grateful for every mile that further distanced her from possible pursuers.

"Maidstone, ma'am?" the ostler at *The Bull* said. "Not from here. You want *Blossom's Inn* in Lawrence Lane. But there'll be no more coaches today."

"Is it far?" Rosa asked faintly.

"Not above a mile, ma'am, but take a hack. Here, I'll find a respectable driver who won't chouse you."

He took her under his capable wing, handed her into his selected hack and passed up her bandbox as if it contained the crown jewels. He waved away her proffered sixpence.

"No thank you, ma'am. You've troubles enough, it seems. And tell them at *Blossom's* that Adam from *The Bull* sent you and they're to treat you right!"

At *Blossom's* they provided her with an early dinner and a clean bedchamber as well as plenty of hot water. She handed her garments to the obliging maid to be brushed and pressed for the next day, then washed methodically. It was wonderful to feel clean again. She had asked for writing materials and while she waited for her clothes to be returned, she painfully recorded the occurrences of the past days to the best of her recollection. Already the scene at the gamekeeper's cottage seemed remote, as if it had happened months previously. She blotted and sanded her paper, folded it carefully and tucked it into her reticule, then climbed wearily between the inviting sheets. She closed her eyes with a brief prayer that Mr Chidlow would be at his chambers tomorrow and sank into oblivion.

Persistent knocking recalled Rosa to consciousness.

"Ma'am? Ma'am? 'Tis a quarter to six. I have your tea and your hot water, ma'am. The coach leaves at half-past."

She was stiff and sore all over, as if she had been beaten with cudgels, and it was a struggle to get out of bed. The palms of her hands burnt and there were blisters on both heels. She wrapped old Mrs Purdue's shawl around her shoulders and hobbled to the door.

"Here you are, ma'am. It's too early for fresh rolls but I made you some toast."

"Thank you, Molly." Rosa pressed a shilling into the woman's hand.

It took her a full half hour to get ready. Her stiff hands protested as she fastened the gown and it was difficult to dress her hair. The bonnet will cover it, she reminded herself, as she fumbled with the hairpins.

This must be what it is like to be old, she thought as she made her painful way down the stairs and out to the coach. She was the last to reach it and had to take a middle seat wedged between two other women who, after initial attempts to include her in their conversation, prattled cheerfully across her for the entire journey. Rosa set her teeth and endured. On the seat opposite, two burly gentlemen extended their legs as far as they could but thankfully remained silent.

At eleven o'clock they rolled into Maidstone. Rosa found shillings for the guard and coachman and laboriously clambered down. Ten minutes later she was at the door to Mr Chidlow's office.

"What name shall I say, ma'am?" the clerk asked politely.

Rosa folded back her black veil. "Miss Fancourt."

"If you will wait a moment, miss."

He vanished and was replaced a moment later by Mr Chidlow himself who came forward, hands outstretched. "Miss Fancourt!" His smile faded as he took in her appearance. "Why, my dear, what is wrong? Come in, come in."

He ushered her into a comfortable room, where the gleaming wood of the desk and bookcases complemented the rich reds and creams of the carpet. In a sudden flash she saw again the incongruous turkey carpet in the gamekeeper's cottage and Lady Loring kneeling between Purdue's legs. She swayed and Mr Chidlow leaped to guide her to a chair.

"Sit here, Miss Rosa. Will you not remove your bonnet and pelisse—it is very mild today. Now, you will take a glass of Madeira and a couple of Shrewsbury cakes before you utter a single word."

Almost mechanically she complied with his suggestion, gritting her teeth as she peeled off her gloves. Some blisters had burst and the fabric was stuck to the raw flesh.

He noticed her wince and came to look.

"God bless my soul! What have you done to yourself? Can you hold the glass?"

She nodded and sipped the sweet wine, grateful for its soothing effect on her aching throat.

"I wrote it down last night," she rasped, setting down the glass to take the sheet of paper from her reticule. "It all seemed so strange, as if I had dreamt it somehow."

He looked at her over his silver spectacles, nudged the plate of cakes nearer to her hand and took a seat opposite her.

"Shameless," he growled when he came to the end of her account. "Utterly shameless, the pair of them! I shall take you home at once. Mrs Chidlow will look after you. Today you must rest and tomorrow we shall consider what is to be done."

"I have come to the conclusion that there is nothing to be done," Rosa said resignedly the following afternoon, gingerly accepting a cup and saucer with her bandaged hands. "It would only be my word against theirs."

"You could lay a charge against Purdue for abduction and false imprisonment," Mr Chidlow suggested.

His wife shook her head. She was a pleasant woman of about sixty whose kind features were marked by traces of constant pain and whose fingers were swollen and misshapen by arthritis. From her stiffness of movement, Rosa suspected that other joints were also affected.

"You forget, my dear, that Miss Fancourt would have to give evidence and once it emerged she had been detained by that scoundrel for two days, her reputation would be in tatters, even if the jury found him guilty. That would mean the end of her hopes to take in pupils. Even a suggestion of scandal is enough to ruin a lady in her situation."

"There is also Chloe," Rosa added. "How will it reflect on her if I reveal the truth? Sir Edward would be within his rights to repudiate his wife and sue Purdue for debauching her. Chloe could hardly make her come-out while her mother was the subject of the latest crim. con."

"But surely they should not escape scot-free!" Mr Chidlow was incensed. "Such iniquitous behaviour must be punished."

Rosa smiled wryly. "Part of me would love to see them pilloried or at least made do public penance on the cutty stool the way they do in Scotland, I believe, but it is better to leave it be. What grieves me most is that I have lost all my possessions, including the keepsakes you retrieved for me."

"That cannot be allowed to happen," Mr Chidlow said firmly. "I shall write to Sir Edward."

"What if he decides to charge me with injuring Chloe?" Rosa said desperately. "He is a magistrate, remember."

Mr Chidlow shrugged. "If he wishes to make his case, her ladyship must be called upon to give evidence and subjected to cross-examination too."

"We need not decide today," Mrs Chidlow intervened. "Miss Fancourt, I have another proposition I would like to put to you. Adam and I discussed it when we learned that you were considering setting up your own establishment. In fact we wrote to you about it only two days ago. We should dearly like it if you would agree to share our home with us." She held up her twisted hands. "You see how it is with me. There is so much I can no longer do—even pouring tea is difficult. I have finally accepted that I need a companion. Would you consider remaining with us? Of course we would make you an appropriate allowance, just as we would do for our own daughter. Indeed, we hope you will become a daughter to us. We do not lead a very exciting life, but Maidstone has a small, neat theatre as well as a concert room and I believe you would find our little society here very pleasant."

Rosa felt the tears well up. They were offering her a home and a family. "How good you are! There is nothing I would like more."

"Is it agreed then?" Mrs Chidlow asked.

"Yes, provided you will not hesitate to tell me if it does not work out."

"I have no doubt that it will, my dear. And if you will not object to telling a little fib, we shall say we are cousins on my mother's side and you have kindly come to stay with me. Let me see, now; if my great-grandmother was your great-great-grandmother—that is distant enough that no-one will expect us to know all the ramifications but near enough that we might have kept up the connection. But no-one will be impolite enough to ask for details."

Mr Chidlow chuckled. "I had not thought you such an excellent conspirator, my dear."

"One must be thorough," his wife answered complacently. "Then that is also agreed." She turned to Rosa, "You must call me Cousin Emmy—my name is really Emmeline but I detest it— and I shall call you Cousin Rosa."

# Chapter Eight

Miss Fancourt did not return to Loring Place and Lady Loring confirmed Mr Purdue's story, or at least so Julian understood. He had not heard her ladyship's account of what had occurred from her own lips. It would have been too distressing for her to relate it to anyone other than her husband.

"She says they caught her on her knees with her hands inside the fellow's breeches," Sir Edward informed him. "It's no wonder she fled."

"No," he agreed bleakly.

He was also forbidden to visit Chloe. She was recovering slowly from her ordeal, he was told, but must not be excited.

Lady Loring spent much of her time sitting at her daughter's bedside. "Poor child, she is still confused and has very little recollection of what happened, which is a blessing," she remarked at dinner one evening. "I tell her she should not exert herself to remember—far better to put it behind her."

"Does she ask for Miss Fancourt?" the dowager enquired. "I cannot believe that she left us so abruptly."

"She would not be the first old maid to have her head turned by a scarlet coat," her daughter-in-law replied with a tinkling laugh.

"The strange thing is that no one else saw the absconding couple," Julian commented to his grandfather afterwards. "One would have thought it would have been generally remarked upon. There is no talk of an officer being absent without leave or having a new ladybird in keeping either."

Lord Swanmere looked at him keenly. "Been making enquiries, have you?"

Julian shrugged. "Why should she get away with such a cowardly attack? For all she knows, she left my sister for dead."

"Perhaps she did not want to be taken up for murder," Swanmere said dryly. "But she will not go unpunished, my boy. She has only the clothes she stood up in and who knows what support, if any, she will get from her lover. Very likely he put her on the first stage to London. Hers will be a rapid descent into vice and depravity."

Julian sighed. "I suppose you are right."

But he could find no comfort in this dismal prophecy. Beneath his concern for Chloe, he strove to ignore another injury inflicted by Miss Fancourt: the betrayal not only of his family but also, on a deeply personal level, of himself. How could he have been so mistaken in her? And yet, at other times he could not accept her guilt. But that would mean his stepmother and Purdue had colluded in a shameful deceit for which there could only be one explanation. He had no reason to suspect his stepmother of adultery and to do so felt disloyal to his father, but was it not also wrong to condemn Miss Fancourt solely on their evidence? She had served the family faithfully for ten years, after all.

His grandmother agreed with him. "I have never known her to flirt or seek to attract male attention, not even during the house-party when there was plenty of opportunity. Mr Haldon was quite *épris* but she did not give him the slightest encouragement. And I do not see how she could have had the occasion not only to make this fellow's acquaintance but also to set up such an assignation. You know how little time she has to herself."

"I'll ride over to Purdue again; see if he can tell me anything more."

"Do, Julian. If we have been told a Banbury story, we must ask ourselves why, and what has happened to her. I cannot help but worry."

But Purdue was not at home and the Hall was locked up.

"There's nobody here, sir," the young groom said cheerfully. "Not that there's many of us left, only Ferry, the master's manservant and me. The rest have all been let go. I'd be gone too, I daresay, but someone has to look after the horses."

"So you won't have had any lady staying here recently?"

The lad laughed. "There's been no females at all here, at least none that I've seen."

"What about officers?"

"Officers?"

"Of the yeomanry or the militia. Sir Edward Loring had a report that some had been seen in the woods."

The groom shook his head. "Nary a one, sir. And why

would there be? I don't say some mightn't take a gun out on the stubble fields in the autumn, for all that they shouldn't, but there's no shooting now, is there?"

"No," Julian agreed.

On an impulse he rode on to the gamekeeper's cottage. Here a confusion of wheel-ruts and hoof-marks showed where a carriage had been turned on soft, wet ground and there were traces of only one rider, most likely Purdue. Still it was almost a week ago, he reminded himself. The door was locked and there was little to be seen when he peered through the small windows.

Julian was overjoyed to find Chloe sitting with their grandmother when he returned to the Place but shocked by the sight of her wan face. Her prettily rounded cheeks were now hollow and her eyes looked strained. She frowned when she saw him.

"Julian, you are a mean beast not to have come and sat with me before now. I vow I thought I was going to expire of boredom!"

He laughed and took her hands, stooping to kiss her. "We were under doctor's orders, pet."

"Pooh! It wasn't Dr Hastings but Mamma who was so insistent that I not overtax my strength, as she put it. But today she wasn't here when he called so Grandmamma came up with him and I asked him there and then did I have to stay in bed and he said, 'not any longer' and so up I got directly and Grandmamma kindly lent me this lace cap because they have positively scalped me."

Julian laughed again as she paused to take a breath. "It is most fetching, even if you do look like a little girl playing dress-up. Hastings assured me that he only cut away as much as was absolutely necessary and once you are healed we shall arrange for a modish *friseur* to come and trim your hair. Your short curls will be in the first style of elegance, I promise you, vying with those of such daring beauties as Lady Caroline Lamb."

She wouldn't be consoled. "You don't understand, Julian, he cut my hair right down to the skin. There is a bald patch the size of a crown piece between my ear and the top of my head!"

He sat beside her and hugged her carefully. "Your hair will grow again, pet, but in the meantime I engage to keep you supplied with all the decorative bits of nonsense you might possibly need to conceal any deficiencies."

"That is a most handsome offer," their grandmother said approvingly. "I should accept it at once, Chloe, if I were you. Tomorrow we shall look through my ribbons and other fripperies and see what we can find to tide you over until Julian takes you to visit the milliners in Bury."

"Which will be as soon as the doctor permits," Julian promised. "Is your head still sore?"

"A very little," the girl admitted, "but only when I touch it."

"That's good. You gave us quite a fright, you know."

"I didn't do it on purpose," she retorted defensively. "In fact, I wish I knew what had happened. All I can remember is running towards the cottage in the rain. At least, that is all I am sure of. Mamma says I am confused."

"Why, what else do you remember?" Julian enquired just as a haggard-looking Lady Loring hurried into the room.

"Chloe! I couldn't believe it when they told me you were out of bed! If this is what you do as soon as my back is turned, you need not blame me if you suffer a setback. I am surprised at you, ma'am, for encouraging her. And, Julian, I will thank you not to make her condition worse by pestering her to recollect things best forgotten. We do not want her to have a relapse. Remember she was at death's door only a week ago."

As Lady Loring completed her attack with this raking shot, her mother-in-law raised a quelling eyebrow. "Dr Hastings permitted it, Delia. In fact he said it would do her good not to be moping by herself and to lie here on my chaise longue would be just the thing for her."

"And what was he doing, coming today when I did not expect him until tomorrow? I would never have gone out if I had known he planned to call."

"He was in the neighbourhood, I think," the dowager said vaguely.

"Well, it's done now," Lady Loring said resignedly. "But you will not dine with us, Chloe. That would be too much for a first day up."

"But, Mamma, I am sick of invalid pap! I cannot face any more barley caudle or calf's foot jelly. And it is so dull eating by oneself from a tray in bed."

"Perhaps you would permit Chloe to dine quietly here with me," the dowager suggested. "I am sure they can send up a tempting little dinner for us."

"Please, Mamma!"

"Very well," Lady Loring conceded. "But you must return to bed immediately dinner is over."

Chloe opened her mouth to protest again but Julian caught her eye and shook his head warningly.

"You have tried your luck enough for one day," he said after Lady Loring had withdrawn. "There is an hour before

I must change for dinner. How may I entertain you?"

"We miss our music, do we not?" Sir Edward said after dinner. "It is a pity you did not keep up your practice, my lady; there was a time when you played very prettily."

His wife, who seemed unable to decide whether to be flattered or outraged by this dubious compliment, did not reply. It was her mother-in-law who filled the silence by enquiring, "How did Miss Fancourt come to you, Delia?"

"I'm sure I have forgotten," Lady Loring answered petulantly. "It can no longer be of importance."

"No, no," her husband contradicted her. "If it was through some sort of register office and you still have its direction, we could perhaps trace the woman through it."

"She would never have the temerity to return there, Sir Edward, especially when to all intents and purposes she was turned off without a character. But why are we talking about the wretched female? She must be expunged from our memories, especially Chloe's! I must insist that Miss Fancourt's name is not mentioned in her presence."

"You are right, I suppose," her husband said, "although to my mind, she is getting off too lightly."

*The lady doth protest too much,* thought Julian scornfully. His stepmother's remarks had only increased his anxiety about Miss Fancourt. It was a pity Chloe had not had time to reply to him earlier. For the moment he would respect her mother's request that he not jog her memory, but he would not stop her if she chose to speak of the events in the cottage.

Delia sighed with relief as she watched her husband ride out with his agent. They would be gone for the rest of the day. As soon as the men were out of sight, she descended to her book room and retrieved the little sheaf of papers relating to Miss Fancourt's employment. The discussion about the governess the previous evening haunted her and she had passed yet another night beset by visions of discovery and disaster. She sat at the desk for some time staring into space, then nodded resolutely and drew a sheet of paper towards her. Prevention was better than cure. She dipped her pen into the ink-well.

*Loring Place, Suffolk*
*May 1814*

*Mrs Ellicott*
*Mrs Ellicott's Academy for Young Ladies,*
*Bath*

*Madam,*

*I consider it incumbent upon me to inform you that we have been sadly disappointed in the character of Miss Rosa Fancourt whom you recommended to us some years ago as a suitable governess and who has left us without warning, having been surprised in most compromising circumstances with a member of the Yeomanry.*

*Decency prevents any further description of this unhappy scene which I mention only to warn you against proposing Miss Fancourt for any other position despite her lack of a character in respect of her employment at Loring Place.*

*I remain, Madam,*
*Yours etc.*
*Lady Loring*

"I wouldn't believe it, not even if the Queen herself had written it," Mrs Ellicott said fiercely, shaking the offending letter so violently that her little cat flicked a lazy ear at this disturbance of their postprandial snooze.

Puss was unceremoniously unseated from her comfortable position on her mistress's lap as Mrs Ellicott crossed majestically to her desk. This impertinent letter was too dangerous to be ignored. She would write immediately to Mr Chidlow—the post left at six o'clock and she must not lose another day.

"I like your new curls." Julian gently tugged one and let it spiral back.

Chloe dimpled. "So do I. Mr Francis says many ladies would kill for my hair as I will never need curl papers. He showed Hughes how to dress it too, threading ribbons through so you do not notice the gap, especially when your silk flowers are pinned on, Julian. And you have no idea how much lighter my head feels. Oh good, there's Meadows to announce dinner. I'm famished."

Now that Julian's concern for his sister had eased and she dined again with them, he felt more keenly another absence from their table. When the family dined alone, Miss Fancourt sat opposite him, beside Chloe, and it had become his habit to seat her before returning to his own chair. Now he missed the faint rustle of her gown and the quiet smile of thanks sent over her shoulder to him as she sat. He had not realised how adept she was at keeping the conversation flowing; although she never put herself forward, her little remarks and apparently simple questions opened new perspectives or encouraged one or the other of the diners to expand upon a topic of particular interest to them. Chloe, in particular, participated less in the conversation now. He would not raise this across the table, but afterwards, when the gentlemen had re-joined the ladies, he drew her aside and asked her why.

"I don't know what to say, Julian," she replied. "Miss Fancourt and I read the newssheets together and discussed them so if a subject came up I was able to join in. Somehow, she made it easy for me to do so."

"Why don't you offer to read the journals to Grandmamma?" he suggested. "I know Miss Fancourt was used to. I'm sure she would be happy to discuss them with you too."

"What a splendid idea! I'll suggest it to her directly."

"You have purchased what, Sir Edward?" Lady Loring's piercing tones focussed all eyes on her husband who stood with his back to the hearth, his cup and saucer in his left hand.

"Old Hall," he repeated obligingly. "Originally it and ours were one estate belonging to one John Barrett. Some hundred years ago he divided his property and sold the greater part to my great-grandfather with the remainder bought by Purdue's ancestor, including the original house. We built this one, of course. But, as Purdue discovered at the last minute, each deed requires that if either wishes to sell up, he must offer the other first refusal at the price he has agreed with a third party. When he mentioned it to me, I snapped it up."

"Sell up," Lady Loring repeated woodenly. "Mr Purdue is selling up?"

"Has sold up, my dear," her husband corrected her jovially. "The deed was signed, sealed and delivered this afternoon."

"Edward, surely you do not mean Mr Purdue has already left the neighbourhood?" the dowager demanded.

"I'm not sure, Mother. He has left the house; that I do know, for I have the keys. But I do not think he intends to linger here. He spoke of going abroad."

"You will have to do some work on the house before you look for a tenant," Julian remarked.

"Or find someone to take it on a repairing lease," Lord Swanmere suggested.

Sir Edward waved away these comments. "Time enough for all that. The first thing is to have a word with my gamekeeper. He will require an assistant and I should like to have a good man in place before August."

"There may be some soldiers returning home," Julian suggested. "A peninsula veteran would be more than a match for our poachers."

Lady Loring, who had gone extremely pale, pressed a lace handkerchief to her lips. "I beg you will excuse me. I'm not feeling at all the thing."

"Come, Mamma," Chloe said fondly. "It is time for me to look after you." She helped her mother to her feet and the two left the drawing-room arm-in-arm.

When both the dowager and Lord Swanmere also decided to retire to their rooms, Julian announced that he needed to shake out the fidgets and if his father would give him the keys to the Old Hall, he would ride over and ensure it was properly locked up for the night. "The last I knew there was only a groom and a manservant left, and who knows what state the place was left in."

Sir Edward frowned. "Take one of the grooms with you. I'll send Mapps over tomorrow."

❧

"Check the kitchen and offices, Ben, then go up to the top floor," Julian instructed his father's groom as he turned the heavy iron key in the lock. "Make sure all the doors and windows are fastened and let me know if you notice anything strange."

"Aye, sir."

Sir Edward had not revealed the terms of the purchase agreement, but it soon became apparent that Purdue had not cleared the house. Massive oak sideboards, blackened by age, still stood in the hall while the library also looked much the same as on Julian's previous visit. The only difference was that the big desk was empty and a pile of ash in the fireplace suggested that a considerable amount of paper had been burnt. After a quick look at the bookshelves, he could understand why the volumes of sermons and religious tracts had been left behind. An empty decanter and a dirty glass stood on the table beside Purdue's chair.

The shabby state of the dining-room and drawing-room spoke of years of neglect. Only a small morning-room, furnished in the style of thirty years ago, was in any way inviting and Julian guessed that this had been the old lady's domain.

Upstairs, Purdue's wardrobe and chests of drawers had been emptied and all personal impedimenta removed from the dressing-room. Nothing else had been taken. It was as if he had simply rid himself of the house as an adder sheds its skin. Of course it had never been his home.

"Sir? Sir Julian?"

"What is it, Ben?"

"You said to call you if I saw anything out of the ordinary. There's this room upstairs, if you'd come and take a look?"

The groom glanced past him into Purdue's bedroom and ducked in to retrieve two candlesticks and a tinder box from the mantelpiece. "The stairs is dark and there's only a very small window," he explained, as he deftly lit the candles.

Julian followed him to a small room at the top of the attic stairs.

"You'll need to come right in, sir, so I can close the door. See?" He pointed to the hole that had been broken into the wall. "From the footprints here and in the loft on the other side, a woman climbed from one to the other. But she would only have to do that if she'd been locked in, sir, wouldn't she?" Concerned brown eyes met Julian's.

Fine hairs rose on the back of Julian's neck. "And quite recently, too. The marks are still very clear."

He handed his candle to Ben and squeezed through into the loft before retrieving it. The footprints led both to the door and to the old trunks at one end of the room. He lifted the lids. One was empty; the other contained women's clothing.

He prowled back to the door of the loft. It opened onto the passage. He walked down the corridor and re-entered the little room.

"Leave me the candles, Ben, and wait outside while I turn this place upside down."

The Spartan garret was quickly searched. After upturning the chair and table, he removed the thin mattress from the simple bedstead and lifted a candle high. Something dark adhered to the edge of the frame as if it had slipped down between the mattress and the wall. Julian very carefully leaned over to retrieve it. It was a lady's glove. He yanked the frame away from the wall and peered down. The other glove was on the floor, behind an untidy pile of broken plaster.

His heart thumped and he felt sick as he carefully spread the gloves on the table. They were Miss Fancourt's. He was sure of it. The Saturday they had ridden to Lavenham, he had noticed the dark brown cotton and deemed it too light to protect her hands from the reins. With one finger he traced the wreath of flowers embroidered in subtly toning shades so that you did not notice the embellishment unless you looked carefully. Like her, he had thought at the time. The narrow hand and long fingers were hers, too. He turned the right-hand glove over and his blood froze. The palm was torn and shredded, with splinters and tiny pieces of plaster caught in the threads. The other glove was in a like state, the fabric stiff at the top of the palm, just below the fingers. He held it closer to the candles. What had caused those darker patches?

His vision dimmed and the blood roared in his ears. She had been held here, had very likely been trapped here while he sat below and drank with her abductor. Had she looked out of this window and watched him ride away from her? He folded the gloves and placed them in his pocket before leaning over the table to peer down into the yard. Was that Purdue's young groom below, perched on a mounting-block? Julian was at the door in two strides.

# Chapter Nine

JULIAN TOOK THE STAIRS TWO at a time, jerked back the bolt of the side door and erupted into the yard. "You, there!"

The boy jumped to his feet, poised to run. Before he could escape, Julian had seized him and spun him around to face him.

"Where's Purdue?"

The boy gulped. "I'm sure I don't know, sir. He left this afternoon—said he had sold everything to Sir Edward Loring. Ferry went with him but he had no use for me, although he took the horses 'n' all. Tossed me a guinea, but I should've got three at the quarter. There's more than two months gone since Ladyday as well as my notice owing. And I got no character nor nothing, though I've worked for him these three years."

"Why are you still here?"

"Got nowhere else to go, have I?" the lad retorted pugnaciously. Then his shoulders drooped. "I thought no one 'ud notice if I stayed awhile—the stable loft is better'n nowhere and mebbe Sir Edward would keep me on. I'm a good worker, horses like me and I can turn my hand to 'most anything. My father was a blacksmith, but he's dead."

"How old are you?"

"Fifteen, sir. Mr Purdue took me on to help the coachman, but he had to go when the carriage was sold."

"Do you know where your master was heading for today?"

"He had business in Bury, I know."

"He saw my father at three o'clock," Julian said, almost to himself.

"Your father, sir?"

"Sir Edward Loring," Julian explained impatiently.

"Sir Edward? Would you mebbe put in a word for me, sir?"

"We'll see. Did Mr Purdue return here after three?"

The boy nodded vigorously. "About four o'clock, I'd say. Had me tie the chestnut to the back of the gig and left again. That was the last I saw of him."

"Had he trunks or other luggage?"

"Just a valise. Everything else was collected yesterday."

"But you didn't suspect anything?"

"No, sir. I thought we'd be heading back to London."

"And he said nothing about where he was going tonight?"

"No, or at least not then. But this morning he did say something about not wanting to miss the cocking."

"Cock-fighting? Where?"

"I dunno, sir."

When the boy shook his head, Ben volunteered, "There's to be a Welch-main this evening at *The Scole Inn*, sir."

Julian thought fast. A Welch-main meant sixteen pairs of cocks pitted against each other in successive battles of reducing numbers until only one bird remained. It was a cruel display, accompanied by heavy drinking and wagering.

"He'll stay the night," he decided. "There's not much of a moon, but it will do. Ben, ride back to the Place and have Josiah take my curricle to *The Angel*. I'll meet him there. Have Fox put together a bag for me. Quickly now!"

The lad ran to untie the older man's horse and held it while he mounted.

"Mind, not a word to anyone about this or about anything we noticed inside." Julian tilted his head meaningfully towards the attic window and Ben nodded in comprehension. "I'll talk to my father tomorrow, but in the meantime, mum's the word. I want you to stay the night here. Ask Cook for some victuals. Enough for two," he added, with a glance at the boy.

"What's your name, lad?" Julian asked when Ben had left.

"Matt, sir. Matt Stone."

"Well, Matt, you may stay here tonight with Ben. Make yourself useful and do what he tells you. If I get a good report of you, I'll speak to Sir Edward."

"Yessir, thank you, sir."

The last red smudged the western sky as the curricle turned onto the turnpike at Bury. Julian dropped his hands, let his pair pick up speed. As they headed northeast, the ribbon of road unfurling before them, the colour gradually leached from the passing landscape until the world was awash in shades of grey and black. Above them, the silvery shine of the waxing moon grew stronger and soon the darkening sky was pricked by tiny golden lights.

It promised to be a clear, dry night, thank God. There would be little traffic at this hour, and it was a good, level road. Still, it would take the best part of three hours to cover the twenty-one miles to the *Scole Inn*.

He concentrated on his team, grateful to be distracted from his ever-increasing concern for Miss Fancourt. He was convinced she had been held at the Old Hall. Had she succeeded in escaping and, if so, where might she have gone? Unprotected, without funds, she could have fallen victim to any number of scoundrels who preyed on lone women.

His grandfather's prophecy of her rapid descent into debauchery haunted him. She clearly had not felt she could return to the Place—presumably Purdue had made sure of that, and many so-called decent people would refuse to help a woman in distress, no matter how grievous her plight. Too many would assume she was to blame for her misery. Society expected females to be at once properly submissive to the lords of creation and strong enough to withstand any attempt to coerce or seduce them from the path of virtue. Any woman deemed to have left it was presumed to be complicit in her own ruin.

Had Purdue compelled her to travel with him? To what other abuses had he subjected her? If she were still in his company, convention would require him to make her an offer, but surely that would simply add insult to injury?

Lanterns ahead. A toll-booth. The blare of Josiah's yard of tin. A sleepy gate-keeper stumbling out to take his shilling and drag the gate aside.

They swept on, darkness enveloping and cocooning them in a strange world that was more motion than progression. The rhythmic drumming of hooves, the swish of the wheels and the swaying of the curricle, the cool breeze against his face, the subtle tension of the reins that linked him to the greys—all drew him in so that he felt an integral part of a whole. The Deus ex machina, the god in the machine hurtling through the night to wreak vengeance and make things right again. Or Perseus hastening to save Andromeda? If only he could.

More lanterns, this time illuminating an inn sign. Slow down as you pass. *The Pickerill* at Ixworth. On again through Stanton and Botesdale. An owl hooted in the distance. Stop for another toll gate. He swigged brandy from his flask before passing it back to his henchman.

"Is all right behind?"

"All's right, sir."

Julian rolled his stiff shoulders and flexed the cramped fingers in the buckskin driving gloves. Her gloves were so thin. What shape must her hands have been in after she freed herself? What a dauntless woman she was! Cross the Waveney River into Norfolk. Less than an hour now. On and on. Purdue had to be there.

"Look out ahead, sir," Josiah called.

A private drag loomed out of the darkness, coach horns blaring, and crammed with sportsmen inside and out, all raucously exhorting the dragsman to 'spring 'em!'

The main must be over, Julian thought as he prudently made way for the coach to pass. Young fools! They'd be lucky not to be overturned before the night was over. Soon more carriages and horsemen neared, followed by stalwarts on foot.

"You're too late, sir," one called jocularly as he passed. "You missed a proper battle royal."

A glare of torches and lanterns illuminated the five

Dutch gables of the *Scole Inn*. Julian turned thankfully into the yard and climbed down while Josiah went to the horses' heads.

"We'll rack up here," Julian said briefly. "Look after them and yourself. Good night."

"Good night, sir."

The taproom reek was like a blow in the face after the crisp, clean night air. Fortunately the fire in the massive hearth had been allowed to die; otherwise the heat would have been unbearable. A throng of excited men, tobacco fumes wreathing above their heads, vociferously re-lived the excitement of the past hours. Here ale was slopped into leather tankards; there a steaming bowl of punch was mixed. In one corner a stout country-man tenderly fed morsels of bread dipped in ale to the bedraggled bird in his lap.

"There now, me old cock," he crooned, as he stroked the tattered feathers, "there now."

The harried landlord came up. "Good evening, Sir Julian. Do you want a room, sir?"

"Yes. Is my friend Purdue still here?"

"Mr Purdue?" The landlord hailed a passing waiter. "Have you seen Mr Purdue, Jem?"

"He went up ten minutes ago. I brought him a bottle of port."

Julian nodded acknowledgement.

"Take Sir Julian to room eleven," the landlord instructed.

The man picked up Julian's bag. "If you'll follow me, sir?"

"Help you with your boots, sir?" the servant asked after

he had lit the candles on the mantelpiece and side table.

"Please." Julian threw his hat and gloves onto the table and thrust his hands through his hair before removing his caped greatcoat. He sat and stretched his legs towards the servant who rubbed his hands on his apron before tugging off the boots.

"There you are, sir. I'll bring up some hot water. Will there be anything else?" he asked as Julian retrieved a pair of slippers from his bag.

"A jug of ale, a bottle of claret and something to eat, in thirty minutes." He tipped the man a half-crown. "But first show me to Mr Purdue's room."

"This way, sir." The servant led Julian up more stairs and into a side wing. He stopped and rapped on a door. "Gentleman to see you, sir!"

A stocking-footed Purdue opened the door. "Loring? I didn't see you below. What can I do for you? Have a drink?" He dropped back into his chair and gestured hospitably to the bottle of port. "I think there's another glass somewhere."

Julian shut the door firmly behind him. "I don't drink with liars and scoundrels."

Purdue raised an eyebrow. "What's this?" he asked, visibly amused. "Surely you're not seeking a dawn appointment?"

Julian seized him by the lapels and jerked him to his feet. "Do you dare deny you lied to me about Miss Fancourt while holding her prisoner? Your account of how my sister came to be injured was also false. It is up to my father to deal with you regarding his wife—that is no concern of mine—but as to the rest! Believe me, I should be more than happy to put a bullet through you, but no action of yours can restore your honour or induce me to take your hand."

He shook Purdue violently and let him fall back into his chair, dusting his hands as if they had been contaminated by the touch.

"Tell me exactly what happened that day, from beginning to end."

Purdue drained his glass and refilled it. "Really, Loring! I had not thought you so prurient. I was never one to kiss and tell."

Julian took the glass and dashed the contents into the fire. "I don't give a damn about your squalid amours." He put his hands on the arms of Purdue's chair, caging him, and leaned down so that they were nose to nose. "I want to know precisely what you did to my sister and her governess. Must I choke it out of you?"

His sudden grip had Purdue clawing at the hand that viciously twisted his neckcloth.

Julian implacably tightened his hold, lifting the other man out of his seat. "Raise your hand if you are willing to speak."

His victim, by now bright red, complied. Julian released him and he collapsed back in the chair, his mouth opening and closing soundlessly. After a moment his gasps became audible and he groped for the bottle of port. He drank slowly, shuddering as he swallowed.

"Well?" Julian snapped impatiently.

Purdue touched his throat delicately as he ventured a deeper breath. At last he croaked, "I never laid a hand on Miss Loring. Miss Fancourt, yes, and I admit to confining her in my house, but she suffered no further injury from me, I swear it."

"So it was you and her ladyship who were caught in the act?"

The other nodded. "Miss Loring stumbled in the door, Miss Fancourt followed. Her ladyship jumped up, irate, and Miss Loring fell as I described to you."

"And you decided her ladyship might be able to brazen it out if Miss Fancourt disappeared?"

Purdue nodded again. "Miss Fancourt assured us of her discretion—said the most important thing was to get help for Miss Loring, but I couldn't be sure she wouldn't let something slip. I'd already lost the previous purchaser who took offence at your father's option. I would have set her free once I had concluded my transaction with him. I couldn't afford to jeopardise that."

"What sort of a gentleman does business with another while tupping his wife?" Julian asked scornfully.

"Don't be so bloody particular," Purdue snarled. "The one had nothing to do with the other. I had agreed to sell to another buyer when we discovered that damned clause in the deed. I felt deuced uncomfortable about it, though." He climbed to his feet and refilled his glass. "Have you never made a false move, Loring, and seen the whole damn house of cards collapse? I had to get the governess out of the way. I was going to give her some money and suggest she take a ship to North America, perhaps the Canadas."

Julian snorted. "With only the clothes she stood up in? How do you think she would have fared?"

Purdue threw up his hands. "I hadn't thought that far."

"When did she make her escape?"

"She was gone on the second morning when I brought her coffee and a sandwich."

"At what time?"

"I suppose about half-past eleven."

"And you last saw her?"

"About half-past eight the previous evening."

"Did you search for her?"

"Of course not," Purdue replied indignantly. "I didn't wish her ill, you know; still don't! I admired her for the way she coped. No sign of the vapours or anything like that; in fact she boxed my ear for me. But she chose to decamp, so she is no longer my concern."

Julian's lip curled. "You are the most miserable mawworm it has ever been my misfortune to meet. You will not shrug off your responsibility so lightly, I assure you."

"If you accuse me, you accuse Lady L."

"You should have thought of that before you were complicit in her adultery," Julian said contemptuously.

"That milk is already spilt. If I could go back and do anything differently, I would, but what?"

"You could lock the door for a start."

Purdue laughed harshly. "By God, yes! But it's too late for that. It's best to let sleeping dogs lie," he added persuasively. "Loring, pray consider how it would reflect on your sister if her mother is exposed."

"That would depend on how it was handled. My father must decide how to deal with his wife but, if asked, I shall advise him to act discreetly. I have no wish to see my family at the centre of the latest crim. con."

Purdue smirked. "I am very sure you don't,"

"You had better hope it is kept out of the courts," Julian returned sardonically. "I recently heard of a case where ten thousand pounds in damages was sought for debauching a wife. My father could beggar you if he chose."

Julian was gratified to see the colour drain from his opponent's countenance. He pressed his advantage. "But that would be nothing compared with the penalty for abduction and false imprisonment of a lady."

"You can't prove anything!"

Julian drew Miss Fancourt's gloves from his pocket. "You overlooked these in that attic cell of yours, Purdue. They had slipped between the mattress and the wall. See how shredded they are and the plaster caught in their threads? Anyone taken to see the hole she was forced to make in the wall and the footprints either side of it could come to only one conclusion—that a woman had been held there against her will. And if she cannot be found— why, the natural suspicion would be that her abductor had done away with her and concealed the body. You would be fortunate only to be transported and not hanged! And if you should, by some mischance, be acquitted, you could never show your face in polite society again."

Purdue sank back in his chair, ashen-faced. "What's your interest in this, Loring? She's only a governess, after all."

"In fact she is a lady, whose father, a naval officer, was killed defending his country, but that is of little importance here. No woman should be subjected to such treatment. Miss Fancourt served my family faithfully these past ten years and does not deserve to have her reputation ruined by a lightskirt and a rake seeking to save their skins. What choices have you left to her? As matters stand, she has no hope of obtaining honourable employment."

"She would not benefit by it all coming out in court," Purdue pointed out astutely.

"No, and that is why I will engage to do my utmost

to prevent it happening, provided you—" Julian broke off tantalisingly.

"Provided I what?"

"First you will write an unvarnished account of what occurred, up to the day Miss Fancourt escaped. Secondly, you will give me five hundred pounds as compensation for her injuries. My family will provide a similar sum, all to be held in trust for her until we find her. If she does not wish to accept the money, she may donate it elsewhere as she wills. Thirdly, you will completely sever your connection with Lady Loring."

"The last is as good as done," Purdue muttered. "As for the second—will you take my vowels?"

"No."

Purdue reddened at Julian's uncompromising tone. He sighed and went to a locked case. "We'll make it guineas," he said and handed Julian five boxes, each holding five rouleaux of twenty gold coins. "For what it's worth, make my apologies to the lady."

"If you wish. And while you're at it, you may give me another four guineas."

"My God, what for?"

"They're owing to your young groom, Matt Stone."

"Who chose you to shoulder the world's burdens?" Purdue asked sourly and counted out the coins. He handed them to Julian and sat down at the table, pulling a travelling writing desk towards him. "May I assume that you are not going to lodge this document with the nearest magistrate?" he asked lightly.

"You may. I will only use it if it becomes necessary to defend Miss Fancourt's good name."

❧

# Chapter Ten

DELIA, LADY LORING PEERED INTO her dressing-table mirror. Should she use a hint of rouge? No. A faint pallor would be natural after yesterday's indisposition which she had ascribed to the richness of the buttered crab. How dastardly of Simon to sell up without even an attempt to bid her farewell. And how foolish she had been to be seduced by his blandishments. She had just been one of his convenients, she thought bitterly, on hand to divert him while he dealt with his uncle's estate. Men were all the same—not to be trusted.

Hughes held up a mirror so that she could see how the pretty lace cap, its frill threaded with apricot ribbon, sat on her brown curls. At the back her hair was still dark, but she could detect more and more silver at her temples. Fortunately Hughes was skilled in concealing it.

"It will do." She turned her head at the tap on the door. "See who that is."

The maid returned with a silver tray. "A Mr Chidlow to see you, my lady."

Delia picked up the card disdainfully. "Maidstone, Kent. Do I know a Mr Adam Chidlow, Hughes?"

"Not that I am aware of, my lady."

Thumb and forefinger flicked the card onto the tray. "I am not at home."

Within a few minutes there was another knock. Could she not have even one morning's peace? "Tell whoever it is to go away. I am still unwell and do not wish to be disturbed."

Hughes went obediently to the door but returned to report, "Meadows says it concerns Miss Fancourt, my lady. Mr Chidlow is insistent he must see you or Sir Edward."

Delia swallowed hard. "I had better see him, I suppose. Sir Edward hates being troubled with domestic matters. Tell Meadows to show him to the small office."

When Delia entered the bare room that held little more than a desk and four chairs, a tall, grey-haired man turned away from the window and bowed politely. His high domed forehead rose above speaking, brown eyes; eyes that regarded her gravely, even severely, with none of the unspoken admiration she was used to encounter in members of the opposite sex.

"Mr Chidlow?"

He bowed again. "Lady Loring?"

"I am she."

She swept behind the desk and sat, regarding him with faintly raised brows. Silence swelled between them. He did not seem discomfited by the absence of an invitation to sit but looked down at her thoughtfully, almost as if he were judging her. How dare he? Her temper rose.

"I understand you wish to speak to me about a former

governess. I am sorry to say that she left us in questionable circumstances."

"I am quite aware of the circumstances which led to Miss Fancourt's departure, Lady Loring."

His quiet reply sent a shiver through her. He couldn't know all. Or could he? What was it Simon had said? Attack is the best defence?

She laughed lightly. "I wonder what stories she has been telling you, Mr Chidlow. She was to leave us at Midsummer, you know; my daughter has left the schoolroom and no longer needs a governess. It is sad that Miss Fancourt was unable to accept this. The news came as quite a shock to her, I am afraid, and she became—resentful." She pursed her lips and shook her head disapprovingly. "It was quite—difficult."

Her visitor was unimpressed. "Lady Loring, I must tell you that I have known Miss Fancourt's family for almost twenty years and have had the honour to act for her since her father, Captain Fancourt, fell in battle. She was shocked and distressed by the regrettable occurrences of two weeks past but, moved by her affection for her pupil and her natural sense of discretion, decided neither to expose you nor seek redress under the law for the injuries inflicted by your companion. She would have been content to keep her silence had you not gravely maligned and libelled her."

Delia tossed her head. "What nonsense! I have spoken to no one outside this house about the woman."

"As to that, I cannot comment. You have however written about her. I refer in particular to the calumnies uttered in your recent letter to Mrs Ellicott of Bath, in which you impressed upon Mrs Ellicott that she should not recommend Miss Fancourt for future employment."

"That was a private letter," she protested.

"Private? Nonsense! Your only previous connection with Mrs Ellicott was a business one and it was in that context that you wrote to her. Let me tell you, my lady, that to say a libel was made in a 'private' letter is no defence and any jury would find in Miss Fancourt's favour."

He put three pieces of paper on Delia's desk, leaning forward so that she shrank back despite herself.

"If you wish to avoid explaining yourself in court, you will immediately sign these documents. They are a retraction to Mrs Ellicott, an apology to Miss Fancourt and a satisfactory certificate of character for Miss Fancourt."

Delia stared unseeing at the items he had laid on the desk, her thoughts skittering to and fro. She stiffened her spine. "I am sorry for you, sir, if you have been drawn into Miss Fancourt's web. You may act for her but how long is it since you have seen her? You cannot know her as well as one who has had her in her home for the past ten years. She will find nobody to support her in such an action."

"And you will?" he asked contemptuously. "Will you encourage your daughter to commit perjury at your side? And your paramour?"

Her eyes flashed. "My daughter remembers nothing of what happened that day. Our neighbour"—she emphasised the term—"Mr Purdue, who kindly came to our assistance, has left the district. It would simply be my word against Miss Fancourt's." She smiled coldly. "I think a jury will believe me rather than the governess I dismissed."

"Do you indeed, Lady Loring? Are you brave enough to put it to the test? What do you think will be left of your reputation by the time my client is heard? Don't forget, too, your daughter may recover her memory and the runners will very likely track down Mr Purdue."

"The runners? What do you mean?"

"The Bow Street Runners. If you refuse to withdraw such a serious allegation, apart from suing you for libel, my client will have no option but to lay information against Mr Purdue accusing him of assault, abduction and false imprisonment. You would of course be called to give evidence at his trial."

It would serve Simon right for abandoning her like that, Delia thought viciously. But her courage shrivelled at the prospect of being summoned to appear in court. How could she explain it to her husband? He would have no mercy, she knew.

Mr Chidlow seemed to have sensed her turmoil. He smiled blandly. "I think the print-shops would leap upon such a subject. Do you not agree?"

Her eyes closed in horror. Caricaturists would vie to depict the titillating tale of a mother and her lover surprised in a rustic cottage by her daughter with her governess. It would ruin not only her but Chloe.

She shaped numb lips into a conciliating smile. "If I sign these, it will be on condition that the—incidents which led to Miss Fancourt's departure never happened. She will never refer to them and neither will I. Are we agreed on this?"

"We are, provided that you have all of Miss Fancourt's belongings brought down. I shall take them with me."

Delia glared at him. If she had thought of it, she would have had the room cleared a week ago. Should she say it had already been done? She studied her implacable opponent. Better not, she thought, ringing the bell for her housekeeper. The woman glanced curiously at Mr Chidlow who was still standing, but Delia was not about to invite him to sit or offer any other courtesies.

"Not so fast, puss," Sir Edward called as Chloe ran down the stairs. "You'll trip on your skirts and fall again!"

"Oh, Papa!" she protested but slowed obediently.

"Where are you going in such a rush?"

"To find Mamma. She must have received word of Miss Fancourt, for she is having her belongings packed up. Hughes says there is someone here to collect them."

"Do you mean to say that the woman had the effrontery to send for her possessions after all that has happened? Where is this messenger? Below stairs?"

Sir Edward glared questioningly at Meadows who coughed discreetly.

"It is a Mr Chidlow, sir. He is with her ladyship in the small office."

"The small office!" Sir Edward snorted and turned on his heel.

"May I come too, Papa?"

He forced himself to smile down at his daughter. "Not now, pet."

"But I want to know about Miss Fancourt. I can't understand why she left so suddenly. She didn't even say goodbye." Chloe's eyes filled with tears.

"I'll see what I can find out," Sir Edward temporised. "In the meantime, you could take the *Morning Chronicle* to your grandmother for me. It is on my desk."

He watched her disappear into the library and went down the hall to the office. As he opened the door, his wife held out a sheet of paper to a stranger who glanced at it and said, "And the certificate of character?"

"Character, what character?" Sir Edward exploded as she handed the man another sheet. "Never tell me you have written a character for that wretched woman! And you, sir, you should be ashamed of yourself, coming here on her behalf. Who are you and what is your connection to her?"

The stranger made a courteous bow. "My name is Chidlow and I am Miss Fancourt's man of business."

"A fine way to describe her fancy man, if not her cock pimp! Leave this house at once, sirrah!"

"Sir Edward! Such language!"

He looked shamefacedly at his wife. "I beg your pardon, my lady. It would have been better if you had requested me to deal with this fellow."

"My business is with Lady Loring, sir."

"Sir Edward, pray leave it to me," Delia implored him. "Miss Fancourt was with us for ten years after all. Are we to condemn her utterly for one error of judgement? Should we not be more merciful?"

"You forget, my dear, that it is an offence to give a false character," he said severely. "And it is a case not only of Miss Fancourt's turpitude but also of her assault on our daughter. Indeed, I ask myself if it is not my duty to prosecute her for it."

"No!" Delia shrieked. "You could not ask me to stand up in court and describe what happened. Only think what the print-shops would make of it. Do you wish to have effigies of your wife and daughter hanging in every window?"

Mr Chidlow cleared his throat. "It was not my wish to bring discord into your home, Sir Edward, but I must tell you that Miss Fancourt and Lady Loring differ considerably in their account of the events that led to Miss Fancourt leaving Suffolk. Should it come to a trial of any description, Miss Fancourt would not hesitate to testify under oath. I need not remind you both that perjury is not only a crime but a grave sin."

Sir Edward looked from Mr Chidlow to his wife who had sunk back in her chair. "My lady?"

She spread her hands despairingly. "You see what he is like. He says it would be my word against hers. And so I thought it simplest to let her have her character."

"This is outrageous," Sir Edward snarled. "If you give in to such extortion once, what will her next demand be?"

Mr Chidlow drew himself up, affronted. "I assure you, sir, that Miss Fancourt's sole aim is to preserve her good name."

"She has forfeited her good name," Sir Edward snapped.

"Pray forgive me for contradicting you, sir." Julian's voice came from behind him. "She has not. She is blameless in all of this."

His son strode across the room to Mr Chidlow. "I understand you are here on Miss Fancourt's behalf, sir," he said urgently. "Is she safe and well?"

Chidlow's stern features softened at Julian's evident concern. "She is, sir. I thank you for your kind enquiry. Adam Chidlow at your service."

"Sir Julian Loring." Julian held out his hand and Chidlow clasped it.

"What do you mean, blameless?" Sir Edward demanded. His belligerence faded as he regarded his son who bore all the signs of one who brings unpalatable news. If Miss Fancourt is innocent, he thought uneasily. His gaze went to his wife. She looked frightened.

Julian said, "I'm sorry, sir, but I chased down Purdue last night and got the true story from him."

Delia eyed the three broad-shouldered men who stood in a tense triangle, exchanging wary glances.

Finally Julian broke the strained silence. "I think, sir," he said to his father, "that at the moment there is no need for me to say anything more than that Miss Fancourt was the innocent victim of an unfounded attack on her good name. If you permit, I shall withdraw with Mr Chidlow and discuss with him what amends must be made to her."

"Very well."

Sir Edward stood unmoving while Mr Chidlow gathered together his papers.

When the door closed behind the two men, a stony-faced husband turned to Delia. "Well, my lady?"

For once she could think of nothing to say. In the end, she rose, head erect and shoulders back, and stepped around him to leave the room. As she passed, he reached out and gripped her wrist hard, whipping her around to face him.

"Not so fast, my dear. You will describe to me how my daughter came to be injured. In addition, you will explain why you felt it necessary to traduce a blameless woman and how and why Miss Fancourt left Suffolk. And, finally, you will tell me what you were doing in that damn cottage."

She tried to jerk her wrist free but he pulled her over to the chair nearest the desk before releasing her.

"Sit!"

As if she were a dog, she thought resentfully, rubbing her wrist. He paid no attention but went to lock the door, removing the key and putting it in his pocket.

"Now, madam."

"I am not your prisoner, sir!"

He leaned against the desk and looked down at her, his arms folded. "No," he agreed softly, "you are my wife. You would do well to remember that the law gives me more power over you than any gaoler has over his prisoners. I will have the truth this time—and don't forget there are two others in this house who can confirm or deny it."

"Edward! Ned!" She held out an imploring hand but he was unmoved by this reminder of their early life together.

"Do not try my patience too far, madam. You will regret it."

There was no escape. Delia moistened her dry lips and began her confession.

Sir Edward's cheeks were flecked with red as he looked grimly at his son.

"I've told the adulterous trollop to stay in her room until I decide what to do with her. You said Purdue had made a clean breast of it. What did he say?"

He listened, frowning, to Julian's report. "Hmmph. Much the same tale, although she says she has no idea what happened to Miss Fancourt—she hasn't seen Purdue since that day and then she was too worried about Chloe to spare any thought for anyone else. But she was happy enough to adopt the story he made up and accuse an innocent woman of her own sins. And then to repeat the slander in writing in a letter to this Bath school teacher!" He laughed grimly. "She was too clever for her own good, for it was that that brought this Chidlow down on her head."

"I had Purdue give me five hundred guineas as compensation for Miss Fancourt," Julian said. "I gave it to Chidlow as well as a draft on my bank for the same amount. He demurred, said she was not seeking financial damages, but I convinced him that it was only just."

"That was well done! I'll reimburse you, of course. I'll be cutting my lady's funds in any event," Sir Edward added sourly. "She will pay for this in every possible way."

Julian went to the decanters and poured two glasses of brandy. When his father was in such a mood, it was the only way to soften him.

"Chidlow and I are agreed that it is in Miss Fancourt's best interest to keep the whole affair to ourselves. If it were to become known, her reputation must suffer despite her innocence. He quite rightly reminded me that a governess must be above suspicion."

Sir Edward gulped his brandy. "I must talk to my solicitor. I am reluctant to go to court—apart from the expense, I have no wish to wash my dirty linen in public. But I don't know if I can allow her to remain here or permit her to associate with Chloe. And that's another thing! What the devil am I to say to Chloe? She is very upset that Miss Fancourt left so abruptly."

"You need not decide anything today," Julian said calmingly. "As to Chloe—is it possible that she will recall more of what happened when her mother is not constantly by her side urging her to forget or telling her she is confused in her memories?"

His father looked startled. "Of course that is what she was doing! That is why she allowed no one near the child for the first week. The scheming jade! To muddle the poor girl's mind under the pretext of caring for her! But it is all of a piece, I suppose."

A timid tap on the library door heralded Chloe herself. "I beg your pardon for disturbing you, Papa, but I do want to hear about Miss Fancourt. Mamma is indisposed so I came to you."

Sir Edward looked despairingly at his son.

"Come in, pet, and sit down." Julian gestured to the deep window seat. He closed the door and went to sit beside his sister, taking her hand as he asked gently, "What do you remember of the day you fell?"

"It's confused," she said. "Mamma said I must not worry about it."

"You are well enough to try now, I think. Let us see what we can put together. It was the day my father and I came home from Newmarket, was it not? You waved us off on the previous Monday and warned us not to wager too much."

She nodded. "After breakfast, I practised the pianoforte and afterwards Miss Fancourt came to accompany my singing. I remember Lord Swanmere came in to listen."

"Does he often do that?"

"He did that week. I think he was bored because you and Papa were not here."

"What did you sing for him?"

"*Where the Bee Sucks, There Suck I*. Then he asked did I know *Oh! The Oak and the Ash*. I don't but Miss Fancourt does and she sang it for him. He said she must sing it again one evening before he went home."

"And then?" Julian prompted her.

Her face fell. "Usually when practice was over, we read aloud in French, but I can't remember if we did that day."

"Nobody remembers everything they did every day," he remarked soothingly. "You will have had your nuncheon?"

"Yes, with Grandmamma and his lordship—Mamma wasn't there. She had gone out earlier. Then Grandmamma went to rest."

"Did you and Miss Fancourt rest too?"

Chloe giggled. "Like a pair of old ladies? No, we always went for a walk after our nuncheon."

"Where did you go that day?" Julian asked softly. "It was a fine day, as I recall."

She looked into the distance. "It was hot and close so we went into the woods. I said I wanted to see if the lily of the valley had blossomed. Remember, Papa, we noticed the leaves last month?"

"A big patch not far from old Lambert's cottage?" Sir Edward had pulled up a chair and was listening intently.

Chloe giggled again. "Except that it was bear's garlic. The flowers are pretty, but you cannot conceive how strongly they smelled! I was so disappointed."

"Did you pick any?"

"Of course not! Who would want a posy reeking of garlic? We went back to the path and then the storm came." She looked frightened. "The sky went black and there was such a flash of lightning! And the thunder! I had to put my hands over my ears. Then the rain just pelted down. Miss Fancourt asked how far it was to the cottage and I said not far and we ran. She said there would probably be a shed or something where we could shelter. But I tried the door first and it opened."

The colour drained from the girl's face. "Mamma was there with Mr Purdue. I don't want to say what she was doing. She was angry when she saw us." She put her hand to her head and said, "I don't remember any more."

Julian put his arm around her. "That must have been

when you hurt your head. They told us that your mother and Mr Purdue brought you back here about half-past three."

She rested her head on his shoulder. "Mamma was angry," she said, like a child. "She said I was spying on her. I said it was no such thing and she had betrayed Papa, then she slapped me and I tripped and fell."

"And hurt your poor head." He pressed a kiss to her brow. "But it is better now, isn't it?"

"Yes."

Julian rocked her gently and her father came to kneel beside her.

"That's my good, brave girl. Now that you have remembered, we need not talk of it again."

She looked at him earnestly. "Are you angry with Mamma, Papa?"

"I am, child," he said heavily. "Apart from the betrayal, as you rightly describe it, she lied to make us think that it was Miss Fancourt who was at fault, not she."

"But we know the truth now and you will be glad to hear that Miss Fancourt is well and staying with friends not far from London," Julian put in.

"I suppose she felt she could not return here," Chloe remarked sadly.

"It would have been very difficult for her."

"Might I write to her, do you think? When we talked about her leaving, she said she would always be glad to hear from me."

Julian could not imagine Miss Fancourt rejecting her former pupil. "I am sure she would be pleased if you wrote. Remember, sweetheart, she knows that none of this was your fault. In fact, she instructed the person who called here earlier to ask how you went on. She was most concerned about your welfare, he said."

"Send her to her mother," the dowager Lady Loring said firmly. "Mrs Eubank and I correspond from time to time and in her most recent letter she told me that the elderly cousin who had been her long-time companion had died and she did not know how she would go on without her. Let her daughter take her place."

"Where does she live?" Julian enquired.

"In Harrogate."

"It seems an odd penance, to send her to a watering-place."

Sir Edward smiled dourly. "That is where we met, you know, in ninety-four. I was visiting my old great-uncle who was taking the cure for the gout and she was attending her mother who even then was something of a valetudinarian; one of those women who glory in the rigours of their medical treatment and keep a very plain table because they suffer so from dyspepsia—you know the sort. She liked to be at the baths by seven each morning. The family is originally from near Brighton, or Brighthelmstone as Mrs Eubank insists on calling it. When Delia's brother inherited after their father died, her mother decided to move to Harrogate. She disapproved of the raffish elements flocking to Brighton in the wake of the Prince of Wales."

"Good God! Could she not at least have gone to Bath?"

His father did not respond to Julian's quip. "I just want Delia out of my sight. I must support her, but shall make it clear that she may not draw on my credit. She will get what is due to her under our marriage settlement and that is all."

"Send her to her mother," the dowager repeated. "That will give you the opportunity to decide what you wish to do without making the breach immediately public or permanent. There is time enough for that later if she does not show a proper remorse. But you must also think of Chloe."

Harrogate! He was sending her back to Harrogate, back to that stagnant house and tedious daily round. Outwardly attentive, Delia let her husband's words flow over her. Reduced to the strict terms of her marriage settlement— use the opportunity for reflection—behave at all times in a seemly manner. He had decided not to inform her mother that she was in disgrace and hoped she appreciated his magnanimity. However she was not to take this as meaning that he in any way condoned her adultery; he had not yet considered whether or under which conditions he might permit her to return to Suffolk.

She thought quickly. The important thing now was to ensure that she would have as much freedom as possible in Harrogate.

"You are very good, Edward," she said meekly. "If you permit, I shall write to my mother, informing her that I have not been well and that a change of scene has been recommended. That would be best, would it not? When do you wish me to go?" She touched a handkerchief to the corner of her eye.

He cleared his throat. "I suppose it will be the end of next week before we hear from Mrs Eubank."

She bowed her head submissively. "I shall set out on Monday week, then. My maid will come with me. I cannot travel alone."

"Of course, of course," he said impatiently and left the room.

As soon as the door closed behind him, she seized a porcelain shepherdess from the mantelpiece and held it high above her head. Nothing would give her greater satisfaction than to shatter it and its companion piece against the marble fireplace. Her fingers itched to hurl it but she forced herself to return the figure undamaged to its place. She must continue to appear meek and humble. He liked that. She would stay in her room today but tomorrow was Sunday and she would go to church. He could hardly forbid her that.

But he could, she found. He came to her room that evening to tell her that, on reflection, he would not permit her to attend church the next day. "It is Whitsun and I cannot think it right for you to take Communion at present."

"So I have been weighed in the balances and found wanting," she said bitterly. "You are very quick to cast the first stone, Edward."

Did he redden a little? His face was so weather-beaten it was hard to see. But he did not relent.

"You will regret it if you try my patience too far, madam. Do not forget that you remain here on sufferance."

She lowered her eyes. "Do you intend to keep me confined to my room until I leave for Harrogate? It will cause talk, you know, and I assume you would prefer to avoid that."

"You may come down tomorrow, but you must remain within the park. Will you obey me, or must I give orders that all instructions to the stables are to be referred to me?"

Delia felt herself flush but forced herself to remain calm. "Oh, very well. I shall have so much to do preparing for a long absence that I shall have very little time to go anywhere. I hope you do not expect Chloe to take over as mistress here."

"Chloe is no longer your concern," he returned evenly. "My mother has taken her to visit my sister. They will not return until after your departure."

"How can you be so cruel as to keep her from me?" she cried before asking less truculently, "What have you said to her?"

"Nothing. I didn't have to. She knows you have displeased me. Besides, do you really think she would continue to forget how her mother struck her?"

Real tears filled Delia's eyes. She stretched out her hand imploringly. "I didn't mean to hurt her, Edward, truly I didn't. She tripped and fell."

He shook his head. "You have made your bed, madam, and now you must lie on it."

# Chapter Eleven

SEATED AT THE LARGE ROUND table in Cousin Emmy's drawing-room, the members of St Mary's Dorcas Society plied their needles and their tongues with equal alacrity. As they sewed clothes for the poor, they dissected local and national news; the dismissal of a servant, the betrothal of the vicar's daughter and the controversy regarding the exclusion of the Princess of Wales from her daughter's presentation all receiving equal attention from the ladies, who ranged in age from almost sixteen to more than seventy.

They had been most welcoming and although talkative in the extreme were without malice. They had murmured sympathetically on learning that young Mr Chidlow had served under Captain Fancourt—both having sadly given their lives for their country—, admired the Captain's portrait now hanging beside that of the young midshipman and exclaimed how happy they were that Miss Fancourt had come to live in their midst. After ten years spent in the limbo reserved by society for governesses and companions, it was a particular delight to Rosa to be received as an equal and she looked forward to establishing closer friendships with some of the younger women.

She carefully snipped her thread and tenderly folded the little cap. What should she start next? There was a constant need for clothing for the unfortunate infants born in the workhouse whose mothers had nothing to dress them in.

"Poor mites," Cousin Emmy had said, "they are not responsible for the sins of their parents and I always say that if we did not have the military camps on Coxheath we would have far fewer such cases. Well, with the war over, we may soon see the last of the soldiery."

"Miss Fancourt, would you be kind enough to show me how to set the sleeves in this gown?" the youngest member of the group asked. "You do it so neatly."

"Of course." Rosa took a paper of pins and showed the girl how to place them in the tiny garment. "Baste it now and make sure it is gathered evenly before you sew the seam."

As she returned to her seat, she noticed John, Cousin Emmy's footman, standing at the door. Why did he not enter? She looked at him questioningly and he tilted his head faintly towards the landing behind him. Was there something he did not wish to announce to the company at large—a kitchen disaster that would delay the tea-board, perhaps? With a murmured excuse, she went towards him.

As soon as he saw her approach, John stepped back out of the drawing-room. "There's a gentleman to see you, miss," he said when she joined him, proffering a card on a tray.

*Sir Julian Loring.* Her heart skipped a beat. What

brought him here? Had Chloe suffered a relapse?

"I beg your pardon if I did wrong, miss, but I thought today it'd be better not to show him up unannounced."

"That was quite right, John," she assured him, smiling inwardly at the thought of Sir Julian's face if he had been propelled unexpectedly into such an assembly, although the ladies would have been enraptured by the arrival of a handsome and titled stranger. "Where is he?"

"I had him wait in the master's study. I couldn't leave such a fine gentleman in the hall."

"No," she agreed. "I'll go down."

"I'll be just outside, miss, in case you need anything."

"Thank you." Rosa smiled at her would-be protector and hurried down the stairs.

At the sound of quick steps in the hall, Julian turned from his inspection of the book-cases that lined the room. For a moment he didn't recognise the smiling woman standing in the doorway. She wore a stylish wrap-over gown of muslin printed with primrose stripes wreathed with fresh green leaves and flowers. A tantalising little frill flirted around the edge of her bodice, emphasising the curve of her elegant neck. Her dark hair was not as severely dressed as before and her little lace cap served to adorn rather than to conceal.

"I apologise for keeping you waiting, Sir Julian." Her smile deepened. "Believe me, it was not lack of attention but masculine fellow-feeling that had John show you in here rather than the drawing-room. The ladies of the parish have gathered there for their weekly sewing circle."

He smiled back at her. "I must be sure to express my appreciation to him. Thank you for receiving me, Miss

Fancourt. I am happy to see you look so well and hope you have fully recovered from your ordeal."

"I have, thank you, sir. How does your sister?"

"Chloe has made a good recovery from her injuries, physically that is, but—it is on her account that I have ventured to call on you."

"Why, what is wrong?" As she spoke, she sank gracefully into a deep armchair and waved him to another.

"Thank you." He sat and gathered his thoughts. "Briefly, she is not the same person she was before. You remember, she was like a little lark—always so happy and so, so effervescent. You couldn't remain in the dumps for long in her company. And she was interested in everything. But now she is always dejected and doesn't seem to know what to do with herself. My grandmother thinks it results from her injury and says to give her time, but I am worried, Miss Fancourt, and I thought you might advise me. You probably know her best of all of us."

She frowned a little. "It seems very unlike her, I agree. Is she sleeping well?"

"I don't know," he said helplessly.

"Has she a good appetite?"

He had to think about that. "Not as good as it was, I would say. She no longer comments on her favourite dishes, for example, and has not regained the pounds she lost when she was ill."

"Hmmm. May I speak frankly, Sir Julian?"

"I hope you will, Miss Fancourt."

She was silent for a few moments, as if choosing her words. "I assume Mr Chidlow's visit to Loring Place was not without consequences for your family as a whole?"

"No. Briefly, my father decided Lady Loring should

join her mother in Harrogate until the end of September at least."

"How was this explained to Chloe?"

"I don't know, precisely. She sought out my father that day—after Mr Chidlow had left—hoping for news of you. In the course of our conversation, she remembered more of what happened the day she was injured." He hesitated. "For obvious reasons, Lady Loring had encouraged her to forget it or to believe that her memories were confused."

"I see."

"That evening, Chloe asked my father if he were angry with her mother and he admitted he was, both because of her behaviour with Purdue and her subsequent deceit in relation to you. The next day Chloe and our grandmother went to visit my aunt Undrell. They did not return until my stepmother had departed."

Miss Fancourt raised her brows. "So Chloe has not spoken to her mother since discovering the truth?"

"No."

"And you don't think all of this must have affected a sensitive girl?"

"I am very sure it did. In addition, my father is inclined to be testy at present and Chloe is too young to deal with him. Last week I drove her over to see her former nurse. Mrs Crewe had helped take care of her after the fall and Chloe was always fond of her. I thought the distraction might do her good."

"An excellent notion," Miss Fancourt said approvingly. "We used to call there regularly on our walks; frequently on baking day when Mrs Crewe would have made a pie or a tart. She said that Miss Chloe's visit gave her the perfect excuse to take the weight off her feet. Chloe used to bring sugar plums for the children and tell them stories."

Julian nodded. "They ran to her as soon as we arrived. Mrs Crewe took one look at Chloe and suggested—in fact it was more an order—that I leave her there for the afternoon. When I returned, she sent Chloe off with the children to see a new litter of kittens and then told me that she was pining, not for her mother but for you. It was only then I realised that although in the beginning your name was frequently on her lips, she had not mentioned you since she learnt you were safe and well with friends. At the time, she just said sadly, '*I suppose she felt she could not return here*'. She doesn't know about Purdue's treatment of you; I imagine she thinks you left immediately and of your own free will, perhaps because of her mother's shocking behaviour."

Miss Fancourt put her hand to her mouth. "In her letter she said she missed me and would I not come back, but I replied it was no longer possible. I'm so sorry if I hurt her, Sir Julian. Lady Loring had given me notice to Midsummer and, even if nothing else had happened, I would have thought it unwise to return only for a few weeks. Your sister was most distressed when she heard I was to leave and I thought it would only make it harder for her if I returned briefly."

He leaned forward. "But supposing, Miss Fancourt, you were to return for good or at least another year? I sincerely doubt that Chloe will be ready to make her come-out next spring. I questioned the idea before— but now! She seems lost somehow, childish even, and I can't see my father agreeing to it, even if he permits Lady Loring to return home."

She stilled, her composed features displaying no

reaction to his proposal. It's her governess face, he thought; the one she hides behind.

Her bosom rose on a deep breath. "I am afraid, Sir Julian, that I have agreed to stay with Mrs Chidlow indefinitely." A faint flush tinged her cheek. "She and Mr Chidlow—they have offered me a home, you see. But apart from that, I would find it difficult to return to Loring Place. My sudden departure is bound to have caused talk. In addition, I cannot think that Lady Loring would welcome my presence when—if she returns."

It was on the tip of Julian's tongue to reply: 'Lady Loring will be fortunate if she is permitted to return,' but that was his father's decision to make.

"And what about Miss Dismore? You can hardly have two governesses at once."

"Miss Dismore? Oh, you mean the so-called finishing governess? She didn't last much more than a day."

"A day? What can you mean?"

She looked so flummoxed that he had to laugh. He sat back and crossed his legs, looking forward to telling his story.

"You may well ask. I only heard about this afterwards and received three, no four, highly-coloured versions of the whole thing, but as far I could understand, what happened was this. Firstly, everyone had forgotten about the lady and there was consternation when she turned up in a hired gig from Bury. No one was at home—my father had ridden out as usual and my grandmother had gone for a drive with Chloe. Meadows sent for Mrs Walton and they paid the driver and put her into the small office, the one where my father sees people he doesn't want shown into the library but won't leave standing in the hall."

"The bleak little room beside Lady Loring's book-room?"

"That's the one. She stared at the wall there for an hour until my grandmother and Chloe returned. My grandmother was horrified and went at once to see her. She apologised, explained that Lady Loring had been called away to her mother who was unwell—which is the story we have put about—and suggested that Miss Dismore first settle into her room and then she would send her maid to bring her, Miss Dismore, I mean—there are too many females in this story—to Grandmother's sitting-room where she would make her known to Chloe."

"What sort of a person was she?"

Julian forbore repeating his father's comment that the woman would have been *'better suited to a whipping parlour'*.

"*'Of a certain age'*, was how Grandmother described her, but *'inclined to dress lamb-fashion'*, whatever that may be. She had *'a pursed mouth and a spine like a poker'*, according to Chloe."

Miss Fancourt smiled at these descriptions. "Good heavens! I can't imagine Chloe finding her agreeable."

"She didn't. She was not pleased by her arrival but she agreed to see how they got on together. Their first encounter was not promising. Miss Dismore looked her up and down and said, *'My dear Miss Loring, I can see there is much work ahead of us. Your hair for a start—it will not do.'* You may imagine how Chloe bristled at this but, she told me later, she would not give the woman the satisfaction of explaining about her short hair. It had been cut so that the wound on her scalp could be treated," he added.

"Poor girl. But I am sure her curls are very pretty and it will grow again."

"Then my father came in and Miss Dismore was presented to him. She began to flutter with arch looks and 'oh, Sir Edwards', and particular emphases. '*So* sorry *to learn* dear *Lady Loring was called away but of course I am only* too happy *to prepare Miss Loring for her come-out. It is such an* important *occasion for a young lady. Why, her* whole *future depends upon it.*' "

Miss Fancourt's eyes brimmed with amusement. "I can picture Sir Edward's face. How did he respond?"

"How do you think?" he challenged her.

She laughed. "With throat-clearings and '*ahems*', I should imagine, and appeals to your grandmother, were they not to get any dinner or something of the sort."

"Precisely. Fortunately dinner was announced. Miss Dismore was inclined to regale them with tales of the *ton* but when Chloe asked her had she seen the allied sovereigns, she had to admit that she had not been in town during their visit. Her latest charge had made a most *suitable* match and her work was *done*, was how she put it. She had gone to visit her dear sister before taking up her *new* position. Not long after the ladies withdrew, Grandmother excused Miss Dismore, saying she knew she would be tired after her journey.

"As soon as she had gone upstairs, Grandmother and Chloe returned to the dining-room to hold a council of war as Grandmother put it because, she said, she was certain my father would not join them that evening. He was all for turning the woman off immediately. Chloe agreed with him, but Grandmother persuaded them to give her a trial. The next day was Sunday. She accompanied the family to church, of course and in the afternoon Chloe suggested they go for a walk. The lady agreed, but could not be persuaded to go beyond the walled garden. Once there, she sat on a bench and instructed Chloe to walk up and down so that she could observe her posture. They then repaired to the music room where she had Chloe play and sing for her and declared that her pieces were sadly old-fashioned and would never do in town. Chloe then excused herself by saying that she must read to her grandmother."

Julian laughed again. "I don't know whether to be glad or sorry I missed the next bit. Grandmother was not yet dressed the following morning when Chloe burst into her bedchamber brandishing a wooden implement. It was an oval piece of wood, about eight inches in diameter, tapering on either side to form something like a broom handle. It was altogether about three feet wide. Miss Dismore had instructed her to put this implement behind her back and hook her elbows around each of the handles so as to hold it in place between her shoulder blades. She was to maintain this position all morning as it would improve her posture and teach her to hold her elbows close to her side. What nonsense! Can you imagine anything more uncomfortable, Miss Fancourt?"

She smiled ruefully. "At school, I used a posture board for fifteen minutes twice a day. We used take it in turns. It wasn't too bad once you got used to it, but to expect Chloe to use the thing for a whole morning is nothing less than torture. And she doesn't need it. She has a graceful, natural posture that is much more elegant than anything enforced. There were some girls at school whose governesses had been devoted to such devices and our dancing master was used to despair of them, their stance was so stiff. We didn't have one in the schoolroom at the Place so Miss Dismore must have brought hers with her. What did Chloe do?"

"She refused, of course. And then this vixen fetched a rod she had also brought with her and said she could see Chloe must be made to mind her."

"What!" Miss Fancourt's cheeks flushed with anger and her eyes flashed fire. "She wanted to whip my Chloe? I am sure she did not succeed."

Her Chloe! Julian's heart turned over. He smiled fiercely at her. "Of course not. Chloe repulsed the attack with the board, ran out of the room and went straight to Grandmother who, of course, was horrified and sent at once for my father. In the meantime, Miss Dismore had bearded him in the library, still brandishing the rod and declaring she must have a free hand with her pupil and be able to punish her disobedience. He immediately summoned Mrs Walton. She was to supervise Miss Dismore while she packed her traps. When Dismore protested, he snatched the rod from her hand and asked her if she would like a taste of it."

Miss Fancourt inhaled sharply but nodded, apparently in approval.

"She yelped how dared he offer violence to a defenceless woman and he retorted that she had been prepared to use it on a defenceless girl. When Mrs Walton heard that, she said, *'Give me that rod, sir, if you please, and I'll deal with her'.*"

Miss Fancourt burst out laughing. "I shouldn't laugh," she gasped, her hand pressed to her breast, "but such a bizarre scene is more suited to the stage than the library at the Place. Miss Dismore capitulated, I take it?"

He nodded. "She was bundled into the carriage fifteen minutes later and driven to Bury."

"Thank goodness. She must have misled Lady Loring, for she did not permit any form of corporal punishment. She told me on my first day that she did not approve of it, especially for girls. Not that she needed to, for I would never have dreamt of using it. Perhaps it never occurred to her that Miss Dismore might attempt it. Chloe is almost an adult after all."

"But the damage was done, Miss Fancourt. Chloe was distraught, crying that she would have no governess or companion if she could not have you and declaring she would rather go to Harrogate to her mother than stay at the Place."

Miss Fancourt looked concerned. "I doubt that would be wise but, with all due respect to your grandmother, she is too old and frail to act as Chloe's only chaperon. You will need to find someone more active, but I think it would be advisable if you were to meet her first."

Julian's blood ran cold. "Interview a governess? I should have no idea how to go about it. I would do almost anything for my sister, Miss Fancourt, but that is where I draw the line."

She raised an eyebrow. "I thought you were doing just that at present, Sir Julian."

"No, I am not, I am appealing for help to a lady whom I greatly admire; one who has lived with my family for over ten years and whom my sister regards as an elder sister, if not an aunt."

She blushed furiously at this forthright retort. Encouraged, he asked, "Would you consider coming to us, not as Chloe's governess, but as a friend who would assist us in finding the right person for her? It need not be at Loring Place. I am sure my grandmother would agree to remove to Swanmere Castle with her for the rest of the summer. Chloe needs you, Miss Fancourt."

"So does Mrs Chidlow."

"Please consider it at least; perhaps discuss it with Mrs Chidlow before you refuse."

She looked at him for a moment and said, "Very well."

He smiled warmly at her. "Thank you. I won't press you any further now, but will call in two days' time if you permit."

"As you wish, Sir Julian."

She walked with him to the hall door and held out her hand. "Goodbye, Sir Julian. If you are writing to your family, please convey my respectful compliments but pray do not raise any hopes that may turn out to be false."

"Of course not—and thank you again."

Her bare hand was warm in his and he relinquished it reluctantly. "Until Thursday, Miss Fancourt."

*My dear Grandmother,*

*Pray excuse this scrawl, written in haste in my carriage so as to catch tonight's mail. I have just left Miss Fancourt who, I am happy to tell you, appears to be in good health and is in excellent looks. I explained our concerns for Chloe but unfortunately she feels unable to return to Loring Place which would solve all our problems. She suggests we look for another lady to be a companion, mentor and chaperon to Chloe. It would be important that Chloe is comfortable with her and that we do not have a repeat of the Dismore episode.*

*I think we should look for someone to be with Chloe for two years. I wondered from the beginning whether she was not too young to come out next year. I am more convinced of this than ever and should be reluctant to see her embark on preparations for it, especially given the uncertainty regarding her mother's future. Do you not agree?*

*Pray do not mention it to Chloe, but I am hopeful that Miss F will agree to come to Swanmere as our guest and assist us in finding the right person. This would, of course, depend on your being prepared to remove there with Chloe for the summer. Pray let me know by return if this would suit you.*

*I must close. Miss Fancourt desires me to convey her respectful compliments to you, but I think it best you do not tell Chloe that I have seen her.*

> *I remain, dear Grandmamma,*
> *Your affectionate grandson,*
> *Julian Loring.*

Julian folded the letter and put it in his pocket—he had no intention of trying to melt sealing wax in a swaying carriage. He had stabled his own team at the *Black Lion* in Farmingham and could seal his letter there while the horses were changed. He leaned back against the squabs and closed his eyes, not dissatisfied with his day's work.

She had looked exceptionally well today. He hoped that if she agreed to come to Swanmere, she would not consider it necessary to resume her former drab costume or her governessy demeanour.

"If I were not so attached to Chloe, I would not even

consider it," Rosa told the Chidlows. "I have no desire to return to that life. But I cannot forget how lonely I was when I was sent to school and how forsaken I felt after my mother died. Poor child, she must be feeling something similar."

"From what you say, you have been as much a mother to her as Lady Loring was and it is very likely that in all the confusion she feels abandoned by you," Cousin Emmy said. "I think Sir Julian is right in that it would benefit her to re-establish a connection with you even if it cannot be on the same footing as previously. But you would be wise to limit your visit to an agreed period and for Miss Loring to know that from the beginning. It would be intolerable if you were still with the family on Lady Loring's return."

"Is there not a risk that a short visit would only provide temporary relief and that Chloe would fall back into the dismals when I leave?"

"It will be your task to prevent that, Rosa," Cousin Emmy said placidly before asking her husband, "What is your opinion, my dear?"

"As always, I am in complete agreement with you, my love." He turned to Rosa. "I think you should oblige Sir Julian if you feel you can. Apart from what you might owe his sister, you are also indebted to him. He went to considerable lengths to extract the truth from Mr Purdue, besides arranging that you were suitably compensated for the distress you suffered. His concern for you was evident; his first words to me were to ask were you safe and well."

Rosa felt her cheeks grow hot. "Oh, I had not realised," she stammered. Although she had written a very proper letter expressing her appreciation of Sir Julian's efforts on her behalf, she had not thought his interest to be as personal as Cousin Adam implied. She had not wanted to accept the 'compensation' but had reluctantly allowed herself to be convinced that to return it could only be construed as a refusal to accept Sir Edward's apology.

'As neither he nor his son is in any way at fault, it would be an unforgiveable affront,' Cousin Adam had said firmly.

"If you are to be a guest at Swanmere Castle for several weeks, you will need a much more extensive wardrobe. There will very likely be all manner of entertainments," Cousin Emmy said practically. "It is fortunate that the same satin slips may be used under various over-gowns and robes and much may be achieved by varying trimmings and embellishments."

"If my gowns are to be re-trimmed or altered every day, I would need my own maid," Rosa pointed out, dismayed. The proposed visit was getting more and more expensive.

"Why not take Polly?" Cousin Emmy suggested. "Are you not satisfied with her?"

"Of course I am. My hair has never looked so well and she has a deft hand with a needle and a good eye. But will you not need her?"

Emmy shook her head. "I think she's getting restless. I don't know how many girls have moved on from here to become ladies' maids. Let Polly have her chance— the others may each move up a rung and we shall have a new scullery maid. I am always pleased to be able to take another girl from the workhouse. So that is settled." She gave a decisive nod and said plaintively, "I should like another cup of tea, my dear."

"Aye, thinking and talking make thirsty work." Her husband collected her cup and took it to Rosa for refilling. When he returned to his wife's side, he stooped to kiss her cheek, saying fondly, "If the country were managed as well as this household, we would all be better off."

Rosa had been thinking something the same. Cousin Emmy had all the reins in her hand and did not hesitate to take control. I must learn from her example, she reflected; remember I am no longer a servant. True independence starts in the mind.

# Chapter Twelve

THREE O'CLOCK. IF HE was to come today as promised, he could not delay much longer. Perhaps the dowager had refused to go to Swanmere—it was a long journey for an old lady—or Sir Edward did not want to part with his daughter for the summer. Rosa tried to imagine what life was like for Chloe with only her grandmother and an irascible father for company. It was no wonder the girl seemed lost. From the day she was born there had always been an attendant to wait on her, keep her company and tell her what to do next. How did young ladies of quality occupy themselves between leaving the schoolroom and marrying? If they were fortunate, they were given a Season, perhaps two, but that would cover only a few months of the year. What did they do the rest of the time?

Hooves stamped in the street below and harness jingled. Rosa went cautiously to the window, standing to one side so that she could not be seen. He was here. She quickly regained her seat. Soon she heard the rap of boot heels on the floorboards and John stood at the door.

"Sir Julian Loring," he announced and stepped back.

Once again he was immaculately turned out, today in a dark brown coat with a cream and fawn silk waistcoat, clinging buff pantaloons and gleaming hessians, but his shirt points remained moderate and his tie austere rather than exuberant. His hair had been trimmed since she saw him last and his curls ruthlessly tamed, she was sorry to note.

"Miss Fancourt," he said and bowed.

She inclined her head. "Sir Julian," she replied as correctly, then, "will you not be seated?"

He sat, rested his hat on his knee and smiled at her. "Well, Miss Fancourt?"

She raised an eyebrow. "Well, Sir Julian?"

He laughed and placed his hat on the floor, then leaned forward, his hands clasped loosely between his knees. "So I am to account for myself? You must have been a stern preceptress."

"It was never necessary. Chloe was always biddable and eager to learn. She was so sweet-natured and it was a joy to help her mind develop. I miss her but a governess knows from the beginning that her charges are only temporarily hers. We are warned not to get too fond, but with Chloe— it was impossible not to love her."

His smile faded. "And yet you seem to have borne the prospect of parting from her with equanimity."

"The last service I could perform for her was to help her accept the inevitability of my departure. My feelings did not matter."

His eyes narrowed at her quiet reply. "I beg your pardon," he said at last. "That was unfair of me."

"Yes." She felt stripped bare by his searching gaze.

"When Lady Loring informed you of her plans—did you think Chloe was ready to leave you?"

"If I had been consulted, I should have suggested waiting another year—after all, Chloe is not yet seventeen. Lady Loring was right, however, in thinking that I would not be able to prepare Chloe properly for her come-out."

"Why do you say that?"

She spread her hands. "I know nothing of fashionable life, sir. I went from a Bath academy to Loring Place where my world was almost as circumscribed as Chloe's. I have been in London twice in my life, once on my way to the Place and once on my departure from Suffolk."

"How did you manage that?" he interrupted. "I cannot describe the horror I felt when I realised you had literally broken out of that attic room. What did you do then?"

"Why were you so sure it was I who had been held there?"

"I knew a woman had been there from the footprints, but then I found your gloves trapped between the mattress and the wall. I recognised them from the day we rode to Lavenham. When I saw the state they were in! If Purdue had been before me, I would have throttled him."

A shiver ran down Rosa's spine at his rough growl. "Perhaps it was fortunate he was not," she answered primly. "I suppose luck was on my side. I found a trunk containing mourning weeds including a veiled bonnet as well as a little purse with some guineas in it. It had been left in a reticule. I slipped out at dawn and walked to *The Angel* in time to catch the six o'clock Fly. Nobody looked askance at me."

He regarded her with open admiration. "Fortune favours the bold. I hope Chloe has acquired some of your resourcefulness and resilience."

"I hope she never needs it. I didn't feel very resilient when I saw you ride out of the stable yard at Old Hall. I banged and banged against the glass but you didn't look up."

He looked horrified. "You saw me and tried to attract my attention? I swear I never noticed a thing."

"I could see that. And later, when you found I had been held there, you went out of your way to discover the whole truth. I cannot tell you how grateful I am that you did not simply write me off like a bad debt."

"I could never have done that," he said simply. "I found Purdue's story hard to believe from the beginning and later, when no one had seen or heard of you that day or the officer he claimed to have seen you with, I became even more concerned, as did my grandmother."

"She did not believe it either?" Rosa was relieved and comforted that she had not lost the old lady's good opinion.

He grinned. "Apart from the fact that it wasn't in your character, she said she did not know how you could have found time to meet this officer, let alone make an assignation with him."

Rosa laughed. "I can just hear her saying it. But you did not come here to discuss my adventures, Sir Julian."

"No." After a moment, he continued, "My grandmother and my father both agree we should defer Chloe's come-out for another year and that she needs a lady who will—"

"Ease her entry into the *beau monde* and help her avoid its pitfalls? I have given this some thought in recent days and I do not think she needs another governess. Is there no family member to whom you could turn? Chloe gained so much confidence during the week of the house-party and I think it would be better to continue in that line, letting her try her wings at little dances and entertainments with other young people."

"I wonder—" he said slowly. "You have given me an idea, Miss Fancourt. I have a distant cousin, a Mrs Overton— the relationship is through our mothers—whose husband was killed at Vitoria last year. Her daughter is Chloe's age and she has a younger son. She might be interested in bringing her family to Swanmere this summer. It would provide a distraction for Chloe and, depending on how she and Ann go on together, something more may come of it. But we'll have to wait and see whether my father decides to take his wife back before deciding anything further."

"Do you think he might not?"

He shrugged. "I have no idea what his intentions are. At present, he does not propose to have recourse to the courts but that is all I know."

"I hope for Chloe's sake he decides to forgive Lady Loring. I don't know how her come-out could be managed otherwise. It would look very odd if she came to town without her mother."

"You are right. In the meantime, are we to have the pleasure of your company at Swanmere? Without you, it will be much more difficult for Chloe to regain solid ground. My grandmother thoroughly approves of the plan and my father has given his consent."

"And Chloe?" Rosa wondered if he was trying to force her hand.

"Nothing has been said to her," he reassured her. "I wouldn't risk subjecting her to such a disappointment for the world."

"If I come, it must be on condition that Chloe knows from the beginning that it is a temporary visit."

"Agreed. May we regard it as settled, then?"

Rosa took a deep breath. "You may, Sir Julian."

His shoulders relaxed as he responded with a dazzling smile and a heart-felt, "Thank you, Miss Fancourt. How soon can you leave?" he continued eagerly. "I shall send my carriage for you, of course. My grandmother suggests that she and Chloe meet you near Cambridge. If you do not object to an early start, that distance can be covered in one day so you will not be obliged to break your journey while travelling alone. From Cambridge, you would go on together and at a more comfortable pace."

Rosa was torn between amusement and indignation at this babble of instruction and arrangement. The Lorings had demonstrated no such qualms when they assumed an eighteen-year-old girl would travel alone across England from Bath to Bury St Edmunds.

"You seem to have it all arranged."

"My grandmother issued a long list of instructions. For example, I am to ask if you will bring your own maid. If not, I am to arrange for one to travel with you."

"My maid comes with me," she replied composedly, inwardly thanking Cousin Emmy for her foresight. She rose and he stood with her. "I should like to make you known to Mrs Chidlow."

Julian resisted the inclination to shift uneasily under Mrs Chidlow's scrutiny. There was nothing he could put a finger on, but it seemed to him that she was anxious to convey that Miss Fancourt's place was with them now, not with the Lorings. Perhaps it was just that she was overly protective of her cousin and, indeed, who could blame her. She enquired about the proposed travel arrangements and nodded approvingly when he revealed that he planned to escort Miss Fancourt, driving his curricle within sight of her carriage.

"Mr Chidlow will bring her as far as London," she said at once. "It would be foolish for you to drive an additional seventy miles just to come and collect her, Sir Julian."

"In that case, ma'am, rather than having Miss Fancourt set out early in the morning, would you be amenable to accompanying them the previous day and staying overnight at Swanmere House? I had not ventured to make such a suggestion, but it would be much easier for her. The next day, it will only be the six and a half hours from town to Cambridge."

"I'm sure it can be arranged. Mr Chidlow should be home shortly. If you are happy to wait, we can put it to him when he arrives."

Of course he was willing to remain.

Mrs Chidlow nodded, satisfied, and turned to Miss Fancourt. "We must finish *Mansfield Park* before you leave, my dear. I am convinced Fanny will relent and marry Mr Crawford."

"I hope not," Miss Fancourt replied. "I think once he knew her to be his, he would quickly tire of her and move on to his next flirtation."

"But Edmund is such a dull stick," Mrs Chidlow objected, "and Fanny is too in awe of him to do anything but agree with him. That is a bad recipe for a marriage. How can she be a proper help-meet to him if she will not stand up to him?"

"What book is this?" Julian enquired.

"*Mansfield Park*," Miss Fancourt informed him. "It is by the author of *Pride and Prejudice*. I think your grandmother would enjoy it."

"Do you think this Fanny should marry the dull stick?"

"She clearly idolises him despite his interest in another lady. Besides, Fanny is very young, too young to be considering matrimony. However, given her circumstances—" she broke off and threw up her hands in despair. "It is too complicated to explain. You will have to read the book yourself, Sir Julian."

"I shall see if I can obtain a copy for our evenings' entertainment at Swanmere provided you promise not to reveal the twists and turns of the story."

"I would never be such a spoilsport," she assured him.

A bustle downstairs signalled the arrival of Mr Chidlow, who ushered another gentleman into the drawing-room. About Julian's age, perhaps a couple of years older, he was of medium height and wiry build, his tanned features marked by deep crow's feet at the corners of his piercing blue eyes. The cut of his coat was old-fashioned and he wore buckskin breeches, not the more modish pantaloons.

"My dear, may I present Captain Philbert of the *Nausicaa*. He served as midshipman with our James and has now purchased the Smale property so he, his mother and sister are to be our neighbours."

Mrs Chidlow's thin face lit up. "You are doubly welcome, Captain. When do you propose to remove here?"

"As soon as possible, ma'am; once I'm assured everything is shipshape."

"Is your family with you at present?"

"Not today, ma'am."

"Then you must stay and dine with us—and you too, Sir Julian. We dine at five so you will have ample time to return to London before dark."

Her tone brooked no resistance and Julian found himself murmuring his thanks and acceptance in chorus with the captain. Mr Chidlow, who had not yet sat down, tugged the bell-pull and his wife instructed the footman to tell Cook that there would be two more for dinner in a matter-of-fact manner that left no doubt of her command of her household.

The captain meanwhile had wandered away to inspect two portraits of naval officers. "There's poor James—a speaking likeness, and—surely that's Captain Fancourt? A brave officer, sadly missed." He looked at Mr Chidlow. "How came you by it, sir?"

"How indeed?" Mr Chidlow answered with a little smile for Miss Fancourt. "Cousin, allow me to present Captain Philbert. Captain, our cousin Miss Fancourt, daughter of the late Captain."

"Miss Fancourt! This is an unexpected pleasure."

"For me too, Captain. You evidently were acquainted with my father."

"Acquainted with him, Miss Fancourt? I served under him for three years."

"Oh! Could you perhaps tell me about him? I have very few memories of him. I have his journals but there is no-one to tell me how he appeared to others."

To Julian's disgust, the captain took this as an invitation to join Miss Fancourt on the settee, flipping his coattails as he sat in what Julian considered an overly familiar fashion.

"Why, I shall be delighted to. I am sure many of my yarns, as we sailors say, will interest our hosts, for their son, James, also served on the *Steadfast*."

The Chidlows hastened to agree and Julian had to console himself by watching Miss Fancourt's fluctuating expressions as she listened to a series of anecdotes that contrived always to place the narrator in the best possible light. Even when he had been 'mastheaded' by the severe lieutenant for some perceived fault, this had proved to be most advantageous, for his keen eye had spotted a sail, thus putting the *Steadfast* in the position of taking a valuable prize.

When Mrs Chidlow claimed Julian's arm to go down to dinner, her husband waived his right to that of Miss Fancourt, insisting that the Captain escort her, "for I have the pleasure of dining with her every evening and she shall sit between us so all's fair."

"You see your dinner, gentlemen," Mrs Chidlow said, once the soup, a creamy concoction fragrant with fresh herbs and young asparagus, had been removed and a plump turbot set before the master of the house. A crisply roasted leg of lamb, a sheet of writing paper wrapped around the shank bone, throned at the opposite end of the table while the centre held spatchcocked chickens as well as a refined array of vegetables, sauces, tarts and pies to tempt the diners. Everything was of the highest quality, Julian noted.

"Would you be so good as to carve the lamb, Sir Julian?" Mrs Chidlow requested after her husband had deftly filleted the fish.

"Gladly, ma'am."

A leg of lamb was not the easiest joint to carve and Julian prided himself on his skill in cutting even slices of just the right thickness while fairly distributing the fat and the lean.

"How well you do that," Mrs Chidlow said admiringly

as he quickly filled the plates that were passed to him.

"At what age does a boy start learning how to carve?" Miss Fancourt asked curiously.

"When he is old enough to be handed a sharp knife and tall enough to use it while seated," Julian replied. "I suppose I would have been about ten when my tutor first asked me to carve a small fowl. I went much too timidly to work, failing to secure it with the fork so that it bounced off the plate and skimmed across the table. Fortunately, he made an excellent catch and saved our dinner if not my pride."

Miss Fancourt laughed. "At least it happened in private and the table-cloth bore the brunt of it. Imagine if it had been your neighbour's gown. I remember my mother describing how something of the sort happened to her not long after she started to go into society. At that time, the gentlemen sat at one end of the table and the ladies at the other, not one beside the other as we do today, so it was generally the youngest, most insignificant persons who met in the middle. The poor young man was so mortified that she had to pretend that she didn't care a rap about her gown, but of course she did; in those days they were far more elaborate and made of much costlier materials than they are now."

This was the first time that Julian had heard her refer to her mother. He would have liked to learn more about her previous life but the captain seized the opportunity to describe the permutations of shipboard dining from the rigours of the midshipmen's berth to the delights of the captain's table. He spoke drolly and Julian found he could not grudge his table-companions this insight into the life so familiar to their deceased son and father. He would have her company for two months, he told himself—enough time to dismantle the barriers she had set up between herself and the world.

"May I have a brief word with you, sir?" Julian asked Mr Chidlow as they left the dining-room to join the ladies.

"Of course. Go on ahead, Captain. You know the way." He led Julian to the study where two days previously he had waited anxiously to see if Miss Fancourt would receive him. "What can I do for you, Sir Julian?"

Within five minutes it was all arranged. Miss Fancourt would be conveyed to town on Monday the twenty-fifth and they would set out for Swanmere the following morning. When she was ready to return home, the Chidlows would come to London to collect her.

"She is our daughter now," Mr Chidlow said simply. "My only regret is that she did not come to us when she left school, but at the time my elderly mother lived with us and my wife was concerned that in caring for her she would not be able to take a young lady about as much as she would have wished. It is a pity, for I am sure Miss Rosa would be married by now, with her own children, but it is not too late for that. My wife already talks of spending the winter in Bath, but perhaps Miss Rosa will find an agreeable suitor nearer home. I hope so. Now, shall we join the ladies?"

Miss Fancourt officiated at the tea-tray and Julian immediately went to take the cups and distribute them, experiencing a very private satisfaction when, after she had ascertained the captain's preferences, she prepared his own cup without any enquiry as to his taste, deftly using the tongs to retrieve the smallest piece of sugar as she had on so many evenings at Loring Place.

"Thank you. No one makes it quite as well as you do."

She acknowledged his murmured remark with a little flickering smile and he took a seat beside her.

"Does Chloe make the tea at the Place now?"

"Yes, but it is a very poor affair." He stopped, hearing what he had said and went on, "I don't mean that the tea is not good. There is no sense of occasion about it. Most ladies make a little ceremony of the tea-tray, but for Chloe it is no more than a tedious duty. As soon as she has drained her cup she asks to be excused. My father then gets grumpy and mutters that he does not know why he comes up and indeed my grandmother tells me that he often does not when it is just the three of them."

"He never came up every evening," she remarked. "In fact, he frequently did not dine at home but ate his mutton, as he put it, wherever he happened to be. It was different when you visited, of course."

"I hadn't realised, although when I look back to school holidays, for example, he was not always there. I never thought to question it."

"Nor I. I just assumed it was what gentlemen did. Even my father, when he was at home, did not dine with us every day."

"Will you show me his portrait? Was it at the Place all this time?"

"Yes. It is kit-kat size, so it fit into my trunk."

She led him to the alcove where James Chidlow smiled proudly in his midshipman's uniform beside Captain Fancourt who posed sternly, blue eyes fixed on a distant horizon. His dark blue coat was trimmed with gold lace and a gold epaulette decorated his left shoulder. A telescope lay along his right forearm and his left hand rested on the hilt of his sword.

"To think you might have lost this, and your other belongings too," he said softly. "Miss Fancourt, I cannot thank you enough for your generosity in agreeing to help Chloe. You would have been more than justified if you had refused to have anything more to do with us."

She made a dismissive gesture. "I hope I would not be so lacking in charity as to condemn a whole family for the faults of one member or to forget the many kindnesses I received, especially from your grandmother, or the joy I found in teaching Chloe." She studied the portrait. "This likeness was taken in '97—we saw him once more after that."

"He was killed at Copenhagen, you said."

"Yes."

"Did it cause a big change in your life? Forgive me, I do not mean to suggest you were unfeeling, but you were used to him being away."

"Not directly, no, but—my mother remarried within the year." She bit her lip. "Afterwards, things were—not the same. We had been so close, just the two of us for so long."

"I understand," he said gently.

She turned. "We should go back to the others."

"I had a brief word with Mr Chidlow before we came up," Julian said quickly. "He suggests bringing you to town on the Monday of the week after next. Is that agreeable to you?"

"Certainly."

"Splendid. I shall send for your trunks on the previous

Saturday," he told her and went to make his farewells.

# Chapter Thirteen

THE ADVENTURE HAD BEGUN. ROSA felt a little prickle of excitement. Until now, despite all the preparations, it had seemed unreal. But here they were at Swanmere House. Tomorrow the Chidlows would return to Maidstone and she would continue northwards with Sir Julian. Tomorrow evening, she would see Chloe again—and stay with the Ransfords, not as a dependent governess but as a lady of independent means.

The carriage door opened and Sir Julian himself stood ready to help them alight. Cousin Adam jumped down first. He would not trust anyone else with Emmy although she seemed to have borne the journey well. Then Sir Julian came forward to offer Rosa his hand, his fingers closing around hers in a warm clasp that was so much more personal than the passive support of a servant.

"Welcome to my home, Miss Fancourt."

"Thank you, Sir Julian. I am happy to be here."

"I hope you will be happy here, and at Swanmere as well," he said as he shepherded her through a vestibule into a high square hall lit by an oval roof lantern. A middle-aged man and woman stood to one side.

"May I present Morris, my butler, and Mrs Morris, who is housekeeper here? Mrs Morris will show you to your rooms so that you can refresh yourselves after your journey. I shall await you in the blue drawing-room."

The housekeeper, a plump woman neatly dressed in a dark gown with a lace cap, fichu and apron, dipped a brief curtsey before leading them into a cream stair-hall and up two flights of an elegant staircase. Rosa would have liked to linger and admire the exquisite plaster wall decorations that framed delightful landscapes but obediently followed until they emerged onto a landing from where they could look down into the hall below. Sir Julian had vanished, she noticed, as they crossed it to enter a wide corridor.

Mrs Morris stopped about three quarters of the way down and threw open a door. "Mr and Mrs Chidlow, you are in here, if you please. There is an adjacent dressing-room and a maid and manservant will bring water shortly and unpack for you. If you ring the bell when you are ready, someone will come to take you to the blue drawing-room. Miss Fancourt's room is directly opposite and you will find a water-closet at the end of the corridor. Let me show it to you."

Rosa had heard of such things but had never seen one. She looked curiously at the round white bowl decorated on the inside with blue flowers. She didn't know if she would use it; a close-stool in her room would be much more private.

"After you have used it, just pull here to flush everything away."

The housekeeper closed the door and escorted them

back to their bedchambers. She cast a stern eye around the Chidlows' room as if to check that everything was in order and then crossed the corridor to usher Rosa into her own apartment. "A maid will be here shortly with your own maid, Miss Fancourt, just to show her the way. Please do not hesitate to request anything you need. Again, ring when you are ready to come down."

"Thank you, Mrs Morris," Rosa said soberly, waiting until the housekeeper had departed before giving way to her astonishment at the style and comfort of the bright, airy bedchamber. It was furnished in cool blues and greens with discreet touches of gilt adding warmth without pomp, and perfumed by a bowl of roses. Celadon green jasperware decorated with dancing nymphs stood on the mantelpiece and was reflected in the gilt-framed overmantel mirror. Several interesting-looking volumes lay on the low, round table in front of an elegant daybed, inviting the visitor to rest and read.

She wandered over to the window and looked down into a symmetrically laid-out garden. Had her roses come from there? She had never thought she would be here in his house. She smiled ruefully, remembering how smitten she had been when she first met him, some weeks after her arrival at Loring Place. How could she not have been? He was the first young man she had been on any sort of familiar terms with. At first she had been too shy even to speak to him but when she saw him on his hands and knees with Chloe riding on his back crying, 'Gee up, horsey', she had had to smile, especially when the child dug her heels into her brother's ribs. He had winced then cocked his head to one side, grinning up at her from beneath tousled curls and she had laughed out loud. He had grinned just the same way when he removed his camel head-dress, she remembered.

'What's funny?' Chloe had demanded and he had answered, 'We are, miss. I think it is time you had a real pony, don't you?'

Over the years, Rosa's infatuation had faded and died but Miss Fancourt and Sir Julian had remained on terms of mutual respect. And now she was to spend the summer as his guest.

"To think I thought Mr Chidlow's house was big, miss," Polly said, awestruck, as she helped Rosa out of her carriage dress. "And we're to spend the summer in a castle! I must be sure to remember everything so I can tell my mam. What gown will you wear tonight, miss?"

"The blue," Rosa said as she went behind a screen decorated with figures in the Grecian style. Here again everything was of the finest. A fresh bar of translucent amber soap lay in a dish decorated with rose-buds and fine linen towels hung on a stand. But first—or perhaps she should use the water closet. Mrs Morris had made a point of showing it to them.

"I'll need a dressing gown, Polly, and please tap on the door of the room opposite and ask Mr and Mrs Chidlow if it is convenient for me to visit the water-closet now."

"Certainly, miss," Polly reported on her return, "and Mrs Chidlow said would you please look in afterwards."

"And Polly, just linger in the corridor while I am there in case anyone should come along."

"It's much the same as using a close-stool," Rosa reported to the Chidlows ten minutes later. "If you tug too gently on the handle nothing happens and then I must have pulled too hard and I jumped when the water rushed in but it didn't splash. I suppose it's more pleasant than having everything in your bedchamber although it is less private."

"A high water service costs considerably more," Mrs Chidlow remarked, "but, apart from the convenience, there will be quite a saving in servants' time if water does not have to be carried up and slops down again. What happens to the slops afterwards, I wonder?"

"I imagine they go into a cess-pit which is emptied as usual," her husband answered.

The blue drawing-room was a delightful room decorated in the Pompeian style with classically themed wall paintings and reliefs bordered by elaborate swags and smaller images.

"My grandmother had it done when my grandfather succeeded to the title," Sir Julian said when Rosa admired them. "This was her private sitting-room. Her apartments are in the same style. I loved to sit with her while she told me the stories depicted in the paintings."

"You drew on it for inspiration, did you not?" Rosa asked. "I noticed the classical elements in the staircase and in my room, although they are more restrained. What is Swanmere like?"

"Quite gothick," he replied with a teasing smile. "The oldest part of the castle dates back to about 1400."

"Oh!" She put her hand on her breast and rounded her eyes and mouth in mock horror. "Will my sleep be disturbed by a headless monk or a weeping lady?"

"No, no, our spectres won't disturb your rest," he replied solemnly. "The knight clad in inky armour sees himself as a protector of all ladies. It is true that Lady Idonia, who killed herself in a fit of jealousy, removes the gory dagger from her breast each midnight but she confines herself to the north tower and we never put ladies there, I promise you."

"That is most thoughtful of you, sir. Is the lady your ancestress?"

"Only a collateral relative. That in fact was the problem. She took umbrage at my ancestor preferring her sister Ismenia and killed herself on their wedding night."

"Tsk, tsk, tsk. Most inconsiderate," Mrs Chidlow shook her head disapprovingly. "She was the elder, I take it, and could not bear to see her sister wed before her. There was no need to take such drastic measures, however," she added severely.

"I shall be sure to point that out to her if I am so fortunate as to encounter her," Rosa promised. "She clearly has not changed if she still seeks attention every night."

"No, Miss Fancourt!" Sir Julian extended an imploring hand. "I beg you not to approach her. The sight of another rival may rouse her to worse action. Do not forget that she is armed. What if she turns her dagger on you?"

"I should fend her off with my fan while summoning the inky knight, of course," she replied blandly.

"How could I have doubted it?" he murmured as the Chidlows applauded.

They breakfasted at eight, but by the time farewells were said and the Chidlows had departed, it was half-past nine when Julian led the way out of London in his curricle. Miss Fancourt and her maid followed in his travelling chariot while his valet and a footman brought up the rear in a third carriage. He didn't know when he would be in town again. As soon as they left, the knocker would be removed from the door, Morris would supervise the shutting up of the house and the remaining servants put on board wages.

He held his team to a steady pace, his tiger under strict instructions to alert him if the chariot fell back out of sight. He felt—liberated was the only word for it. The last time he had felt like this was when leaving school for the last time. Yesterday evening had been charming in its domesticity. He couldn't remember when ladies had last stayed at the house or even called there. His cousin Meg had come once or twice with her husband Hal before the Fourteenth had been sent to the Peninsula in '08. She had offered to act as his hostess anytime he wished to entertain, but Hal had laughed and said she would be sadly out of place as bachelor's fare was all Julian had to offer.

Although supposed to be the weaker sex, women reached maturity much sooner than men, he reflected. He and Meg were the same age but, at eighteen, she had been a wife and mother while he was still at Cambridge. Now she was a widow and he was for the first time contemplating matrimony.

After twenty miles, he turned into the yard of *The Bull* at Ware. From here they would use post horses. He was a regular patron of the inn, on occasion stabling his cattle here if he knew he would be returning quickly, but this time his grooms would bring the horses on to Swanmere at a slower pace.

The landlady bustled out to receive them and take Miss Fancourt to a room where she could 'make herself comfortable'. She was smiling when she joined him for a quick nuncheon.

"What has amused you?"

"The landlady insisted on showing me the famous bed. It's truly gigantic—fit for Polyphemus."

"I see you were properly impressed."

"I don't think my entire bedchamber at Loring Place was any larger. The work is very fine, if a little grotesque to our taste, but I suppose people must take the room or they would not keep it."

"Did you not ask her?"

"I was afraid to," she said frankly. "She told me four couples could sleep comfortably in it and many more had squeezed in. Only consider what sort of groups might wish to hire it."

"Young bucks and their doxies on a spree, very likely," he said absently.

She didn't reply but stared rigidly across the room although when he followed her gaze he could see nothing that might have caused her to stiffen so. A white-haired man, a boy at his side, stood in the doorway looking around for a seat while three clergymen moved ponderously towards a round table, causing a waiter with a laden tray to swerve dangerously. Surely she had not been offended by his quip? He hadn't thought her so prudish.

"Miss Fancourt?"

She looked back. "I beg your pardon. I was wool-gathering."

"Will you take some of this veal and ham pie?"

"Just a small slice, please." She helped herself to a salad of cucumbers and lettuce and passed him the bowl.

"Now that we're past the dirt and congestion of London,

would you like to travel the next stage in the curricle?"

"That would be splendid, Sir Julian. It is too beautiful a day to be shut in. When do you hope to arrive?"

"Ransford's seat is near Cambridge so we have about another three hours ahead of us. Mrs Overton and her son and daughter will join us there. She is also bringing a schoolfriend of her son's as it had been arranged that he would come to them during the holidays."

"So you will have two girls of sixteen and two boys some years younger. It is fortunate that the friend is coming too. It will make it easier to keep them amused, especially on a wet day."

"How the deuce are we to do that—on any day?" he demanded. "I hadn't given it much thought, but Meg writes that she won't bring a governess or tutor—she says she has no further need for either. You are not responsible for the children," he added before she could say anything, "which is not to say that I should not be grateful for your advice."

"Young ladies on the brink of coming out will have different interests to schoolboys," she pointed out. "That is why it is good there are two of each. But boys in particular must be kept occupied."

"They could ride or go fishing, I suppose. At eleven or twelve, they are old enough to learn to shoot or take out a boat on the mere."

"But not unsupervised," she said firmly. "Is there a steady groom you could trust or some young man in the neighbourhood who would be prepared to act as tutor while they are there? It would also be useful if an old schoolroom or similar room could be made available as a retreat for them."

"We'll consult my steward and housekeeper as soon as

we arrive."

"Would it not be better to send a note from here? That way they will have time to consider everything before the guests arrive."

"You see how unused I am to these matters," he said ruefully. "I'll write now while you sample these strawberry tarts. One of the grooms can ride ahead." He called a waiter over and requested writing materials. "What of the girls?" he asked as they waited.

"They will spend much of their time with the ladies, but I imagine they would be flattered if you gave them their own sitting-room as well. Then they must keep up their music and I'm sure Chloe will wish to paint the castle and its surroundings."

He dashed off his note, folded and sealed it. She had finished eating and looked around the room, frowning.

"Is something the matter?"

She started. "No. I thought I saw someone I once knew but I was mistaken. Are you ready?"

"I must find my groom and then we can be off."

"Would your maid like to sit on the box with Jebb?" Julian asked as they walked back to the carriages.

Polly looked hopefully at her mistress.

"Is that what you would like, Polly?"

"Yes, miss, if you please."

He handed Polly over to the coachman of the servants' carriage before leading Miss Fancourt to the curricle. She stepped up lightly, her hand barely resting in his, and settled herself on the bench seat. He sprang up beside her and spread a rug over her lap before threading the ribbons through his fingers and picking up his whip.

He smiled down at his passenger. "Are you comfortable?"

"Yes, thank you."

"Let 'em go," he ordered Josiah who stood at the horses' heads. The tiger at once released his grip on the reins and darted past to clamber onto his perch at the back.

Miss Fancourt remained silent as he guided the fresh team out of the crowded inn yard onto the turnpike where he skilfully wove his way through a tangle of traffic before overtaking a heavily laden long waggon laboriously drawn by five pairs of plodding horses. He raised his whip in salute to the mounted waggoner who rode alongside the leading pair and eased his grip on the reins.

Once they were bowling along at a steady pace, she stirred and asked, "Is Chloe happy to go to Swanmere?"

"She is over the moon, or so she writes, both at the thought of seeing you again and the prospect of leaving the Place for a couple of months."

"I am sure she looks forward to spending the summer with you. She has always looked up to you and was at her happiest when you visited the Place."

Julian was taken aback by this quiet comment. "I could have done more for her, I think. I was already at Cambridge when she was born and hardly saw her those first few years, but when I did come home she used run to me and lift up her arms. 'Up, Dulian!' For a long time she couldn't manage to say 'J' properly."

"I remember. We used to practise silly phrases like, 'jaunty Julian jibs at jam' and 'jolly Jill enjoys jelly'. It became easier once she learned her letters and could see the difference between J and D."

"You are a born educator, Miss Fancourt," he said admiringly. "A stricter governess might have sought to enforce compliance rather than look for playful ways to help her pupil."

She acknowledged this remark with a pleased smile before asking, "Who taught you to read and write, Sir Julian?"

"My mother. She taught me until I was six and then I had a tutor." He flicked his whip to warn a stray dog away from his wheels. "Then school and Cambridge. And you?"

"My mother was my first teacher also. Later I attended a day-school near our home in Chichester but when my mother remarried I was sent to Mrs Ellicott's Academy in Bath. After her death I remained there as a pupil-teacher until I was experienced enough to seek a position as governess."

"And then you came to us?"

"Precisely. There you have my story."

He glanced down at the gloved hands clenched on the rug. Not all of it, he thought. There was more to learn, but not today. "We must think of entertainments to please the ladies. How do you like to amuse yourself, Miss Fancourt?"

"I?" She was silent for some minutes and then said, "You will think it very foolish of me, Sir Julian, but I don't really know. I have never had much time to myself."

"But if you had?" he coaxed her. "What would you enjoy?"

"This." She gestured around her. "To drive or ride out on a fine summer's day and see somewhere new. Perhaps stop at a picturesque spot for a pick-nick and be able to set up my easel without fear of being disturbed. Have more time for music and reading."

"What about acting some scenes from a play?"

"I'm sure the young people would like that."

"I remember you mentioned that it would be good for Chloe to attend some little entertainments and dances."

"Yes. Are you planning to invite your neighbours?"

"We'll see. I'm not really sure how many young people there are," he confessed. "I know you ride well but do you drive?"

"No."

"Would you like to learn?"

"I don't know," she confessed.

"We'll find out, but not on the turnpike. It is too busy for a first lesson," he added as he pulled out to pass a lumbering coach, his tiger blowing furiously on the yard of tin.

"My goodness," she gasped.

"Too fast?"

"No." She sounded surprised. "It's exhilarating. You feel the speed much more in an open carriage.

He laughed and dropped his hands. "It's not a bad team. Let's spring 'em."

Rosa sat back, cradled by the hood and sides of the curricle, the rug tucked cosily around her, although she hardly needed it. Sir Julian's comforting bulk radiated warmth and she welcomed the cool breeze that streamed past her face as they sped along. How strange to be so close to him, so at ease with him. The swaying curricle rocked her into a sort of half-doze. Deep down, the prickle of excitement grew stronger. His questions had provoked her, and something new had unfolded in her as she answered them. The real Rosa had hidden herself for so long. I must find her again, she thought drowsily as her eyes closed.

❧

The rhythm of the horses' hooves changed as they slowed to a canter and then a walk.

"Awake, Miss Fancourt?"

She could hear the smile in his voice. Her face grew warm. How could she have fallen asleep beside him? It smacked too much of intimacy to be proper.

"I beg your pardon."

"There's no need. I was charmed—and flattered."

Her face burned. Was he amusing himself at her expense? She dared to look at him and found he was smiling gently at her.

"We stop here for the next change. Would you prefer to wait for the other carriages to catch up with us? You can probably rest more comfortably inside."

Unsure of what was happening, she was tempted to say yes, but there was something she needed to ask him. "No, I am quite happy to go on."

"I was wondering, Sir Julian," Rosa glanced over her shoulder. She didn't think the tiger would be able to hear them through the hood, but still—

"Yes?" he asked encouragingly.

She lowered her voice. "I hope you don't consider it too forward of me to ask, but what have you said to your cousin about Chloe's mother? Does she know what happened?"

"Ah." He slowed the horses and matched his tone to hers. "I'm glad you thought to enquire. No, she doesn't. The only people who know the full story are we two, my father and my grandmother. Chloe and my grandfather know that Lady Loring disgraced herself and tried to blame you, but no more, and all Mrs Overton knows is that Lady Loring is spending the summer with her mother in Harrogate."

"How have you explained my presence to Mrs Overton?"

"That Chloe begged you to come and stay with her for the summer and you kindly agreed. My grandmother will explain all this to Chloe."

It would have to serve, Rosa thought, though only heaven knew what the servants would make of it.

# Chapter Fourteen

LADY RANSFORD BRUSHED ASIDE SIR Julian's apologies for treating her home as a convenient staging post for the Swanmere house-party.

"Nonsense, Julian. I know it was my Aunt Loring's notion—and a very good one it was too. We are delighted to see her and Chloe again. What a pretty girl she is, even if a little peakish at present. I'm sure the change of air will do her good. She has gone for a walk with Cynthia but you will see her at dinner. My aunt is resting at present and Mrs Overton has not yet arrived."

She offered Rosa her hand. "Miss Fancourt, I am happy to see you again. Now you will wish to refresh yourselves after your journey. We dine at six."

She handed them over to a maid and footman who led Rosa and Sir Julian upstairs, separating them on the first floor landing.

"You are down here, miss," the maid explained. "Miss Loring is beside you and Lady Loring beside her."

"Well, Polly, did you enjoy your drive?" Rosa asked some ten minutes later.

Her maid nodded vigorously. "Mr Jebb is so kind. And, excuse me, miss, when I told him my name, he said it was a pretty name but a lady's maid ought to be called by her surname. The other servants will think less of me if I'm called Polly, he said. So I'm to be Lambton and the lower servants will call me Miss Lambton." She closed her eyes as if to savour her delight at this development.

"I'm sorry." Rosa was vexed at herself for having overlooked this important change in Polly's circumstances. "I should have remembered. I shall call you Lambton in future."

"But he said he hoped as I would allow him to call me Polly in private."

"What did you say to that?"

"I said I'd see and I wasn't a girl as would permit any liberties. And he laughed and said he could see I was a good girl and his name was Samuel but his mother called him Sam."

"I see." Rosa was alarmed by these artless revelations. Polly was a pretty girl and unused to a large establishment. "There will be many more men-servants here and at Swanmere Castle than at Mrs Chidlow's, Lambton. Some may try to make free with you. Don't hesitate to come to me if you encounter any difficulties."

"Yes, miss. No, miss." Lambton giggled. "Mr Jebb said the same, only he warned me against the quality and said I was to come to him if any of them tried to take advantage. He would mention it to the master, he said."

"You are well protected, then." Rosa looked at the clock. It was half-past four. She was determined not to appear as the dowdy governess tonight. "I'll wear the plum-pink gown with the long sleeves, Lambton. Brush out my hair now so that it can relax before you put it up again for the evening."

"Miss Fancourt? May I come in?" a light voice asked from the door.

"Chloe!" Rosa hurried to meet the girl who flung herself into her arms.

"Oh, Miss Fancourt, I am so happy to see you again."

Rosa hugged her gently. "And I you, my dear." She nodded to the maid. "That will be all, Lambton, thank you."

There were tears in Chloe's eyes. "I was afraid you'd hate me. I'm so sorry, Miss Fancourt. It was all my fault. None of it would have happened if I hadn't rushed into the cottage that day, or answered Mamma back later."

"That is nonsense, Chloe. How can it be your fault if others were both indiscreet and determined to hide their behaviour? They must take responsibility for their actions."

"But Mamma has been sent away because of me," Chloe whispered.

"Not because of you but because of her indiscretions," Rosa said gently. "Chloe, when we are children, we assume that our parents will always do what is right but as we grow older we must learn that they too are fallible. None of us is perfect. We may all yield to temptation but we must then be prepared to bear the consequences. Anything else would be unfair."

"Papa should forgive Mamma and let her come home again."

"Let us hope he will, but that is between them." Rosa soaked a handkerchief in cold water and wrung it out. "Sit down and press this to your eyes for a minute or two before we go down."

"Yes, Miss Fancourt." Chloe leaned her head back against the chair, smiling beneath the little blindfold. "It feels so right to have you telling me what to do."

Rosa patted her hand. "I know, but another part of growing up is learning to think for oneself and make one's own decisions."

"While considering the possible consequences of one's actions?"

"Precisely."

Chloe was silent for another minute and then uncovered her eyes. She ducked to peer into the dressing-table mirror, smoothed her eyebrows and said, "Shall we go down?"

"Chloe!" Sir Julian stooped to kiss his sister.

She put a hand on his shoulder and smiled up at him. "Julian, you are so good to arrange all this for me," she whispered and gestured to Rosa. "See, I have found her already."

His eyes met Rosa's over his sister's head and they smiled in mutual satisfaction.

"Julian!" A whirl of subtle shades of silver and lavender interposed itself between them and resolved itself into a sprite-like figure with the palest blonde hair Rosa had ever seen. Cut in short curls and threaded through with narrow ribbons, it crowned a triangular face set with almond-shaped, pale blue eyes.

She looks like Titania, Rosa thought as the lady stood

on her tip-toes to press her lips to Julian's cheek.

"How good of you to think of us! The children are thrilled to visit a real castle, aren't you, my darlings?" She turned to address the stocky, dark-haired girl and the fair, slim boy who stood behind her.

"Yes, Mamma," they chorused dutifully.

"Ann and Henry, make your bows to your cousin Julian."

She hardly waited for them to comply before continuing with a glittering smile, "Is this your Chloe? I see the resemblance."

"Yes. Chloe, you have heard me speak of my cousin, Mrs Overton."

Chloe curtseyed. "Good evening, Mrs Overton."

A trill of laughter protested against this salutation. "Oh, not Mrs Overton—Cousin Meg, please. Are we not to spend the summer together? I am sure you and Ann will be great friends."

Chloe murmured something indistinct, then said more clearly, "May I present my dear friend, Miss Fancourt, who comes to Swanmere with us?"

Mrs Overton nodded curtly in response to Rosa's bow, her vivacious smile dimming as she looked her up and down. "Pleased, I'm sure, Miss Fancourt. Julian, you must make me known to the others." She slipped her arm through his and walked him away.

Rosa watched the two girls eye each other cautiously. "Did you travel far today, Miss Overton?" she asked pleasantly.

"About fifty-five miles. We spent the night near Buckingham."

"Where do you live?" Chloe asked.

"Near Stratford-upon-Avon."

"The birthplace of Shakespeare!" Chloe cried. "How I should love to see it—and his grave too."

"It is cursed," Henry said with relish. "It's written on it: *'cursed be he that moves my bones'.*"

"That doesn't mean that the grave is cursed," his sister pointed out, "only whoever would desecrate it."

The boy ignored her comment. "It's jolly kind of your brother to have us, Miss Loring," he said. "Is it an old castle? Will there be weapons and suits of armour?"

"Do say Chloe, please," Chloe implored him. "When you say 'Miss Loring' I feel as if I'm my own maiden aunt, or would be if I had one."

"Only if you'll say 'Hal'. Henry is a fusty old man who spills his snuff."

"You shouldn't sneer at Great-Uncle Henry—he has the shaking palsy and can't help it."

Hal looked mutinous at his sister's rebuke but then his face cleared. "Here are the Kennards at last. I thought they would never arrive. Excuse me."

Kennard? It couldn't be! Rosa's stomach churned. You must find out, she told herself fiercely. Don't be such a coward!

She swivelled to observe Hal's progress across the room. Her breath seized in her throat. The chestnut-haired boy at the inn in Ware—the one whose smile had reminded her of Mamma's—stood at the door and, yes, the man with him was indeed her former stepfather. So that was her brother! Her heart raced so violently that she put her hand to her breast in a vain attempt to still it. She must avoid them at all costs. Her vision dimmed at the thought of meeting them here, before everyone. She felt first hot, then cold, and the room spun around her. Was there some other door through which she could escape, to a terrace, perhaps? She turned blindly, trying to make her way through the crowd. Suddenly her hand was taken and tucked into the crook of a gentleman's arm. The superfine sleeve was smooth to her touch but beneath it she felt an underlying strength. A familiar, aromatic scent reached her nostrils, steadying her.

"Miss Fancourt." Sir Julian's deep voice sounded above her head. "Are you feeling quite the thing? Miss Fancourt?"

She drew a wavering breath and then another. "I suddenly felt a little faint, but it was just a momentary weakness. I am better already."

"My grandmother is seated over there, near the window. Come, let me take you to her. You will find the air fresher there."

Lady Loring held out both her hands and pulled Rosa down to brush cheeks with her. "How delightful to see you again, Miss Fancourt. Come and sit here beside me." She lowered her voice. "We were so relieved to hear you were safe and well. But no more of that here. We shall have all summer to talk. I think this is going to be very good for Chloe," she added, looking over to where the girl chatted to Ann Overton and Lady Ransford's granddaughter Cynthia Glazebrook.

"Mrs Overton's daughter must take after her husband's family. She hasn't made much of an effort with her, has she? I wonder is it carelessness or spite. Some exercise and a proper pair of stays would work wonders for the child, but then a young widow might prefer not to have a daughter almost old enough to make her come-out. I wonder how long it will take her to remind us she was a mere child when she married."

Rosa managed a trembling smile at this devastating indictment but the dowager swept on.

"Now, tell me how you go on. I'm sorry I didn't meet your Mr Chidlow when he called to Suffolk, but Julian tells me you are in good hands."

"Yes. He and his wife have been so kind. We pretend there is a connection—it was Cousin Emmy's idea so that we do not have to explain my presence, and they treat me like their daughter."

"Who are your people, Miss Fancourt?"

"As you know, my father was a naval officer and my mother died two years after he lost his life at Copenhagen. His family was from Dorset, I believe, although I have never met them. My mother's father was a Canon Bletsoe in Chichester and her mother was a Miss Rowan. I think they married quite late in life. Mamma was their only child and they both died before I was born."

"I am ashamed that I never asked you before," Lady Loring said quietly. "I can see that Loring Place provided a safe haven for you, but perhaps it is no harm that you have been forced to spread your wings."

Rosa smiled faintly. "Perhaps."

"Aunt, Miss Fancourt." Major Raven, resplendent in a new dress uniform, bowed before them.

"So you're home again, are you, Frederick?" Lady Loring said. "I hope it will be a little longer this time."

He shrugged. "I hope so too, ma'am, but we must go where we are sent. I am charmed to see you again so soon, and Miss Fancourt too. Have you decided to remain with my cousins a while longer, Miss Fancourt?"

"No, Major. I now live with my own cousins, near Maidstone."

"We are delighted that Miss Fancourt accompanies us to Swanmere for a little holiday," Lady Loring intervened.

"A well-earned one, I am sure, after so many years," the Major replied, just as dinner was announced. His father came up to escort Lady Loring and the Major lost no time in offering Rosa his arm.

The schoolboys had vanished, presumably to eat elsewhere, and, to Rosa's great relief, she was seated far enough from Mr Kennard that no communication between them was possible. The soup revived her and a glass of wine completed the cure.

"Were you home in time to experience the visit of the Allied Sovereigns, Major?" Rosa enquired.

"Fortunately not," he replied. "Although I believe poor Blücher was almost treed in Hyde Park. That would have been a sight to behold."

"What I would like to have seen is the Proclamation of the Peace on the twentieth of June. I understand there was a magnificent procession, suitable to such a momentous occasion. It is hard to believe that after twenty years the war with France is truly over."

"It is certainly strange to be at home after so many years on the march. But a soldier looks on peace with half a smile only. It is his nature *to seek the bubble reputation, even in the cannon's mouth.* It is then that he is most alive. Without war, without the spice that action brings, life is duller and advancement slower."

Mrs Overton, who was sitting opposite on Sir Julian's right, shuddered artistically and said across the table, "You military men all live for danger. My poor Harry was the same."

Rosa was suddenly back in her old home in Chichester. Bags packed and ready to leave at first light, her father sat at dinner with her mother and her fourteen-year-old self. He poured himself another glass of wine, filled her mother's glass and then went to the sideboard for a third glass which he set in front of Rosa.

"She's too young for wine, Charles," her mother objected.

"Nonsense, Mattie," he said. He half-filled Rosa's glass and then raised his own. "Drink with me, my dear ones. Here's to a bloody war or a sickly season!"

"Charles!"

"What?" His eyes sparkled with mischief. "That is our regular Thursday toast on board ship. How else are we to be promoted? With a little bit of luck I'll be post-captain when we meet again and then, my darling, it is only a matter of time until you are an admiral's lady." He took her mother's hand and kissed it, retaining it while he lifted his glass again. "Come, drink with me!"

They had obeyed, but even at the time Rosa had felt he was tempting fate. He had indeed 'made post' but had not lived long enough to enjoy the automatic progression that went with it.

The scene changed to some days later. Unwell, she had come home early from school to find Mr Kennard had called.

"So he's gone again, is he?" he was saying as she came into the parlour. "Martha." He saw Rosa and broke off.

It had never occurred to her before to wonder how often he came when she was not there. Or why he addressed her mother by her first name.

"Don't you agree, Miss Fancourt?"

She blinked and looked to her left. "I beg your pardon, Major, but what did you say?"

Before he could reply, Mrs Overton interrupted, "Were you in the Peninsula, Major Raven?"

"I was, ma'am."

"Perhaps you were acquainted with my late husband, Major Overton of the 14th?"

"I was indeed, ma'am. An excellent officer. My condolences on your loss."

She touched a lace handkerchief to the corner of an eye. "It was almost too much to bear, but one must go on for the sake of one's children."

"I'm sure they are a great comfort to you," Sir Julian remarked.

"Yes, and so kind of you, dear Julian, to take us in," the grieving widow sighed, laying a small hand on his arm and gazing soulfully at him.

Rosa noticed him stiffen and his voice was markedly cooler when he replied, "My sister is happy you, Ann and Henry could come to us for some weeks." He didn't wait for a response but spoke in turn across the table. "I obtained a copy of *Mansfield Park*, Miss Fancourt, and look forward to our readings."

She smiled brightly at him. "That is wonderful, Sir Julian! My cousin and I did not finish it so I am glad I will not have to languish until the end of summer ignorant of the outcome. I made her promise she would not reveal the denouement in her letters."

"I cannot imagine her doing something so unkind," he answered and turned to listen to the lady who sat at his left hand.

What had put a damper on Miss Fancourt's spirits? When Julian saw her entering the drawing-room with Chloe, he had thought her delectable in a dark pink silk gown trimmed with narrow gold ribbon and he had experienced an answering joy when he heard her laughing with his sister. She had smiled so tenderly at Chloe's pleasure at their reunion and he had wanted to include her in their embrace; know her and his sister safe in his arms. Perhaps it was just as well Meg had interrupted them.

A scant fifteen minutes later, he had caught sight of her moving haltingly through the room, looking shocked to the core. He had gone to her at once, of course, and she had clung to his arm as a drowning man might clutch a rope. He brought her to his grandmother, and once she sat safely beside her, moved away but not so far that he could not keep an eye on her. The dazed look soon faded and a trace of colour stole into her white face.

Meg had descended on him, declaring he was to take her in to dinner. He hadn't thought her so forward but had had no choice but to comply. Then she had made that remark about his taking them in, as though it were a permanent arrangement. He had instinctively wished to make clear she and the children were there for Chloe and for a limited period only. Miss Fancourt had responded ably to his comment about *Mansfield Park*, but afterwards she became abstracted, paying no attention to the conversation in a way that was most unlike her.

Lady Ransford rose. Julian stood with the other gentlemen while the ladies withdrew in a perfumed flurry of silk and muslin. He hoped Ransford wouldn't linger too long over the port, but that odd fellow Kennard bored them all recounting how a broken trace had delayed them on the last stage, a story that encouraged others to relate their tales of similar misfortunes.

At last Ransford pushed back his chair. "Shall we join the ladies?"

"I understand my son is to spend some weeks with you at Swanmere, Sir Julian," Mr Kennard said as the gentlemen left the dining-room. "It was most kind of you to include him in your invitation to young Overton."

Julian, who had not invited Master Kennard, but merely been informed that he would be coming with his cousin's family, muttered a polite rejoinder.

Chloe, Ann and Cynthia were gathered around the pianoforte, comparing music and trying snatches of melody. Once the gentlemen had arrived, Cynthia took her seat at the harp and they embarked on a selection of Mr Moore's Irish melodies, at times singing together, at times each one taking a solo verse. Their voices blended charmingly and when they finished with a poignant yet defiant rendition of *The Minstrel Boy* there was heartfelt applause and congratulations.

"Tell me, Miss Overton," Lady Ransford said to Ann who had directed the little group from the pianoforte, "from where had you the accompaniment that linked the songs together? It was so cleverly done with all the little variations and ornaments."

Ann blushed. "It just comes to me," she said. "It feels right so I play it."

"You mean you improvised it as you were playing?" Miss Fancourt said admiringly. "You are a true musician, Miss Overton."

"Oh Ann spends far too much time at the piano," Meg

said carelessly. "I am forever telling her it spoils her posture and will make her hunch-backed in time."

Chloe and Cynthia exchanged glances over Ann's bowed head and drew nearer to her while Julian said, "Ann, I hope you and Chloe will explore the music room at Swanmere. Apart from an interesting collection of instruments, there are several old music books as well as piles of loose sheets that I would be delighted to have deciphered."

Ann beamed as if he had promised her a pair of diamond bracelets. "May I really, Sir Julian? I'll be very careful, I promise."

"You shall be doing me a service, I assure you."

"Now, Julian, you must not encourage her to ruin her eyes poring over old manuscripts," Meg said with a light laugh.

"Will you not play a sonata for us, Miss Overton?" Lady Ransford asked kindly. "Some Mozart, perhaps?"

Ann readily turned back to the keyboard. She held her hands poised for a moment and then began an infectiously light and happy melody. From his position to one side, Julian could see that she played without any overly dramatic effect, her nimble fingers scampering over the ivory and ebony keys as merrily as dancing mice. The features that had tensed at her mother's cattish remarks eased again and the little smile that played on her lips was mirrored on the faces of her listeners.

When the tea-tray was brought in, Julian collected two cups and strolled towards Miss Fancourt. Mr Kennard was there before him, bending low to murmur something in her ear. She frowned up at him, shook her head slightly and turned away. He was not put off by this rejection, but bent nearer. Angered that he dared pester her, Julian came closer.

"We must speak before I leave," Kennard said.

"I have nothing to say to you, sir," she hissed.

"For the boy's sake," Kennard whispered desperately.

"You mean my—?" She looked up and saw Julian.

"I brought you some tea, Miss Fancourt."

When she accepted the cup with a smile and a murmur of thanks, Kennard glared and moved away.

"Was that fellow annoying you?" Julian demanded.

"A little. I knew him slightly a long time ago and have no wish to renew the acquaintance. Fortunately he leaves in the morning."

"I'll make sure it is before we do," he said promptly. "Why don't you breakfast in your room? I'll send word via your maid as to when we are to depart."

# Chapter Fifteen

LADY LORING PUT DOWN HER cup. "I'll bid you good night. I fear my old bones still feel the jolting of the carriage."

Rosa rose instantly to her feet. "I'll go up with you, ma'am."

"Thank you, Miss Fancourt. I should be grateful for your arm and I daresay you are weary too from travelling. No, you stay here, child," Lady Loring added to Chloe who had also stood.

They progressed slowly up the stairs and along the corridor. "Thank you, Miss Fancourt," Lady Loring said again when they reached her door. She stopped and looked directly at Rosa. "You must not feel you should attend me at Swanmere. You are our guest, just as Mrs Overton is."

"I know, ma'am," Rosa replied, "but we know each other these ten years and I trust a guest may offer some little assistance out of respect and affection."

Lady Loring patted her cheek. "A guest may indeed, my dear. You are most kind."

Rosa closed the door of her own room and leaned her

back against it. She could hardly stand but resolutely put all thought of the Kennards out of her mind. Polly—no, Lambton—she must remember that—would be up at any moment to help her undress. She moved away from the door just in time. She stood and sat passively while the maid's deft fingers unbuttoned and unlaced her garments and unpinned and unravelled her hair, brushing it out before plaiting it loosely for the night.

Her pale reflection stared back at her from the mirror. She wanted to finger her mouth and jaw—did she have Mamma's smile too?

"There, miss." Lambton tied the end of the braid neatly and went to turn down the covers.

Bone-weary, Rosa climbed into the big bed.

"Will I draw the bed-curtains, miss?"

"No, thank you, Lambton."

"Will I quench the candles, miss?"

"Please. Good night, Lambton. Sir Julian will ensure you are told at what time we are to leave tomorrow morning. Bring my breakfast an hour beforehand."

Rosa stared at the faint rectangle of grey that marked the window, her mind in such turmoil that she had little hope of sleep. What was she to do? That boy—he was her only living relative and she didn't even know his name! She would have passed him unsuspecting at Ware if Kennard had not been with him. Her own brother! Did he know she existed? Most likely not. And if not, should she tell him? What could she say? Would he believe her? Would he care?

She turned restlessly. The impertinence of Kennard approaching her like that. She was surprised he had recognised her. She was generally thought to favour Papa, but perhaps he had seen something of Mamma in her and enquired who she was. Sir Julian had been so kind. Again. She had enjoyed the drive in his curricle. She wasn't going to let Kennard spoil her pleasure in her stay at Swanmere. He had robbed her of so much in life. She wouldn't let him take more.

It was wonderful to be with Chloe and the dowager again. She hadn't realised the extent to which they had stolen into her heart. And they had made no secret of their delight in their reunion. If only Sir Julian had not invited the Overtons, there would have been no Kennards to cut up her peace. Mrs Overton appeared to be on very close terms with Sir Julian. She was a widow and her year of mourning was up. Rosa's eyebrows twitched together. *'Perhaps something more may come of it'*, he had said about the Overton visit. She had assumed he spoke in reference to Chloe, but of course, if he were to marry, his wife could sponsor Chloe's come-out. Nothing would be more natural, especially when she had a daughter of the same age. Mrs Overton did not seem overly maternal. Rosa was sorry for the girl—Ann. The boy didn't seem so defensive. How had he come to invite young Kennard?

At last she fell into a dream-tossed sleep from which she woke unrefreshed and haunted by a strange sense of loss.

She looked like a ghost. Anxious to avoid any questions, Rosa gently patted and plucked at her white cheeks until a little colour stole into them. Fortunately the rose-coloured silk that lined the brim of her bonnet cast a flattering reflection on her face and the matching ribbons helped too. Steeling herself, she pulled on her gloves and picked up her shawl and reticule while Lambton put the last items into the portmanteaux. She must go down to the others.

Her brother stood in the hall with the Overtons. Head held high, Rosa went to make his acquaintance.

It was Hal who said, "Miss Fancourt, may I present my friend Robert Kennard who comes with us to Swanmere?"

Rosa looked down into smiling brown eyes—her mother's eyes.

The boy bowed a little awkwardly. "Good morning, Miss Fancourt."

"Good morning, Robert. Are you at school with Hal?"

"Yes, since last year. We're chums."

"Chums?"

"Chamber-fellows," Hal explained.

"A good friend is important at school," Rosa remarked, remembering how lonely she had been when she first went to Mrs Ellicott's. "Don't you agree, Miss Overton?"

"I was educated at home," the girl replied.

"Would you have liked to go to school?"

"Too much education is bad for girls," Mrs Overton interrupted tartly. "No man wants a wife who always has her head in a book." Her peevish expression vanished when Sir Julian came into the hall. She took a couple of light steps towards him, her skirts swaying. "Well, Julian? How do you plan to dispose of us?" she asked gaily.

"Dispose of you?"

"Who travels in which carriage, for I have none, you must know." She sighed. "My parents-in-law lent us their travelling coach as far as here, but it must go back today."

Sir Julian raised an eyebrow. "It is a pity you did not think to mention this yesterday. How many servants have you brought?"

"Just Jenkins, my maid."

"I see." He stood for a moment deep in thought, then went to his grandmother who sat to one side with Chloe. "Which carriage are you using, ma'am?"

"The berline."

"You could take me up in your curricle, Julian," Chloe suggested eagerly.

He smiled down at her. "I should be delighted to have your company, pet, then if our grandmother has no objection to joining Miss Fancourt in my travelling chariot—"

"Not in the slightest," Lady Loring assured him, with a warm smile for Rosa.

"We can make the berline available to Mrs Overton and her party," Sir Julian concluded. "Grandmother, if your maid travels in the smaller carriage with my servants, Mrs Overton's and Miss Fancourt's maids may occupy the berline rumble seat."

"Oh, but why not let Chloe and my three young people travel together in the berline?" Mrs Overton suggested. "I have no objection to a curricle."

Chloe looked appealingly at Sir Julian.

She was caught in a nice dilemma, Rosa realised. To protest would mean she set her own wishes over those of an older, married woman who was also her brother's guest and at the same time imply that she did not wish for the company of Ann and the two boys. But Sir Julian was not to be moved.

"Chloe comes with me," he said firmly. "I'll just have a word with the coachmen."

Mrs Overton did not seem happy at the thought of another

day spent in her children's company. Rosa was conscious of dagger-looks cast in her direction as she and Lady Loring crossed to the travelling chariot that stood directly behind the curricle. Sir Julian waited at the door to hand them in.

"Chloe!" Rosa held out her shawl to the girl who wore only a blue cotton spencer over her light muslin gown. "Take this; you may be glad of it."

"But you'll need it," Chloe protested.

Rosa shook her head. "I had not realised how warm it is but there is always a little wind in an open carriage."

"It's very pretty," the girl said, admiring the border of pink and blue flowers, although she seemed puzzled by the way it was stitched onto the large square, with the wrong side of the pattern showing along two sides.

"You turn it over." Rosa showed her how to fold the shawl so that it formed two deep overlapping triangles, then draped it over Chloe's shoulders.

"How ingenious. Thank you, Miss Fancourt."

Sir Julian pressed Rosa's hand as she stepped up into the chariot. "Have you everything you need?"

"Everything," Lady Loring replied firmly, nodding towards the basket at her feet. "Drive safely, Julian."

He touched his hand to his hat. "Yes, ma'am."

Rosa could hear him whistling as he strode to the curricle.

"She was always so thoughtful," Chloe said to her brother as they moved off at the head of the procession of carriages. "Such small things that I took for granted until they were no longer there." She fingered the shawl. "She tells me I must learn to think for myself; it is part of growing up."

"I think you are beginning to," he answered. "You have

a new awareness of what is happening around you."

"Yes. Julian, what made you invite Mrs Overton?"

"I remembered her daughter was about your age and thought you might like the company."

Chloe wrinkled her nose. "I don't know. Mrs Overton isn't very kind, I think; look at the way she constantly disparages Ann."

"It is not pleasant, I agree. Will you try and be friends with her?"

"With Ann? Yes, if her mother doesn't make it impossible."

Julian frowned. What had made him think of Meg? He had written to her when he read of Harry Overton's death but she had only recently acknowledged his condolences. There had been an air of melancholy in her letter when she recalled happier days spent at Swanmere when they were both young and free, and she had also hinted that her husband's family was not well disposed towards her and her children.

And I rose like a trout to her fly, he thought disgustedly. I'll be on my guard from now on.

In the berline, Meg Overton frowned at her daughter who hummed to herself as she worked out the fingering of an intricate passage. "Ann, do be quiet and for heaven's sake stop fidgeting."

Ann subsided dutifully while the two boys who sat opposite the ladies exchanged wary glances.

Meg sighed. Another tedious day lay ahead. It was unpardonable of Chloe not to give up her seat in the curricle. Lady Loring should have intervened if Julian would not. And who was this Miss Fancourt, who was accorded precedence over Julian's cousin, travelling ahead of her in the chariot while Meg was relegated to this antiquated carriage? Meg's eyes narrowed. Lady Loring must be eighty if she was a day. What could have induced her to leave Loring Place? Did she hope to provide her grandson with a bride? Was Miss Fancourt an heiress and she, Meg, simply invited to lend an additional air of propriety to the proceedings?

We'll see about that, she resolved. She must not let Julian slip through her fingers again. That was the problem with men of one's own age. When they were both eighteen he had seemed only a boy, especially when compared with the romantically haggard officer newly returned from the West Indies, one of the few survivors of a devastated regiment. She had been flattered when Harry Overton set his sights on her and had seen herself destined to heal his ravaged soul. Perhaps she had. Perhaps she had succeeded too well, for as his sleep improved and his strength returned, he spent less time with her. 'Duty calls', he used say, stooping to kiss her carelessly, although she had never understood what it was that he did all day, and most of the night too.

It hadn't been so bad while they still had the house in London but Harry had given that up when the regiment left for the Peninsula in '08. His grandmother had died and he arranged with his father that his wife and children would move into the newly-vacant dower house. *'I won't have you in town on your own,'* he had declared. It was unfortunate that the regiment had been posted just after she had been compelled to seek his assistance to pay her gambling debts. Up until then she had managed to stay more or less above water but a run of bad luck had brought her to Point Nonplus.

She had never seen him so angry. '*Our name is not Devonshire, madam,*' he had stormed at her. '*I make you a generous allowance and I expect you to live within it.*' But what was five thousand pounds, after all? Many a man—and woman—wagered that on the turn of a card.

And then his will! She was restricted to the meagre jointure set out in the marriage settlement while the bulk of his fortune was left in trust for his son and daughter, with their guardianship entrusted to his brother rather than his wife. While she might draw on the trust for their expenses, the trustees, including her horrid brother-in-law, were not prepared to accept a Dutch reckoning but insisted on a strict accounting for every shilling so she could not even include items for herself in, say, a milliner's bill for Ann. Well, if she was to be restricted, the children would be too. She could not prevent Hal going to school, but she had dismissed her daughter's governess and music-master, saying the girl was too old for them.

She must re-marry and marry well. And who better than Lord Swanmere's heir? Was Miss Fancourt a rival? She would set Jenkins to discover what she could about her.

In the last carriage, Lady Loring's maid sat comfortably opposite Sir Julian's valet and senior footman.

"How are all at the Place, Miss Dover?" the valet enquired.

"Well enough, Mr Fox, thank you. Mrs Walton and Mr Meadows send their compliments. The house is very quiet, of course."

"And Sir Edward?"

"He has been quite peevish, or so Mr Meadows says, especially when he is in his cups."

"Any word from Harrogate?" the footman asked.

Dover shook her head. "Not that I have heard."

They looked at each other in silence.

"Miss Fancourt is in exceedingly good looks," the valet remarked.

Dover nodded. "I always felt she would do better in brighter colours. My lady and Miss Chloe are so happy to see her again."

"Her maid, Polly Lambton, seems a good girl, if inexperienced," Fox commented. "She is very respectful and eager to learn. Jebb gave her a hint about her name."

"Jebb?" Dover repeated. "It isn't like him to take an interest in the maids."

The valet laughed. "She's refreshing, is what he said, and not used to the quality. He doesn't want to see her taken advantage of. A shilling says he'll have her on the box beside him again when we change horses."

"Done," Dover agreed. "If you lose, we'll suggest she travels with us. I didn't take to Mrs Overton's maid. She's one of the prying sort."

Swanmere Castle was not as monumental or forbidding as Rosa had imagined. As she stepped down into the sunny enclosed courtyard, she was assailed by the heady scent of hundreds of roses blooming in a riot of shades along walls that ran right and left to the half-timbered gatehouse that spanned the entrance. This must be what attar of roses smelled like—rich, sweet, fragrant but with an underlying spiciness so that it did not cloy. Opposite stood a glorious hotch-potch of buildings that somehow formed a harmonious, living whole. A wide, single-storey house formed the centre, its steeply pitched roof penetrated by the pointed arches of four gables set with tall leaded windows. Square towers throned at either end; the lower was crowned by a half-timbered upper storey while the crenelated top of the taller one ranged high above all other roofs. A charming oriel window set high on the lower tower suggested that a lady of bygone days might have waited here for her returning lord. How wonderful to sit there, dreaming, while the scent of roses wafted up to you.

Below, a wing extended at right angles to the main line of buildings, providing shelter to the returning prodigal and arriving guests. A soft whisper seemed to float on the air: *You are home.*

Her lips curved as Sir Julian came out of the gabled house, his sister by his side. "Welcome to Swanmere, Grandmother, Miss Fancourt."

"Thank you, sir. What an enchanting place! It is like something out of a fairy-tale. Are there still swans here?"

"Yes. They nest on the banks of the mere on the other side of the castle. You can see it from the great hall."

He ushered them through a heavy oak door into a vast space spanned by immense curving beams. A soft light shimmered through the old glass of the mullioned windows, deepening the muted colours of timeworn wall hangings and bringing out the jewel shades in a large Axminster carpet. Dark, carved oak chests were ranged along the side walls between the windows, two high-backed settles faced each other across the huge fireplace and a large refectory table took up the centre of the floor.

Rosa squinted up into the shadowed space where

serried ranks of shorter rafters led the eye to the apex of the high roof. "It's as if you were looking into an up-turned boat."

He laughed. "Noah's ark, perhaps. I imagine the boys will be disappointed that it is more hall than armoury."

"You mean there are no relics of the inky knight? I might have known it was all a hum."

He pointed to a suit of armour beside a door in the end wall. "On the contrary, there Sir Gilbert stands, guarding access to the north tower."

Rosa had to smile at his thrilling tone. "What? Not on the battlements?"

He spread his hands. "He used to patrol there until Cromwell's forces slighted the castle. While they didn't do much damage to the buildings, the battlements were razed apart from those on the tower itself and the perimeter wall lowered considerably. Sir Gilbert immediately changed his habits. He watches here but just before midnight ascends to the top of the tower. Do not be alarmed if one night you hear him clank away."

She burst out laughing at the idea of an armoured knight laboriously mounting stone steps. "Your trick, I think, sir."

He grinned and bowed in acknowledgement.

Chloe turned back from the window to stare at them. "What are you talking about?"

"Nonsense," Sir Julian replied at the same time as Rosa said, "A silly joke."

"To work." He looked enquiringly at his steward who bowed slightly.

"Mr Thomas Musgrave is waiting to see you, sir. He is home for the long vacation."

"And might not be averse to bear-leading the two boys?"

Sir Julian turned to the housekeeper. "Where would we put him up, if he is willing to stay here rather than at the vicarage?"

"We thought in the north tower, sir, with the young gentlemen."

Sir Julian nodded approval. "I defy any boy not to be happy there. And the ladies?"

"We've made up rooms in the new wing, sir. Her ladyship will have the rose suite on the ground floor. Upstairs, the tulip suite has two bedrooms separated by a sitting-room and we thought the jonquil and bluebell bedchambers for the remaining two ladies."

Sir Julian looked at his sister. "Would you like to share the suite with Ann? It would give you a private sitting-room."

Chloe shook her head. "I don't think Mrs Overton would consider it private from her, do you?"

"I suppose not."

"Put Mrs Overton and Ann in there—or—Miss Fancourt, would you object to sharing with me?"

"I should be very happy to," Rosa replied. So she was not the only one who had taken a dislike to Mrs Overton. She glanced at Chloe's brother who showed no sign of discomfiture.

"Very well," he said. "We'll do it that way, Godin. In addition, there are three lady's maids, a coachman and a groom who also acts as footman to Lady Loring. Where is Musgrave?"

"In the muniments room, sir."

He strode down the room to a door left of the hearth while the housekeeper bustled out through the north door, presumably to instruct the maids about the disposition of rooms. She returned some minutes later followed by a footman with a tray of glasses and an earthenware pitcher beaded with moisture.

Rosa gratefully accepted the offer of cool lemonade. She sipped, relishing the tart, tangy flavour as she joined Chloe at an open window. The ground fell away on this side of the castle and spread into a grassy expanse which led to a lake surrounded by reeds. They looked out in comfortable silence, admiring the way the breeze rippled the surface of the water and listening to the trills and pipings of hidden birds. A swan glided majestically into view.

"It is so tranquil and remote," Chloe remarked. "I feel like a demoiselle of old in her bower."

"Waiting for a troubadour to appear beneath her window?" Rosa asked with a smile. "She will drop a white rose at his feet. Tomorrow she must wed another and the poor troubadour will die of love for her."

"*Men have died from time to time and worms have eaten them, but not for love*'," Lady Loring quoted dryly behind them.

"Grandmamma, you are completely lacking in sensibility!"

Chloe jumped up when Lord Swanmere entered, followed by Sir Julian and a lanky, fair-haired young man with an engaging smile.

"Lady Loring, my humblest apologies for my failure to greet you on arrival," Lord Swanmere said. "Welcome, welcome."

"I am happy to be here again, Swanmere," she answered, taking his outstretched hands and accepting his kiss on her cheek.

He smiled warmly at her. "It has been far too long, has

it not? This is a splendid notion of Julian's." He released her hands and turned to his other guests. "Miss Chloe, I am delighted to see you looking so well—and you, Miss Fancourt. Welcome to Swanmere, ma'am."

Rosa curtsied. "Thank you, my lord. It seems to be a very special place."

"We think so, indeed."

There was just time to present Mr Musgrave to the ladies before the berline pulled up outside. It seemed natural for the whole group to go out to receive the newcomers. Hal Overton jumped down first and turned to assist the ladies to alight. Robert Kennard came last, looking as awestruck by the castle as Rosa had felt. The little party bore all the signs of having spent too long together in a confined space, but their peevish expressions soon eased under Swanmere's soothing spell. The boys disappeared to explore the north tower with Mr Musgrave and the housekeeper escorted the ladies to the new wing which, Rosa was amused to discover, was one hundred and fifty years old.

"Built after the restoration of good King Charles, ma'am," Mrs Godin explained.

Chloe stretched out both arms and twirled around the sitting-room, her curls bobbing. "Isn't it exciting, Miss Fancourt? I have always hoped Julian would invite me here but, I suppose, before I was too young. He wouldn't have known how to entertain me. Mr Musgrave seems very amiable, does he not? It's not fair, though. The boys are much younger than Ann and I, yet they will be allowed to spend their days doing all sorts of interesting things while we shall be confined to the house."

"I am sure we ladies will find plenty to amuse us," Rosa replied. "There must be lovely walks here and my fingers itch to sketch the Castle."

Chloe looked a little more cheerful. "Perhaps Julian will take us driving, but first I am going to insist he shows us around. These are handsome apartments but I had hoped for something more picturesque, gothick even. Are you ready, Miss Fancourt? Shall we explore a little before we meet the others for dinner?"

Rosa smiled at her former pupil. "If you continue to address me as Miss Fancourt, I shall feel obliged to call you Miss Loring. I should be very happy if you would say Rosa."

Chloe's face lit up. "May I really? Thank you, Miss—" the girl caught herself, "Rosa. It will be a little strange in the beginning, but no doubt I'll quickly become accustomed."

# Chapter Sixteen

"ALL SETTLED, ARE THEY?" LORD Swanmere asked when Julian came into the library.

"For now."

Julian poured two glasses of Madeira and handed one to his grandfather. "It's good to be home. I seem to be on the road since the first Spring Meeting." He sank into his favourite chair and stretched his legs out in front of him with a sigh of relief.

"An interesting little house-party you've acquired."

Julian grimaced. "The Overtons may have been a mistake."

"In what way?"

"Meg is as frivolous as ever, but what was attractive in the girl is almost desperate in the woman."

"Acting the fizgig, is she?"

"It's more than that. I had not thought I would have to be on my guard against her. At the Ransfords I found myself obliged to make clear that their visit was temporary, and the invitation issued on Chloe's behalf."

"Hmph. She wants to marry again, I suppose. You would be an excellent catch for her."

Julian snorted. "She may troll the bait as much as she likes, she won't hook me on her line."

Swanmere laughed. "Many a man has said the same only to find himself at the altar. But, all jesting aside, Julian, it's high time you were married."

"I know, sir, but it won't be to Meg." Julian raised his glass to the light, admiring the golden fire conjured by the late afternoon sun in the rich depths of the wine. He drank deeply, then caught his grandfather's eye. "It won't be to Meg," he repeated, "and I will thank you not to encourage any foolish notions she may have."

"Trust me." Swanmere got to his feet and refilled their glasses. "Before we join our guests in the drawing-room, let us drink to your unknown bride."

When the two men entered the drawing-room, they found Miss Fancourt and Chloe talking to Mr Musgrave and the two boys. Robert and Hal were full of the delights of sleeping in the tower. Chloe was envious that they had already climbed to the top and she immediately demanded that her brother give the ladies a tour of the castle the next day, "including the battlements, Julian."

He glanced sideways at Miss Fancourt. "Will you dare the tower battlements, Miss Fancourt?"

"It depends on the stairs, Sir Julian."

"And on your shoes," Mr Musgrave said. "I should think ladies' slippers would be uncomfortable on the stone."

"Rosa and I are prodigious walkers and the possessors of stout half-boots," Chloe informed him.

"Like my sister," Musgrave said approvingly.

"Your sister? Does she live here too?"

"Yes."

"Do you think she would show us her favourite walks?"

"I am sure she would be delighted to, Miss Loring."

"I'll take you and Ann to call on Mrs and Miss Musgrave," Julian intervened. If he weren't careful, Chloe would take the bit between her teeth and arrange everything to her satisfaction and probably to his exclusion.

"My mother would be delighted," Mr Musgrave said, "just, if I might suggest, not tomorrow. The Dorcas Society meets at the vicarage on Thursdays."

"The sewing circle," Miss Fancourt explained helpfully to Julian, her eyes dancing at this private joke. "Good evening, Miss Overton. Have you recovered from the journey?"

"Yes, thank you."

"Julian, you were going to show Ann the music room," Chloe reminded him. "Is it in this wing?"

"Yes, just here." He led them through a connecting door into the next room. "There is no pianoforte, I'm afraid, but we have a spinet, harpsichord and harp. And here," he opened a tall cabinet, "are miscellaneous instruments."

Ann was instantly at his side. "Flutes, a violin and a lute. May I?" At Julian's 'of course', she carefully lifted down the lute.

"It needs new strings, but I shall have it re-strung if you would like to play it," he offered.

"I would love to try."

"All the music is in the drawers below, but I have no idea what is there."

"Perhaps I could go through it and catalogue it for you?"

"Are you sure you wouldn't find it too tedious a task?"

Her eyes gleamed. "Oh, no, I would love to. You never know what you might find."

"Then I should be greatly obliged to you. I hereby make you free of the music room, Ann, but you must promise me not to spend all your time in here or feel obliged to complete the task if it becomes too onerous."

"She'll enjoy that much more than a private sitting-room," Chloe muttered to her brother as they returned to the drawing-room.

He flicked her chin. "I rely on you to ensure she leaves the castle at least once a day."

"Oh, am I the last? I do apologise if I have kept you waiting, Cousin Swanmere, but the journey was so fatiguing and Jenkins positively insisted I lie down for half an hour. She is so devoted to me, you know. Nothing would do her but to make me one of her tisanes, which did the trick, I am happy to say, and here I am." Meg beamed on the assembled company as if they could not but rejoice in her presence and drifted over to slip her hand into Julian's arm.

"I am delighted to see you recovered, Cousin," he said politely, "but you must not tire yourself again by standing. Come and sit with my grandmother." He led her to Lady Loring and deposited her on that lady's sofa just as the steward appeared.

"Dinner is served, my lord."

Lord Swanmere immediately approached Lady Loring. "Will you do me the honour of taking the head of the table while you are my guest, ma'am? Julian will take you in."

As soon as Julian had assisted his grandmother to rise,

Swanmere offered his arm to her neighbour. Meg could not refuse her host although it would place the length and width of the table between her and his heir, as Julian recognised appreciatively. When the couple led the way out of the drawing-room, the others, recognising the impossibility of such a disparate group pairing off in an orderly fashion, followed; first Miss Fancourt with Adrian Haughton, Julian's secretary, then Chloe and Ann, with Musgrave and his charges coming last.

"If there is soup, you must serve it for me, Julian," his grandmother said quietly as they crossed the vestibule that linked the new wing with the south tower and the great hall. "My hand is no longer so steady."

He patted the hand in question. "Of course, Grandmamma. There is no need for you to do anything more than give the signal for the ladies to withdraw."

Lord Swanmere beckoned Chloe to the chair on his left. Lady Loring called Hal to her side and instructed Ann to sit between her brother and Musgrave on Meg's right. Robert was sent to sit between Miss Fancourt and Haughton who sat next to Chloe. To Julian's great satisfaction, this left Miss Fancourt the seat on his right.

Meg, in the place of honour on her host's right, had looked surprised when Robert and Hal appeared. "Surely you don't mean the boys to dine with us, Cousin?"

"If they are not able to behave as gentlemen, it is time they learned," Swanmere told her. "I dined with my parents when I came home from school and Julian did the same."

"It was a welcome change from school fare, as I recall," Julian remarked, with a friendly smile for his young cousin and his friend.

"It was the same for me," Musgrave said, "I don't know what it is about school food—I think they must study to make it unpalatable."

Julian removed the lid of the tureen in front of Lady Loring. "Will you take soup, Grandmother?"

Perhaps as a result of the little exchange, the boys were on their best behaviour, but as the meal progressed they became less nervous. Miss Fancourt made a point of seeing to Robert's comfort, Julian noticed, while across the table Ann and Musgrave saw that Hal's schoolboy appetite was satisfied.

When Robert was supplied with a slice of apple tart and a few macaroons, Miss Fancourt turned to Julian.

"I have been poor company, I fear, but it was a little daunting for the boys at first."

He nodded. "I don't know which was worse—Mrs Overton's objection or my grandfather's expectation that they would behave as gentlemen. The question now is, do they withdraw with the ladies or remain with the gentlemen?"

"What did you do when you were their age?"

"I withdrew, but was then at liberty to do what I pleased. My mother used say, '*We will say goodnight to you, Julian*.'"

"Of course. That was what her mother said to Chloe when she first dined with the family as well."

"What did you do then?"

"I stayed with Chloe until she went to bed and then I generally sat with your grandmother."

"You must have had no free time."

"Sitting with Lady Loring was not an arduous task," she said fondly. "Looking back, I suspect she requested my company as much for my sake as for her own. I should have been very lonely without her—and I learnt a lot from her."

"How old were you when you came to us?"

"Eighteen."

"Only two years older than Chloe and Ann are now."

He looked down the table at his sister and tried to imagine her in such circumstances. Meg had married at eighteen, he remembered.

"I said to Miss Dover that if you didn't mind, I could help with Miss Loring as well, miss," Lambton said as she brushed Rosa's hair. "It makes more sense seeing as the rose suite is downstairs, which is better for her ladyship but more difficult for Miss Dover if she's to see to Miss Loring as well. She was wondering how she'd manage, especially as the stairs is at the other end of the wing. She's not the youngest either."

"What did she say?" Rosa asked, remembering that Chloe had not yet been assigned a lady's maid of her own but had been assisted by Hughes who presumably had accompanied Lady Loring to Harrogate.

"She said she'd be grateful if I could help Miss Loring dress and undress, seeing as I'd be up here with you anyway. She would see to her clothes and to tidying her things once she had done Lady Loring's. And she said it was kind of me to offer and if I liked she'd show me how to go on, as this is my first position and I mightn't be used to staying in such a house, which I'm not. But I'm not being kind. I'd rather be busy and that's the truth."

Lambton paused to draw breath and Rosa said hastily, "I have no objection, Lambton, but let me see what Miss Loring says."

Chloe was very taken by the suggestion. "As long

as you are agreeable, Rosa. It takes forever to dress Grandmamma, I know. If—when Mamma comes home, I'll talk to her about having my own maid."

*I'd rather be busy.* Rosa smiled wryly when Lambton had left her. So would she. But what was she to do? Sir Julian had made it clear she was his guest, not Chloe's governess, and Lady Loring had emphasised she was not to wait on her. Chloe and Ann would very likely find their own amusements, perhaps together with Miss Musgrave, and she would be *de trop*. She had no intention of spending more time in Mrs Overton's company than politeness demanded.

Each evening she would set herself a new task for the day ahead, she resolved, so that she would not flounder if asked at breakfast what her plans were. Of course she would participate in any communal activities, but she wanted to be able to say firmly, "I thought to do such-and-such" and not appear to depend on being included by the others. She would keep a journal and sketchbook of her visit. She must write to Cousin Emmy, of course, and she should also thank Lady Ransford for her hospitality.

Presumably the music room would not be occupied all day so she could practise her playing and singing, and she had needlework and books with her too.

"What is that on the horizon?" Rosa asked Sir Julian who stood beside her at the top of the north tower. The wind was noticeably stronger up here and she had to hold her bonnet to prevent it flying away.

"The spires of Peterborough Cathedral."

"My goodness! How far away are they?"

"About ten miles as the crow flies. It holds the grave of Katharine of Aragon, Henry the Eighth's first wife."

"So that is where she rests, poor woman."

"Would you like to drive over and see it one day?"

On his other side, Mrs Overton clapped her hands. "Do let's, Julian. If we go on a fine day, we can take the curricle."

He ignored this interjection, his eyebrow cocked almost challengingly at Rosa as if to emphasise, *I was talking to you*.

She raised her chin and smiled. "That would be delightful, Sir Julian. Thank you."

"We'll arrange it for next week, then."

She heard Mrs Overton inhale sharply but before she could say anything more, Chloe had called her brother over to the other side of the tower.

"You seem very—familiar with my cousins, Miss Fancourt," Mrs Overton remarked. She didn't turn to face Rosa, but continued to stare out over the mere. "Have you known them long?"

"For over ten years, now," Rosa replied pleasantly.

"Ah yes. I've known Julian all my life. We were boy and girl together." She sighed sentimentally. "I believe he was inconsolable when I married and indeed he has remained single all this time. But perhaps now—" She sighed again. "He is an excellent host, is he not? Sometimes I feel his guests take advantage of his good nature."

Rosa laughed. "He is most good-natured, I agree, but I doubt if he would let anyone take advantage of him for long. I think we're going down again," she added, crossing to the turret door which Sir Julian held open for Chloe and Ann.

"Take your time and descend in single file, staying at the wall," he instructed them.

"I'll go last with you, Julian," Mrs Overton declared. "You must go before me and take my hand. I feel quite dizzy when I think of the drop. Pray go ahead of me, Miss Fancourt."

As Rosa ducked under the low arch of the doorway, she heard Mrs Overton whisper, "She's very tall, isn't she? Quite mannish, really. I suppose that's why she never married."

Much as Rosa would have liked to hear Sir Julian's response, pride propelled her forward, so that all she heard was the irritating little titter that followed this pronouncement floating down the steps after her.

Once they were safely on the ground, Sir Julian excused himself with the plea that his land steward was waiting for him.

Mrs Overton pouted. "Surely you are not going to leave us alone on our first day here, Julian?"

"I have been away so long I'm afraid I must—for a few hours at least. Please make yourselves at home and ask Godin for anything you want."

"I'm surprised you didn't have your steward here earlier," Chloe remarked. "Papa would have. May I borrow a newspaper to read to Grandmamma?"

"Of course. If you come with me, I'll give it to you."

Mrs Overton turned to her daughter. "What do you propose to do with yourself, miss?"

"I think I'll start sorting out the music, Mamma."

Sir Julian overheard and looked back. "Shall I have them put a table in the music room for you, Ann?"

"If you please, Cousin."

"She'll need pens and pencils and paper as well, Julian," Chloe reminded him.

He nodded. "I'll ask Haughton to bring a selection of stationery."

Chloe tucked her hand into his arm and he bent his fair head towards hers as they walked away.

"First you'll take a turn about the courtyard with me, Ann," Mrs Overton ordered. "You should not be cooped up indoors all the time. We might also visit the lady's garden that Julian pointed out."

She pointedly did not extend an invitation to Rosa to join them but Rosa was relieved rather than offended by this omission. She would prefer to attempt a water-colour of the mere, but there did not appear to be a suitable vantage point. The edges looked quite marshy and even if there was more solid ground, the tall reeds would block the view. Perhaps I could do it from the great hall—the window embrasures are deep enough to take a table and two chairs, she thought. If I have one chair removed, there should be ample space to work.

Thirty minutes later Rosa contentedly smoothed a sheet of paper and attached it to her drawing-board. She looked out of the open window. Far above, a fleet of cloud-ships scudded across the high, pale sky while below reeds and rushes bent with the quickening wind that sent little wavelets lapping at the shore. To the left, three old pollard willows raised their grotesque heads and further away a jagged stump stood proud above the water. On it, an ungainly black bird perched, its large wings spread out like sails.

Taking a sketchbook and pencil, she quickly drew an outline of the scene, scribbling notes to remind herself of the distinctive hues. It took her some time to capture the large bird. She had never seen one like it. It looked quite menacing, she thought. Strange how it stood so still. She gently touched her sheet. A faint wash of palest blue to begin. She dribbled some water onto the little cake of paint, mixing the solution on the porcelain palette until she had just the right shade. A quick glance at her sketch and another out the window and she slipped into another world.

"Excuse me, Miss Fancourt."

"Yes, Mrs Godin?"

"I beg your pardon for disturbing you. I've sent in ale and sandwiches as usual for the gentlemen and we're setting out a nuncheon in the morning room for the ladies; nothing too heavy, just a tasty dish or two and some bread and cake with little tarts and preserves. Do you wish to join them, miss, or would you prefer a tray here?"

"A tray here would be perfect, Mrs Godin. Thank you."

Julian quietly entered the great hall. Miss Fancourt— Rosa, as Chloe was now permitted to call her—sat at right angles to a window, bathed in the light reflected from the small diamond-shaped panes of its open casements. She was oblivious to his presence—wholly engrossed in her work as she glanced out and then down at her paper, her ivory nape bared temptingly by her bent head. She was wrapped in a large apron and had unbuttoned and turned back the cuffs at her slim wrists. He could close his fingers around one, he was sure.

A tray on the big table suggested that Mrs Godin had supplied her material wants. He hoped the other ladies had been thought of as well. He softly pulled out a chair and sat down to wait. After some ten minutes, she laid down her brush, put her hands in the small of her back and, sighing, arched her spine, drawing his eyes to her rounded bosom. When she shook her shoulders to loosen them, it was time to make his presence known.

"Are you finished? May I see?"

She jumped at the sound of his voice and turned her head. A few tendrils had come loose from beneath her lace cap and danced on a forehead that, he was amused to note, was streaked with blue and green, as were her hands. Her eyes shone with an inner happiness.

"Forgive me for alarming you, but I was afraid to break your concentration. One drop in the wrong place can ruin a painting."

"Especially a water-colour," she agreed. "I've done all I can, but it is never enough."

He came to look over her shoulder. There was a lack of exactness about the soft colours and outlines that pleased him. "You've captured the essence of the place. It is always in flux. It is almost impossible to determine the precise transition from land to water as it changes daily."

"Can one get down to the shore? I would love to paint it from that aspect."

"In places. I'll set some of the men to work with scythes to clear a path suitable for ladies. And that reminds me. When Chloe asked for the newspaper, I realised we had put nothing of the sort into the drawing-room. It is a room we don't generally use. What else should be there to entertain the ladies?"

"And the gentlemen," she pointed out. "You are not going to desert us in the evenings, I trust."

"No, but I was thinking more of a wet day, for example. Will you come to the library and help me make a selection of books and so forth?" He hesitated and added, somewhat awkwardly, "It is my grandfather's retreat and I don't want to make it available to all the guests, but I know he would always be glad to see you there, as would I."

She flushed a little under his intent gaze, but simply said, "I shall be glad to help you, Sir Julian, but first I must clear up here."

"You may also wish to attend to—" He pointed to his own forehead and she turned a delicious pink.

"My teachers were forever scolding me about that. It happens when I become absorbed in a painting."

"I think neatness would suffocate your talent, Miss Fancourt, which would be a pity. May I have this?"

Her gaze flew to his. "If you wish. Be careful to keep it flat and pinned to the board until it is completely dry."

"I shall."

Once she had cleaned and tidied her brushes and paint-box, she stood and reached behind her to untie her apron. She lifted it over her head, unveiling her graceful form, and shook out her skirts. This enticing glimpse of future familiarity had him long for the right to escort her to her room and himself remove the coloured traces from her face and hands, perhaps see if an errant drop had trickled further.

"Sir Julian?"

He reluctantly relinquished this tantalising vision. "I beg your pardon?"

"I said I'll let Mrs Godin know I'm finished here and shall be with you in fifteen minutes."

"I'll wait for you in the vestibule of the south tower and take you to the library."

# Chapter Seventeen

SIR JULIAN USHERED ROSA INTO the library where Lord Swanmere sat in a deep armchair. He looked up with a sweet smile.

"Good day, Miss Fancourt. I have been admiring your work—it is very fine indeed. Julian tells me you are to advise us how to entertain the ladies. He must be a dull dog, I said to him, if he has to seek instruction on how to do that."

"One cannot be all things to all women," Sir Julian murmured.

Lord Swanmere gave a crack of laughter. "Aye, the readiness—or the willingness is all. Come and sit down, my dear. Will you take a glass of Madeira with us, or should I ring for tea?"

"Madeira, if you please," she answered, smiling her thanks to Sir Julian when he handed her a glass.

The room was as much sitting-room as library, with comfortable high-backed chairs angled towards the huge fireplace and card and chess tables ready for use. Other tables were stacked high with newspapers and journals while books were piled higgledy-piggledy in the shelves that reached from the tiled floor to the heavy beams of the ceiling, but the surface of the big desk was clear. If this was Swanmere's lair, did Sir Julian have one too?

She looked up to find him studying her.

"A penny for your thoughts?"

She laughed. "I doubt if they are worth it. This seems to be one of the older parts of the castle."

"Yes, it was built to provide private apartments for the lord and his family. He could retire here but still be aware of what was happening in the great hall. Come and see." He beckoned her over and slid back a panel beside the elaborately carved mantel to display the squint set in the wall.

Rosa peered in. It gave a surprisingly good view of the room beyond. "Perhaps the lady used it to keep an eye on her husband," she suggested, laughing.

"Her rooms were upstairs, but that may not have stopped her. In fact, a clever man might have asked his wife to observe certain gatherings. But what are we to do with our ladies?"

"I don't think the evenings pose much of a problem. Just put out card tables and fish for speculation, perhaps a chess or backgammon set, and pencils and paper for conundrums and other word games. Have you thought of asking each person to suggest an evening's entertainment in turn? I am sure that Ann and Chloe will be happy to play and sing for us, but they should not be called upon to do so all the time."

"That is a truly splendid notion," he exclaimed. "Why should we rack our brains each night?"

"I hope you will sing for us one evening," Swanmere put in. "You have a delightful voice—a true mezzo-soprano which to my ear is much more pleasant than a shrill soprano."

"Thank you, my lord. When it is your turn to choose, you may request some music."

"Should we not include the two boys and Thomas?" Sir Julian asked. "Half-past eight is very early to be sent to bed."

"It would probably be for the best as I doubt very much they'll retire at that hour," Rosa commented. "More likely they'll be up to all sorts of mischief. Include them by all means, but perhaps not if you have invited other guests."

"Yes, we must think about that too."

"Are neighbouring ladies likely to call on your grandmother, do you think?" she asked and then had to smile at the look on his face. "You did want Chloe to move a little in society," she reminded him. "There is no point bringing her here if you are merely going to replicate her life at the Place."

He threw up his hands in defeat. "Frankly, I am out of my depth, Miss Fancourt. If I invite a group of fellows for some fowling, for example, I don't have to worry about these things. We have no problem amusing ourselves."

His grandfather snorted. "With shooting, fishing, gaming and carousing—all ladylike occupations."

"Surely you would make up a party if there were something of interest happening in the neighbourhood—a cock fight or races or—what is it you gentlemen call it—a mill?" Rosa asked. "And you might invite neighbouring gentlemen to an evening of cards."

"True. What is the feminine equivalent of such pastimes?"

"Dancing, visiting, sight-seeing, tea-drinking, a pick-nick, shopping, cards as well."

"I throw myself on your mercy, Miss Fancourt. If you will engage to join us here at five o'clock each afternoon, we'll put our heads together and come up with some ideas for the next day. There is no one else to help me. Chloe is too young and my grandmother likes to rest before dinner. Without you I'll be completely dished and my reputation as a host forever tarnished."

There was something very enticing in this invitation to be one of an inner circle. "If you really think I can be of assistance," she said doubtfully.

"I am sure of it. Thank you."

Chloe was already dressed by the time Rosa hurried into their sitting-room. "Is it so late? Go on down, don't wait for me," she gasped, as she vanished into her bedchamber where Lambton waited. The maid worked quickly with none of her usual chatter but, despite this, Rosa was the last to arrive in the drawing-room.

Robert accosted her as soon as she appeared. "Excuse me, Miss Fancourt, but Chloe says you know all about perspective and shadow. I want to draw the castle, but it just won't work—it's too flat and I can't get the proportions right. Will you show me how?"

"Certainly I will. There are some simple tricks—once you know them, you will find it quite easy, I assure you. We shall arrange a time for tomorrow once we know what everyone's plans are. What did you do today?"

She listened intently while he explained how Mr Musgrave had first asked them what they liked doing and was there anything they would be interested in learning or improving their skills in, for example shooting or riding, and had then said he could see they were going to have a splendid summer. And he had even suggested they sit at their books for half an hour or so each morning so they wouldn't have forgotten everything when they went back to school. It wasn't swotting, he had assured them, but just a sensible precaution and he would be happy to explain anything they might not have quite understood in the previous year.

"He doesn't really know about perspective either, Miss Fancourt, but otherwise, he's a great gun."

"I can see that he is," Rosa said, deeply appreciative of the guile that contrived to make the notion of schoolwork in the holidays attractive. But why was the boy here instead of spending those holidays at home? Had Mr Kennard married again or had he remained a widower, unsure how to occupy a growing boy?

"Do you have any brothers or sisters, Robert?"

He made a face. "One of each, but they are very young still. My brother is four and my sister only one. That is why I was so pleased when Hal invited me to spend some time with him. At home I must always be quiet and not disturb the babies. There is nothing for me to do and a fellow can't sit mum all day, now can he? And what's worse, they gave the babies to my old nurse but I'm not allowed to visit the nursery either or play with them. I could help, couldn't I? A boy of four can play ball," he finished indignantly.

"I'm sure you could," Rosa said. "Perhaps things will change when your brother is a little older."

He shook his head. "Their mother is not mine, you see. She married my father when I was six. I think she would prefer if I wasn't there. She talks of sending me to the Military Academy at Woolwich."

Rosa had no idea what this meant. "Would you not like that?"

"I might," he conceded. "It would probably be better than mouldy Greek and stuffy Latin, but I don't see why I should be sent away for good, for that is what it would amount to. Once I had passed my examinations, I would be commissioned as an officer and could be sent anywhere with the army. I don't know if I want that." He looked around the room.

"I like it that we are all together here. I don't eat with them at home, you know, I'm not old enough, she says. But then she says I am too old and boisterous to have my meals in the nursery. Since the babies were born, I get a tray in my old schoolroom. Sometimes Abbie—that's what I call Mrs Abbott, my nurse—sneaks in to see me, but as Johnnie grew older, it became more difficult. In the beginning, she still woke me and told me when I should go to bed, but with two babies it was harder for her to manage. Now, when I'm at home, one of the maids comes in every morning to put out my clothes and I go to bed when I like. Sir Julian said from now on Hal and I are to come to the drawing-room after dinner and not go to bed like babies."

He looked so forlorn that Rosa longed to tell him that he had another sister who would welcome him into her life. If only Mr Kennard had permitted her to look after him from the beginning, how different things would have been for both of them.

"Life can be very hard when you are young," she began hesitantly. "I hardly knew my father—he was a naval officer who was at sea for many years before he was mortally wounded—and when my mother died two years later, I had no-one. But I have found that even in our darkest hour there is always some light; someone who holds out a friendly hand to us. You may find that person at school or here this summer. Don't despair, Robert."

He smiled tentatively at her. "I won't, Miss Fancourt." He paused. "You won't say anything to anyone else, will you? Hal knows, of course, that's probably why he invited me, but the others don't have to know they don't want me at home."

"I promise I won't say a word," she assured him. "You know, when you go home, you could mention to your father that you dined each evening with Lord Swanmere."

"That's a good idea. She could hardly say then that I am too young. She was quite impressed that I was invited here. She wanted to come to Lady Ransford's too, but my father said she should stay with the children."

At dinner they took the seats assigned to them the previous evening. Like a real family, Rosa thought happily, thanking the good fortune that had placed her between her brother and Sir Julian. Robert seemed to accept her as a lady to whom he might speak freely and Sir Julian clearly valued her advice. Perhaps it was petty of her, but she could not but be pleased that he had apparently never considered consulting Mrs Overton.

That lady was entertaining her end of the table with stories of her childhood escapades during previous visits to Swanmere. Her cousin featured large in these descriptions that were peppered with phrases such as 'Julian and I' or 'of course, Julian'.

"Did she spend a lot of time here?" Rosa asked him under cover of the laughter that followed the story of how Julian had rescued a kitten Mrs Overton had thought to set sailing in a toy boat. 'From that day he was my hero,' she had declared.

"I would not say so," he answered. "We—that is my

parents and I—generally came here for some weeks in the summer and Meg's family, the Eardleys, were often invited during our visit. Her mother and mine were cousins and great friends. But to be frank, I was closer to her brother Richard who is two years older than Meg and I. She was always a dainty little thing, fussing about her dress, and we felt she should play with her younger sister and leave us boys to more masculine pursuits. When I was twelve, my mother became ill and I did not visit again until after her death which was two years later. To the best of my knowledge, Meg has not visited these past twenty years. We met from time to time in town, although not recently, and I knew her husband, but not very well."

"That first visit after your mother's death cannot have been easy."

"No. I was fifteen by then. My father remarried soon afterwards and after that I came by myself."

"It is hard when a parent remarries so quickly."

"Did you find it so?"

"Yes. It was not even a year." She bit her lip. "When I was older and better able to understand, I thought perhaps she had tired of being on her own, for my father was rarely at home. It was not his fault, of course, but that did not alter the fact that for most of their married life she was far more a widow than a wife. She only had one year in her new marriage, but I hope she found some happiness."

"What are you and Miss Fancourt talking about so seriously, Julian?" Mrs Overton called gaily down the table. "It will not do, you know. If you distress the lady, we shall have to separate you."

Before either of those addressed could respond, Robert, who had been talking to Mr Haughton, turned and glared accusingly at Sir Julian.

Rosa patted his hand reassuringly. "Mrs Overton is just teasing Sir Julian. They knew each other as children, remember?"

The boy's face cleared. "Oh, you mean the way Ann sometimes teases Hal?"

Rosa felt Sir Julian convulse beside her. She stole a glance at him and saw he had raised his napkin to his lips. She quickly turned back to Robert. "Just like Ann and Hal," she confirmed.

"And you are really not distressed?"

She laughed. "Not in the slightest but it is kind of you to be concerned about me."

She didn't know how much of the exchange reached Mrs Overton, but that lady was more subdued for the remainder of the meal.

When the second course had been removed and dessert set out, Sir Julian stood up.

"You look very imposing, Julian," Chloe said. "Are you about to make a speech?"

"In a way, I suppose I am. I have an announcement to make. As we are to spend several weeks together, it would be unfair to expect Chloe and Ann to provide us with entertainment every evening, delightful as their music is. I propose we take it in turn to suggest a pastime or prepare something to amuse the others. I shall begin this evening and, after the gentlemen join the ladies in the drawing-room, I shall ask you to draw lots to determine the order for succeeding evenings."

Chloe was aghast at the suggestion. "You surely don't mean we must keep everyone entertained for two or three hours?"

"No, you may practise something with others or suggest

a game or a pastime where all can join in. But if others help you, you must be prepared to help them."

She nodded. "Of course. What about Robert and Hal?"

"I think the boys should count as one adult," Rosa suggested. "I am sure that between them they will have some very good ideas."

"You may be sure we shall!"

It must have been the gleam in Hal's eyes as he said this that caused Mr Musgrave to intervene. "If you are agreeable, Sir Julian, we shall make it a triumvirate and draw two lots where the others take one each."

"What have you prepared for us, Julian?" his grandmother asked once tea had been drunk and the lots drawn.

"Tonight's entertainment comes in two parts. First I shall read to you the first chapters of a new three volume novel,"—Chloe and Ann perked up at this—"and then I thought we might play commerce or loo, in any event a game where all can participate."

"Excellent. Come and sit beside me at this table, so I can hear you. Swanmere, you may have his other side."

The others hurried to find places and Julian picked up his book.

"*Mansfield Park. Volume the First.*"

"Well, I wonder that you should choose such a dull book about such a dull family, Julian," Mrs Overton exclaimed when he closed the book at the end of the third chapter. "There is nothing horrid or thrilling about it, nothing exciting—why, you might be reading about any of your neighbours."

"That's what I like about it," Ann said. "Many books are

so far-fetched that you know they couldn't be true."

"In describing something so close to home, the author both gives validity to our own stories and makes it possible for us to learn from hers," Rosa said quietly.

"The children seem real," Robert contributed. "Children in stories are mostly either terrible prigs or very wicked and neither is generally true."

"I daresay it will become more interesting now that the girls are grown up," Chloe reflected. "It is my turn tomorrow and I intend to start by reading the next chapters."

"An excellent suggestion," Lady Loring approved. "I would propose that we all do so, but my eyesight is so poor that I should be unable to take my turn."

Sir Julian smiled at her. "I shall be happy to read for you, Grandmamma, and hereby second your proposal. All in favour?"

"The Ayes have it," Swanmere announced a few moments later. "Now who will take a glass of wine before we move to cards?"


Jenkins knelt to remove her mistress's shoes and stockings and slid delicate silk slippers onto her feet before helping her disrobe and don a nightgown. She held up a dressing-gown of amethyst silk. "Are you sure you won't get into bed, ma'am? You're that tired."

Meg shook her head as she slipped her arms into the sleeves. "I'll just sit here a little while."

How tedious this visit promised to be. Little or no company during the day and in the evening dull novels and duller cards played not even for chicken-stakes but for fish. She must think of something livelier for her evening's entertainment.

"Will that be all, ma'am?"

"Yes, Jenkins. Tell me," she asked as the maid reached the door, "what do they say below stairs about Miss Fancourt?"

"Not much, ma'am. She seems a pleasant lady. But that reminds me." Jenkins went to a drawer and took out a letter. "This was in the reticule that matches your carriage dress. Should I take it to Miss Fancourt?"

"Oh, I had forgotten that. It's late now; leave it there. Good night."

Meg was too restless to think of sleep, too consumed by the enigma of Miss Fancourt. It was very sly of Julian not to have mentioned her in his letter of invitation. It would have been only natural, polite even, to say '*Miss Fancourt, who is the daughter of——, will also join us.*' And what connection could she have with Mr Kennard that he would request Meg to pass a letter discreetly to a lady she had only just met?

'*Just a small matter left unfinished, I am ashamed to say, Mrs Overton,*' he had told her. '*I hoped to see her this morning before I left, but she has not yet come down.*'

There was definitely something smoky there. Robert had not known her previously, she had discovered, although they seemed to have quickly made friends, but the woman was on very familiar terms with the Lorings. A blind ass could see that they all held her in great affection. Last night, when the tea-tray had been brought in and placed in front of Lady Loring, she had immediately asked Miss Fancourt to preside, which was a deliberate affront both to Julian's sister and cousin, Meg considered.

It had not escaped her notice that the other woman had

asked neither the Lorings nor Swanmere how they took their tea but had prepared each cup as matter-of-factedly as if she were in her own home. Tonight the tray had been brought directly to her, as if she were the acknowledged mistress of the house.

Now that Meg thought about it, she could not have travelled from Loring Place with the Loring ladies. Sir Julian had had to ask his grandmother which carriage she was using and had then suggested she share the chariot with Miss Fancourt. So he and Miss Fancourt must have arrived together. But from where? She could not imagine him introducing his *chère amie* to his female relations. In addition, she was sharing a suite with Chloe, which made any nocturnal visits impossible.

It would have been more appropriate to offer me the suite; Ann could have had the other bedroom, she thought. I am the elder and a widow and should have been given the sitting-room. That woman must be thirty if she's a day. An ape-leader, if ever I laid eyes on one. I'll set Jenkins to find out more. The letter? It can remain forgotten for the moment.

❧

# Chapter Eighteen

"Nonsense, Julian. It would present a very off appearance for Ann to call on Mrs Musgrave without me. I cannot allow it. She is not yet out—although I shall soon have to think about it, I suppose. I don't know how I shall manage." Meg glanced at Julian from under her eyelashes. "I suppose Chloe will have a formal come-out."

"I imagine she will when she is eighteen. For my part, I would like her to become more accustomed to society before she goes to town. I have seen too many girls overwhelmed by the whole affair."

"Yes, or swept off their feet, as I was by Harry. Girls are very vulnerable to charming, older men but it does not make for an ideal marriage." She sighed. "I would not make the same mistake again."

Julian thought his cousin would leap at the bait of any charming older man providing he was well-born and wealthy enough, but forbore from saying so and returned to the proposed call on the vicarage.

"I had thought to walk—it is a fine day."

"How far is it?"

"About two miles."

She gave a little shriek. "Impossible. We cannot arrive wind-blown and with reddened faces. Pray order the carriage. For half-past two, shall we say?"

He bowed to the inevitable. "Very well." Thank God Miss Fancourt had already declined his invitation to accompany them, saying that she had promised to give Robert a drawing lesson.

Mrs Musgrave appeared gratified by the call from the Castle, Miss Musgrave was happy to engage to show Miss Loring and Miss Overton her favourite walks and the vicar, looking in to welcome Sir Julian home, professed himself delighted to meet Mrs Overton and the two girls. The Musgraves accepted an invitation to dine the following Tuesday and the call was over.

"We'll see you at church tomorrow morning, I hope," the vicar said as Julian made his farewells.

"Certainly, sir." Julian bowed and shepherded his little flock to the waiting carriage.

"I suppose you'll read the lesson, Julian," Meg said as they drove away.

"I generally do when I am at home," he replied, ignoring the little note of spite in her arch tone.

"I vow you are become a staid old bachelor. I am surprised Cousin Swanmere tolerates it."

"Do you think he would prefer it if I were a rakehell?"

"Don't be so dense! He must be anxious to see the succession secured. It is high time you set up your nursery."

"Is it indeed?"

"You know very well it is. I can see I shall have to take you in hand next season, sir."

"God forbid," Julian exclaimed, infuriated by the slanted eyes and coquettish laugh that suggested an unspoken understanding between them. "I never thought to see you act the meddling matchmaker, Meg. If you are not careful, you will turn into one of those old tabbies whom everyone avoids."

"Well!" Meg's bosom swelled.

Before her mother could say anything more, Ann asked quickly, "Did you like Miss Musgrave, Chloe?"

"Very much. She is as amiable as her brother. I am looking forward to exploring the countryside with her."

Ann nodded. "She has promised to show me how to play the church organ. I have always wanted to try one."

Julian was grateful for the change of subject. The poor girl had obviously recognised the warning signs. "That reminds me that I must send to town for new strings for the lute. Will you be able to fit them, Ann?"

"I don't know, but I'll try. I am sure Mr Haughton would help me. He plays the violin, you know."

"Have you found any music of interest?" he asked before Meg could recapture the conversation and listened attentively to Ann's excited description of the treasures of the music room until they arrived back at the Castle.

"I should like to have a word, Julian."

He raised his brows at Meg's acerbic tone. "In here." He ushered her into the great hall and firmly closed the door. "What may I do for you, Meg?"

She had stalked over to the window but now whirled to face him. "How dare you speak to me like that? In front of my daughter, too!"

He looked blandly at her. "My dear Meg, if you will

encroach on my personal affairs, you must expect to be told to keep your undoubtedly pretty nose out of them."

"Well!" She inhaled audibly. "I may speak my mind within my own family, I trust."

"If you insist, but not with me."

"Julian!" Tears trembled on her eyelashes. "Are we not family?"

He shook his head. "Not in the way you mean. The connection between us is by no means as close as you apparently consider it to be. You have no more right than any other matron of my acquaintance to pry into or interfere with my personal life and I should be obliged if you would refrain from doing so."

She raised a handkerchief to her eyes. "How can you say that after all we have been to one another?"

"All what?" he demanded, exasperated. "Our great-grandmothers were sisters. Our mothers were cousins and friends and at times we were childhood playfellows or, more properly, your brother and I were. We meet now and again in society. That is the sum of it and a small sum it is."

"But—why did you invite me here?"

"I invited you and your family because I wished Chloe to meet Ann and," he continued more gently, "I thought all three of you might like a change of scene after your year of mourning. I remember how difficult I found it when my mother died and how lost my father seemed to be."

"You mean you were sorry for the poor widow and her children?" she said, outraged.

"Should I not have been, Meg?"

She stared at him, the tears spilling down her cheeks. "He should have been coming home now with all the others," she sobbed. "It is so unfair!"

He was about to put a consoling arm around her when she peeped coyly up at him over the edge of her lace handkerchief, just as the eight-year-old Meg used do. It had been one of her most formidable childhood weapons and its employment generally resulted in her wishes being granted or her peccadilloes overlooked.

His arm dropped to his side. "It is unfair," he agreed. "Come Meg, let us not quarrel. I am sorry if I offended you."

"If?" She sniffed. "You are a boor, sir."

Julian just looked at her steadily. He was not about to recant.

After a few moments, she sniffed again and moved away. "I must look a sight."

He shook his head. "Tears never spoiled your beauty."

She dimpled becomingly as he held the door open for her but then her eyes narrowed with suspicion.

"Julian!"

"What?"

"Nothing."

She had obviously thought better about picking another fight. He grinned as the door closed behind her. That could not have gone better if he had planned it. Now, where was Miss Fancourt?

Julian found her in the lady's garden, ensconced beside Robert on a bench in a shady arbour, their heads bent over his sketchbook. A broad-brimmed straw hat lay on the seat beside her, its blue ribbons lifting and falling lazily in the light breeze.

They both looked up at the sound of gravel crunching under his boots, each raising a hand to shade their eyes in an uncannily identical gesture. The tilt of their heads had to do with the angle of the sun, he supposed, but for a moment they might have been mother and son. Then Robert looked down again at his page and the illusion vanished.

Miss Fancourt's lips curved in a welcoming smile. "Good day, Sir Julian. Was your call at the vicarage successful?"

"It was indeed." He gestured at the bench. "May I?"

"Please."

He moved her bonnet to the end of the bench so he could sit next to her, then removed his own hat, stripped off his gloves and thrust a hand through his hair.

"You two seem very busy."

"Miss Fancourt is teaching me perspective," Robert answered without glancing up. "Look, ma'am, I think I've got it now."

"That is much better, Robert. Now you can rub out some of the guide-lines so that your drawing is not too cluttered. Look at it carefully and make the outlines of your building a little darker before you begin and be sure not to erase your vanishing points as you may wish to add some more detail later."

He nodded, frowning with concentration as he bent to his task.

Julian stretched out his legs and closed his eyes, content to sit beside her, his shoulder touching hers. He could feel each little movement as she leaned forward to instruct the boy, hear her low voice as she explained things to him, relish the brush of her skirts against his thigh. A faint fragrance rose to his nostrils, one that he recognised as uniquely hers; a gentle blend of flowers with a hint of spice.

"Gillyflowers," he murmured.

"I beg your pardon?"

"Your scent—it reminds me of gillyflowers," he responded drowsily. At her shocked gasp, his eyes snapped open. She was staring at him, a soft flush on her cheek.

"I beg your pardon. I was thinking aloud."

"Oh." Her blush deepened and she looked anxiously at Robert but the boy remained immersed in his work.

Julian followed her glance and said no more. There was no point in attracting the lad's attention to his careless remark, but it was too tempting to remain so close to her. It was almost as if they were in bed together. He got to his feet. "Will you take a turn around the garden with me?"

"Certainly, unless—do you need me at the moment, Robert?"

"No, thank you, Miss Fancourt. I'm just finished. What is the time, do you know?"

Julian pulled out his watch. "Four o'clock."

"I must go. Mr Musgrave and Hal should be back any minute and Mrs Godin has cake and lemonade for us about now." Robert carefully brushed his drawing to dislodge any crumbs of rubber and closed the book before replacing his pencils in their case.

"Thank you again, Miss Fancourt. I understand it a lot better now."

"It was my pleasure, Robert. If you like, we can start working on the different sections of the castle tomorrow, so you get some practice before you attempt to draw it as a whole."

"That would be splendid." He hesitated, made an awkward bow and ran off.

"A well-mannered lad," Julian commented.

"Yes. It is a pity his father won't arrange for drawing lessons. He has a natural talent that should be encouraged."

"Was yours?"

"Yes." She set her hat on her head and tied the ribbons. "When it comes to the finer arts, I think girls have more advantages. Every school has a drawing-master and a music-master and they also call to private houses, as Chloe's did. I had to chaperon her during her lessons, so of course I benefited from them too. Her mother was generous in that respect and did not object to my receiving instruction as well." She looked around. "Where did I put my gloves?"

"Here." He retrieved them from under the bench and picked up his own belongings. "Would you like to walk down to the mere? I saw as I came back that they have mown the path."

She took his arm and they fell into an easy rhythm that seemed a continuation of the little intimacy they had enjoyed in the arbour.

"You must not commit all your time to your pupil," he said as they strolled down the grassy slope. "From Monday you will have lessons of your own to attend."

"I beg your pardon?"

"Have you forgotten I am to teach you how to drive? We have a neat little gig that will do perfectly for a first lesson. Depending on how well you do, you may later graduate to the curricle."

"I'm sure the gig will more than satisfy me," she said firmly, "but I should like to learn."

# Chapter Nineteen

HE DID NOT EVEN WITHDRAW that hateful remark about the old tabby, Meg thought resentfully as she dressed for dinner. Being sorry if he had offended her was not the same as being sorry for what he had said. And how dare he call her a matron!

What a waste of the summer! She would have been better advised to leave her children with their grandparents and take rooms at one of the bathing-places that had sprung up along the south coast. Not Brighton—she could not afford Brighton—but anywhere that had assembly rooms and a circulating library must be an improvement on Swanmere.

"About Miss Fancourt, ma'am?"

"Yes, Jenkins?"

"I ran into her maid this morning in the ironing-room."

"Oh? Of what quality is Miss Fancourt's linen?"

"Very good but quite plain from what I could see."

"Hmm. Go on."

"Lambton's not been with her very long, so all she could tell me is that she lives in Kent with her cousin, a

Mrs Chidlow who is married to a solicitor. Her father was a naval captain, it seems, and is dead these many years."

"Kent, you say? Did they travel to Lady Ransford's in one day? It would have been quite a journey. "

"No, ma'am. They spent a night at Swanmere House. Mr and Mrs Chidlow came with them and returned home the next morning."

"Hmm. Does this Lambton know the nature of Miss Fancourt's acquaintanceship with the Lorings?"

"I don't think so, ma'am. Dover, Lady Loring's maid, came in then and I thought it best not to press the girl any further."

"That was wise. Thank you, Jenkins. Perhaps you should talk to Dover or any other servants who came from Loring Place."

"I'll do my best, ma'am. I suppose Sir Julian visits there as well, so his man might know, but they are all quite close-mouthed here."


"Rosa, Lord Swanmere said he would like to hear us sing together," Chloe said after dinner. "Should you have any objection?"

"No, of course not."

"I thought we might perform the duet from the *Messiah*."

"*He Shall Feed his Flock?*"

"Yes. We have time to run through it before the gentlemen come in—Ann will play for us."

Meg frowned as the two moved towards the music room. When had Swanmere heard Miss Fancourt sing? He rarely left home nowadays, he had told her, but he had gone to Loring Place for Sir Edward's birthday festivities.

Had she been there too? Meg sniffed. Julian had not thought of having his cousins included in the celebrations although, from what she had overheard Chloe tell Ann, there had been several girls of their age among the guests. It was all of a piece. She knew now where she stood with him. For two pins, she would leave in the morning. But how would she explain her early return to her parents-in-law?

"How did you come to know Miss Fancourt, Cousin Swanmere? Was it at Loring Place?" Meg enquired later as the two singers acknowledged their applause.

"Yes, of course. Don't you know that she was Chloe's governess for the past ten years? A most estimable woman! She has left the Lorings now, of course, but I am delighted Julian had this notion of inviting her to stay this summer. That was beautiful, my dears," he said to the performers. "Miss Rosa, would you further oblige me by singing *The Oak and The Ash* again? It was a favourite of my mother's."

A governess, Meg thought disgustedly as the woman complied with Swanmere's request. She doesn't look or behave like any governess I've ever seen. She is not expected to chaperon Chloe and Ann or attend Lady Loring but is treated as a guest in all respects. And it was Julian's notion to invite her.

The music over, the company settled to the reading of the next chapters of *Mansfield Park* which saw the introduction of the Crawfords to the Bertram family. Afterwards, Miss Crawford's question as to whether Miss Fanny Price was 'out' or not led to a discussion on the appropriate behaviour for young ladies and the best way for them to emerge from the schoolroom.

"Are you to come out next year, Chloe?" Meg enquired.

The girl looked at her brother. "I don't think so," she answered. "Not until I am eighteen."

"Like Ann. Very wise." Meg's hand went to her breast and she widened her eyes as if suddenly seized by inspiration. "Why, you may come out together! Is that not a splendid notion? What do you say, girls? To have a friend at your side will make your come-out much less daunting."

When neither Chloe nor Ann responded—really, the girl was past praying for if she could not take a cue from her mother on this—Meg was forced to pursue the theme herself. Repressing her irritation, she turned to his lordship. "Cousin Swanmere, you will remember that that is what Julian's mother and mine did. Dear Mamma often described what a splendid occasion it was. Such a beautiful ballroom at Swanmere House, she always said. It is a pity it has not been used for so long, but this will be the perfect opportunity to start anew." She glanced blithely from him to Julian. "I know you gentlemen hate arranging such things, but you may leave it all to me. I should also be more than happy to advise you on any refurbishments, for I suspect very little has been done since dear Lady Swanmere's day. Now, what say you?"

"Nothing," Julian answered immediately. "The decision is not mine to make; it is for Chloe's parents to decide on the nature of her come-out."

Meg felt her cheeks grow warm. How dare he snub her like that? She glanced at Miss Fancourt who had not yet contributed to the conversation. Pasting a sweet smile on her lips, she asked, "How was your *début*, Miss Fancourt?"

To her chagrin, the other woman showed no sign of embarrassment.

"Following the deaths of my parents, it became necessary for me to earn my living, Mrs Overton. I suppose I made my come-out when I advanced from being pupil to pupil-teacher." She smiled faintly. "I can assure you that no court presentation could be more terrifying than the first time you stand in front of a class, conscious that until recently you yourself were seated among the pupils."

Thomas Musgrave whistled. "In the same school, you mean? By Jove, I can imagine nothing more horrifying. I suppose your former sins must rise to haunt you. How did you cope, ma'am?"

"As is often the case, the reality was nothing like as dreadful as anticipation painted it. They were all new girls, and so homesick that I forgot my own apprehension in comforting them."

"That is so like you, Rosa," Chloe remarked.

"How long did you remain there as a teacher?" Julian asked.

"A year."

"And then you came to me." Chloe smiled warmly at her former governess.

"For which we were all extremely grateful," Lady Loring put in. "Nobody could keep up with your questions."

Julian grinned. "I remember you asked me once why we could separate our fingers and toes but animals could not."

"And you showed me a picture of a monkey doing just that," Chloe remembered, "so I asked why people did not have tails."

When the general laughter had subsided, Chloe leaped to her feet. "Let us play charades! Shall we have two or three teams?"

"You either put yourself forward too much or are too silent," Meg admonished her daughter whom she had bidden to her bedchamber at the end of the evening. "Earlier, in the carriage, you interrupted Julian and me and this evening you had nothing to say for yourself. Even when I was trying to arrange a come-out ball for you, you could not support me. All you had to do was clasp your hands and say, 'oh, that would be truly famous, would it not Chloe?' You would have left her with no choice but to say yes. Who knows what might have come of it."

"But you always say you cannot afford a London Season for me."

"Stupid girl! This way Swanmere and the Lorings would stand most of the nonsense. If we were to stay at Swanmere House, all we would need is a few gowns. The least your grandparents can do is pay for them."

"Grandmamma has said they will give a dance for me when I am seventeen and I can go to the assemblies at home as well. I don't care about having a grand come-out. If there is money for London gowns, I would far rather have it spent on my music."

"Nonsense! A Season is an investment in your future. Music will not find you a husband. You take it too far, Ann. I have warned you before—no gentleman wants a wife whose sole interest is the pianoforte. He might as well marry a blue-stocking. And that reminds me! You would do well to keep a little distance in your dealings with Miss Fancourt. I do not understand why she was invited here. I suppose it is a reward for her long service, but it does not do to permit such people to get ideas above their station."

"I don't agree. Her station is no different from mine,"

Ann said flatly. "We are both daughters of deceased officers and gentlemen. In fact her father as a naval captain would have taken precedence over Papa who was a major. I don't think you should have asked about her come-out, Mamma. I heard Lord Swanmere telling you she had been Chloe's governess and you might have guessed she hadn't had one—or were you deliberately trying to discomfit her? If that was the case, you failed. I would say everyone admires her even more now."

"What do you mean, admire?"

"She is both accomplished and kind. I don't know how to describe it—maybe it comes from her having been a governess—but she makes it easy for you to join in the conversation as an equal, not like many adults who are either condescending or dismissive. And I like the way she dresses, she has a simple elegance that becomes her very well."

"I should like to know how she can afford it on a governess's salary. I hope she won't regret having spent her savings just so she can act the lady here for a month."

Ann rolled her eyes. "She doesn't act the lady, she is a lady. If you ask me, you are the one whose behaviour is unladylike, trying to trick Lord Swanmere into giving me a Season."

Meg's spine stiffened. "You will speak to me with the proper respect, miss, or you will suffer for it. You are not too old to be whipped."

Ann seemed to grow even taller. Since when could she loom over her mother? Meg took an involuntary step back.

"Do you really think so, ma'am? I should not advise you to put it to the test."

Meg raised her hand at this impertinence but Ann caught her by the wrist.

"You will receive the respect you deserve, no more. Good night." She dropped her mother's arm and left the room.

Just wait until I have you home again, Meg thought as the door closed behind her daughter. It had been a mistake to bring her here. Ann had never stood up to her before. It was Miss Fancourt's fault, of course. The girl had taken her insolence as a model.

There was still something strange there. The Loring connection had been explained, but what about the Kennard one? She looked thoughtfully at the drawer where Mr Kennard's letter lay. She must consider what to do about that. It wasn't sealed, just folded. It would be easy to open it carefully and return it to its original state. Really, she should not be expected to pass on correspondence when she had no knowledge of the content.

# Chapter Twenty

To Rosa's relief, Ann announced at breakfast on Monday that her mother was indisposed and would keep to her room for the day.

For some reason Mrs Overton had taken her in dislike and, beneath a veneer of civility, pricked her with subtle verbal assaults, never so much as to cause overt offence but sufficient that Rosa found she had to be constantly on her guard when in the other woman's company. Fortunately she could generally avoid her during the day but Sunday had been particularly trying and she had been subjected to a flow of petty remarks punctuated by tittering gusts of shrill laughter. She hoped Mrs Overton's temper would improve once she had recovered from her complaint.

Lady Loring said something similar when Rosa called to her sitting-room to say good morning. "Indisposed, is she? I hope she returns to us in a better disposition than she has exhibited until now. I have always admired your good sense, Miss Rosa, but never more than yesterday when you refused to allow yourself to be put out of countenance by her or even acknowledge her little jabs. Now, what are your plans for this morning?"

"Sir Julian has offered to teach me to drive, ma'am."

"Has he indeed? Not in his curricle, I trust?"

"He did threaten me with it, but only once I master the gig."

Lady Loring chuckled. "We shall see you driving the curricle by the end of the month."

"I doubt it, ma'am. I shall be happy if I don't overturn the gig."

"This way." Sir Julian conducted Rosa through the door into the south tower. "In a moment we'll go to the stable yard, but first I hope you will allow me to give you this."

She took the small package automatically and then stared down at it. Her hands shook as she carefully unfolded the wrapping paper to reveal a pair of elegant tan driving gloves made of soft kid and lined with silk. She had never seen anything so fine.

"It is a liberty, I know," he said apologetically as she gazed at them, dumbfounded, "but one I hope you will overlook. I should hate to be responsible for more blisters on your hands."

Rosa had to swallow a colossal lump in her throat before she could stammer, "They are beautiful, Sir Julian, and it is most thoughtful of you, but I really should not—"

"I mean no disrespect, I assure you, Miss Fancourt. With the right gloves you will find it much easier to handle the ribbons. Will you not try them on?"

A lady should not accept a gift from a gentleman who was not a relative but she could not bring herself to refuse. She stripped off her cotton gloves and eased her hands into the new pair. They fit so perfectly that he must have had them made especially for her. The deep cuffs were embroidered with an elaborate golden pattern. She looked closer. It was a monogram of *RF* in a wreath of roses.

"They are exquisite and so comfortable. How did you know the size?"

"Have you forgotten you left some gloves behind when you escaped from the Old Hall?"

"Sssh!"

His smile dimmed. "What is it? What's wrong, Rosa?"

"If anyone found out about—that, I would be ruined!"

He took her hands reassuringly. "There is no-one here but ourselves. You know I would never do anything to harm you."

"But if someone—your cousin—were to overhear—"

He closed his eyes briefly. "You are right. I'm sorry. It is best never to refer to it. It—and the gloves—shall be our secret."

A sigh of relief escaped her. "Thank you—and thank you so much for them, Sir Julian. It was so kind." Perilously close to tears, she searched for the right words. He had gone to such trouble to ensure her comfort.

His clasp on her hands grew tighter. "Do you think you could forget the 'Sir' and just say Julian?" he asked huskily.

She shook her head. "It would be most improper."

"In private, at least," he coaxed her, "and permit me to call you Rosa as Chloe does? I don't think you would like me to join my grandparents in saying 'Miss Rosa.'"

Rosa had to smile at his ingenuity. From a gentleman of his age, such an appellation would stamp her as a spinster and old maid. "In private, then—Julian." It was sweet to say his name unadorned and, judging by his smile, he liked hearing it from her.

"Shall we, Rosa?"

She hastily folded the blue gloves and stowed them in her reticule before taking his arm. He led her to a tack room where a pair of reins was attached to a board. "We'll start here so that you can get a feel for holding the ribbons."

Following his instructions, she threaded them through the fingers of her left hand and secured them, then practised signalling to the horse to turn right or left.

"Very good," he approved. "Now, I think they are ready for us outside."

In the stable yard, a sturdy cob stood harnessed to a trim gig.

"What a fine fellow," Rosa remarked, then turned her head at a familiar whinny. "Oh, it can't be!" She rushed across the cobbles to where, ears pricked up, a big, bay head looked eagerly over the door of a box. "Captain!"

Tears stung her eyes but she laughed as she stroked the white-blazed forehead while the big gelding turned his head as if he wanted to nuzzle against her.

"Captain," she whispered, "how did you come to be here?"

"Chloe insisted we bring her mare and I thought you might like to have your own mount here as well," Julian explained.

"How kind of you," she sighed. "I never thought to see him again. Yes, you like that, don't you?" she said to Captain as she scratched his favourite spot behind his ear. "And this. It was meant for another horse, so today you must share." She took some sugar from her reticule and held it out to him.

"We'll ride out another day," she told him after he had delicately lipped the piece from her palm, "but I must leave you for now."

A final pat and they moved away. "To think I almost did not pack my riding habit," she said to Sir Julian. "I cannot wait to ride again. I have had no opportunity in Maidstone; in fact I have not ridden since that day we went to Lavenham."

"In that case, we shall ride and drive on alternate days. And here is Henry, strictly speaking Henry the Eighth, but we are rarely so formal."

"I do not imagine that he stands on ceremony. Yes, I kept some sugar for your majesty," she added as the horse snuffled at her pelisse. "Do you call all your horses after the Kings of England?"

"It's more the way some people call all their coachmen 'John'. When he leaves us, there will be a Henry the Ninth."

"I hope that is many years in the future. Will you explain to me how the harness works? Isn't it strange how one can see something every day and never properly understand it?"

"It's quite straightforward, especially when there is only one horse," he told her as he led her around the equipage, finishing at the step to the seat. "Excuse me for going before you." He stepped lithely into the little carriage and held down his hand to help her climb up.

"Comfortable?" At her nod, he held out the reins. "Take them up first in your right hand and then transfer them to the left as we practised. The back of your hand should be towards the horse. That's right. Take the whip in your right; not that way—like this." He adjusted her grip.

"See how better balanced it is?"

"Yes."

"Now give him the office, just a little signal with the ribbons. If you wish, you can tell him as well. Just say, 'walk on'." The horse started to move. "We'll walk him a little first, until you are accustomed to the reins and the few commands."

"He doesn't appear to need any further instructions," she remarked as the gelding ambled calmly out of the yard.

"We'll go right here; take the back lanes. Well done—I knew you'd soon get the knack of it."

"I wonder who is conducting whom," Rosa said as the horse plodded on. "You hear of horses who take their drunken master home every night."

"Or stop as a matter of course when they reach his favourite inn. Henry is very placid—inclined to be a little lazy, perhaps, but he keeps going. We turn left here."

Rosa cautiously guided Henry onto a wider lane. The castle towered high above them while below the mere sparkled in the morning sun.

"What a superb vista, so picturesque!" She pulled up so that she could admire it in comfort. "The castle is much more impressive, more forbidding from below. This would be a splendid place for Robert to attempt his sketch."

"You and he have become firm friends."

"Yes." She said no more, but let Henry walk on. She still had not decided whether to reveal her relationship to her brother. It was not that she felt she owed Kennard any consideration—if there was any debt between them, it was due from him to her, but she could not be sure that Robert's joy at discovering he had a loving sister would not be overshadowed by the knowledge of his father's treatment of her. He felt unwanted at home. Would his position seem even more precarious when he learned that his father had already washed his hands of a stepdaughter?

She glanced sideways at her companion. While his relationship with his stepmother could best be described as chilly, his love for his sister was very apparent. "Were you happy when your father remarried?"

"I was happy enough that he had a wife, but I did not want a new mother, especially one just ten years older than I. Later—things became more complicated."

"In what way?"

"I always knew I was heir to both Swanmere and Loring Place but it didn't matter while my mother was alive. She was a sweet, gentle woman and, although she would have been Baroness Swanmere in her own right, I imagine my father would have been just as much master here as at the Place. After her death—I did not properly understand this until later, but afterwards he came to resent the fact that I would supplant him, as he saw it, when my grandfather dies. Not only that, he hates the idea that the baronetcy will be subsumed into the barony."

"He must have known that would happen when he married your mother," Rosa pointed out.

Julian laughed shortly. "One would assume so. He fell madly in love with her, by all accounts—perhaps it didn't matter so much when he knew he would rule by her side. But as soon as my stepmother was with child, he informed me that if she bore him a second son, he would require my consent to the barring of the fee tail as soon as I came of age. The estate would then be resettled in my brother's favour. I must inherit the title, of course—he can do nothing about that, but would not receive any Loring property."

"And he expected you to agree to disinherit yourself?" Rosa asked incredulously. She stopped the gig again and turned to look at him.

He had been gazing bleakly into the distance, but now looked down and covered her hand with his. "I have never spoken to anyone else about it." He shrugged. "The years passed and there was still no second son and so the issue became moot."

"But you must have felt betrayed, as good as cast off by your father?"

"Yes. If it had been a question of resettling the estate to provide for younger siblings, I would have had no objection, but he wanted to go much further than that. I would have been left with nothing from my father's family except his name. The Place, its contents, the tenant farms—everything would have gone to my half-brother."

"Would you have agreed?"

"I don't know. I doubt it now, but then? Had I refused, he might have banned me completely from the Place."

She turned her hand to clasp his. "It wasn't the material things as much as the sense of belonging."

"Precisely. But the damage was done. Ever since there has been a distance between us."

"Do you no longer regard the Place as home?"

"No. The Castle and Swanmere House are my homes now. Loring Place is where I grew up. I value it for my memories of my mother, but that is all."

Henry tossed his head at a buzzing fly and Rosa loosened the reins, telling him to walk on.

"The odd thing is," Julian said, "that when I came of

age, he insisted I claim the knighthood to which I was entitled as his eldest son under the Letters Patent. I must honour my true heritage, he said. Now, my grandfather wants me to promise to take the name of Swann when I succeed him, something my father would greatly resent."

"Poor Julian, you must feel torn between them."

"Sometimes," he admitted. "What should I do, Rosa?"

"Remember that you are your own man and do what you feel is right," she said stoutly. "You may owe a duty of filial affection to them both, but—*'to thine own self be true'*. If one or the other decides you have been false to him, then it is because his demands were unfair. The fault will be his, not yours."

*"O wise young judge!"*

"You are mixing your plays, sir," she said severely.

"Am I?" He smiled briefly. "What a stern preceptress you must have been. But, seriously, what would you recommend?"

She looked out at the rippling water. "It must be your decision," she said finally. "But while I like the idea of there still being Swanns at Swanmere, I can also appreciate your father's point of view. Must it be one or the other, Julian? Why not acknowledge both your heritages? You are as much your mother's son as your father's. 'Swann Loring' has a pleasant ring to it and is only three syllables, after all."

"A new beginning. That seems right." He took off his glove and gently touched her cheek. "Thank you, Rosa. I had not realised how much it bothered me."

She flicked a smile at him. "You're welcome."

The warmth of his bare fingers lingered, thawing the shield she had put up against an uninterested world. If he could confide in her, could she not confide in him? Not now, but later.

Rosa squinted against the midday sun and pointed with her whip at a flat boat on the mere. It was occupied by two boys with fishing rods and a tall man who stood at the back, steering by means of a long pole. "Are they the boys and Mr Musgrave?"

"Probably. Thomas mentioned they would take the boat out today."

"Do you think we could do it one day? I'm sure Chloe and Ann would love it, even if they do not want to fish."

"I don't see why not. We might even get up a party to go to Whittlesey Mere. It is much bigger than this—some five miles across. One can hire bigger boats and yachts there."

"That sounds exciting, but I like the idea of just floating peacefully here as well," she said dreamily.

Julian had a sudden image of her reclining on piled-up cushions at his feet while he poled their skiff to a secluded spot. She might sing or read to him as they drifted across the water. "We'll do both," he promised her. "Do you feel up to trying a trot for the last stretch?"

"Why not?"

Henry responded willingly, almost as if he knew they were nearing home, and they turned in to the stable yard. A groom came running to Henry's head. Julian jumped down and held out his hand to Rosa.

"Well done!"

She took it, her smile radiant. "Thank you for my lesson. I enjoyed it so much." She went to pat Henry's neck. "He was a perfect gentleman."

"Tomorrow we'll go riding," Julian said as they walked to the castle. "What are your plans for the rest of the day?"

"I'll stay indoors. It is very likely we shall have some callers this afternoon—we met so many people at church yesterday—and I should like to be on hand to support your grandmother, especially as the girls have gone for a walk with Miss Musgrave. I think I'll try the harpsichord; I want to see how it differs from the pianoforte."

# Chapter Twenty-one

"THIS IS VERY SNUG, JUST the four of us," Lord Swanmere announced. "You may carve me some of that ham, James," he said to the footman, "and we shall have some hock."

"Yes, my lord."

"Bring some soda water as well, James," Julian added. "Mixed with hock it is most refreshing," he told Rosa. "I think you might prefer it in the middle of the day."

"Especially when we are expecting callers. It would never do for them to find us tipsy."

He laughed. "I think you will be safe. Byron swears by it when he has overindulged."

"That must, of course, recommend it to me," she said drolly, helping herself to a dish of eggs.

"You are not an admirer of his, I take it?"

"No. I do not deny that he has written some beautiful passages but I have no patience with either his falsely archaic language or his style. Just listen:

"*Childe Harold was he hight:—but whence his name
And lineage long, it suits me not to say;*'

He strikes me as one who is supremely self-indulgent and that is reflected in his work."

"There can be no doubt of that," Julian agreed.

"Which of our modern poets do you prefer?" Lady Loring asked.

"Mr Wordsworth," she said immediately. "There sublime language is matched by nobility of mind."

"After such an encomium, you must supply us with an example, Miss Rosa," Swanmere said jovially. "What have you got for us, hey?"

"Will you accept a sonnet, my lord?"

"If you please. But you must tell us why you selected it."

"Just hear what he makes of the scene he viewed one morning while crossing Westminster Bridge—in the Dover coach, I believe. Such a commonplace occurrence, one would think, but not to one who has eyes to see.

*"'Earth hath not anything to show more fair:*

*Dull would he be of soul who could pass by*

*A sight so touching in its majesty:*

*This City now doth, like a garment, wear*

*The beauty of the morning; silent, bare,*

*Ships, towers, domes, theatres and temples lie*

*Open unto the fields, and to the sky;*

*All bright and glittering in the smokeless air.*

*Never did sun more beautifully steep*

*In his first splendour, valley, rock, or hill;*

*Ne'er saw I, never felt, a calm so deep!*
*The river glideth at his own sweet will:*
*Dear God! The very houses seem asleep;*
*And all that mighty heart is lying still!' "*

"Superb," Lady Loring said after a moment.

Lord Swanmere nodded agreement. "He teaches us to look about us with new eyes."

"You are more lenient to your favourite," Julian said teasingly. "'Doth' and 'glideth'—some would call that usage archaic."

She tilted her head and smiled at him. "Others would call some pedantic or sadly wanting in sensibility."

He grinned back. "Surely you must disapprove of excessive sensibility; it can only lead to self-indulgence."

She sighed dramatically. "*'Hoist with my own petard'.*"

"Have some hock and soda," he suggested, nodding to the footman who stood waiting to pour the wine.

"Things are progressing very nicely," Lady Loring said to Lord Swanmere later.

"What things?"

"Between Julian and Miss Rosa. Have you not noticed his interest in her?"

"His interest? No—not if you mean he is pursuing her."

"Surely you have no objection? You should be glad to see the boy settled."

"She is an estimable woman, I have never denied it. But—married to his sister's governess? I had hoped for a better match for him, my lady."

"A worldlier match, you mean. What additional advantage would that bring him? He wants neither money nor connections. She is a lady through and through with an elegance of mind and body that must appeal to anyone of discernment. To be sure, she has not moved so far in the first circles, but I see no problem in introducing her into them. She did very well during the May festivities, you will agree. The thing is, Swanmere, she will be happy to make her home here—and she will make him happy. I have never seen him as content as he is with her."

"That is true. What will his father say?"

"He can say very little after his own disastrous marriage," Sir Edward's mother said acerbically. "Julian is too old for a girl who has just come out. I don't approve of these May and September matches. Far better a modest lady who has no thought of marriage and is used to occupying herself fruitfully than an ape-leader who has been on the town this many years and only knows how to fritter away her time frivolously or a widow who looks to improve her circumstances."

"Are you sure she has no thought of marriage?"

"Not to Julian at any rate." Lady Loring smiled. "I remember when she first came to us, she blushed painfully when he spoke to her, but she soon grew out of that. If anything she looks upon him as an older brother. But I think—I hope—that she is beginning to drop her guard."

"Her guard?"

"The guard any young woman must maintain when she earns her living in other people's houses. She told me once— this was after she had been with us for several years—that before she left to take up her position as governess, her schoolmistress warned her that she must assume that the attentions of any gentleman she might encounter, either in her pupils' home or otherwise in the course of her duties, were dishonourable. A happy ending such as *Pamela*'s—if indeed hers may be described as such—did not occur outside the pages of novels."

"Harsh but true, I suppose."

"So now, before she can even consider the possibility of Julian's interest in her, she must dismantle the defences behind which she has sheltered all these years. Only then can she see him in a new light."

"She seems younger here than at the Place. There, I would have said she was more than thirty. I want to see my great-grandson before I die, my lady."

"As do I, Swanmere. Miss Rosa is eight-and-twenty, which is young enough. She is in very good health and anyone who has seen her with Chloe must be persuaded that she will be an excellent mother."

"You have convinced me," Swanmere said. "What can we do to drive the affair forward?"

"Very little except make it easy for them to spend some time together. You did well, placing Mrs Overton at your side at table."

He laughed. "That was to remove her from his, it is true, but not in order to place Miss Rosa there. You were quick to seize that opportunity."

She inclined her head in acknowledgement. "I am as fond of her as if she were my granddaughter and should be delighted to welcome her as my granddaughter in truth. Yes, Dover?"

"Miss Fancourt asked me to let you know that Mrs and Miss Aubrey have called, my lady."

Lady Loring struggled to her feet. "I'll come at once."

# Chapter Twenty-two

Jenkins cautiously lifted the linen towel out of the bowl of steaming water. Wincing a little, she wrung it out as tightly as she could, folded it and wrapped it first in another towel and then in a fine woollen shawl.

"Here you are, ma'am."

Mrs Overton laid the warm pad on her lower belly. "Thank you, Jenkins. I don't know why I must suffer so. It would almost be worth being with child again, to be spared."

Jenkins smiled sourly. There would be no question of her taking to her bed each month—that privilege was reserved for ladies. "Will you take another dose of the tisane, ma'am?"

"Very well. Pour me some ratafia as well to take the taste away."

There was a tap on the door. Jenkins opened it to find Miss Fancourt's maid on the threshold. "What do you want?" she asked gruffly.

"Miss Fancourt sent me to enquire how Mrs Overton

went on and ask if there was anything she could do for her."

Jenkins glanced over to the bed. Her mistress, who was listening avidly to the clear, young voice, raised an eyebrow and shook her head firmly.

"Madam is resting and has no need of anything," she said curtly, shutting the door in the girl's face.

"Hmph. You were quite right to snub the chit. One would think the Fancourt woman was mistress of Swanmere, the way she puts herself forward." Mrs Overton sipped the ratafia with relish. "I don't know what is in your witches' brew, but it is effective, Jenkins. I won't risk going down this evening, but I should be better by tomorrow."

"Shall I have them bring up a tray, ma'am?"

"Yes. Nothing too heavy." Mrs Overton settled herself against her pillows. "How did the other ladies occupy themselves today?"

"I believe Miss Fancourt went out with Sir Julian this morning. Later she and Lady Loring received callers together with his lordship."

"Drat it!"

Jenkins hurried to blot the spilled ratafia.

"Leave that and pour me another glass," Mrs Overton said crossly. "Governesses receiving callers indeed! I am surprised my cousin Swanmere permits it."

To Julian's relief, Meg did not come down to dinner. The boys were full of their boating expedition and Julian offered to explore the possibility of an outing to Whittlesey Mere, a suggestion that was met with great acclaim.

It was Ann's turn to provide the after-dinner entertainment and when they had gathered in the drawing-room, she said, "If you have no objection, I shall not continue with *Mansfield Park* tonight but leave it until tomorrow, when I hope Mamma will be feeling more the thing."

"Very proper, Miss Ann," Lady Loring commented. "For all her complaints, she is eager enough to dissect the characters and the plot. What do you propose instead?"

"I mean to put everyone to work, ma'am. I have found a collection of old songs and we shall learn a most amusing catch from France. It depicts two country-women boasting how handsome and good their husbands are."

Lady Loring snorted. "How strange! But that is the French for you. You must excuse Lord Swanmere and me, if you please. We shall play a game of piquet and later be your audience."

"Of course, ma'am. Chloe and I copied out the parts earlier so if the rest of you would join me in the music room?"

Ann lost no time in marshalling her forces and soon four couples had retreated to separate corners to rehearse. Robert, who was paired with Rosa, was struggling with the strange language, Julian noticed, and she explained it to him, murmuring the translation so that he giggled at the thought that a good husband was one who did the housework and fed the hens. She laughed with him and for an instant their two faces were alive with mirth, their expressions so similar that Julian caught his breath.

Perhaps there was a distant relationship, Julian said to himself as he prepared for bed. That must be it! She had said she knew nothing of her parents' families and some resemblances recurred down the generations. Cheered, he began to unwind his neckcloth, but suddenly stopped. That would mean the Kennards were strangers to her but at Ransford she had said that she knew the father slightly. Had her frozen distress earlier that evening been due to his unforeseen arrival? Later, he had importuned her to speak to him. Julian had intervened but had only caught snippets of their conversation. *'For the boy's sake,'* Kennard had said. And she had answered, *'You mean my—'*. She had broken off when she saw Julian.

Swallowing an oath, he hastily removed the rest of his clothes, shrugged into a banyan and dismissed his valet for the night.

An image of Rosa swathed in sumptuous brown silk rose before him. Her shoulder touched his and her eyes sparkled with suppressed mirth as they squeezed beneath arched hands in *Sir Roger. Tall enough to meet his eyes, intelligent enough not to bore him and with that certain something that meant he could imagine spending the rest of his life with her*—it was no longer an anonymous description but a vivid portrait of the lady he had hoped to make his wife.

But now? The dates fit—Robert was eleven and it was just over ten years since she came to the Place. She had come to them directly from school, she had said. But a complaisant schoolmistress, or one who feared for the reputation of her establishment, might have been prevailed upon to overlook a fall from grace and provide her pupil with a certificate of character before sending her to a remote house on the other side of the country. And yet, he thought fondly, despite Rosa's evident distress at his unexpected reappearance in her life, she had not rebuffed the boy when he turned to her. Was the maternal link so strong that he had, unknowingly, recognised it? Who could blame her for availing herself of an unforeseen opportunity to know her lost son? He paused in his pacing to pour a glass of whisky, swallowing half in one gulp.

There were many ugly names for a woman who had borne another man's by-blow. Swearing violently, he hurled the glass into the fireplace. He would thrash any man who used them of her. He would not condemn her, but did it change things?

Rosa sang to herself as she settled to write her journal. "*Il est bel et bon, bon, bon, bon, bon, commère; il est bel et bon, bon, bon, bon, bon, mon mari.*"

What an enjoyable evening it had been. Ann had perhaps been a trifle ambitious in her choice of song but they had all set about it with a will, the more experienced singers helping the less proficient. Robert, who didn't know any French and had had very little musical tuition, was lost at first but his quick ear had helped him pick up his part. The group's first attempts at the whole had failed as they dissolved in laughter when required to imitate the clucking of chickens but finally they had got through it *con brio* and without any mishaps.

"Now that we are in good voice, let us sing another," Mr Haughton had suggested. "What about *Come Let Us All A-Maying Go*? That has a cuckoo as well."

They had sung that and *The British Grenadiers* before turning to riddles and rhymes. It had been the most light-hearted evening at Swanmere so far. It was strange how the absence of one person could make such a difference.

She must start her account of the day with the morning. Unable to resist, she got up and went to the drawer where she had stored Julian's gift. She took the gloves out and gently smoothed them, a soft smile on her lips. How kind, how thoughtful he was.

The inhabitants of Swanmere Castle woke to grey skies and a steady, drumming rain that offered no promise of ceasing. There would be no riding today, Rosa thought glumly as she told Lambton to put out a warmer gown and her green kerseymere spencer.

Chloe was equally dispirited. "Ann will vanish into the music room, I have no doubt," she complained, "but what are we to do?"

"What would you do on a wet day at home?" Rosa asked patiently. Really, it was time the girl learned to rely upon herself.

"I don't know—write letters, read, do some needlework, practise my music, read to Grandmamma. What about you?"

"The same, more or less," Rosa admitted. "I have started to keep a journal here but generally write it before retiring. I might read some French or German or I might draw or paint. At home, I assist my cousin Mrs Chidlow as she suffers grievously from rheumatism and the wet weather makes it worse."

"It's very dull being a woman, isn't it, Rosa?"

"Say, rather, being a lady," Rosa answered wryly. "A farmer's wife, for example, has enough to do running her household and looking after her children."

"Like Nanny Crewe. I'll read to Grandmamma after breakfast and then start embroidering the panels for a new reticule. Perhaps the sun will come out later and we can go for a walk."

"Let us hope so. In the meantime, I'll try to sketch the great hall."

"I'll bring my embroidery there and keep you company. There will be as good light at the windows as anywhere."

Robert and Hal rushed into the great hall, stumbling to a halt when they spotted Rosa and Chloe intent on their tasks. Mr Musgrave followed more slowly.

"Oh. We didn't think there would be anyone here," Hal said. "We were going to play marbles."

"Will we be in your way?" Rosa asked, surprised.

"No, no, but would we not disturb you?"

"I think the hall is large enough to accommodate all of us. What will you do for a ring?"

"I have some chalk tied to precisely the correct length of string so that I can draw a circle," he said proudly. "I don't think Cousin Julian would object to some light marks on the stone floor, do you?"

"I am sure he wouldn't." Rosa thought it more likely that Julian would get down on his knees to play with the boys.

While Hal set about his preparations, Robert came over to look at Rosa's sketch.

"I wanted to draw the rafters, but today is so grey and murky that there isn't really enough light to provide contrast," she said.

"Why not imagine it?" Hal suggested from the floor. "You could make it more gothick, with something emerging from the shadows."

Chloe looked over. "Yes, Rosa. A mad monk or—"

Rosa smiled to herself. "A knight clad in inky armour?"

"Yes! And a fair maiden fleeing from him, her visage ghastly and pale."

Hal jumped up. "Hang a blood-red curtain at the top of the stairs so that he appears from behind it, and have bats swooping around the gloomy rafters."

"Open one window so that a gibbous moon lights the awful scene. And don't forget the owl flying across it," Mr Musgrave put in, grinning.

"Who is our hero?" Rosa asked. "Who will save our fair maiden?"

"Her trusty squire and her faithful hound," Robert said at once. "The squire pushes the knight down the stairs. Lying on the floor in his armour he is as helpless as an upturned turtle. The hound holds the monk at bay until the squire rushes over with the knight's sword and dispatches him."

"Chloe and I were wondering what to do on such a wet day. Why don't we write the story together and illustrate it?"

"With coloured plates?" Robert demanded eagerly.

"Why not?"

"Miss Fancourt, if Robert and I each write a copy, would you draw two sets of pictures so we could have one each?" Hal asked hopefully.

"If you wish. We may not finish it today, though."

Julian signed the last letter and stretched. "I'll leave the rest to you, Adrian. I must see to my guests."

The drawing-room was empty but Ann looked over from the harpsichord when he came into the music room. "Try the great hall, Cousin," she recommended. "Miss Fancourt said something about sketching there this morning."

Whistling, he retraced his steps. If she was immersed in her work, they could have a tray sent in, just for the two of them. He opened the door to the great hall to a burst of laughter from the vivacious group gathered around the big table.

"What colour is Clara's gown?" Rosa asked.

"White," the boys said as one.

"A white underskirt and long, full sleeves caught tight at intervals with blue ribands," Chloe elaborated, "and a blue gown confined by a golden girdle. Her flowing locks are covered by a lace veil."

"The monk's cowl must fall back to reveal skull-like features," Mr Musgrave said solemnly, "And his fingers should be long and bony."

"A skeletal monk!" Chloe shuddered with delight. "That is a very good suggestion, Thomas," she commended Mr Musgrave before continuing in her most dramatic tones, "his eyes are orbs of blackest fire and his lips look as if they have been dipped in blood."

"But why is he there?" Robert asked. "It is the knight who is pursuing Clara."

This pragmatic question reduced his listeners to puzzled silence.

"The inky knight has summoned the monk to perform the marriage ceremony," Rosa said finally. "Clara's mother is dead and her father has gone hunting, leaving the knight and her squire to protect her. But the knight is overtaken by his evil passions and decides to take advantage of the situation to force Clara into marriage."

"Because," Hal cried triumphantly, "the monk is an emissary of the devil and the knight has sold his soul to him in return for gaining Clara as his bride."

He jumped up and bowed as the others broke into applause.

"That would be a truly splendid scene," Robert pronounced. "Set in a gloomy grotto. The knight must kneel before an inverted cross and swear in his own blood."

"Dripped onto a volume from the Minerva Press, I assume," Julian interjected.

"We are recording the Dread Secret of Swanmere," Rosa informed him.

He recoiled, a hand to his heart. "Not the tale that must never be told?" he asked in hollow tones.

"No, not that one," she reassured him. "That—er, hasn't been told yet, you see."

He brushed the back of his hand across his brow. "I am immeasurably relieved," he declared and went to sit beside her. "How far have you got?"

Thomas Musgrave looked up from his notes. "I think we have the whole story now."

"Except the real end," Chloe said. "What happens afterwards?"

"When Clara's father returns, he knights the squire," Hal said at once, "and offers him her hand in marriage."

The others nodded approval but Rosa asked quietly, "Would that be a happy ending for Clara?"

"What do you mean?" Chloe demanded.

"Her father doesn't give her a choice. She is still young. She might not love the squire; she could be in love with someone else or not yet have met the man she would like to marry."

Chloe frowned. "I wouldn't like it if Papa just decided I was to marry someone or offered me to him as a reward."

"The squire might not want to get married so young either," Robert pointed out. "Now that he has won his spurs, he would probably prefer to go on a quest."

"They are both young. Perhaps one day, when they have spread their wings and seen something of the world, they will meet again and the time will be right for them to fall in love," Julian suggested.

Hal frowned. "So we should leave the ending unresolved?"

"Not exactly unresolved, but still open," Thomas suggested. "End with the squire being knighted and riding off into the world. Who knows what adventures he may have."

"Why can't Clara go into the world too?" Chloe asked. "Why should she have to sit at home by herself when her father goes hunting?"

Rosa nodded approvingly. "Perhaps he realises that he has neglected her and arranges for her to attend his overlord's wife as a maid of honour. The overlord would command a much larger household and she would learn how to go on in the world."

Chloe was satisfied. "Her father could escort her there. The last picture should be of them setting out together."

# Chapter Twenty-three

"ARE YOU RELATED TO THE Berkshire Fancourts, Miss Fancourt?"

Meg, her health restored, broke in on a lively discussion about some depiction of a monk of all things. Lady Loring had not come to breakfast and Meg had assumed the mantle of the lady of the house, issuing instructions to the footman and directing the conversation as she saw fit.

Miss Fancourt met her eyes across the table. "Not that I am aware of, Mrs Overton. My father's family is from Dorset."

"And your mother's as well? Pray forgive my curiosity— it is strange how often one discovers a distant connection, is it not?"

"Indeed. My mother was a Miss Bletsoe. I believe the family was originally from Bedfordshire. What of you, Mrs Overton? Your mother and Sir Julian's were cousins, I know. Was your father from this part of the world?"

"No, from Northamptonshire," Meg said shortly. "I was Miss Eardley before I married."

"Then I think it unlikely we shall discover ourselves to be long-lost cousins, Mrs Overton," Miss Fancourt said coolly as she helped herself to a slice of pound cake.

"Another cup, miss?" The footman was immediately at her side with the chocolate pot.

"Please, Matthew," she answered with a noticeably friendlier smile and then turned back to Chloe to resume her interrupted conversation.

Such impertinence! Meg fumed as she returned to her bedchamber where she immediately went to the little drawer that held Mr Kennard's letter. Really, she owed it to Julian to discover what sort of a woman had inveigled herself into his family. Flown with righteousness, she removed the paper and sat down at the little writing table to unfold it carefully.

*Dear Rosa,*

*You refused to talk to me last night and it has become clear that I shall not see you before my departure this morning. I therefore write to beg your indulgence and forbearance on behalf of Robert who is both innocent and ignorant of all that happened between us. What is past is past. Say nothing to him of it, I implore you. What good would it do to drag up past injuries and shatter his faith in his father?*

*As I watch him grow taller each passing year, I regret more and more my treatment of you. There is little I can do to make amends but you should know that you can apply to me at any time if you find yourself in distress.*

*I scribble this note in haste and shall entrust it to Mrs Overton.*

*Be kind to Robert, I beg you, Rosa.*
> *Yours etc.*
>> *Stephen Kennard*

Meg moistened her lips as she avidly reread the letter. Here was the proof that she was right! *Robert is both innocent and ignorant of all that happened between us.* It could only mean one thing—but best to make doubly sure. There's no need to be hasty, she admonished herself as she meticulously returned the letter to its original form and placed it in the drawer. Her good humour was completely restored when Jenkins arrived with an invitation to play a hand of tredille with Lady Loring and Lord Swanmere in her ladyship's sitting-room.

"Finished," Chloe announced triumphantly from her seat at the big desk in the library which, for the past days, had become the scriptorium, as Thomas Musgrave described it. Lord Swanmere had raised no objection to the invasion of his sanctum but, after observing the proceedings with an indulgent smile for half an hour or so, had announced that he would see how her ladyship went on. Since then, he was more likely to be found in her sitting-room.

"So are we," Robert declared.

Rosa looked up from where she was inscribing a title page in ornate calligraphy. "We should leave everything spread out until tomorrow to be sure it is completely dry before we collate the pages."

"I shall never come into the great hall again without wondering what might lurk in the rafters or conceal itself at the top of the stairs," Julian remarked as he admired the carefully penned sheets and dramatic illustrations that perfectly captured the high spirited embellishments and exaggerations of the youthful story-tellers. "I think I must request another copy that will be placed with the annals of the castle and have you all sign it."

"You must write the story yourself, in your best copperplate, not your usual scrawl," Chloe said. "Nothing less will do justice to Rosa's and my paintings. Don't you agree, Rosa?"

"I'll rule the lines for you," Hal offered with an impish grin.

Rosa shook her head. "Better let Robert do it; he is less slapdash than you are, Hal."

Julian's eyes gleamed. "Perhaps we could come to an agreement that you would write it for me too, Robert. You have a very neat hand."

Robert replied gravely, "I should be honoured to do it for you, Sir Julian, to say thank you for permitting me to accompany Hal on his visit here."

"He had no choice," the irrepressible Hal put in. "I told Mamma we could not come without you."

"Then I am doubly in his debt," his friend retorted.

"You are not in my debt at all, Robert; you are a most welcome guest," Julian assured him. "But I shall accept your offer of assistance."

"It was kind of you to take Robert seriously," Rosa said after the others had departed.

"He is a serious lad," Julian replied. "Hal tends to be as frivolous as his mother." He stood and stretched. "I'll have them send in a nuncheon for us here and then, if it has stopped raining, we shall see what you have remembered of your driving lessons."

"Could we not ride instead? Poor Captain must be longing to leave his stall."

"And poor Rosa, as well?" he teased her. "Why not?"

❧

"Have you written to your parents, Robert?" Meg asked before dinner that evening

The boy looked conscience-stricken. "No, Mrs Overton, I suppose I should."

"I am sure they will wish to know how you go on," she said. "Have you brothers and sisters?"

"A sister and a brother, but their mother is not my mother. She died when I was born."

"That is sad. What was her name?"

"Mrs Kennard."

Meg ignored the little ripple of amusement at this innocent reply. "Yes, but I mean her name before that. A lady changes her name when she marries. I was Margaret Eardley, for example."

"Oh. I suppose I knew that, but I never thought about it, if you know what I mean. I never heard what my mother's name was. My father doesn't talk about her."

There was a tiny intake of breath and Miss Fancourt raised a handkerchief to her lips. Meg looked over to where she gazed fixedly at her lap, as if to hide her face. When she raised her head again, she was pale and her features void of all expression.

That settles it, Meg said to herself. Now I must wait for the right moment. What would be better—to mention it confidentially to Julian or to make her disgrace public, as she deserves?

"We'll write letters tomorrow," Thomas Musgrave decreed. "To whom shall you write, Hal?"

"My uncle. He always answers, and generally puts half a guinea under the seal."

❧

"These past weeks have shown me the disadvantage of being an only child," Julian remarked to Rosa the next day as they sat alone in the library. "I had not realised how much more entertaining and stimulating it is to be part of a larger family group. What about you? Did you ever regret not having brothers and sisters?"

"Frequently," she said wistfully. "I had schoolfriends of course, but it is not the same as a family of one's own." She took a deep breath. "Julian. I want to talk to you about Robert. I've never been able to tell anyone before; it has been too painful—"

She broke off, looking so distressed that Julian longed to comfort her. Her reaction to Meg's question to Robert about his mother had convinced him of her relationship to the boy. Society said she should be shunned as a result but was it fair to judge her more strictly than he judged himself? He did not consider himself a rake but, like any gentleman, he had had his share of liaisons. He did not believe that these previous amours made him unfit for marriage. To the best of his knowledge, he had not fathered a child, but could he be sure? He had never seduced an innocent but was there a woman, carelessly encountered and as carelessly left, who had had to pay a high price for their pleasure? What was past was past, for him as well as for her. He was honoured that she wished to confide in him but at least he could spare her having to divulge the whole story, especially as he was not sure he wished to hear it.

What was Kennard's role in this? Had he just adopted the child or was he also her seducer? Julian's fists balled at the thought. Seducer or worse? Poor Rosa. Orphaned, homeless and not much older than Chloe was now, she would have been easy prey to an unscrupulous villain.

"There is no need to tell me, Rosa," he said gently. "I have guessed your secret."

"Guessed? How could you?" she asked faintly.

"There is a considerable resemblance between you and Robert. Oh, your colouring is not the same, but there are many similarities, for example the setting of your eyes or the way you laugh or hold your heads. Once I had spotted one, I soon saw more."

"Oh! Do you think others might have noticed it?"

"I don't think so. I doubt if anyone else observes you as closely as I do—and I knew how distressed you were by Kennard's presence at the Ransfords'."

She flushed faintly but did not pursue this remark. "I had accepted I would never know him but now fate has thrown us together and I wonder whether I should tell him the truth."

Julian could not think this a good idea. "That is understandable," he began,

She did not let him finish but continued in a rush, "He has told me of his unhappiness at home—how his stepmother rejects him—and I would like him to know there is someone who cares for him, someone to whom he can turn if he is in distress. On the other hand, I fear he would be upset if he learned of his father's treatment of me. He has come to like me, I think, and I don't want to be the cause of a further estrangement between them. I do not seek revenge, Julian," she assured him earnestly. "I have long since come to terms with what happened. I just want what is best for Robert."

He came to kneel beside her chair. "Rosa, my dearest Rosa, I do not doubt that for an instant. However, I strongly advise you to let sleeping dogs lie. Revealing the truth now would bring little benefit and could cause a lot of pain. You are a good friend to the boy. He clearly admires and respects you. Is that not much more than you ever hoped for?"

"I suppose it is," she said on a long sigh. "But he is my only blood-kin, Julian. I had not realised how important it was to me." She came abruptly to her feet and walked to the window where she stood with her back to him.

He followed and took her into his arms. "Poor Rosa." For a moment she didn't react, then she rested against him. His arms closed triumphantly about her.

"Poor Rosa," he said again. "You have been strong for so long. Will you not lean on me; let me support you through this final challenge?"

"I shall have to say goodbye to him and never see or hear of him again.

"Perhaps when he is an adult you can tell him the whole story but now is not the right time."

"But how shall I find him again? His stepmother talks of sending him to the Military Academy at Woolwich and from there he could be sent anywhere."

"You would be able to follow his progress in the *Gazette*," Julian pointed out. "And I can take an interest in the boy. I like him and it will do him no harm to have a patron."

She turned in his arms and looked up at him, wide-eyed. "Would you really do that, Julian? And let me know how he does?"

"Of course."

Her lips quivered and he gently touched them with his own. The faint movement stilled but she did not draw away and he kissed her more firmly. At first she passively accepted his caress but suddenly her lips clung to his and she gripped his shoulders. When he lifted his head, she was flushed and dreamy-eyed and her fingers went instinctively to her mouth as if his still rested there. He captured her hand and raised it to his lips but she snatched it away at the sound of the opening door.

Julian moved a step in front of Rosa and looked over to the housekeeper. "Yes, Godin?"

"A person by the name of Hughes wishes to speak to you, Sir Julian. She says she is Lady Loring's abigail but her ladyship is not with her. She is however travelling in her ladyship's carriage, driven by her coachman. She seems quite distressed."

Rosa gasped. "Hughes has been with Lady Loring as long as I know them. Something must be very wrong or she would not have come here on her own."

Julian nodded. "I had better see her then. Where have you put her, Godin?"

"In the muniments room, sir."

"We'll be there shortly. Thank you."

As soon as the door closed behind the housekeeper, he turned to Rosa. "You will come with me, won't you? I imagine you will be much better able to deal with her than I will."

Still half-dazed by Julian's kiss, Rosa preceded him through a small door into a corner room that was lit by two windows and lined floor to ceiling with shelves and presses filled with books and folios. Mr Haughton sat writing at a desk while Hughes perched on a chair at the wall beside the door to the hall. She was huddled in a large shawl that covered a Pomona-green robe-pelisse of fine wool. Rosa recognised it as one Lady Loring had worn some three years previously.

"Can you take that into the library, Adrian?"

"Certainly, Sir Julian.

Hughes didn't seem to recognise Rosa for a moment and then a look of incredulous relief crossed her pinched face.

"Miss Fancourt!" She darted across the room to seize Rosa's hands. "I hadn't expected to see you—thank God, miss—oh, I don't know what I am to do."

"Sit down and let us know what the trouble is, and then we shall see how we can help you." Rosa urged the maid forward to a chair Julian had placed in front of the desk. "Will you not remove your bonnet and shawl?"

"No, thank you, miss. I'm that cold—I can't get warm."

Rosa looked at Julian over Hughes's bent head. "Perhaps some tea?"

He nodded and disappeared into the library while Rosa took a seat beside the maid, still holding her hand in a comforting clasp.

"What has happened?" Julian asked when he returned to the muniments room. "Is my stepmother in good health?"

Hughes laughed harshly. "As to that, I suppose she's well enough. It's just—well the long and the short of it is, sir, that she has eloped."

"Eloped?" he repeated blankly.

"Yes, with Lord Stephen FitzCharles."

"What? How the deuce did she come to meet him?"

The maid shrugged. "I don't know why he was in Harrogate, sir. He could have met my mistress at a ball or some other entertainment in any one of the hotels."

"When did this happen—the elopement, I mean?"

"The day before yesterday, sir. He had his yacht at Bridlington and they left to get the evening tide." Hughes began to tremble and tears gathered in her eyes.

"I thought we was going home. She told me to pack the trunks and tell John Coachman she needed the carriage. And then, once we left, she told me different. We was only taking her to where *he* was waiting with his travelling chariot—at the side of the road it was, about four miles on—and then she said I wasn't to go with her—she would hire a new maid in France."

She stopped talking when the tea-tray arrived and closed her hands around the cup, almost shuddering with relief at its heat. By the time she had drained it she seemed less tense and accepted a second cup with a murmur of thanks.

"Her ladyship signalled to John to pull up and her trunks were moved to the other carriage—and off they went, as bold as brass." She dabbed at her eyes with her handkerchief. "I beg your pardon, Sir Julian, for coming here, but I didn't know where to turn. Twenty years I've been with her, since her marriage. I dressed her for her wedding, I did, and looked after her all these years and she turns me off like that." She snapped her fingers dramatically.

"Oh, she was as sweet as honey, thanking me and saying that she knew I wouldn't want to leave England, and she gave me my quarter's wages, and another quarter instead of my notice, but I knew she wanted to be rid of me. John Coachman was to take the carriage home and I might travel with him as far as I liked, she said. And she gave us money for the horses and the postboys and two letters, one for Sir Edward and one for Miss Chloe." She handed her cup and saucer to Rosa and took the sealed missives from her reticule.

After a cursory glance, Julian dropped them onto the desk.

"Do you happen to know how Lady Loring explained her departure to her mother?" Rosa asked.

"I don't, miss. It's most likely she let her think she was going home, otherwise she would have had Lord Stephen collect her at the house, wouldn't she?"

"So there was nothing to cause talk in Harrogate?"

"I don't think so, miss. John and I didn't say anything, neither."

"I am grateful for your discretion, Hughes," Julian said. "My housekeeper will look after you for the moment, but all she or anyone else needs to know is that Lady Loring sent you here on an errand. Nothing more. We'll talk again tomorrow."

"Yes sir. I won't say a word, I promise." She yawned. "Oh, excuse me, sir."

"You're very tired, Hughes," Rosa said. "Would you like to lie down?"

The maid nodded. "I didn't sleep these past two nights, miss."

"We'll ask Mrs Godin to find you a bed and I suggest you retire as soon as you have had something to eat."

"What a coil!" Julian said when they were alone again. "I'll have to travel to the Place tomorrow and tell my father. But what of Chloe? Should I say anything to her before I leave? He might prefer not to tell her what has happened;

just let her assume he has refused her mother permission to return to the Place. Have I the right to prevent him from doing so?"

"She will never forgive you if she discovers you—or he—have deliberately deceived her. A lie by omission is still a lie."

"Even if you think it is better for the person concerned to remain in ignorance of the truth?"

"Better for whom?" Rosa demanded, conscious of her own dilemma about Robert. "Sir Edward is a proud man. He may wish to spare himself the embarrassment of admitting that his wife has left him; that he has lost control of her, if you like. But would it really be better for Chloe, or indeed for him, if she believes he is keeping her mother from her? I know she hopes he will forgive her and allow her to come home. What will she think of her father if he remains obdurate, as she will see it?"

"You mean she might blame him for her mother's continued absence?"

"I think it very likely. But apart from that, while you may be able to hush things up for the moment, sooner or later the truth will out. Lord Stephen is not unknown in society, is he?"

"On the contrary! He's the younger brother of the previous Duke of Gracechurch, uncle of the present one, and one of Prinnie's set into the bargain."

Rosa made a face. "He will see no need to make a secret of a new mistress. Word will get back to England quickly enough."

"I fear you are right, especially as so many of the *ton* have moved to the continent since the peace. I'll tell Chloe—it is better if she is prepared. Should I give her her mother's letter?"

Rosa took longer to answer this question. At last she said, "I think you have to, don't you? She is no longer a child and it may help her accept what has happened. While Lady Loring was not a particularly demonstrative parent, I never had the impression that she wanted anything other than the best for her daughter. What happened that day in the cottage was completely out of character for her. She did not constantly set Chloe down, as Mrs Overton does Ann, and hired the best music and drawing masters for her."

"The Overtons. Not one of my best ideas," he sighed. "Without them or, to be fair, without Meg, everything would be much easier. How are we to get through dinner, for instance? Can we wait to tell Chloe until afterwards?"

"It might be best, but what if she learns that her mother's servants are here? Their presence cannot be hidden—too many will already be aware of the carriage and how Hughes introduced herself. And who knows what the coachman has been saying."

Julian looked at the clock. "Leave him to me. I'll have a quick word with him and then go to my grandmother. Can you bring Chloe to her sitting-room in about thirty minutes? We'll break the news to her there."

# Chapter Twenty-four

"WELL? HAVE YOU FINALLY MADE Miss Rosa an offer?" Julian's grandmother demanded as she swept into her sitting-room. "I can't think of anything else so important that you would disturb me when I am dressing for dinner."

Despite his satisfaction that his grandmother clearly approved of Rosa, Julian did not allow himself to be distracted. "I'm sorry, Grandmother," he said soberly, "but I fear I am the bearer of ill news."

She turned white and collapsed onto the sofa. "Who is it? Edward? Or has something happened to Eloisa or her family? Tell me quickly, Julian!"

"No, no, ma'am. It's nothing like that. My stepmother has eloped to the continent."

"The devil she has! What fool was mad enough to take her?"

He grinned at this trenchant remark. "Lord Stephen FitzCharles."

"Gracechurch's uncle? A charming rake, but I suppose an improvement on Purdue. Have you told Chloe?"

"Not yet. Rosa is bringing her down here so that we can tell her together."

"How did you find out? Did your father write?"

He shook his head. "Her maid came here from Harrogate in the Loring carriage. I must go to the Place tomorrow."

"To tell Edward? If it weren't for the scandal, I would say he is well rid of her."

"Perhaps, ma'am, but Chloe must be our first concern."

Dazed, Chloe looked from her brother to her grandmother to Rosa. "I don't understand. I thought you eloped to get married. Mamma is married already."

"It can also mean just to run away with someone, as your mother has done," Rosa put in.

"Run away for good? Do you mean Mamma will never come back?"

"As to that, we don't know. But—Chloe, the sad truth is that even if she returns to England and seeks his forgiveness, it is highly unlikely your father will take her back into his home. It would be too much to ask of any husband. It is not her first such escapade, after all," the dowager explained.

"Not take her back? But—shall I never see her again?"

Julian put his arm around his sister. "We don't know, pet. It depends on so many imponderables that we cannot say. Who knows what may happen in the future?"

"That is perhaps true but it would be foolish to raise false hopes. With her departure, she cuts herself off from you—from all of us," Lady Loring stated. "She will never again be received in polite society and it would be ruinous if you were known to associate with her, especially if you wish to make a respectable marriage."

Chloe smoothed the tassels of the reticule on her lap. Without looking up, she asked, "What if Papa divorced her and she married this Lord Stephen?"

Lady Loring was adamant. "She would still remain at the edge of society. There could be no question of her being received at court, for example, and no decent woman would want to have anything to do with her."

Life at the edge of polite society could be quite amusing, Julian thought impiously, and in years to come it might be possible for Chloe to meet her mother privately. But that was for the future. Now he held his sister close.

"How could she simply turn her back on me?" she asked piteously. "Three months ago she was planning for my come-out and now she says, 'I have no daughter'."

"She sent you a letter," Julian told her. "Perhaps you will understand better when you have read it."

Chloe shook her head. "I don't want it."

"Why don't I leave it with Rosa? You can ask her for it when you are ready."

"You don't have to decide anything tonight," Rosa said compassionately. "I am sure Julian would make our excuses in the drawing-room. He can say you are suffering from a migraine and I have stayed to look after you."

Chloe looked at Julian. "May I? I don't think I could face anyone tonight."

"Of course you may, pet," he said, hugging her. "Tomorrow I must drive to the Place to tell our father what has occurred. I'll return as quickly as I can."

"Very well," Chloe said listlessly. She began to rub her arms as if she were cold.

"Come, my dear," Rosa said gently.

Julian got to his feet. "I'll come up after dinner to see how you go on, if I may."

"Do, Julian. I can't think just now."

Lady Loring rose laboriously and opened her arms to her granddaughter. "Good night, my dearest girl. You have had a shock as we all have, but remember you are not alone. We love you, as does your father."

Chloe clung to her for a moment and then went to hug Julian.

"I'll walk with you to the stairs," he said, tucking her hand into his arm.

As soon as they reached the haven of their sitting-room, Chloe flung herself into Rosa's arms. Rosa drew her down onto the chaise longue and held her, murmuring soothingly while she sobbed her heart out.

Finally the girl sat up. "I'm sorry, Rosa. She's not worth my tears, is she?"

"Perhaps not, but her transgression does not debase your love or make your hurt at being abandoned less painful. If anything, the knowledge that you were so deceived in her must make it worse."

"I just can't understand her—first Mr Purdue and now this Lord Stephen. Do you think there were others we know nothing about?"

"I cannot say."

"We'd never have known about Mr Purdue if we hadn't burst into the cottage that day. If we hadn't surprised her, Papa would not have sent her away and she would never have met Lord Stephen."

"We have already discussed this, Chloe," Rosa said firmly. "If they hadn't been there, we could not have surprised them. It was your mother's choice to meet Mr Purdue in the cottage, just as it was her choice to elope with Lord Stephen."

"I know," Chloe wailed, "but somehow I would rather believe it was my fault she had to go away than that she decided she didn't love me enough to stay." She paused, startled. "When I say that, it seems very foolish."

"No. As children we assume that our parents are everything that is wise and good and that they will ensure that nothing bad can ever happen to us. It is very frightening when we first realise how little control we have over our lives or that the parent we love unquestioningly may not always put us first. It happened to me when my mother remarried and I was sent away to school. Like you, I felt I was being punished although I had done nothing wrong."

"That's it exactly," Chloe cried. "It's one thing if one is deprived of a mother by fate, as Julian was. But for our mother to choose not to be with us—"

"Is very bitter," Rosa finished. "I could mourn my father but I resented my mother's preferring a new husband to me. But—and, in saying this, I do not want to condone or excuse Lady Loring's behaviour—later I came to understand that my mother was also a woman who had her own life, separate from me."

"Your father was dead," Chloe pointed out. "Mamma still has her husband. That's a big difference."

"I agree."

Chloe yawned. "I think I'll lie down for a little, Rosa. All the crying has given me a headache."

"I'll help you into a dressing gown. Wash your face and I'll make a lavender compress for your forehead."

"You always did that for me when I was ill," Chloe said with a wan smile.

"Shall I bring up a tray later, Miss Fancourt?" Lambton asked before she left the tulip suite. She had helped Rosa out of her evening dress and into a morning gown with long sleeves and then tiptoed into Chloe's bedroom to tidy her things.

"Do, Lambton," Rosa said wearily, "but at Cook's convenience. I have very little appetite and I imagine Miss Loring feels the same."

Unable to settle, she walked to the window. The western sky was streaked with red. They all longed for an improvement in the weather although between paying and receiving calls and their various indoor pursuits, the house-party had generally managed to keep cheerful and occupied.

Two additional morning readings of *Mansfield Park* had seen poor Fanny Price returned in disgrace to her childhood home in Portsmouth. Even Mrs Overton was caught up in the narrative, declaring only yesterday evening that while Fanny was a fool to refuse Henry Crawford, he was an even greater fool to continue to pursue a girl who plainly could not like him.

"It's the thrill of the chase," Thomas Musgrave had explained. "If she had worshipped at his feet from the beginning, he would have taken it as his due and disregarded her completely. It was her lack of interest that provoked him. He said so himself."

Was he right? Rosa wondered. Did gentlemen value more what was hard won?

Lambton placed a decanter, a cordial glass and a plate of Naples biscuits on the table beside the chaise longue. "Mrs Godin sent this up, Miss Fancourt. It's her orange wine—she said a glass will help you feel more the thing."

"Thank her for me, Lambton."

The maid disappeared into Rosa's bedroom and returned with a shawl. "Put your feet up and rest, miss," she instructed her mistress. "Here's another cushion." She piled the cushions behind Rosa's head and spread the shawl over her. "Drink your wine," she added severely as she left the room.

"Thank you, Lambton."

Rosa made a face as she sipped from the little glass. She preferred the Madeira Julian gave her every afternoon. Julian. She didn't know whether to be relieved or disappointed that Mrs Godin had interrupted them. She had never imagined a man's kiss could be so thrilling—it was more than just a brief pressure of lips; she had felt the tip of his tongue just before the housekeeper came in. Earlier, he had called her his dearest Rosa.

It had been a relief to be able to speak of Robert. She had never guessed that Julian had noticed a resemblance between them. It had hurt when he was so insistent that she keep silent. Could he not see how much it mattered to her? She had turned away so he would not notice her distress but he followed her. She could not resist when he drew her to him; it felt so right to be in his arms. He would be willing to take an interest in Robert—act as his patron, even. Her heart had jumped and then his kiss had obliterated all thought. She touched her fingers to her lips, remembering.

"Your supper, Miss Fancourt. Shall we set for Miss Loring?"

Lambton lit the candles on the mantelpiece and the table under the window while a footman stood by with another tray.

"Please do. I'll just see if she is awake."

Chloe was curled up on a window seat looking out into the twilit lady's garden. "I couldn't sleep. It's a pity there is no cure for heartache."

"None except time, but distraction sometimes helps. Come and eat a little supper and tell me about your call on the Clarksons."

"My goodness!" Chloe exclaimed, admiring the fare arrayed on dainty floral china. "Petty patties with rich gravy, fricassee of chicken and mushrooms, some new potatoes and a dish of cucumbers."

"Mrs Godin mentioned that Cook enjoys cooking for ladies." Rosa ladled a delicate concoction of fresh peas and herbs into the soup plates.

"Mmm. This is delicious. And chocolate creams and cherries for dessert," Chloe said contentedly. "This is cosy; it reminds me of our schoolroom suppers." She laughed at Rosa's expression. "Because it's just the two of us up here, I mean. I don't think I shall ever again eat a plain rice pudding."

"Nor I. And I had to eat it to give you a good example."

"Poor Rosa. Have some wine to take the taste out of your mouth."

"What will happen now?" Chloe asked after she had sampled all the dishes and was nibbling the cherries. "If Mamma doesn't come back, who will bring me out? I love

Grandmamma dearly, but I know it would be too much for her if she had to stay up late every night for a whole Season. I just hope it's not Mrs Overton. You heard her suggest that Ann and I come out together. I think I'd rather die!" She carefully placed the last cherry stone on her plate and arranged them in a neat circle.

"You should have seen her today at the Clarksons, Rosa. Miss Clarkson, Ann and I were expected to be seen and not heard while she flirted not only with Mr Clarkson but also with his son who cannot be more than twenty-two. Poor Mrs Clarkson was reduced to silence but I could see she was not pleased. I was never so embarrassed or so grateful when the half-hour was up."

She picked up her spoon and began to count, "Soldier, sailor, tinker, tailor," stopping when they heard a gentle tap at the door.

Rosa got up to answer it. "That's probably Julian."

"Julian, you won't have Mrs Overton introduce me to society, will you?" Chloe cried as soon as her brother came into the room.

"Certainly not. You have my solemn promise on it. What made you ask?"

"Nothing. I was just wondering—" She shrugged and returned to her cherry stones, muttering under her breath. "Ploughboy," she said as she touched her spoon to the last one. "If I am to throw my cap over the windmill like that, Papa will be spared the cost of a come-out."

Julian laughed. "Promise me I may be there when you explain that to him."

She smiled back at him but then grew more solemn. "What will happen now? Will there be a huge scandal?"

He drew up a chair to sit beside her. "I don't know, pet.

It all depends on whether the scandal sheets get hold of the story. Lord Stephen is well known among the *ton* and there may well be a paragraph about his new liaison, but generally they publish initials rather than spell names fully. Your mother has never moved in society and readers may not realise who is meant or connect her to you. However, if Father decides to seek a divorce or sue Lord Stephen for criminal conversation, then it must become public."

"Do you think he will?" Rosa asked. "Surely it would not be wise to court such notoriety."

"I agree, but if it is splashed all over the newssheets, he will probably feel he has no choice but to revenge himself on the man who seduced his wife. We must pray it won't come to that."

Chloe looked dismayed. "I do hope it won't become public. It would be terrible to be known as the daughter of an adulteress."

"You would not be the only one in the *ton*," Julian said wryly. "Don't worry about your come-out, sweetheart. Father has already agreed that I may give a ball for you at Swanmere House when the time comes."

"He has?" She jumped up and hugged him. "Julian, you are the very best of brothers. And I may invite Rosa to stay there too, may I not? You will come, won't you, Rosa?"

"If I can," Rosa temporised. Who knew what might happen in almost two years?

"I must leave you. I slipped up while the others are at their port, but it is time we joined the ladies, although a dull evening we shall have of it without the two of you." Julian cocked an eyebrow at Rosa. "I don't suppose you will take pity on me and come down now?"

She shook her head. "I'm not dressed for the evening."

"Do go, Rosa," Chloe urged. "You are dressed but for your gown and I'll help you change quickly."

"Are you sure?"

"Yes. I would prefer to be alone when I read my mother's letter."

# Chapter Twenty-five

A FOOTMAN PLACED A SUBSTANTIAL platter of ham and eggs in front of Julian while Bates offered Rosa a smaller plate. "Cook thought you might like an omelette, Miss Fancourt."

"How thoughtful. Please thank him, Bates."

"That will be all, Bates," Julian said, once the remainder of the dishes had been placed on the library table. "We'll serve ourselves."

"Very good, sir." The steward placed the tea and coffee pots at Rosa's right hand and withdrew.

Rosa wondered what the servants made of this early breakfast *à deux*. They did not disapprove at any rate, she thought as she cut into the yellow pillow of eggs flecked with herbs. "This is delicious."

Julian smiled at her. "Cook evidently considers you are in need of additional sustenance if you must rise at such an early hour. I feel I should apologise but I was determined to talk to you before I left."

"When she heard I was to join you, Chloe gave me her mother's letter to show you."

"Have you seen it?"

"Yes, but we didn't discuss it. She was too tired last night."

"I must read it, I suppose."

"I think it would be best. We must also consider what is to be done with Hughes."

"I had forgotten about Hughes," he admitted. "I'm not sure whether it is best to keep her here or have her depart before my father has a chance to talk to her."

"Why?"

"We are agreed that it would be best if he does not sue Lord Stephen. Without Hughes, his case must be weaker and there would be less risk of salacious evidence coming to light."

"That is very true. We must be grateful that she left Harrogate rather than remain to fuel gossip there. She was very upset at being turned off without notice after twenty years' service. I know Lady Loring paid her what was owing to her, and more, but her feelings are badly hurt. A resentful servant can cause a great deal of damage."

"My God, yes."

"I wonder why she thought to come here in the first place. I doubt if your paths crossed much, Julian."

He grinned. "That was John Coachman. '*I couldn't think what to do with her, Mr Julian,*' he told me. '*There she was, wringing her hands on the side of the road, saying "my lady" and "what'll I do?" and crying fit to bust. So I said, 'I have to pass near Swanmere. You come with me and we'll see if Sir Julian is at home,' and that shut her up*'."

"You have a staunch ally there."

"There is a fellowship among horsemen, you know,

and he was a young groom when I was a boy spending a lot of time in the stables."

"Did he have anything more to add—about Lady Loring, I mean?"

"No, nothing. She always came and went in the carriage, he said—never sent him home ahead of her. When he saw her trunks, he assumed they were returning to the Place."

"How far is it to the Place from here? When can you hope to arrive?"

"It's about eighty miles, so eight hours' driving if I can keep up a steady ten miles an hour. I'll take my own pair as far as Peterborough and leave them at *The Angel* there. There are another six changes and it all depends on what sort of nags they can offer me. If I make it in under ten hours I'll be happy—you just need one long waggon ahead of you on a narrow road and all your plans are for naught."

"Why don't you take the carriage—let Jebb drive?"

He laughed. "I like driving. I would probably end up on the box, taking the ribbons myself. Jebb and the carriages are at your disposal while I am away—you only need to give the order."

"Thank you."

Rosa poured him another cup of coffee, enjoying the intimacy of this early-morning meal. When he had finished eating, she reluctantly handed him Lady Loring's letter. "To come back to our muttons."

"If we must, we must," he said with a sigh and unfolded the sheet.

*My dearest Chloe,*

*I am sure you are asking yourself how can I call you my*

*dearest when I am about to leave you, perhaps forever. I know the Law—and Society—will consider my conscious decision to abandon my marriage unjustifiable. Very likely you will too. I want to try and explain nonetheless and hope that when you are older you might understand a little.*

*It is hard to know where to start and I will not force on your notice or weary you with details of the twenty years I spent as your father's wife. Suffice it to say that not even for the dubious security provided by matrimony can I continue to remain subject to him, as much a bondwoman as any unfortunate in the colonies. When, unexpectedly, the doors to my cage were opened and a new world appeared, I chose freedom.*

*In placing my trust in Lord Stephen, I may be disappointed, but he will never be able to remind me, as Sir Edward did, that the law gives a husband more power over his wife than any gaoler has over his prisoners. If Lord Stephen and I remain together, it will be of our free will, because we have a kindness for each other and take pleasure in one another's company. My only regret is that the price I must pay for this new happiness is my continued separation from you.*

*But you should know that I cannot be sure that Sir Edward will permit me to see you again, even if I crawl to him and beg him on my knees. 'Chloe is no longer your concern', he told me coldly. His last words to me were that I may not write to you but I have chosen to disregard this prohibition.*

*Chloe, please do not think too harshly of me. Remember me, especially when the time comes for you to choose a husband. Do not permit yourself to be hurried into marriage without doing your best to satisfy yourself that your husband will truly love, comfort and honour you until the end of your life—that he will consider these vows as binding on him as they are on you. Sadly, in our world, only a wife pays a price for breaking them. Her husband's broken vows do not diminish in any way his power over her.*

*My darling girl, I beg your forgiveness for everything. Think kindly of your mother. Perhaps, one day, Heaven will grant that we meet again. Never doubt that I love you and always will.*

*Mamma*

"A neat piece of special pleading," Julian commented.

Rosa shivered. "Part of me says there can be no justification for breaking one's marriage vows but another part cannot but recognise the general truth in what she says—about a husband's power under the law, I mean. I cannot comment on anything more particular."

"Yes. Much is implied rather than spelled out." He looked down at the sheet, frowning. "It makes me uneasy, feel guilty even."

"Why?"

"That day—after Chidlow called to the Place and Lady Loring had been forced to confess all to my father—she was confined to her room while we, that is my father, my grandmother and I, considered what was to be done with her—as if she were a common criminal like a poacher or a thief. We all accepted that my father had the right to dispose of her as he wished. We sat in judgement on her and no one spoke in her defence."

"*'Judge not that ye not be judged'*?"

"That's it. I was furious about the way you had been treated, but that must chiefly be laid at Purdue's door and I accept now that Chloe's injury was as much an accident as anything. Delia must have known she could expect no mercy from my father. She was like an animal caught in a trap; everything she did after she and Purdue were discovered was to protect herself from my father's wrath."

"It is a wonder she agreed to an *affaire* in the first place."

He shrugged. "It is common enough in the *ton* for a wife to seek consolation or relief from her loneliness elsewhere. It is generally tolerated provided she is discreet."

Had he done his share of consoling? A man of his age must have had some liaisons or kept a mistress, she supposed, although really she knew nothing about such matters.

"Christ forgave the woman taken in adultery," she said softly.

Julian shook his head. "My father never would or, if he did, it would be a cold sort of forgiveness. Even if he could bring himself to permit her to return home, he would never forget. She would pay for her sin for the rest of their lives together."

Rosa shivered again. "What a grim prospect."

"The thing is, I am conscious that I added to her isolation. I resented her from the beginning and never responded to any overtures she might have made."

"Overtures?" Rosa's voice rose and she put her hand over her mouth as if to hush herself.

He laughed. "Not that sort of overture but—I could have been kinder to her. I was never more than courteous towards her. My grandmother was the same. She is closer to you than she ever was to—" He broke off. "It seems wrong to refer to her as Delia now, when I refused to use her name."

"I used wonder about that. I assumed she would not permit it."

"No. It was my choice," he said heavily. "The only thing I can say in my defence is that neither my father nor my grandmother challenged me on it—or on my behaviour in general."

"It is very difficult to defend oneself against such petty unkindnesses," she reflected. "They are almost impossible to prove, to begin with."

He flinched. "I know, and they quickly become a habit. You are not like that, Rosa—you are kindness personified."

"I have never found you anything but kind," she objected. He judged himself far too harshly.

"I'm glad, but I think it was a passive sort of kindness; an absence of unkindness if you like. But I was unkind to her. Your kindness is more positive; it is the true charity that the apostle Paul speaks of."

"Julian!"

He touched a finger to her cheek and she thrilled at the soft caress.

"You have turned as pink as a kitten's tongue, Rosa. You must not be used to receiving compliments."

She smiled and shook her head, then jumped when the longcase clock sonorously struck the hour. "Eight o'clock already. You will want to be on your way. What about Hughes?"

"Something must be done for her, I suppose. Do we have any position here?"

Rosa frowned. "I cannot speak for Swanmere of course

but, frankly, I would be happier to see her leave. We don't know what she might reveal to Chloe of her mother. A woman has no secrets from her maid, after all."

"Nor a man from his valet. You are right. Some form of compensation, then. Perhaps it would be better for you to speak privately to her, Rosa. She seemed happy to confide in you yesterday."

"Perhaps." Rosa had never had much to do with her employer's maid, but she was a familiar face, she supposed.

"Miss Hughes?" Mrs Godin said when sent for. "She came down fifteen minutes ago. I let her have her sleep out as she has no work here. She's in my room now, Miss Fancourt, having her breakfast. I thought it best to keep her away from the others for the moment."

"Thank you, Mrs Godin. When she has finished eating, please bring her to the muniments room."

Hughes was pale and heavy-eyed this morning. "I beg your pardon, Miss Fancourt," she said as soon as Rosa came into the room. "I can't think what came over me to sleep so late."

"It has been a difficult few days," Rosa said sympathetically.

"That it has, miss. Somehow I can't see my way forward yet."

"Are you worried how you will manage until you find another position?"

"Yes, miss. After twenty years with her ladyship, I don't know which are the best register offices or where to find respectable lodgings. I have some savings, but they could disappear very fast, especially if I cannot find something by next quarter day."

"What about your family? I understand that you would not want to be beholden to anyone, but could you go to them if you could pay your way?"

"Yes and no, miss. I have a brother and a sister in Norwich. Nan is married to a cobbler and they wouldn't really have room for me. My brother has a butcher's shop. He lost his wife last year and wrote to say I should come and keep house for him and the children but I wouldn't go. He wouldn't think to pay me a proper wage and if he got married again, a new wife wouldn't want me in her way. I would rather have my independence. Quite cross, he was, when I said no. He said it was my Christian duty, but he didn't show me any Christian duty when our Dad died. He got the shop and said as he'd care for Mam but Nan and me would have to go into service. Nine and ten, we was. I was lucky; I went to work for Miss Jessup—she had a milliner's shop and she trained me up properly."

"You certainly have the knack of trimming bonnets and making little caps and head-dresses," Rosa put in admiringly.

"But I took a fancy to being a lady's maid," Hughes rambled on. "I learned how to dress hair and got a position with a customer who was going to Harrogate to take the waters. She died there, poor soul, but I was lucky and was taken on by my lady. Miss Eubank she was then and about to marry Sir Edward. Perhaps I should have stayed with Miss Jessup. She and I always got on well. She's over sixty now and her sight is fading. It's hard to do the fine work, she says. I've over eighty pounds saved. If I had another fifty, she'd take me on as a partner. I would have to look after her, of course, as she gets older, but the shop would be mine in the end."

"Is that what you would like to do?"

"I wouldn't mind. I'd be near Nan, too. But I'd never be able to save the money in time. Even if I could manage a pound a quarter, it would take me more than twelve years."

"Could you stay with Miss Jessup while you were looking for a position in Norwich?" Rosa suggested.

The maid brightened. "I hadn't thought of that. I'm sure I could."

It was time to address the matter at hand. "Hughes, if Sir Edward Loring were to ask you about your mistress and Lord Stephen, what could you tell him?"

"Nothing, miss," Hughes said promptly. "You could have knocked me down with a feather when she told me she was going with him. Well it stands to reason, don't it? She was staying with her mother and she wasn't going to dirty her own nest. She went out a lot—to card parties and balls and such, but as they all took place in the different hotels, it would have been easy enough for her to go apart with him without it being noticed. She never said anything to me. She wasn't one for confiding."

"But you might have guessed she was seeing someone," Rosa suggested. "There are signs a lady's maid might have noticed; laces done up differently perhaps—"

Hughes shook her head. "There was nothing like that."

We're both unmarried and have been sequestered in the country for years, Rosa said to herself. How should we know the signs of adulterous intimacy? Perhaps she didn't undress—she was fully clothed in the cottage that day.

"I did notice these last weeks that she was happier than she has been for a long time," Hughes offered. "I put it down to her being away from Sir Edward and the Place."

"We must hope there will not be too much talk about this," Rosa remarked. "I am sure the family can rely on your discretion, especially for Miss Chloe's sake."

"Of course, miss. I don't think it would do me any good either if people got to know about it," Hughes said frankly. "There's too many as would say, 'flighty mistress, flighty maid'. 'Tis hard enough for a woman on her own, as you know."

"That is very true," Rosa agreed with a friendly smile. "Well, Hughes, I know Sir Julian wishes to show his appreciation of your loyal service to the Lorings. I'm sure he would allow John Coachman take you to Norwich today if you wish. Shall I ask him?"

"Oh, would you, Miss Fancourt? I would be very much obliged to him—and you."

"How much should I give her?" Julian asked.

"Would fifty pounds be too much? She has some savings and with another fifty pounds, she has the chance of buying into a milliner's shop in Norwich, near where her sister lives. It is the ideal solution, Julian. We don't want a prospective new mistress wondering why she cannot apply to Lady Loring for a character but must write to your grandmother or Chloe or even Mrs Walton."

He nodded understandingly. "Fifty it is, then. I don't have it on me; I'll be back in a trice."

Hughes burst into tears when Julian handed her the roll of notes. "Thank you, sir, and Miss Fancourt, too. I never dreamt—I hope you don't think I was angling for it, miss. I don't know why I told you all that. I'm still not myself this morning."

"No, no, I quite understand," Rosa murmured. "John Coachman is having the horses put to. Are you ready to leave?"

"I just have to fetch my box, miss."

Rosa held out her hand. "Goodbye, Miss Hughes. I am sure Jessup and Hughes Milliners will be a great success."

Hughes smiled broadly, suddenly looking years younger. "Jessup and Hughes Milliners," she repeated rapturously. "I can't thank you enough, Miss Fancourt. If you're ever in Norwich, Jessup and Hughes will be delighted to serve you."

# Chapter Twenty-six

"YOU'RE LATE," MEG SNAPPED when Jenkins hurried in with her morning chocolate.

"I'm sorry, ma'am. I thought I might be able to find out some more, but she's gone. Miss Fancourt asked to see her about eight o'clock and the next thing she and the coachman had left."

As she spoke, she put down the tray and piled pillows behind her mistress's back before carefully draping a shawl around her shoulders and handing her a delicate cup and saucer. "What will you wear today, ma'am?"

"I don't know yet. First, tell me again from the beginning. I was too tired last night to take it all in. No, stop that. I cannot understand you if you have your head in the wardrobe."

Jenkins obediently faced the bed. "There was a strange coachman at the servants' supper and I wondered because there were no guests. He came from Harrogate with Lady Loring's maid, someone said, but without her ladyship. He didn't say much himself. The maid wasn't at supper but one of the footmen told me afterwards that she had asked to see Sir Julian. She was all in a dither, he said."

"Did Sir Julian see her?"

"I suppose so, ma'am, for later she was in one of the maids' rooms in this wing. So when you were at dinner, I thought I would look in and see if she needed anything— just friendly-like."

"That was kind of you, Jenkins." Meg awarded her henchwoman a conspiratorial smile.

"She'd been crying, ma'am, I could see that, so I took the liberty of fetching the decanter from your bedroom, hoping it might soothe her."

Meg eyed the ratafia, the level of which was considerably lower than it had been the previous evening. "I think we should say it was spilled, Jenkins. I have no wish to be thought a toper."

"No, ma'am."

"Did the ratafia—soothe her?"

The maid looked frustrated. "She didn't say much. I asked her what was wrong and all she would do was moan, '*oh, don't ask me*'. Where was her mistress, I asked. '*I have no mistress,*' she said. Had she been turned off? I asked, and she began to cry again. So I gave her another glass before asking why she had come here. '*To see if Sir Julian would tell me what to do*'."

"What sort of woman is she? Might he have given her a slip on the shoulder and her mistress found out?"

Jenkins looked startled. "That never occurred to me, ma'am. It's possible, I suppose. She'd be about my age with a neat enough figure but her face was all blotched and red from the crying."

"Hmmm. Go on."

"I asked her what Sir Julian had said. When she didn't answer, I poured another glass of ratafia and slipped just a couple of drops of laudanum into it as a composer. That seemed to soothe her. Suddenly, she said, '*I was that pleased to see Miss Fancourt*'."

"Miss Fancourt?" Meg repeated incredulously. "That woman is everywhere!"

Jenkins nodded vigorously. "'*She was so kind*,' she said. '*I never believed that about the officer*'. What officer? I asked her, straight-out. And then, ma'am, she said, '*The one Miss Fancourt was supposed to have eloped with*'."

"What?" Meg leaned forward, the cup and saucer tilting precariously. She had hoped to discover something discreditable about the other woman, but this surpassed all her expectations. "What else did she say?"

"She was nodding off by then. Eloped? I said, just to prompt her, like, but all I got was, '*They said it was why she left the Place so sudden but it can't have been true because if it was she wouldn't be here, would she?*' And with that, ma'am, she was sound asleep and I could get no more from her.

"She was still asleep when I went down to breakfast and just now, when I went to fetch your chocolate, she came out of the private wing with Miss Fancourt. I couldn't hear what they said and she hurried past me with just a nod. The coachman was in the kitchen and he said they were leaving immediately. I hung back a little, hoping he might say something more, but she came in and off they went."

"How very strange." Meg handed her maid the cup and saucer and pushed aside the bed clothes. "You did your best, Jenkins. Dress me quickly so that I am not too late for breakfast."

After breakfast, she would write to her friend Ellen Kitchell in Bury. Why hadn't she thought of her before? She need only mention that Miss Fancourt was at Swanmere and she would learn all there was to know. Eloped with an officer! It would be beyond everything if it were true.

Despite Jenkins's best efforts, breakfast was almost over when Meg came into the morning room. Mr Musgrave and the two boys rose politely but as soon as she sat, Hal and Robert returned to their argument with Chloe and Ann. She looked crossly at them.

"Hal and Robert, you may leave the table if you cannot behave in a more gentlemanly manner. What is all this about, pray?"

"We're discussing what to do first, now that the sun is shining," Hal explained. "We want to take a pick-nick and explore the old priory. The girls say everything will still be wet, but who gives a fig for that?"

"It's all very well for you in your breeches and boots, but our skirts will drag through the grass," Ann pointed out.

Miss Fancourt put down her cup and asked, "Boys, could we perhaps leave the priory until tomorrow? I had thought we ladies might take the opportunity to do a little shopping in Oundle. I am told it is a pretty town, but I am sure Thomas can find something wet and perhaps even muddy for the two of you if you prefer."

"'*A Daniel come to judgement.*'" Thomas Musgrave touched his forehead in a mock salute. "As a matter of fact I had arranged for the gamekeeper to give them a lesson with the guns."

Hearing this, Hal and Robert abandoned speech in

favour of clearing their plates as quickly as possible, then begged to be excused. Left alone, the ladies began to plan their own expedition.

"I presume Julian will escort us," Meg said.

Lady Loring shook her head. "I am sure he would have been delighted to, but unfortunately he has been called away for a few days. He makes his apologies and is sure you will understand. We shall take Ephraim. Frankly, I have always considered a footman much more use than a gentleman when one is shopping. Gentlemen tend to get so impatient and cannot understand that one must try on another bonnet."

"I must agree with you, ma'am," Meg declared. "There can be no denying that a gentleman's presence is flattering, but they have no patience for what they term our fripperies, although the cut of their boots or the minutest details of their regimentals are matters of utmost importance. And if you remark on it, they inform you loftily that *'that is different'*."

"Which, in their opinion, clinches the argument," Ann said with a sigh, "and if you do not accept it, it just proves that you are a silly female and unable to understand."

"That is an attitude one encounters frequently," Meg told her daughter. "You will have to learn to accept it or you will never find a husband."

"I don't want a husband who treats me like that," Chloe protested. "I'd rather stay single."

"You may say that now, but wait a few years and you will see things differently," Meg retorted. "Do you want to spend your life in other women's homes, always reliant on their goodwill?" She could not resist glancing at Miss Fancourt as she spoke, but the governess ignored this barb, as did her former pupil.

"When should we leave, Rosa?" Chloe asked.

"I thought at half-past ten. Would that be convenient for you, Mrs Overton? It's a drive of just over an hour, I believe."

"Certainly, Miss Fancourt," Meg replied graciously. "Please be good enough to order the carriage."

She rather felt she had come off the victor in that exchange, Meg thought triumphantly as Miss Fancourt left the room. The younger woman's '*Certainly, Mrs Overton*' had been as gracious as her own response, but she had made no bones about doing Meg's bidding. Perhaps while Julian is away I can turn the tables a little, she said to herself. After all, her holiday here will soon be over and she will require a new position. I could offer to recommend her to my sister-in-law. That would put both of them in my debt. That is if I don't reveal the full story of her past, she thought with a secret thrill. It was delicious to know she held the other woman's fate in her hands.

Mrs Overton raised an eyebrow. "Two carriages? Is that not rather extravagant, Miss Fancourt? Surely you could have taken the outside seat? It is perfectly comfortable, or so my maid tells me."

There was an icy pause. Chloe looked furious and Ann mortified. Lady Loring opened her mouth but her response remained unspoken when Rosa calmly informed them that they would call at the vicarage to take up Mrs and Miss Musgrave. She no longer paid attention to Mrs Overton's pin-pricks. If anything, she was sorry for the woman whose petty spite spoke of a deeper malaise.

"What a splendid idea, Rosa," Chloe said. "They are bound to know the best shops."

"Mrs Overton, you, I and Mrs Musgrave shall take

Swanmere's carriage," Lady Loring pronounced regally. "Miss Musgrave may join the other young ladies in the berline."

For a moment Rosa thought that Mrs Overton would fly into a rage at this decree which not only placed her among the older generation but required her, as the youngest and least important of the three matrons, to take the rear-facing seat but, although she looked as if she had bitten into an extremely sour lemon, she said no more.

"It is rather old-fashioned and not the most comfortable of conveyances but we shan't notice that, I am sure," Chloe said as she took her place beside Ann in the berline, the two girls facing backwards without complaint. "Do you object if we open the windows, Rosa? It is such a beautiful morning."

Oundle was a small town whose few, neat streets harboured enough purveyors of the modish, quaint, charming and uncommon to satisfy the Swanmere visitors. Others had also taken advantage of the fine weather to visit the shops and Rosa was delighted to meet several neighbours as they explored the little town. She was touched by the friendly greetings and amused by several sly comments about her progress as a whip. She could not have expected her outings with Julian to go unnoticed, she supposed, as she denied any aspiration to drive unicorn.

"What interesting work," Chloe exclaimed as she peered at the array of boxes and other decorative items displayed in a bow-fronted window.

"It is straw marquetry done by the French prisoners at Norman Cross," Mrs Musgrave informed her. "If you are interested, you would be well advised to acquire it now, for the barracks will soon be empty. Most of them have already left and I understand they will all be gone by the end of the summer."

"Do let us go in," Chloe begged.

"Such exquisite work," Rosa said. "Only look at the vivid colours and such fine detail—on the inside as well," she added, displaying the picturesque scene depicted on the inside lid of a sewing-box. "Perhaps this is his home town and in his mind he returned there while he worked."

"Here is a lovely Noah's Ark," Ann said. "I've never seen one with so many animals. I'm sure the maker pictured his own children playing with them."

"I don't know, miss," the shopkeeper said. "Jann, who made that, was here for over eight years. His children would be well-grown by now."

"But he will still have thought of them as small," Rosa said softly. "One does when one hasn't seen a child for years. Even though you know they must have grown, in your mind they are as you left them."

"They were hard workers, the frenchies," the shop-keeper said. "Some of them will take a couple of hundred pounds home with them."

Rosa tried to imagine the joy of a family whose father and husband was restored to them. Or would it be an unwelcome surprise? Perhaps they already had given him up for dead. What sort of home-coming would he have? The little box was too full of someone else's dreams. With a silent prayer that 'Jann' and his fellows had found their families safe and waiting for them, she gently closed the lid and handed the box back. As she stepped away from the counter, she saw that Lady Loring was sitting on a chair, her eyes closed.

"Are you feeling quite well, ma'am?"

"I am a little fatigued," her ladyship admitted. "I think I shall wait for you at the inn."

"We'll come with you and have the horses put to immediately," Rosa said as Chloe hurried to her grandmother's side.

"I think it is best her ladyship and I go ahead on our own," Mrs Musgrave intervened. "She will be the better for a short rest."

Rosa could see the force of this argument. "Very well, ma'am. Ephraim will go with you and pray send him at once if you need me. We shall join you later."

"I cannot like these Oldenburgh bonnets," Mrs Overton said. "I know they are all the rage, but it is as if one were wearing blinkers." She replaced the offending article with a delicate cap of lilac satin and blond lace. "This is much better. What do you think, girls?"

"It's most becoming, Mamma," Ann told her.

"Look, Rosa." Chloe had tried on a bonnet of split straw lined with pale blue silk. "It can be ornamented either with bows of riband or clusters of flowers. I think these cornflowers are very pretty."

"They match your eyes," Rosa agreed. "Shall you take it?"

The girl nodded. "Grandmamma said I was to buy myself something pretty," she whispered as she untied the ribbons. "I didn't find anything until now."

"Of course there will be no problem in trimming the bonnet immediately and sending it to Miss Loring at *The Talbot*," the milliner assured them. "Should the boy bring the other purchases as well?"

◦❧

"Did you not find anything you liked, Miss Fancourt?" Mrs Overton asked as they left the shop.

"Nothing I liked well enough."

"You are wise to be careful, especially when you are between positions. How long do you remain at Swanmere?"

"I am not sure. It has not yet been decided."

"It is very kind of Lady Loring to give you a little holiday before you take up a new position. Now, I have the perfect opportunity for you, Miss Fancourt. My sister-in-law writes that she requires a new governess immediately and I should be happy to recommend you to her. There are four daughters, between the ages of four and twelve, and a five-year old boy as well so, providing you give satisfaction, you may look forward to another lengthy engagement such as you had with the Lorings."

Mrs Overton concluded this speech with a smile worthy of Lady Bountiful herself and paused, clearly in expectation of receiving Rosa's humble thanks. When none were immediately forthcoming, she continued more testily, "You cannot risk losing such an opportunity, Miss Fancourt. You must not presume too long on Sir Julian's hospitality, you know."

It was time to put a stop to this nonsense. Rosa looked down her nose at her companion. "It is not necessary for you to concern yourself with my affairs, Mrs Overton, but thank you just the same. I have no doubt your suggestion was well-meant."

At this set-down the other woman began to gobble like a turkey-cock. Words like 'ungrateful,' 'temerity'and 'impertinence', reached Rosa's ears but she chose to ignore them. Chloe, Ann and Miss Musgrave had paused to look into another window and when the five women moved on, Ann walked beside her mother who had lapsed into a fraught silence.

# Chapter Twenty-seven

THE FIRM RAP OF JULIAN'S BOOT heels broke the somnolent silence of Loring Place and caused the footman in the front hall to spring up from the chair where he had been dozing.

"Sir Julian! 'Beg your pardon, sir. The master's from home and we wasn't expecting anyone."

"Is Sir Edward dining elsewhere?"

"Yes, that is, I'm sure I don't know, sir."

Julian's brows twitched together. What sort of an answer was that? "Fetch Meadows," he ordered.

The man cleared his throat nervously. "I'm sorry, sir, but Sir Edward gave him a week's holidays."

"Is Mrs Walton here?"

"Yes, sir," the man answered with obvious relief.

"I want to see her in the library immediately."

His father's desk was bare—something Julian could not recall ever having seen before—and the library smelled stale as if it had not been aired for a couple of days. As he flung open the windows, he heard a movement behind him. The housekeeper had come into the room and stood waiting, her hands folded at her waist.

"Where is my father, Mrs Walton?"

"He has gone away for a few days, sir," she replied placidly.

What the devil? Now of all times! John Coachman would arrive tomorrow with the carriage and then the fat would be in the fire. While he had been able to withstand the interest of the Swanmere servants, his familiars at the Place would not be put off as easily.

"When is he expected back?"

"He didn't say, sir."

"Did he say where he was going?"

"No, sir."

"Have you no idea where he might be, Mrs Walton?" When she hesitated, he added, "It is imperative I speak to him as soon as possible."

He said no more but frowned at her until she blurted out, "Perhaps you should talk to Mr Mapps, Sir Julian."

"Is he at home?"

"I think so, sir."

"Send a groom over. My compliments and he is to attend me here immediately. I'll want something to eat after I've spoken to him."

"I'm afraid it might take some time, Sir Julian," the housekeeper said apologetically. "Cook will do her best, but the fires have been slaked, you see. We could serve a cold supper sooner."

"That will do, but send up some ale now."

The land-steward was a meek man in his fifties who

operated in the shadow of his forceful employer and denied any knowledge of Sir Edward's whereabouts.

"Don't be ridiculous, Mapps. You must have some idea where he is, otherwise Mrs Walton would not have suggested I speak to you. It is vital that I see him as soon as possible. Come now, man to man—"

Mapps puffed and capitulated. "Man-to-man, Sir Julian, he is in Ipswich."

"Ipswich?"

"Yes. He has owned a small property there for over twenty years. It is a—a gentleman's retreat, one might say. He is known there as Mr Edwards."

Julian's jaw dropped. "Am I to take it that there is a Mrs Edwards?"

Mapps shuffled his feet. "In a manner of speaking, sir."

At ten o'clock the next morning Julian drew up in front of a secluded house in Ipswich. He jumped down from the curricle and rapped on the dark green door.

"Yes, sir?"

Julian brushed past the manservant. "Tell your master Sir Julian Loring wishes to speak to him on a matter of urgency."

A door on his right opened and his father came out, napkin in hand. "What the devil are you doing here?"

"I might ask the same, sir," Julian retorted.

Before Sir Edward could answer, a small plump woman followed him into the hall. She was neatly but not stylishly dressed, her only extravagance the elaborate lace cap that crowned her grey curls.

Her face softened when she spied the visitor. "Why, it's Master Julian! Come in, come in."

"You have the advantage of me, madam," he said stiffly.

"Come in here where we can talk privately," his father ordered, stepping back into a pleasant dining parlour. "What has happened? Good news would not have brought you here."

"Your family is well, sir," Julian said coldly as he followed him into the room. "For the rest, I prefer to wait until we are on our own."

"Of course, pray excuse me," the woman said. "Shall I send in fresh coffee?"

Sir Edward looked enquiringly at his son who shook his head.

"Who is she?" Julian demanded as soon as the door had closed.

"Margaret Robson. You don't remember her? She was your mother's maid."

"And all this time—?" Julian asked, sickened. "Did you deceive my mother as well as Delia?"

"Not Katharine," Sir Edward said defensively. "It was only afterwards—Margaret looked after her until the end and then—well, I suppose we comforted one another."

"Why didn't you make an honest woman of her?"

"Marry a lady's maid? Have you taken leave of your senses? All the other servants would have left for a start. She would have been a fish out of water. She is much happier here where, as far as the world is concerned, she has a respectable position as my housekeeper. Besides, she was too old to give me a child. It was my duty to take a younger wife."

"Whom you had the temerity to chastise because she took a lover after twenty years," Julian said witheringly.

"That's different," Sir Edward said, but refused to meet his son's eyes.

"I had not thought you to be such a hypocrite! Did she know about this little arrangement?"

"Not initially, but later, yes. It had nothing to do with her, I told her; her position remained unaltered by it."

"As a matter of fact, sir, she has taken it upon herself to alter her position." Julian took Lady Loring's letter from his pocket and flicked it across the table to his father. "She has left you for Lord Stephen FitzCharles."

Sir Edward picked up the letter and broke the seal. There were only three or four lines, Julian saw. Lady Loring had apparently not thought it necessary to justify herself to her husband.

"The effrontery!" his father spluttered, flinging down the sheet of paper. "Purdue was bad enough, but to make a public display of herself like this! Lord Stephen will pay, I assure you."

"That might be difficult to achieve," Julian pointed out. "You cannot claim he has deprived you of the benefit of her society, given that you have already banished her from your home. Also, would you not first have to sue Purdue? I doubt if there is much to be collected there. Do you seriously want to crown yourself with a twin set of cuckold's horns?"

"No, I don't," Sir Edward said resignedly. "I spoke to my solicitor about obtaining a *divorce a mensa et thoro* from the ecclesiastical courts. He said that even with the testimonies of Miss Fancourt and Chloe it might be difficult to prove adultery. There must be penetration, he said."

"It is unthinkable that Miss Fancourt and Chloe should be asked about such matters, let alone in court."

"I would never expect it of them. It would be to no avail. The courts are so strict that, apparently, even a confession of adultery—which this letter might be presumed to be—

might not suffice without corroborating testimony and how the devil am I to get that if they are abroad?"

"Even if you succeeded in obtaining your evidence, you would be vulnerable to a plea of recrimination," Julian said reflectively. "Her adultery might be overlooked if she could prove that you first violated the marriage vow and, indeed, have kept a mistress from the beginning." He met his father's eyes. "Have done with her, sir, and let it go."

"No doubt you are right. Let us hope the newssheets don't get wind of the affair."

Sir Edward, caught off-balance by his unexpected arrival, was proving more amenable to reason than Julian had feared. "Amen to that,"

"Sit down and have some breakfast," his father said brusquely. "I never meant you to find out about Margaret and you need never see her again, but you need not mount your high horse over her either. We may as well thrash everything out while you are here."

Seeing the sense in this, Julian pulled out a chair while his father went to the door and called for food.

"Now," he said when he returned, "While we are waiting, tell me how my girl has got on with you. Is she in better spirits?"

"She is much improved," Julian said. "The news about her mother was a shock, of course, and it was fortunate that Miss Fancourt was with her."

"Tell me the story from the beginning. How did you find out about Delia?"

Julian described the events of the previous days, pausing only to permit the manservant to place the contents of a laden tray before him.

"Will that be all, sir?

Sir Edward waved the man away and turned back to his son.

"So John Coachman returns to the Place today. I had better go over and see him. Our people are close-mouthed enough, but word will spread. Poor Chloe. She is the one who will suffer most, I fear. What am I to do about her now? It's a pity you are not married—then your wife could take her on. I would miss her, you know," Sir Edward added gruffly, "but she should not be left with her grandmother and me. We are poor companions for a girl of her age. I shall have to try and find some sort of duenna for her. Unless—I don't suppose Miss Fancourt would consider returning to us now that Delia has left for good?" he continued hopefully. "We could make it worth her while."

"I doubt it, sir. The Chidlows have offered her a home, she says. She will not give that up for a temporary position."

Julian hoped to convince her to give it up for a permanent one, but would not mention that to his father until he was sure of his bride. He knew his own mind now—if Godin had not interrupted them, he would have claimed Rosa yesterday after she had responded so sweetly to his kiss. He hoped she did not think he had been trifling with her or, worse, that he considered her fair game because some scoundrel had given her a slip on the shoulder. He would make his intentions clear at the first possible opportunity, he resolved.

"Julian? Julian! What the devil is the matter with you?"

His father's voice brought him back to the present. "Nothing, sir. Of course Chloe may remain at Swanmere for the moment. Do you think my cousin Amelia would invite her to stay for the winter? She and Amelia's daughter seem to deal capitally together." While it might be inevitable that he and Rosa would ultimately assume responsibility for his sister, he was determined to have his wife to himself for the first months of their marriage.

"Perhaps—or my mother might like to take her to visit Eloisa. But we need not decide that now. It is more important that I make a new will. I must ensure that Delia has as little claim as possible on the estate and it is time I made proper provision for my daughter." Sir Edward eyed his son from beneath beetling brows. "While we're about it, we should discuss settlements for the event of your marriage, or have you an aversion to the married state?"

"Not at all, sir. Once I find the right woman, I'll have her fronting the altar in no time."

"Hmph! No need to be too hasty either. That is what got me into this predicament."

"Trust me." Julian poured himself more coffee. "While we are talking about legal matters, I should mention that my grandfather is eager that I take the name of Swann."

"Damned impertinent of him!"

"Not at all, sir. Like you, he is keen to see his name continue. However, I have no wish to deny either part of my heritage and propose to adopt the name Swann Loring."

"Swann Loring, eh?" Sir Edward repeated broodingly. "This would be permanent—your children would also be Swann Loring?"

"Yes."

His father suddenly looked a lot more cheerful. "Well, it could be worse, I suppose. You will need a royal licence, with two titles coming into play, but that should not prove difficult. Is Swanmere happy with this?"

"I have not yet mentioned it to him, but I am sure he will not object."

# Chapter Twenty-eight

*Bury St Edmunds*
*12th August 1814*

*My dearest Meg,*

*So you are fixed at Swanmere Castle for the summer. How did you contrive to secure an invitation from the delectable Sir Julian Loring? I know you say you are cousins, but the connection is quite distant, is it not? No matter, I am sure you are doing your utmost to make it a closer one.*

*You asked about Miss Fancourt who is a fellow guest and was previously governess to Miss Loring. She was at Loring Place since before I was married and is very well respected in the neighbourhood. I last saw her at Sir Edward's birthday celebrations where she was in attendance on her ladyship, including at the ball, although she did not dance until the finishing dance when I was surprised to see Sir Julian stand up with her. I suppose it was a kindness on his part to one who had been employed by his family for so long. Of course, he was the last to seek a partner so all the more eligible ladies had already been engaged.*

*Lady Loring was in exceptional looks that evening. She danced several of the dances, and stood up at least twice with one Purdue who removed here (or so we thought) around that time. His arrival caused quite a flutter among the mammas. He had inherited Old Hall and the appearance of a personable single man among us was not to be overlooked. Indeed, I overheard one lady comment that it was most fortuitous that the Lorings' fête enabled everyone to make P's acquaintance, for he did not attend church and we ladies could hardly intrude upon his bachelor solitude. Be that as it may, in the end he disappointed everyone by selling up to Sir Edward who had a right of refusal because the Old Hall was the original house on what is now the Loring estate, and vanished as suddenly as he had come.*

*Around this time, Miss Loring fell and suffered a severe injury to her head and our local physician was constantly at the Place. They were very concerned about her for some days and her former nurse was called in to tend her. There was talk that this was because Miss Fancourt had disappeared—eloped either with an officer or with Purdue; both stories made the rounds. Frankly, I never believed them. No one had previously mentioned an officer in connection with her and while I might have lent credence to the appearance of one impetuous admirer, the sudden emergence of two at once simply defies belief, especially in connection with a governess. In addition, the officer must have arrived here and departed again very quickly, for no-one could put a name or even a regiment to*

*him and all our regulars were accounted for. Mr Purdue
was not known to have singled her out in any way. What
is more, Kitchell met him at a cocking-main soon after and
I think it highly unlikely that he would have returned here
so quickly after enticing a woman into running away with
him. And, really, if he was interested in her, why would he
not make her an offer? Her family is perfectly respectable,
I believe. Well, if she has been invited to Swanmere Castle,
there can be no doubt that she parted from the Lorings on
the best of terms and the rumours are unfounded. I am
indebted to you for the information.*

*Kitchell sends his compliments, or would if he knew I
was writing to you. Now that you are out of mourning,
would you like to come and stay for our Fair Week in
October? There will be three assemblies and all sorts of
entertainments."*

Meg crumpled the letter into a ball. Ellen Kitchell took
with one hand what she gave with the other. And what
was even more galling, Meg's report of the Fancourt's
presence at Swanmere would serve to obliterate any
lingering stain on her reputation. There was something
behind it all, she was sure of it. Unless—she smoothed the
paper out again. Perhaps she could hint at something, see
if she could trick the woman into betraying her secrets.
What was that name again? Purdue? There were plenty of
men who would discard a woman as quickly as they had
seduced her. Why would this Purdue marry a woman with
no prospects? Ellen had always had more hair than wit.

"Has my brother returned?" Chloe asked as soon as she
dismounted.

"No, miss, not yet."

Chloe frowned and slipped her hand into Rosa's arm as they walked towards the castle. "I wonder how my father took the news. I dread the thought of going home. It may be selfish of me, but everything is so dull there. I don't suppose you would come back with us, Rosa?"

Rosa hesitated. Even if she were willing to agree, she did not think this would be best for Chloe—the girl was very young to assume the role of mistress at Loring Place. Perhaps the dowager would take over initially, but Chloe would soon slip into the position, especially if she had Rosa at her side. And there she would remain until a cuckolded Sir Edward was willing to brave the *ton* and arrange for his daughter's come-out. If necessary, Julian would have to stiffen his father's spine.

"It is too soon to make any plans, Chloe. Let us wait until your brother returns and we hear what he has to say. What would you like to do this afternoon, if there are no callers?"

"Ann wants us to practise another song. She is so lucky to have her music."

"You have music too."

"Not in the same way as Ann. It consumes her completely. She forgets everything when she is playing or arranging or singing. She even composes her own pieces."

But she can never perform beyond that which is permitted to a lady in a drawing-room, Rosa reflected as they entered the castle. Would that satisfy her in the long run?

"Ah, there you are! I hope you had a pleasant ride." Mrs Overton, who was crossing the hall, stopped and smiled at them.

Rosa's and Chloe's eyes met in surprise.

"Yes, indeed," Rosa answered, "but we stayed out a little too long. We must hurry and change out of our habits."

Mrs Overton wrinkled her nose. "You certainly cannot go into the drawing-room reeking of the stables." She moved past them and then looked back. "I must not forget to pass on the compliments of my friend, Mrs Kitchell."

"Mrs Kitchell of Bury?" Chloe asked.

"Yes, we have known each other forever. I had a letter from her today and she sends her compliments and regards."

"Thank you."

Mrs Overton waved her thanks away. "She told me all about Mr Purdue—"

"Mr Purdue?" Chloe looked surprised. "He died last winter. He was a horrible, snuff-stained old man."

"No, no," Mrs Overton said with a tinkling laugh. "The one who had all the ladies in a flutter."

Rosa frowned, as if in thought. "Oh, you must mean the nephew who inherited everything. He sold the house to Sir Edward Loring some months ago."

"He was quite old, as well—forty, I think. We met him at Papa's birthday celebrations, remember, Rosa?" Chloe caught up the train of her habit. "If you write to Mrs Kitchell, ma'am, pray convey Grandmamma's and my compliments."

Without waiting for a reply, Chloe began to mount the stairs. Rosa followed her, but they remained silent until they reached the tulip suite.

"Horrid woman," Chloe sighed as soon as the door was closed. "I am sure she wrote to Mrs Kitchell looking for the slightest whisper of scandal about us. What made her mention Purdue?"

"I have no idea, but I imagine she was fishing for

information. You dealt with it very well."

"It was not deliberate. When I heard 'Mr Purdue', I thought immediately of the old man. But I did try to cut her short, Rosa. I couldn't bear it if she found out about my mother. She would be so disparaging, and in sort of a falsely sweet way, as if she were trying to console me but in fact was triumphing over me."

"I know. I think it unlikely she will learn of it while she is here, but if she does, we shall let your grandmother deal with her. Or, perhaps Lord Swanmere would be better. She values the connection and will not want to be in his black books."

Chloe smiled at this and disappeared into her bedchamber. Rosa followed suit, hoping fervently that any news of Lady Loring's disgrace would be linked only to Lord Stephen FitzCharles and that her escapade with Purdue remained forgotten. She wandered restlessly to the window that overlooked the courtyard. Still no sign of Julian. She had not thought he would be away so long. She missed him sorely. Left to her own devices, she was at a loss to know what to do with herself—the castle seemed empty without him and the days interminable.

She shook her head. In less than two weeks he had made himself indispensable to her. His presence was both a necessity and a constant delight and yet, until that last day, she had not given a second thought to the hours they spent alone—riding, driving or just sitting comfortably together in the library. She touched her lips, felt them curve as they remembered his kiss. Before it, she would have said he regarded her as some sort of undefined female relative— close enough that he need not stand on ceremony with her or, within his own home, pay more than lip-service to the rules of propriety. But his kiss had been neither brotherly nor cousinly. Sensible Miss Fancourt knew better than to indulge in such imaginings, but foolish Rosa built castles in the air.

Julian sighed with satisfaction when they reached the last turn before Swanmere. Home at last. He and his father had parted on better terms than they had been these many years. At Sir Edward's suggestion, the Old Hall estate had been added to the entail so that the original Barrett property would remain united. In addition, his father had set aside a generous dowry for Chloe. They had agreed in principle on a settlement for Julian's future wife that would ultimately revert to her younger children. Sir Edward had made two requests—that Julian would continue to provide for Margaret Robson if his father died before her and that he would not desert Loring Place.

"Promise me you will visit regularly with your family. You must not become a stranger to our people here."

"I won't, sir, I promise. And you must come to us, both at Swanmere and in town. When Chloe makes her come-out, she will want her father at her side."

He did not drive through the gatehouse arch but went straight to the stable yard. A groom appeared immediately and Julian climbed down, stretching with relief when he reached the ground.

"Thank you, Josiah. Let Tom see to them. You've earned a respite." He clapped his tiger on the shoulder and headed for the side door.

Luck was with him. He found Rosa just outside the library. She looked over her shoulder at the sound of his footsteps. "You are home."

She loved him, he was sure of it. Her face was transfigured by it; it shone from her eyes and curved her lips. A few quick strides brought him to her. She came into his arms as if it were the most natural thing in the world and lifted her face for his kiss. Wordlessly, he reached behind her to open the library door, and walked her backwards until they were inside. Fortunately the big room was empty. He shouldered the door shut and turned the key.

"Rosa!"

His arms locked across her back like bars of iron and his mouth came down on hers in an imperious claiming. She did not object—he felt her breasts crush against him as if she needed this fierce connection as much as he did—and her lips opened in instinctive surrender. When her hands closed behind his neck, he softened the kiss, exploring her mouth with his tongue, tempting her to taste him. He growled under his breath when he felt her tongue move against his and slowed to match her more hesitant pace. If she loved him, there was *world enough, and time*. When she gasped, he slackened his hold, letting her pull away a little.

"Rosa?" When she looked up, he said simply, "I need you by my side day and night, as my companion, my helpmeet and my love. Will you be my wife and the mother of my children?"

She leaned back against his arms. Her eyes searched his—he felt she was trying to see to his very soul. One hand moved from his nape to cup his cheek and he turned his head to kiss her palm.

And then her intent expression softened into another ravishingly tender smile. "Yes, Julian, I'll be honoured to be your wife and, God willing, bear your children."

He kissed her lovingly. "You will never regret it, I promise you."

"I know I will not."

He was shocked to see a tear slip down her cheek. "Sweetheart?"

She sniffed and fumbled for a handkerchief. "It's just— I've been alone so long."

"But never again." He took the handkerchief and dried her eyes then inspected her ruefully. "I'm sorry; I came to you covered with the dust of the road. Your face is streaked and you may want to shake out your gown."

She gasped and turned that delicious pink, then seized the handkerchief and scrubbed her face and bosom before brushing at her bodice and skirts. "Is that better?"

"I suppose so."

"You only suppose so? There is no looking-glass in here, is there?"

"No."

"I must go back upstairs before the others see me."

He kissed her again and, his arm around her waist, urged her towards the window seat that was just large enough for two. "Later. Come and sit with me first. I missed our afternoon assignations."

"So did I. I found myself coming in here at five o'clock only to be disappointed when you weren't there."

He smiled and hugged her to him. "How did your expedition to Oundle go?"

"Quite well, although your grandmother suddenly became very tired. Mrs Musgrave went ahead to *The Talbot* with her so that she could rest before we drove back and she retired to her room once we returned here."

"Has she recovered?" Julian was alarmed. He knew he must lose both his grandparents one day, but prayed it would not be too soon.

"She says so, but I was able to convince her not to come down to breakfast since. I think the news about Lady Loring was more of a shock to her than we knew."

"Probably. And she has borne the brunt of Meg's company as well."

"That is true. She, Mrs Overton, I mean, has never sought mine nor, if I am to be fair, have I sought hers. Well, I couldn't because you tended to kidnap me."

He laughed. "I have you now and shall never release you."

She put her head on his shoulder. "I hope not. How long do the Overtons remain here?"

"We have not discussed it, but not beyond the end of the month."

"Another three weeks at most," Rosa said reflectively. "We shall have to try and distract her—give your grandmother some relief."

"I thought of inviting her brother and his family for a week or so. Their presence might mend her manners."

"Let us hope so. How did your father take your news?"

"First he was furious, then resigned. I was able to convince him not to pursue his wife or take any action against her, apart from changing his will and ensuring that she can make no claim on Chloe, should something happen to him before she comes of age—in such an event, I am to be her guardian and trustee."

"That is only proper. Whatever connection Chloe might have with her mother in ten years' time, there can be no public association between them while she is still a girl."

"Do you think they could meet privately?"

She shrugged. "It would depend on the circumstances, but if it were done discreetly—I think it would be very cruel to part them completely. Would you not give anything to see your mother again? I know I would."

It was twenty years since his mother's death, but the wound was suddenly as fresh as if it were yesterday. To sit again with her, even for a few hours—"You are right, but I hope we are spared the necessity as long as possible."

He poured two glasses of Madeira. "How is Chloe?"

"Fretting," she answered after a moment's thought. "She wonders what will become of her now, and dreads the return to Suffolk."

"My father will try and arrange for her to stay with the Undrells or the Glazebrooks for the autumn, but afterwards—should you object if she makes her home with us?"

"Of course not. It would be the perfect solution, if Sir Edward permits. But why not immediately?"

He slipped an arm around her. "Because, Miss Fancourt, I want to have my bride to myself for the first few months at least. If Chloe lives with us, it will be like having an adult daughter—we won't have the same sort of freedom or privacy—even just to be together like this."

"Then we must shape our lives to suit our circumstances," she said determinedly. "We can arrange special times each day when we shall be private, just as we meet now every afternoon."

His eyes gleamed. "But then we shall not be restricted to the public rooms." He kissed her lingeringly. "My love, you shall have a boudoir for intimate five-o'clock trysts. It will be an iron rule that we are not to be disturbed."

She traced the outline of his lips with her forefinger. "We'll make time for us," she whispered. "I promise you. And don't forget that Chloe has already begun to make friends here so she will not be wholly dependent on our company."

He captured her hand and kissed it. "Shall we have the banns called next Sunday?"

"So soon?"

"I don't want you to leave Swanmere, not even for the shortest time. This is your home now. Do you not feel so too?"

She nodded. "I have loved being here. I felt welcome from the moment I stepped down from your carriage."

"Listen to your heart, Rosa. We've known each other for ten years. Why should we delay any longer?"

"When you put it like that, it seems so simple. We can discuss it later—now I must tidy myself and you must change your clothes for dinner."

# Chapter Twenty-nine

ROBERT PATTED THE SEAT OF the settee then held out his sketchbook invitingly. "Come and sit beside me, Rosa. I came down early to show you my latest drawings."

"Let me see."

"Here I have imagined the castle before it was slighted, besieged by Cromwell's forces," Robert explained, pointing out the surrounding wall and crenelated battlements. "Here is Lady Swanmere on the north tower. She defended the castle, you know, while her husband was away fighting for the king."

"It's very good, Robert," Rosa said sincerely. "You have got the trick of drawing in perspective now."

He beamed at her. "Because you explained it so well."

She smiled back and took the sketchbook from him. "May I?" At his nod, she began to leaf through it while Chloe and Hal leaned over the back of the settee to look as well.

"That is very clever," Chloe exclaimed, laughing at a sketch of Hal poling a skiff, in imminent danger of parting company with his vessel. She turned the page. "Here he is, clinging to the pole like a monkey and here comes doughty Thomas to the rescue."

Hal sniffed loudly. "That is pure exaggeration, I assure you."

"It was touch and go for a minute," Robert said with a grin. "He probably would have abandoned the pole and left us to drift to the far bank, but I thought this more dramatic."

Rosa turned another page and stopped at a drawing of herself. She was painting, but her apron was fashioned like a breastplate, her hair was topped by a helmet and she held her brush as if it were a sword. "*En garde*" was written underneath.

"You have captured that fierce look exactly, Rob," Chloe commented. "You must do another one for me, please. Come and look, Ann," she called to her friend.

"I'd love to, but first I want to run through that song one last time with you and the boys."

"You're never satisfied, Sis," Hal grumbled but obligingly departed with the others.

"We won't be long, Rosa," Ann said apologetically. "Just five minutes."

Left alone, Rosa continued to page through the book on her lap. She was vaguely aware of someone taking Robert's place at her side but did not look up. She closed the book and set it aside then glanced at her companion.

"Good evening, Mrs Overton." Determined to be more conciliatory, she opened the sketchbook again and tilted it towards her neighbour. "Have you seen Robert's drawings? They are very clever."

Mrs Overton favoured her with a toothy smile and

edged nearer. "Dear Miss Fancourt, I know you will forgive me if I venture to give you a little advice—just a tiny hint to be more circumspect."

"I'm afraid I don't understand you, Mrs Overton."

The other woman shook her head. "Come, come, my dear," she said in a conspiratorial undertone. "It will not do, you know. Believe me, I feel for you, but you must not flaunt such a relationship. You cannot risk exposing yourself—and him."

Rosa raised her eyebrows. What maggot could possibly have got into Mrs Overton's brain? Although her betrothal to Julian was very new, there was nothing illicit about it and while she had resolved to keep her connection to Robert secret, she need not fear it being revealed.

She rose calmly to her feet. "I have no idea what you are talking about, Mrs Overton. Permit me to tell you that either you are utterly mistaken about something or you have windmills in your head. Whichever is the case, I see no reason to continue such an absurd conversation."

Mrs Overton clutched Rosa's skirts, holding her fast. "You cannot think to brazen it out!" she cried shrilly. "I don't know what my cousin Swanmere is about to permit you to associate with your bastard under his roof. It is an affront to decency and an insult to us all."

"My what—? You've run mad!"

Rosa jerked her skirts free and whirled to confront the other woman who scrambled up, brandishing a sheet of paper.

"Run mad, have I? Why else would Robert's father write to you, regretting more and more his treatment of you and begging you for the boy's sake to say nothing of what had been between you?" She opened her fingers disdainfully and let the paper fall at Rosa's feet. "Now do you dare to deny the relationship between you and that boy? You belong in the nearest Magdalen and not among decent people."

"Enough, you harpy!"

Rosa hadn't noticed Julian come in. He stood in the doorway with his grandparents. Lady Loring looked appalled and Lord Swanmere furious. Surely they would not believe such a calumny?

Julian rounded the settee and drew Rosa to him. "You do not owe anyone an explanation, let alone a malicious, spiteful hell cat."

Mrs Overton glared at him. "How dare you, Julian! But I suppose I might have expected you to condone such behaviour."

"Enough, I said!" He took a step towards her and she subsided onto the settee.

Rosa looked to where a white-faced Robert stood at the door to the music room. Thomas Musgrave had his arm about the boy's shoulders and Ann, Chloe and Hal clustered protectively around him.

"There is one person who is entitled to an explanation," she reminded Julian softly.

He followed her gaze. "Did he hear? Do you wish to speak to him privately?"

"No. She has made it public, whether we like it or not. It is time for the truth to be told."

"Come, then."

When she looked up, surprised, he shook her slightly. "You are no longer alone. Have you forgotten?"

Her heart melted. "I must get used to it."

"Come then."

His arm about her waist, they walked slowly down the long drawing-room. As they neared the little group at the far end, Rosa saw Chloe glance fascinated from her brother to her former governess. Then Thomas released Robert and nudged him gently forward, before taking a pace back to stand with the other three.

When they reached Robert, Rosa stepped out of Julian's embrace and knelt so that the boy could easily meet her eyes. "It is not true," she told him gently. "We are related, but I am not your mother, Robert. I am your sister."

Behind her, she heard Julian catch his breath. Had he thought the same as Mrs Overton? It didn't matter. She spared him a fleeting glance but turned back at once to Robert. He must be her first concern.

"As you know, your mother died when you were born. Her name was Martha Kennard. Her parents were called Mr and Mrs Bletsoe but before she married your father in 1802, she was married to my father, Captain Charles Fancourt. He was killed at the Battle of Copenhagen in 1801. If you ask your father to show you their marriage lines, you will see that what I say is true and that your mother was called Martha Fancourt when she married him."

"If you are my sister, why have I never heard of you?" Robert asked bluntly.

"When they married, your father didn't want a half-grown stepdaughter intruding on their new life together so I was sent to boarding school. When Mamma died a year later, he did not wish to receive me into his household, although I would have been so happy to come and look after you. I was so excited to have a brother at last," she whispered. "I would have loved you."

"Is that what he meant about his treatment of you?" the boy asked hesitantly.

"Yes."

"I'm sorry," he said simply. They might have been alone in the big room.

Rosa shook her head. "We are not responsible for our parents' mistakes, Robert. I have longed to tell you of our relationship but I did not want to cause discord between you and your father. I never received that letter," she indicated it with a backwards tilt of her head, "but I planned to write and seek his permission to tell you before you left. I wanted, want," she corrected herself, "you to know that you have a sister who loves you and to whom you may always turn if you need help of any sort."

Tears pooled in the boy's eyes and she opened her arms to him. He held himself aloof at first and then moved cautiously into them, like a half-tame animal or a child who has learned the futility of hope. She held him close and after a moment his arms came around her in a fierce hug. After long seconds he pulled away.

"Where did Mrs Overton get the letter?" he asked gruffly.

"A good question," Julian said as he helped Rosa to stand. "Come and sit down. You too, Robert," he added to the boy and led them to a small sofa. He retrieved the letter and handed it to her.

She spread it out, holding it so that she and Robert could pore over it, heads together.

"He wrote it at the Ransfords'," she said. "He had wanted to talk to me there, but I was too shocked by the sight of him after all these years. Not to mention seeing you for the first time. You have our mother's eyes."

"Will you tell me about her, Rosa?" he asked shyly. "My father has never spoken of her."

"I would love to, Robert. I have her miniature in a little case she gave to my father. But Mr Kennard does care about you. See, here, where he says, *'Be kind to Robert, I beg you, Rosa'*. He wrote the letter because he was concerned about you."

"And *'entrusted'* it to Mrs Overton." Robert directed a look of loathing at his friend's mother. "Not only did she not give it to you, but she read it and used it to bolster a lie. What a shabby thing to do!"

The boy's honest condemnation rang through the hushed room. In the group around Mr Musgrave someone suppressed a sob.

"Is there anything you wish to say to Miss Fancourt and Robert, Mrs Overton?" Lady Loring asked icily.

Mrs Overton shifted uneasily on her settee. Her defiance had gone and her eyes flickered from one to the other like those of an animal caught in a trap. Her daughter and son looked distraught. They had remained with Chloe and Thomas and now moved closer together so that their shoulders touched. As the silence continued, Hal slipped his hand into Ann's.

"I apologise for my earlier remarks, Miss Fancourt, and withdraw them unreservedly," Mrs Overton said tonelessly. "I apologise, Robert."

Rosa inclined her head. "Thank you, Mrs Overton."

"Thank you, Mrs Overton," Robert echoed.

Mrs Overton rose to her feet. She looked around the room as if unsure what to do next, then walked stiffly to the door.

The click of the lock as the footman shut it behind her

was like a gunshot in the still room. Ann and Hal were the first to move. After an exchange of glances, Ann whispered to Hal, then hand-in-hand they crossed to Rosa and Robert.

"We want you to know we're sorry," Ann said diffidently. "We didn't know she was going to do that or that she had your letter, Rosa."

"How could you?"

When Rosa took her hand, the girl clung to it. She had tears in her eyes. "I'm so ashamed," she whispered.

"So am I," her brother muttered. "I don't suppose you'll want to be friends with me now, Rob. I wouldn't blame you."

"Don't be such a gudgeon," Robert said fiercely. "If my sister," he smiled at Rosa, "does not blame me for how my father treated her, how can I blame you for what your mother did?" He offered his hand and Hal took it.

"Maybe it was all for the best," Robert added. "My father might have forbidden Rosa to tell me and then where would we have been?"

The resulting burst of laughter cleared the air.

"Are we to have no dinner tonight?" Lord Swanmere demanded.

The footman disappeared, returning so quickly with Bates that the house steward must have been waiting outside.

"Dinner is served, my lord."

"Swanmere, you may give me your arm," Lady Loring said. "Miss Rosa, pray oblige me by taking my place. And Bates, have a tray taken up to Mrs Overton."

"Go ahead, Bates. We'll be just a moment."

As soon as the house-steward had left the drawing-room, Julian shut the door and set his back to it, then pulled Rosa into his arms, bending to take her mouth in an ardent kiss. "You were magnificent," he said when he raised his head at last. "I had not thought it was possible for me to love you more, admire you more than I did, but—" He kissed her again, more slowly this time, until she melted against him.

She put her hand on his chest and looked up at him, misty-eyed. "I don't think a woman was ever more honoured—or more loved. The way you rushed to my side and stood up for me; then stood by me and did not condemn me. You thought the same as Mrs Overton, didn't you?"

"I must apologise," he began.

She shook her head and silenced him with a finger on his lips. "No, Julian. You owe me no apology, for your only instinct was to protect me, was it not?"

"Yes. How could I blame you if some scoundrel took advantage of you when you were at your most vulnerable?"

"My dearest Julian," she said and drew down his head to kiss him softly.

His arms tightened but after a few moments she put her hands on his chest and pulled away. "They will be wondering what is keeping us. I don't want to, but we must go in."

"I know," he agreed reluctantly. "Shall we announce our betrothal now?"

"I think it might be better, don't you? Especially after you very publicly declared your allegiance just fifteen minutes ago."

He kissed her again. "It was my pleasure and my

privilege," he said, tucking her hand into the crook of his arm.

"Champagne with the dessert, Bates," he murmured, deeply content, as they passed the house-steward, then led Rosa ceremoniously to the head of the table and seated her there before taking his place on her right.

They received some curious looks, from Chloe in particular but it appeared that no one wished to be the first to comment on the events in the drawing-room.

"I trust you were able to conclude your business successfully, Julian?" his grandmother called down the table.

"Extremely so, ma'am." He smiled reassuringly at her and Chloe before asking, "How did you occupy yourselves while I was away?"

He was able to make a good dinner as he listened to a jumbled description of shooting, shopping, kite-flying and pick-nicks. Hal and Robert soon recovered their spirits, but Ann remained very subdued, merely picking at her food and taking no part in the conversation. Rosa turned and murmured something to her and the girl sniffed and muttered an inaudible reply. Rosa answered in a low voice, covering Ann's hand in a comforting clasp. Ann nodded and looked a little more cheerful.

"Is Ann still upset?" Julian muttered to Rosa once the girl had turned to Hal and Thomas Musgrave to support Chloe's demand that they also be given an opportunity to fly the kites.

"She is mortified by her mother's behaviour and afraid that Mrs Overton might decide to leave in a huff tomorrow. I reminded her that she has neither a carriage nor horses so cannot do anything hasty and said that you would talk to her, Mrs Overton, I mean, in the morning."

"I will, will I?" he asked resignedly.

"I don't think we shall ever be bosom friends but we must come to some sort of accommodation with her for the children's sakes. Also, I would be very reluctant to see Robert leave with her under such circumstances."

"That's true. We must consider how to deal with his situation as well. But let us leave all that until tomorrow. Tonight is ours."

She smiled gloriously and his hand sought hers. She wore the plum-pink gown he had seen for the first time at the Ransfords'. Her breasts swelled above the low bodice, glowing in the soft light of the candles, inviting the touch of his fingers and his lips. He noticed his grandmother's eye on him and deliberately lifted Rosa's hand to his lips before rising to his feet.

"I am honoured beyond measure to tell you that Rosa has agreed to be my wife," he said simply. He held out his hand and gently urged her to stand beside him. "I give you the future Lady Swann Loring—your new granddaughter, sister and cousin; the new mistress of Swanmere. I also welcome my new brother," he continued. "As we forge new bonds, let us look forward together to a bright future."

Her fingers tightened in his and she smiled so lovingly at him that he could have stood there forever looking into her eyes.

"Ahem!" His grandfather stood, glass in hand. "To Julian and Rosa! May they enjoy long life, health and happiness together."

When the toast was drunk, Swanmere walked the length of the table and held out both hands to Rosa. "Welcome, my dear," he said and kissed her cheek before turning to embrace his grandson. "Congratulations, my boy."

This was the signal for a general breaking of ranks. Chloe ran to throw her arms around them. "You are very sly, not to tell me before," she scolded Julian before hugging Rosa. "To think we shall be sisters!"

"C-congratulations," Robert stuttered.

"Thank you, Robert." Rosa stooped and tilted her cheek for his shy kiss.

When she had straightened, Julian held out his hand to the boy. "I meant it," he said quietly as he and Robert shook hands. "Rosa's brother will be my brother."

"And I shall be your sister," Chloe said excitedly to Robert. "I always wanted to have a younger brother or sister."

"Two new, elder sisters in one day? You're in for it now, Rob," Hal announced gleefully.

Thomas Musgrave flicked a fingernail against the boy's skull. "That's enough from you, Mr Rudesby."

"I was only funning," Hal protested, rubbing his head while Ann and Chloe united in glaring at him, and Robert just grinned.

"How surprisingly resilient the young people are," Julian's grandmother murmured before taking the hands of her grandson and his betrothed. "Oh, my dears, I am so pleased. I wish you every happiness together."

It really was all Mr Kennard's fault, Meg assured herself. If he had been more explicit in his letter, she could not have made such a mistake. And, after all, she had been correct in her assumption of a relationship between the Fancourt woman and Robert. Julian need not have spoken so harshly to her. It was better for all concerned that it was out in the open. Why, she had done the woman a favour, for others could easily have made the same mistake. Restored to good humour, she poured a glass of ratafia and picked up the latest issue of *Ackermann's Repository*. She would have a quiet evening here in her room and by tomorrow everything would have blown over.

It was almost too dark to read. Where was Jenkins? She should have returned long since to remove the dinner tray and light the candles. Meg tugged the bell-pull and waited, toe tapping impatiently, for the maid to appear.

"I'm sorry, ma'am," she said as she hurried in and picked up the tinder-box. "Such excitement downstairs, you wouldn't believe it!"

"Why, what has happened?"

Jenkins touched a spill to the candles on the mantelpiece and went to light the ones on the table. "Sir Julian announced his betrothal to Miss Fancourt."

Meg's knees gave way and she collapsed onto the nearest chair. What had she done? They would never forgive her. Not only that, if the future Lord and Lady Swanmere refused to recognise her, she could lose the *entrée* to the best circles. She would have to apologise again tomorrow morning, she concluded grimly, always provided she did not wake to the news that a carriage had been ordered for her and the children.

"I had long since given up any thought of marriage," Rosa said to Julian in the library the following afternoon, "but when I was a girl, it seemed somehow like a fairy-tale—a handsome prince would make me an offer and all mundane problems would be resolved, although why I thought that when I saw my mother's life, I don't know."

"Perhaps I am not handsome enough," he answered solemnly. "You may reconsider your decision if you wish." His kiss belied the sincerity of this offer.

She rested her head on his shoulder and laughed softly. "I am not so foolish, sir. I understand it now. I saw it first last night when you hurried to my side, but today, after dealing with your cousin and writing to Mr Kennard and working out the arrangements for Chloe—although it was worth everything to see her face when we told her she could live here with us if she wished—I see that the important thing is that one must not face all these things alone. *'Mutual society, help and comfort'* is no small thing, Julian. It is the expression of love."

# Epilogue

Rosa waved one last time before the travelling chariot passed under the gate lodge arch and leaned back against the dark blue squabs with a sigh of relief. "That must have been the most chaotic month of my life."

Julian grinned as he took off his hat. "You should be grateful to have had a whole month. If it hadn't been for the lawyers, we could have had the banns called that first Sunday and been married two weeks later." He pulled off his gloves and dropped them into the upturned hat then turned and framed her face with his hands. His smile faded and he rested his brow against hers.

"It's done now and you're mine, Lady Swann Loring. Did you enjoy your wedding?"

"It was beautiful," she sighed happily. "Will you tell me at last where we are going?"

"I'll give you three guesses, but you must pay a forfeit for every wrong guess."

"That's not fair," she protested. "You wouldn't give me the slightest hint, not even when Lambton wanted to know what she should pack. All you would say was that it didn't matter."

"Was that not a hint?" he asked blandly.

She looked at him suspiciously. "Either we are going somewhere so rustic that it doesn't matter what I wear—"

"Wrong! You must pay the forfeit."

Her lips clung to his, parting to admit his probing tongue. He raised his head. "Mine," he said triumphantly and bent to kiss her again.

"Julian!" She pushed him away. "We are no longer in the park. Soon we'll be passing through the village. Anyone may see."

"I could pull down the blinds," he offered as he sat up.

"I think it would be safer not to." She straightened her bonnet and retreated primly to the corner of the seat.

"You must guess again," he teased her. "You may have as many guesses as you like."

"If it matters what I wear but doesn't matter what I brought with me, we must be going somewhere I can purchase anything I need."

"True."

She frowned for a moment, then smiled and waved to three women who paused in their conversation to bob curtsies as the carriage passed. "We're going to Swanmere House," she concluded. "That is why you wanted an early ceremony—so we could make the journey in one day."

"I remembered you said that you didn't know London and thought you might like to have the opportunity to become a little acquainted with it while town is thin of company. I always find this one of the more pleasant times of the year there—the summer heat is over and we do not yet have winter's fogs and dark days. We shall be undisturbed as long as we do not put the knocker on the door. Later, if you like, we could go somewhere else—visit one of the bathing-places, perhaps Weymouth or Lyme Regis."

"I've never bathed in the sea," she said doubtfully. "Is it very cold?"

"The first immersion is a shock, but afterwards it's exhilarating."

He unbuttoned her pale Limerick glove then leisurely peeled it off, touching his lips to each finger before turning her bare hand so that he could press a deep kiss in the palm. She shivered and he raised his eyes fleetingly to hers before unhurriedly removing the second glove.

Where once propriety would have required her to resist, now a happy duty demanded her compliance. How could something so simple be so seductive, she thought as he drew the glove away and repeated the little series of kisses. This time, when his lips touched her palm she curved her fingers to caress his cheek. He smiled at her and rubbed it gently against her hand so that she could feel a slight abrasion from an imperceptible beard, then interlaced their fingers so that his warm palm caressed hers. The carriage swayed, throwing them together so that their bodies touched from knee to shoulder and he rested their joined hands on his strong thigh.

She lifted them, turning them so she could look at her ring. "No longer two but one. It's strange, isn't it?"

"You do not already regret it, I hope?"

He was only half-teasing, she saw; although he smiled, his eyes were serious.

She tightened her clasp. "It's just—how can something be so ordinary and yet so unfathomable?"

He released her hand so he could put his arm around her. "Don't be frightened, Rosa. We'll explore this excellent mystery together."

She leaned against him. "Together. That is the secret."

It was past eight o'clock when they drew up under the portico of Swanmere House. The lanterns on either side of the door had been lit and liveried footmen lined the wide, shallow steps. As before, Morris and Mrs Morris stood ready in the hall, but today they were not alone. Behind them, the entire staff waited to be presented to their new mistress.

Rosa slowly did the rounds, smilingly acknowledging the bows and curtseys, the murmurs of 'my lady'. It would take her some time to get used to this new form of address. Now she felt inclined to look over her shoulder to see if the dowager or Chloe's mother were behind her. Thank heavens Julian had decided to adopt his new name on his marriage. She could never have become accustomed to being Lady Loring.

This time it was Julian who led her upstairs, across the first floor landing and through a heavy oak door. "These are our apartments—yours on the right and mine on the left."

"It's charming—so fresh and airy," Rosa commented, looking around her new bedchamber. Although not as elaborate as the blue parlour, the Pompeian influence was evident both in the plaster work and painting of the walls and ceiling, and the light, gilt-wood furniture.

"You have seen the lady's room at the castle. My grandmother wanted something completely different here. But you may change it if you wish."

"I couldn't—I think it so beautiful," she said honestly. She had never thought such a room would be hers.

He opened a door beside the fireplace. "Your dressing-room is here."

This was equally beautiful but a more intimate space where a lady might receive close friends or simply retreat from the world. Julian crossed it to open yet another door.

"Your bathroom," he said briefly.

Rosa gaped at the decadent extravagance of the gold-canopied bath set against the wall and framed by cream and gilt panels decorated with dancing nymphs. "How resplendent," she said faintly.

"You must blame Mrs Morris."

"Mrs Morris?" She would never have pictured the prosaic housekeeper indulging in such fantasies.

"She wanted a new, closed range for the kitchen and to have water brought into the scullery instead of having to use the pump outside." He spread his hands. "One thing led to another. I had an eager young architect who was interested in all things mechanical and he suggested we put in a high water service, and extend the house to provide bathrooms and water closets as well as a servants' staircase. Of course your bathroom had to match the classical style of the other rooms. Mine is more restrained, although it does include a shower bath."

It was too much for Rosa and she began to laugh, thinking of the little apartment she had hoped to rent when she left the Place.

"Other women bring up families in much less space than these rooms have," she explained when he looked enquiringly at her. "I suppose yours are just as large. It seems excessive, somehow."

He shrugged. "I suppose it is. I've never thought about it. The house is not entailed. We could sell it and buy something smaller if you prefer."

"No, no" she said, alarmed. She didn't want to begin by criticising everything. "I'm sorry. I'm tired, I think, and confused. It has been a long day."

He enfolded her in a reassuring hug. "I know. Have Lambton help you into a *robe de chambre*. They'll bring up a supper in half an hour. Then we may shut them all out until we ring in the morning."

An intimate supper with her husband wearing a *robe de chambre*? Married life was going to be full of surprises, Rosa reflected, grateful that she would not have to endure a formal meal in the dining-room with everyone conscious that it was her wedding night. Lambton helped her undress with a minimum of words, permitting herself only a speaking glance when she said, "Good night, my lady."

"Good night, Lambton. I'll ring when I need you in the morning."

"Yes, my lady."

When the door closed behind her maid, Rosa turned back to the long cheval mirror. Thank heavens Cousin Emmy had insisted she purchase some pretty negligees. A governess had no need for fripperies suitable only for the boudoir. She smiled as she admired her petticoat and tunic of fine, white jaconet muslin, enjoying the graceful drape of the overlapping layers of fabric and the way her long, loose hair flared out and settled back in place when she turned. She spread out her arms and revolved again, delighting in the billow and puff of the finely-plaited, full bishop's sleeves. They were caught tightly at the wrist and trimmed with blue ribbon threaded through the same lace that edged the neckline and the hem of the tunic with creamy ruffles. Little bows of the ribbon held the wrap-over front together.

Who was this woman whose wide eyes and trembling lips betrayed the apprehension and anticipation that caused her colour to come and go? Her lips had never been so plump and red, swollen by the kisses her husband had claimed throughout the day. Smiling, she looked at the gold ring he had placed on her finger that morning. This was the final step—from maid to wife. *Be not afraid*, she said to herself and opened the door to the bedroom.

He stood beside the table at the window, wrapped in a rich green and gold banyan that suggested the robe of an oriental prince, the strong column of his bare throat rising proudly from its open neck. He swallowed when he saw her.

"Rosa," he whispered huskily and held out his hand.

She walked slowly towards him, drawn relentlessly by the ardour in the eyes that never left hers. When she was near enough, she placed her hand in his but he did not move, waiting patiently until she took the final step that brought her into his arms.

"You are so beautiful. You enchant me."

His voice, deeper than usual, held her spellbound. She felt beautiful; beautiful and strong and alluring. She might be still a virgin but she was no longer a girl. She was a woman and he was all man.

"Rosa." He waited again.

Her lips curved. "Julian."

It was enough. His mouth captured hers. She put her hands on his shoulders then slid them up to close behind his neck. Steel arms locked her to him so that they stood torso to torso, thigh to thigh, her breasts crushed against his chest. His banyan had opened and she could feel a rigid column against her belly.

"Come to bed, Rosa, come to me."

His arm around her, he urged her to the high bed. Leaning against the mattress, he pulled her to stand between his open legs and began slowly to untie the bows that held the tunic together. He spread the two sides apart as he worked, bending to press soft kisses on her bared skin and grumbling when he reached the lace trimming of her petticoat.

"Unfair," he whispered, his warm breath skimming across her skin, and drew the tunic down over her shoulders, baring the top of her breasts. His caresses made her sway and she steadied herself with a hand on his shoulder as she looked down at his bent head. A tiny frill of gold curls outlined the base of his skull and she gently combed her fingers through them. He jerked as if an electric wire had been applied to him. She stroked her thumb down the deep furrow that ran from his skull to his spine and he looked up at her, eyes gleaming, before he untied the last bow just below her bosom.

He drew the tunic down her arms, muttering under his breath when it caught at her wrists. Fortunately Lambton had tied the ribbons with simple bow knots and he quickly tugged them loose and let the tunic puddle on the floor. In return, she pushed the sides of his banyan wide. Beneath it he wore only pale, silk dress breeches and she swallowed at the sight of his bare chest dusted with golden hairs. They were crisp to the touch and his skin below felt like satin. Unable to resist, she plucked at the male nipples that were so much smaller than her own. Did they ache as much, she wondered.

He caught her hands and pressed them to his chest for an instant before untying the bow at the top of her petticoat. She swayed again as he loosened the ribbon and he steadied her between his thighs before slowly easing the petticoat down until it fell to the floor. She shivered under the intensity of his gaze. He lifted her and laid her on the cool sheet, pushing the covers away as he followed her down to kiss again. His hand was on her leg, above her knee, and she felt him untie her garter and roll the stocking down her leg and off. He ran his hand caressingly up her bared calf and she twitched at the strange sensation—not quite a tickle; something more exciting. And then her other stocking was gone and only the fine lawn of her chemise protected her modesty. He shrugged his banyan off his shoulders and drew his arms free.

"Rosa." His voice was so deep that she seemed to feel rather than hear it.

She raised her arms invitingly and he sank into them. She gasped when his seeking lips closed over the aching tip of her breast, at first soothing and then inciting an even greater need. Almost of their own volition, her hands clutched him to her before stroking down his muscled back over his narrow hips to shape the firm curves of his silk-clad buttocks. She felt him push up her chemise, bunching the fabric together and silently encouraging her to raise first her hips, then her shoulders and finally her head so that he could whisk it away. She felt herself blush as she lay bare for his delight, He stood briefly to strip off his breeches and faced her, magnificently male; Adam to her Eve.

"You are so beautiful," he whispered and began to kiss her again, stroking and caressing her until her body was on fire.

She felt a new ache, lower, deep in her belly. As if he had noticed, his hands dipped lower too, gently stroking up her thighs to their apex, just touching and withdrawing before touching again. Involuntarily, she spread her legs, opening her most private place for him to explore with subtle yet demanding fingers so that she lifted herself towards him begging wordlessly: *more, deeper, more, yes, there!*

Now he moved to lie between her legs and she felt something bigger, blunter, seek entrance to her body. She stiffened.

"Easy, sweetheart, easy," he murmured. "Let me in."

"You're so big," she gasped, then, "ohh," as he pushed in a little more.

He stopped moving. "You're like a hot, silk glove," he groaned, then took her mouth again, his lips demanding, his tongue tangling and retreating so that hers pursued it. He kissed her more deeply and at the same time surged into her. She felt a sharp sting and then he was buried deep inside her, stretching and filling her.

"Rosa," he groaned. He held still for a moment but then began to move again, pulling out and pushing in, dragging himself through her newly sensitive channel in an insistent rhythm that had her hips rising to mirror his advance and retreat, each time getting nearer to something unknown, some unfulfilled craving; *more, deeper, more, yes, there!* She clutched him, holding him in place while her internal flesh pulsed around him, and she half-groaned, half-purred deep in her throat, a primeval sound that he echoed as he plunged into her with short, sharp strokes. He rose up over her, his head thrown back and his neck corded as he was seized by a final paroxysm before he slumped onto her. She could feel his heart racing as he gasped for breath.

"Rosa, my God, Rosa," he said after some minutes and shifted to lie beside her, his head on her breast.

"Julian." Even to her own ears, her voice sounded different, almost hoarse.

He pressed a kiss to her breast.

She lifted heavy eyelids to look down at him. His eyes were half-closed, frilled by a fan of ridiculously long eyelashes, his features soft and a half-smile played on his lips.

"My dearest love," he murmured and then, "did I hurt you?"

"Just that one moment—frankly, I was expecting worse."

He laughed softly and tugged up the sheet and blanket to cover them, then kissed the finger that bore his ring. "My lady. My wife."

"My husband," she said dreamily.

"How could I not have seen you all these years?"

"I was hiding, I think. Or perhaps you weren't ready."

"A bit of both, perhaps." He yawned.

"I don't know. Certainly, with all my concerns and worries about what would happen after Midsummer, it never occurred to me that I would be in your bed before Michaelmas. And when you think about it, it's all thanks to your stepmother."

He grinned. "Strictly speaking, I'm in your bed, Lady Swann Loring. Tomorrow we'll try mine."

ᘐ🦋

# Background Notes

THIS IS A WORK OF FICTION, but set in a real time and place, and all characters are fictional.

While it would be impossible to list all the sources consulted, I wish to thank Mr Neil Robinson, Research Officer, Marylebone Cricket Club for information regarding the laws of cricket as they would have applied in 1814.

Thanks are also due to Commander Perry Abbott OBE RN, Secretary, Standing Council of the Baronetage for information regarding the right to knighthood of eldest sons of baronets. If any reader is interested in exploring this further, I refer them to *A History of the Baronetage* by F W Pixley, first published in 1900.

The nursery rhyme 'There was a crooked man who walked a crooked mile' was first published in 1842 in *The Nursery Rhymes of England, collected principally from oral tradition. Ed. by J. O. Halliwell.* Halliwell studied at Cambridge and I think it not unreasonable to assume that Chloe knew of the rhyme some thirty years before it first appeared in print.

# About the Author

CATHERINE KULLMANN WAS BORN AND educated in Dublin. Following a three-year courtship conducted mostly by letter, she moved to Germany where she lived for twenty-five years before returning to Ireland. She has worked in the Irish and New Zealand public services and in the private sector.

Catherine has a keen sense of history and of connection with the past which, she says, so often determines the present. She has always loved writing and is fascinated by people. She loves a good story, especially when characters come to life in a book. But then come the 'whys' and 'what ifs'. She is particularly interested in what happens after the first happy end—how life goes on around the protagonists and sometimes catches up with them.

Writing historical fiction allows her to explore these questions against the background of the early nineteenth century—one of the most significant periods of European and American history. The Act of Union between Great Britain and Ireland of 1800, the Anglo-American war of 1812 and the final defeat of Napoleon at the Battle of Waterloo in 1815 are all events that continue to shape our modern world. At the same time, the aristocracy-led society that drove these events was already under attack from those who recognised the need for social and political reform, while the industrial revolution saw the beginning of the transfer of wealth and ultimately power to those who knew how to exploit the new technologies.

It was still a patriarchal world where women had few or no rights but they lived and loved and died, making the best lives they could for themselves and their children, often with their husbands away for years with the army or at sea. And they began to raise their voices, demanding equality and emancipation.

You will find more information about Catherine on her website www.catherinekullmann.com

Her Facebook author page is fb.me/catherinekullmannauthor

*Read on for information about Catherine's other books.*

# The Murmur of Masks

*From the ballrooms of the Regency to the battlefield of*
*Waterloo: A Second Chance at Love*

NINETEEN-YEAR-OLD OLIVIA'S NAVAL captain father is 'somewhere at sea' fighting the French. She and her mother plan to settle in Weymouth but her mother dies suddenly on the eve of the move. Desperately in need of security and safety, a distraught Olivia accepts Jack Rembleton's offer of a marriage of convenience, hoping that love will grow between them. She does not know that Jack's affections are elsewhere engaged.

Ten years later, Olivia has made the best of her situation. She loves her children and has found her place in the *ton*. An unexpected encounter at a masquerade with the intriguing Luke Fitzmaurice leads to a second chance at love. Dare she grasp it? Before she can decide, Napoleon escapes from Elba and Luke joins Wellington's army in Brussels. Will war once again dash Olivia's hopes of happiness?

A thrilling and touching story about love and war—an eternal triangle with a difference, *The Murmur of Masks* was shortlisted for Best Novel, Carousel Aware Prize (CAP Awards) 2017. Recipient of a Chill with a Book Award, it is now available worldwide from Amazon.

# Perception & Illusion

*Does a fairy-tale ending always guarantee
Happy Ever After?*

ENGLAND 1814: LALLIE GREY is unaware that she is an heiress. When her father realises that he will soon lose control of his daughter's income, he conspires to marry her off to his crony, Frederick Malvin in exchange for a share of her capital. But Lallie has fallen in love with Hugo Tamrisk, heir to one of the oldest titles in England. When Hugo not only comes to her aid as she flees the arranged marriage, but later proposes to her, all Lallie's dreams have come true. She readily agrees to marry him at once.

But past events casts long shadows. Hugo resents the interest his three elder sisters take in his new wife and thinks they have turned her against him. And then there is his former mistress, Sabina, Lady Albright. As Lallie finds her feet in the *ton*, the newly-weds are caught up in a comedy of errors that threatens their future happiness.

*"Deliciously romantic with wonderful characters, elegant writing and perfect period detail. Hugely enjoyable!"* Nicola Cornick. Winner of Chill with a Book and Discovered Diamond awards, *Perception & Illusion* is now available worldwide from Amazon.

# The Potential for Love

*"THERE IS AN ESSENTIAL SOMETHING that calls us to another, something that we recognise or that resounds within us on the most intimate level."*

*"Love, you mean?"*

*"Rather the possibility or potential for love." Her father shook his head. "It's impossible to describe, Arabella, and it may take us some time to recognise it, but we do know when it is not there."*

When Arabella Malvin sees the figure of an officer silhouetted against the sun, for one interminable moment, she thinks he is her dead brother, safely returned against all odds from Waterloo. But it is Major Thomas Ferraunt, the rector's son newly returned from occupied Paris, who stands in front of her. For over six years, Thomas's thoughts have been all of war. Now he must ask himself what his place is in this new world and what he wants from it. More and more, his thoughts turn to Miss Malvin, but will Lord Malvin agree to such a miss-match for his daughter, especially when she is being courted by Lord Henry Danlow?

As Arabella embarks on her fourth season, she finds herself more in demand than ever before. She is tired of the life of a debutante, waiting in the wings for her real life to begin, and wants to marry. But which of her suitors has the potential for love and who will agree to the type of marriage she wants?

As she struggles to make her choice, she is faced with danger from an unexpected quarter while Thomas is stunned by a new challenge. Will these events bring them together or drive them apart? Can their potential for love be realised or will they fall at the first fence?

*The Potential for Love* will be published in 2019.